# The Price of Fame

### Edie Black

**Birdie Cracker Books**

# Copyright

Published 2014 by Birdie Cracker Books
www.birdiecracker.com

Cover design: Janine Mielke - http://www.jmade.de

ISBN-13: 978-0692306567
ISBN-10: 0692306560

For Axel

# Chapter 1: Present day

Monroe Bisque. That was the name of the paint color on my bedroom walls. I was lying in bed staring at it for hours. It was sort of creamy beige and it seemingly changed colors based on the amount of natural light coming from the windows. The color promised warmth and relaxation, but not today. Nothing could relax me today.

I pushed the overly tight sheets off me. I was sweating; my heartbeat was erratic, and my head was pounding. I took a deep breath and felt an immediate, intense relief. I would not let myself freak out! I got up to get aspirin and decided that I might as well start my day. It was early; the sun was just rising, thus a peaceful quiet time to enjoy some solitude and take a run. Well, not exactly solitude as the security detail was never far behind, but I blocked that from my mind. I pulled on my favorite Lululemon running shorts and tank top. I glanced at the mirror and saw dark circles under my eyes and a snag in my shirt; actually it was more like a tiny hole, forming below my chest.

"Damn it!" I muttered out loud to my reflection.

I quickly bunched my thick wavy hair into a pony tale, grabbed my baseball hat and sunglasses. This was *not* starting out as a good day, and of all days, I needed it to be perfect, especially when I was face to face with him. I couldn't believe that I was actually going to see him. For so long I had simultaneously wished and feared for this day, and today it was here. I thought about how long it had been and my stomach fluttered. I was, I guess, anxious to see him. I guess that's why I couldn't sleep. How *ridiculous*...my heart was racing. It had been almost five years since we spoke. The thought occurred to me that we had been almost inseparable back then...*almost*. I pressed the code to the keypad and the gates to the driveway opened up. I stretched quickly and started to run faster than I should have. According to my personal trainer, the trick with running, or any endurance exercise for that matter, is to be patient. Today, however, I pushed myself hard above the limit, but I didn't care, as thoughts of him, of that time, of us, flooded through my thoughts. We were so young, innocent, and starry-eyed. I didn't want to remember; after all it was *not* a happy ending.

A blaring horn interrupted my thoughts, and I realized I was far from home; I better turn around to get ready for the "reunion" meeting with James. What was I going to say to him? *What was I going to do?*

The script was good, no doubt about it. The best-selling novel it was based on had been a real page-turner, and I wouldn't be surprised if the movie became the next big blockbuster. The principal female character was strong and I could see myself portraying her, but could we work together again and what would it cost me?

When I returned to the house, Lydia Walters, who was my manager and closest friend, entered the room.

"Alex, what are you doing? Have you taken a shower yet? Dante and the entire team will be here soon. You really need to start moving!" She said with authority. "Directly after the morning meeting for the…well, you know…reunion with uh, James, you have the fitting for the Vogue thing at Noon, and then from there, the photo shoot for the *L.A. Weekly's* 2015 People Issue. Also, we have that work dinner with Thomas Larsson, the Scandinavian director, about a new script."

I nodded my head, but before I could leave the room, Lydia grabbed my arm.

"If you don't want to do this, you still have time to back out?"

I looked straight into Lydia's eyes and at that moment I appreciated her more than she knew. She was more than a great manager to me; she was a source of comfort and support. I knew that I had to be convincing today.

I gave her a reassuring smile. "Of course I want to do this, I'm fine. Don't worry, I know what I'm doing." I said brightly trying to project a confidence I didn't feel.

With that, I grabbed a towel and headed to the bathroom before the stylist and the rest of the team showed up.

Dante performed his magic and my long dark hair fell down my back in soft silky waves. Then, Denise, the make up artist, added mascara to extend my lashes, which made my blue eyes stand out. As my dad always called me: "Blueberry eyes." "Did you pull a Lindsay Lohan last night?" Denise asked as she covered the shadows under my eyes. "Tis, tis...you really need to get enough sleep if you don't want to look old before your time," she scolded. "I don't recall asking for your opinion Denise!" I snapped. "I'll concentrate on my own sleep habits...thanks." Then I picked up my iPad to read Women's Wear Daily, effectively shutting her out.

Denise looked hurt and I felt bad for my ill temper, but I just couldn't make the effort to apologize, at least not today when my nerves were shot. Denise worked quickly the rest of our time together, and didn't say another word, obviously eager to get away from me.

Gretchen, who was my stylist, had three outfits with matching accessories lined up. "Hey, Alex...I'm going to be nice and let you choose which outfit to wear," she exclaimed.

Just at that moment, Sandy, my publicist walked in carrying the latest print editions of *Variety* and *Hollywood Reporter* in one hand and her cell phone in the other. "Wear the white ribbed tank dress by Alexander Wang with the black Louboutin high-heel sandals!" she ordered. I looked up at my bossy publicist, sarcastically flipping her off with my middle finger. I sighed, but said nothing, as Gretchen dressed me in the white.

Sandy gave me a victorious cat like grin and then went back to talking on her cell phone while dropping the trades in my lap.

Sometimes all the fuss and attention frustrated me. Often I felt like a toddler being told what to wear, how to look and where to be. Today, however, I was glad that I didn't need to make any decisions.

We pulled up at the Beverly Hills Hotel exactly at ten. I always liked the hotel as it reminded me of the classic glamour and golden age of Hollywood. I could almost imagine the times when Marilyn Monroe stayed here. In true Hollywood fashion, the hotel was coined the pink palace, for it's pink exterior, exotic color palette and lush, tropical, exotic gardens. The movie studio had booked us the lavish Presidential Bungalow for the meeting. It had more space then we needed for a conversation, but I did appreciate the utter privacy and separate courtyard entrance. The one condition that we both had for the meeting was privacy: No entourage – no agents, no managers, no publicists, no studio executives. Whatever was decided in this meeting was between James and I. Period. My security team did a sweep of the perimeter and then they went into the bungalow. A few minutes later I was given the green light to go in.

As I got out of the car, Sandy said, "I told you the white was the right choice, you look stunning."

I just glanced at her and rolled my eyes.

Sandy turned to Lydia and said "Why are the beautiful ones so insecure?"

With that, I put a smile on my face in case any cameras were near-by, and left the car, making my way along the winding pathway past the lush greenery toward the bungalow.

When I entered the spacious living quarters of the bungalow the first thing I noticed were the floor to ceiling windows, which looked lazily out onto a quiet, secluded patio, jacuzzi, and lap pool flanked by potted lemon trees, hyacinths and seahorse topiaries. The windows were open, and a cool breeze floated through, momentarily relaxing me. I took a deep breath, smelling the air, and the faint fragrance of exotic flowers filled the room. At first I thought I was alone, and I enjoyed the moment of privacy, something I seldom got to experience.

Then he spoke, "Can I get you something to drink?"

I knew his voice in an instant and for one second I closed my eyes. It was the voice of a familiar, beloved stranger.

I was still too unsettled to look at him, so I answered instead. "A sparkling water would be great."

As he prepared the drinks, I stole my first glance. He was breath-taking as I had remembered and suddenly I felt very ordinary, very vulnerable in his presence. The years washed away as I looked at his thick wavy hair, and strong cheekbones. He had an athletic, graceful body, and he moved liked a panther. Then he looked up and our eyes met. I was lost in the depth of those clear green eyes. Neither one of us said anything; we just continued to look at each other from across the room.

## Chapter 2: Rising Star

From a very young age, I had always liked to perform. I would dance and sing in front of anyone who would listen. My parents were my biggest fans and they were always very supportive of my dream to become an actress. They sat through endless school and community productions watching me perform. My brothers would also watch from time to time, but with less enthusiasm. I could tell they were impatient, as football and friends were more interesting to them then their little sister who liked to entertain. We were a happy family and it was to my great advantage that I grew up in LA with parents working in the entertainment industry. They were not famous, but they had enough connections to know when there would be an audition or casting call that I should pursue. My parents encouraged me and drove me to acting classes, singing lessons, ballet and hip-hop, piano lessons, poetry readings – all things art. I loved it! I often fell behind in my schoolwork, and my attempts at sports were clumsy uncoordinated embarrassments. Put me on stage though, and I lit up like a Christmas tree. I just knew that I could do a good job acting. It was, like, hard to explain, but when I was playing a role I felt as if a fire inside was ignited. I became strong and fearless, and I liked the way I felt pretending to be someone else.

My big break came during a school concert when I was ten-years old; a talent scout in the audience spotted and recruited me. From that point forward, I got a steady stream of work. At the beginning, the roles were small and forgettable. I had minor parts in commercials, TV shows, films, but nothing huge. I wasn't complaining, it was a good balance; I was doing work I loved and actually getting paid for it, while still going to school and maintaining a normal life. However, it started to change when I landed a big budget movie starring Tom Hanks at the age of twelve. It was a fairly large role for a child and the movie received critical acclaim as well as box office success. Unexpectedly, I was getting attention. I went from virtually being unknown to suddenly a serious child actor. I was nominated for a Young Artist Award the next year and movie scripts were beginning to be sent to me for lead child roles. I started getting wooed by bigger talent agents. By the age of seventeen, I had shot seven films and received four nominations and one win for the Young Artist Award for Best Young Actress. With my career on the rise, I had to drop out of school and have private tutors accompany me on the road so that I could complete my high school studies while filming movies. Although my star was rising, I was still relatively unheard of by the public. Most of the movies I had acted in were small; low budget Indy films; only two were big Hollywood hits. Overall I was not recognized and I could still lead a semi-normal teen-age life. That was all about to change the day I got a call to audition for the lead role of fictional character Amanda Blake in the film production of *Galaxy Drifters* based on the mega successful young adult best selling book series.

*Galaxy Drifters* was a sci-fi romance fantasy story with all the winning ingredients you'd expect to see. It had an epic teen-age love story, young beautiful people, good and evil, action, adventure, and suspense. The best-selling book series was a worldwide success with a massive fan-base. Expectations for the movie were high and the roles were coveted.

You could see why. The plot had everything! It was basically about the Samuel's, a family from an advanced civilization in another solar system. The Samuel's were on a mission to explore our solar system. The mission goes horribly wrong and the family who looks like humans, but have super-natural powers, ends up crash landing on Earth. The super-natural family is made up of Christian Samuel, a heroic astronaut and space explorer, and his wife, Diane Samuel, a brilliant Astrophysicist, and their two teenage kids: Julia, age sixteen, and Matt, age eighteen. After the crash landing on Earth, the Samuel's are discovered and rescued by the Blake Family. Dr. Daniel Blake is a surgeon and his wife, Katherine Blake, is a teacher. Their kids are Amanda, age sixteen, Shane, age eighteen, and Trevor, age twenty. The story centers on the friendship and intense *Romeo & Juliet* style romance between Amanda Blake and Matt Samuel as the Blake's try to help the stranded Samuel family find a way home while acclimating them to life on Earth and keeping their identities hidden.

The competition was fierce for the role of Amanda and I heard that thousands of young actresses were vying for the part. In reality, only a dozen actresses had been asked to audition and I was among the select group chosen by the casting director. A former co-star and friend, Audrey Hampton, had recommended me to Ben Avery, the legendary director for the film, and today was the big day that I would meet Mr. Avery and the creative team. In preparation for the audition, Mr. Avery had sent me pages from the script in advance with a few highlighted notes and I felt like those pages were scorched on my brain after reading and memorizing them so often. Our conversation was to be informal over breakfast at his Bel-Air Mansion followed by a more formal audition.

I arrived at his home breathless and flustered from the heavy traffic that I had encountered that morning, but relieved, because I wasn't late. I was greeted immediately, offered a beverage and introduced to Mr. Avery and the team.

Ben Avery was just shy of fifty. He had a tall frame, lean physique and dark hair tinged with grey. He had grown up in Virginia and had a reputation for being soft spoken, humble, and deeply intelligent. When Audrey had worked with the famous director, she told me that while he was always in control on the set and famous for being detail-oriented, he also liked to prepare for unexpected developments and opportunities. He told Audrey that "you can't plan too much, otherwise it get's boring."

"Good to meet you Alexandra," Ben said as he shook my hand. "I liked your work on your previous films and Audrey thought you would be a perfect *fit* for the role of Amanda."

Meeting the legendary director overwhelmed me and I started fiddling anxiously with my necklace. "Thank you Mr. Avery. You're, like, my dream director. I…I cannot believe that I'm actually meeting you!" The words tumbled out of my mouth in a rush, like a run on sentence. "And, um…I will need to thank Audrey for recommending me." I added as an afterthought.

Mr. Avery looked amused by my outburst. "Audrey thought you had a lot of natural raw talent and that this role was made for you. From what I've seen of your work Alexandra, I think she may be right. Should we see if she is correct now or would you like to grab breakfast first?"

"I'm…I'm ready to get started if you are," I answered nervously, wiping my sweaty palms on my sundress.

He took me into what I think was his living room. It was a beautiful space and I was momentarily distracted by my lush surroundings. Someone offered me coffee, but I refused, as I really just wanted to perform.

"Who is your agent?" The director asked.

"Toby Sawyer from the Gauthier Group."

"Excellent!"

The pleasantries continued like this for about twenty minutes and I liked Ben Avery and started to feel more comfortable. He was genial and openly communicative as he explained what we were going to do during the audition. A video camera was set up in the adjoining room for the audition. I expected that I would have fifteen or thirty minutes to audition, but once we started he kept asking me to read another line. If I did one reading one way, he asked me to do the next reading a different way. If I did one line with a lot of energy, the next line he would ask me to do slowly or disinterestedly. It went on like that for hours. Sometimes I would perform solo, and other times he would surprise me and have actors perform with me.

At the conclusion of the fourth hour, he suddenly paused and looked up at me with a grin and said, "Congratulations Alexandra…you've got the lead role!"

Tears of joy ran down my face and I felt tiny goose bumps rising along my arms. "I think I love you Mr. Avery!" I shouted with excitement, hugging the startled director, who started to laugh, and told me that if I loved him, I had better start calling him by his first name, which was Ben. I smiled and nodded. "Thank you Ben! Thank you! Thank you!"

Amada Blake was born that day. A part so BIG that it would change my life forever and catapult me to overnight stardom.

But not right away. First the role of Matt had to be filled, and speculation in the press was intense: Who would get the part? Zac Efron and Ryan Gosling wanted it, my agent heard. So did Henry Cavill. But Ben took his time. The weeks started to blur one into another, with a parade of unknown heartthrobs auditioning for the sought after role. Ben and I met frequently during the process and finally by month four, he had it narrowed down to a half dozen contenders. It was a rainy cold December morning, even for LA standards, when I arrived at Ben's house.

"Today is the day we find our Matt!" declared Ben. "The studio, producers and I have agreed on six options and each actor will screen test with you. By the end of today, I'll make a decision as I want to start filming this by spring," he said with finality.

We met with each actor in Ben's dining room first. Ben usually started by asking each actor a lot of questions about their goals, favorite productions, and worst productions, how they got into acting, what classes they were taking, etc. After that, Ben would usually sit back and watch as I engaged in conversation with them. I could almost see the wheels in his head moving as Ben observed us to see if we could work well together. Once the actors were at ease, and the interviews complete, Ben had us perform two key scenes: first a goodbye scene and then a love scene. First and foremost, he was trying to determine how convincing the actors were in the role of Matt Samuel and secondly he was trying to observe the chemistry between us to see if we were believable together as star-crossed lovers.

We were half way through the auditions, when James Alexander Prescott arrived. He had just flown in from Boston. I wasn't familiar with his work and I had not been present at the initial audition, so I didn't know what to expect.

When Ben introduced us, I was momentarily speechless. *James Alexander Prescott was breathtaking – quite simply, he was sex on two legs!*

"Oh my," I said quietly.

"What?" James smirked. "I didn't catch that?"

"I...I just..." I trailed off, feeling like an idiot and shaking my head to get my brain cells to work again. "It's nice to meet you." I finished lamely.

"Likewise," he grinned, shaking my hand. "I'm James."

"Alex," I said, returning his smile. I found it hard to break my gaze from his and for a moment, I was flustered. But I quickly recovered from my initial surprise and exchanged pleasantries with him, willing myself to forget it and move on.

Ben made some corny jokes about my first name and James middle name "*Alexandra Alexander.*"

I rolled my eyes and chuckled. "Ha, ha, Ben...you really need some better joke material. Don't quit your day job!"

From there, we went into the dining room for the interview. It was funny, because I was suddenly nervous and I was trying to figure out why. After all it wasn't my audition. I kept looking at James trying to determine why I felt as I did? He was over the top good-looking, but all the actors in the casting were heartthrobs, and none of them had made me feel this way. Then I realized it was his intensity and commanding presence that drew me in. On some deep subconscious level, I was drawn to him. I found myself mesmerized by his looks, his voice, and his movements. When I looked up, I realized he was watching me and I blushed. It took me a few minutes to get it together. I took some calming breaths, and willed myself to pay attention to the conversation between James and Ben. This was embarrassing. I had always prided myself on staying calm, cool, and professional, and I was acting like a schoolgirl with a silly crush. I hoped no one had noticed my behavior. I promised myself that it would not happen again.

Ben had asked James a question, which I had totally missed, but I think it was something about the character of Matt Samuel...

James was saying, "At first I found him very cool and arrogant, maybe a little distant. Although the more I read it, I think it's more a defensive mechanism and that Matt has built a wall around him. I think it takes a lot for someone to hold his attention. He yearns to establish an emotional connection with someone, but it eludes him. Matt is deep, and intelligent, and there are many layers to him. When he meets Amanda, he is intrigued by her almost immediately, and as the story unfolds, their relationship deepens and he is surprised by the intensity of his feelings for her."

I could tell that Ben liked his answer as much as I did.

"That's a good read on his character James," replied Ben. "I'm curious what do you think of Amanda Blake?"

"Amanda is also complex," James replied. "She is a strong independent young woman. I think you immediately notice the obvious...her beauty, her innocence, her spirit and strength, but like Matt she is yearning for something? I think she is restless and searching, but doesn't know what or whom she is searching for. At times she seems unsure of herself, confused and naive, other times, she seems wise beyond her years."

"How so?" Ben asked.

The actor paused for a moment like he was searching for the right words, and then he continued, "Amanda has depth and wisdom that you wouldn't expect in someone so young. She is an old soul."

*Wow*...his assessment blew me away. I thought he was dead accurate on all accounts.

Ben interrupted my thoughts and said, "You have a good read on the central characters James."

Ben turned to me and asked if I had any questions for James. I didn't so we proceeded with the screen test.

I'm not sure why, but Ben reversed the order of the scenes and decided that we would perform a love scene first. I had been in this room with three other actors already today. It was a lovely atrium with plants and a fountain with a stunning rustic iron orb chandelier hanging from high above, and in the middle of the room, was a curved sectional sofa outfitted with comfy eggshell-colored seat cushions and pillows. The modular sofa pieces were arranged together to form a large circular daybed where we would perform the scene. The video cameras were set up to roll and the crew came in and introduced themselves to James. After a few minutes of instructions from Ben, James and I were asked to take a seat and to perform our lines.

"Ladies first!" James said as he offered me his hand and led me to the super-sized daybed.

Ben shouted, "Silence on the set. Alex, James, please start when you're ready."

Before I knew what was happening, James had grabbed my hands in his and started performing the scene.

"I'm going to kiss you now Amanda" he said.

His gaze was smoldering and his voice was filled with passion. His face was inches from me and I felt his intense green eyes on me.

At that moment, I pulled away from him.

"Matt, why start something we can't finish?" I asked with a shaky voice.

"Is that how you really feel?" he demanded.

We were kneeling on the sofa together, so close that I felt his breath on me.

"I…I'm confused," I stuttered.

"Then let me clear your mind for you," he stated.

He moved in and started to kiss me. At first the kiss was tentative, almost demure, but then he pressed his body against me and deepened the kiss. His soft lips were suddenly demanding, almost rough, and then his tongue was in my mouth. Desire exploded through me and I was momentarily lost, forgetting the cameras and on-lookers as I kissed him back with fervor and abandonment that I didn't know existed. We both seemed so caught up in the heat of the moment that we grabbed each other and started to meld our bodies in unison as we intensified the kiss. The kiss lingered longer then it should have and we continued to hang on to one another in a passionate grip.

Ben was murmuring something in the background and then the sectional cushion that we kneeled on moved and separated from the other cushions and we fell off the sofa together in one big THUD!

Suddenly, I was aware of everyone watching us and I made an embarrassed laugh. I got off the floor and offered James my hand as he to quickly sprang to his feet.

"Well, that was interesting. Chemistry certainly isn't an issue," Ben joked. "Let's take five and then let's do the other scene."

During the break, I stubbornly willed myself to act as casual as possible, but I was flustered and had to take a deep breath to steady myself. *Dang! That boy sure could kiss.* James had said something to me and I had totally missed it.

"I'm sorry, could you repeat that?"

"Sure." he acknowledged. "I was just saying how much I liked your performance in *Keeping Bad Company.*" He added quietly. "I was somewhat nervous to meet you today."

Despite what he told me, I was surprised and found it hard to believe. I mean he just didn't seem like the type of guy to get nervous about anything. I looked up into his eyes and for the first time, I noticed his beautiful long lashes...*holy smokes*. He really was breathtakingly good looking.

"T-Thanks, " I acknowledged, attempting to keep the slight tremor from my voice. "But no reason to be nervous, I promise I don't bite."

"Are you sure about that?" he said with a wink and a hint of mischief.

*Was he flirting with me?* Before I could respond, we were interrupted and the audition continued. There was such an easy way about the dialogue between us, that it felt immediately natural. Ben asked James to perform countless additional scenes and his audition lasted for two hours. We were good together and I thought that we had found our leading man, but we still had two more auditions left for the day. James and Ben were in a corner huddled together talking, and then James came over to me to say good-bye. We shook hands and again I felt the heat of our earlier exchange. We lingered together longer than necessary. Each of us seemed to want to say something, but neither one of us did.

James spoke first. "Well, thanks, Alex. I'm glad we met and I'd love..." He paused and regarded me for a moment, "...to work with you. I really hope I get that chance."

"Yeah, me too. It was a good audition James and your chances are strong."

"I hope so," he said, and then he gave my hand one final squeeze and slowly released it.

I watched him leave, but I couldn't shake him from my mind. Thoughts of our kisses clouded my brain and faint pink colored my cheeks. I could still feel the warmth of his touch on my skin and I realized that I hoped I would see him again.

We finally wrapped up the last of the screen tests late that evening.

"It's a tough choice. What do you think?" questioned Ben.

"Do you think it's a tough choice?" I responded surprised. "I think it's very clear."

"James?" Ben confirmed.

I nodded my confirmation.

James Alexander Prescott was offered and accepted the role of Matt Samuel the next morning. The runner up, Sean Ames was offered a supporting male role as Shane Blake, Amanda's brother. The entire cast was signed and confirmed over the next two weeks and pre-production preparation, training, and rehearsals would start shortly in LA. After that, filming was scheduled to begin in April for ten to twelve weeks in Vancouver.

## Chapter 3: The Boyfriend

I had met Lance Smith when I was fifteen year's old at the MTV Movie Awards Show. We were both nominated for our performances that year. Lance was cute and funny, and a talented young actor. We had mutual friends and started to hang out a lot. On my sixteenth birthday, he gave me a surfboard with a gift certificate for lessons from him. He obviously didn't know that I had two left feet, but the activity brought us closer. Soon after we started to date.

Lance was my first real boyfriend and my family and friends all liked him. The only problem was that he divided his time between living in New York and LA, so we often found ourselves having a long-distance relationship. Otherwise, he was fun to be with and after speaking with my parents and my agent; Lance was the first person I told about landing the coveted role. I kept him apprised of the auditions for the rest of the cast, which was a dizzying task, but I valued his opinion as an actor and trusted friend so it was nice to share it. When the entire cast was finally signed, he surprised me by flying in that evening. I opened the door and there he was with a dozen balloons and flowers with a huge sign that said: *Knock em' Dead.* We celebrated with my family that evening and I was going to be sad when I had to say good-bye to him. I was starting work on *Galaxy Drifters* the next month and Lance had to be in New York for a Broadway play that he was performing in.

We took a walk together after having dinner with my family. I was only seventeen years old, so I still lived at home with my parents and siblings in Brentwood, which is a district in the Westside of LA. Lance was four years older. He had a condo that he owned in New York City and he shared a beach house in Laguna Beach with a good buddy whenever he was in California. It was a lovely warm evening with a gentle marine breeze off the Pacific Ocean. We walked hand in hand enjoying each other's company. We stopped under an oak tree at my favorite park a few block's from my parent's house.

"I'm going to miss you baby."

"I'm going to miss you too," I said sadly.

"Hey don't be sad. It's a great opportunity. Maybe even a once in a lifetime opportunity."

"Do you think so Lance?" I asked.

"I do." He paused and then asked, "What do you think of the cast members?"

I was embarrassed to admit that the only cast member I could think about was James and I started to blush as recollections of our brief encounter flooded my memory. I tried blocking James from my thoughts as I concentrated on answering his question.

"Hmm-mmm...it's mostly an unknown cast, so I'm not familiar with most of their previous work. But, um, after seeing the sheer volume of performers competing for the roles, the actors who were chosen really earned it. I mean they rocked it during auditions. It's hard, like, to describe, but the casting crew took painstaking attention to find the right actors for each role and when I performed with them, it just ah, felt right, and the scenes came to life. I know that might sound lame, but that's how it felt. Ben told me that in the end it all hinges on instinct and my instinct tells me that we have a winning cast. So yeah, I think it's gonna be good."

"What's the leading man like?" he asked with curiosity.

"Oh, I don't know..." I said, my face growing hot. "I guess I would say that James is...ah, intense. "Yeah...intense is a good word to describe him. I think he is a natural and gifted actor and there's no doubt about it, he nailed the role. He seems to have a realness about him that he really puts out there and I felt an immediate kinship with him during the audition..." I trailed off, fearful that I had disclosed too much.

"Well, it sounds like it's going to be a good time on the set." Lance said sincerely, taking a step closer. He grabbed me then and we shared lingering kisses under the big Oak for a longtime that evening. Lance was fun to make out with, and life seemed very sweet and promising as we each prepared to go on our new, but separate adventures.

Lance stayed in California for two weeks. I promised him that I would come to New York for the opening of his show and from there I was headed to rehearsals for *Galaxy Drifters*.

## Chapter 4: New York

Lance twirled me around JFK airport kissing me passionately. "I'm so happy you're here," he said with genuine enthusiasm. "Me too," I said kissing him back.

Lance had a break from his rehearsal schedule for three days, and then he would have to work during the last few days of my visit in preparation for the show's opening. I would stay to watch his performance on opening night, and then I had to fly out to LA the next day. I pushed all thoughts of work aside, and concentrated on enjoying three whole days together without any obligations. I was so excited that I could hardly contain myself. I rarely got a vacation and I wanted to make good use of each precious moment with Lance. I knew that we wouldn't get an opportunity like this again for a while.

"Get ready for a real New York experience," he promised as he escorted me to a waiting cab.

It was a cold winter day, but the sun was shining brightly as we walked hand in hand through central park. That first afternoon we went ice-skating and I kept falling, but Lance always caught me. He took me to his favorite coffee house where we lingered for hours talking and laughing. After that, we strolled haplessly around, no particular destination just happy to be together and carefree.

That evening we had dinner at a little bistro in the Village and then we walked home to Lance's place through Washington Square Park, which was one of my favorite spots in the city. It started to snow and we were huddled together for warmth. Lance had his arm around me, occasionally letting it drop to stroke my backside. It was very romantic, and I was eager, yet nervous, to be alone with him in his apartment.

Lance lived in a spacious modern loft in a pre-war luxury building a few blocks from Union Square. His place was large and open with hardwood floors and a gourmet kitchen fit for a chef. When we arrived at his place, he grabbed a bottle of red wine and two glasses and led me to a rooftop terrace.

"*Wow*...this view is amazing," I exclaimed.

"Yeah, this is the reason I bought the place," he said proudly. "It's almost as amazing as you," he said taking a step closer and wrapping his arms around me in a tight embrace.

I leaned against him watching the snowfall and we stood together like that for a longtime.

"I know we've always taken things slow, and I don't want to rush you baby, but I'd really like to have sex with you tonight."

My heart started to beat erratically and my palms were sweaty. I was nervous, really, *really* nervous, but I wanted him.

I turned to Lance and nodded my consent and he silently took my hand and led me back to his apartment.

He turned on music and started to light candles creating a romantic atmosphere.

"Hey...are you trying to seduce me?" I joked, but the tremor in my voice gave away my inexperience and anxiety.

"I'm just trying to make it perfect Alex. I know it's your first-time, and we will take it slow ok?" he murmured gently in my ear.

He didn't wait for my response.

"Dance with me?" he said tenderly taking my hand in his.

Lance began to kiss me and we started to dance in a slow sensual rhythm to *Thank You* by Dido. The kisses became more fervent and Lance started to unbutton my blouse as we made our way to the couch. We fumbled together trying to take each other's clothes off in a heated rush. I sat on his lap with my legs tightly wound around his waist as our bodies joined in a frenzied tempo. Swiftly Lance got off the couch with me still wrapped around his waist and he carried me to the bedroom.

"Are you on birth control Alex?" he whispered in my ear.

"Yes, my mom dragged me to the gynecologist after we started dating," I confessed.

We started to make out again on the bed, but I pulled away.

"What's wrong?" Lance asked concerned.

"Nothing, but, um, maybe we should still use a condom? I don't know how many people you've been with," I told him in a heated embarrassed rush.

He grabbed my face so that we could look at each other. "If it makes you feel better, I'll wear a condom. But I've always been safe, Alex. Before you, I had two girlfriends and we were careful. Aside from those relationships, I've had some casual sex, but I've always worn condoms on those occasions, and I've been tested, so you're safe with me, " he said earnestly.

"I-I trust you Lance, but would you mind wearing a condom as it will make me feel better?" I asked tentatively.

"Of course baby, whatever makes you feel comfortable," he said.

Talking stopped as desire took over. The first time was a little awkward and uncomfortable.

"How are you feeling?" he asked.

"A little sore," I admitted. I looked at the blood on the mattress cover and was embarrassed by the proof of my lost virginity.

He saw the flush on my cheeks and heard the catch in my voice. He lifted my chin and looked into my eyes. "Don't be embarrassed Alex. You're beautiful and sexy. The first time is always challenging, but I assure you it gets better and better," he promised.

"Prove it." I whispered softly.

For the rest of the night, he did prove it over and over again.

I woke the next morning sore, but satisfied and happy.

Lance got out of the shower and came over to the bed and kissed me sweetly.

"Did you sleep well?" he asked.

"When you let me," I joked.

A sly smile broke out over his face.

"How are you feeling?" he inquired gently but with curiosity.

"Great!" I said as I got off the bed wrapped in his bed sheets.

He kissed my forehead and told me to go take a shower while he fixed breakfast for us. "I have a fun-filled day planned for us Alex. Do you think you'll be able to keep up?"

"I think I can manage, but I was hoping to make one small tweak in your plans…" "Oh yeah, what's that?" he asked with a smirk.

"I was hoping you would join me in the shower, but look's like you already took one…" I said as seductively as possible as I headed into the bathroom.

Lance caught up to me then and gave me a gentle swat on my behind and started to kiss me as the bed sheet that I was wrapped in fell to the ground.

"A man can never get too clean!" he said eagerly.

The rest of the week flew by in a haze of activity and lovemaking. Lance was a sweet and kind lover and a good teacher as he educated me in all things sex! When we finally got out of bed, Lance played tour guide taking me to Rockefeller Center, the Empire State Building, SoHo, and Fifth Ave. On our last free afternoon together we hit golf balls at Chelsea Piers.

During the last few days of the trip Lance had to be in rehearsals and I took that time to memorize lines in preparation for my own rehearsal the following week. When I wasn't working, I aimlessly walked around New York myself. I went shopping, got my hair and nails done, and it was cool, because no one recognized me. For once in my life, I was completely off the grid without a tight schedule. It felt great and in that moment, I was so happy to be young and carefree.

That last evening with Lance I watched his performance on opening night as the willfully alcoholic, unresponsive husband Brick in the Broadway revival of Tennessee Williams *Cat on a Hot Tin Roof*. "Cat" had become a frequent visitor to Broadway and I thought the revival was entertaining, but lacked focus and seemed a bit flabby. However, I thought Lance brought an eye-opening freshness to the role. His acting and delivery was very strong and I was certain that it would gain him some critical acclaim. It was a late night and Lance introduced me to the other performers after the show. We finally made it back to his place in the middle of the night. I could tell that he was exhausted, but he kissed me excitedly and we had sex for the rest of the night until just before dawn.

"I'm going to miss you so much baby," Lance murmured into my ear.

"Me too," I said swallowing back unshed tears. I didn't want to get emotional, as I knew that I had to be on a plane in a few hours and I really needed to be well rested.

"I swear that I'll come visit you during the first break I have," he promised.

"I know and I'll do the same. It's going to be tough, but it won't be forever," I assured. "We will just have to be extra creative with carving out free time for one another."

Neither one of us said goodbye instead we shared a kiss filled with the hopeful promises of young love.

## Chapter 5: Galaxy Drifters

My relationship with Lance went on the back burner as my life was immersed for the foreseeable future with *Galaxy Drifters*. The studio was planning a release date sometime between Halloween and Christmas, so we were kept on a tight production schedule. The hopes were to wrap up filming by the beginning of summer and then we would have July and most of August off. After that we were expected to go on an extensive press tour, think TORTURE, through a dizzying array of cities in the U.S. and abroad. My schedule would be stuffed with *god-awful-mind numbing* interviews, press conferences, photo shoots, and promo events throughout the late summer and fall until the big Premiere tentatively slated for mid-November in California. Although there were high hopes for the film after the blockbuster success of the books, no one could predict the success or failure of the movie, thus *Galaxy Drifters* had to keep to a tight budget and we had no idea if the next installments in the series would ever be made. It all hinged on the almighty box office and those glorious dollar signs – it was anybody's guess?

LA is well known for its generally beautiful sunny weather, but when I returned home from New York, I was greeted with the all-time coldest temperatures ever recorded in LA since 1949. My mother told me it was 28 degrees on this unseasonably cold day in February and I was freezing, as I unpacked my bags in my bedroom. I was scheduled to meet tomorrow with the entire cast including the producers, directors, writers and studio executives to do a read-through of the script and I was both excited and nervous about it. It would be the first time that everyone involved in the production would be gathered together in the same space. After the read-through, I was invited with the other fellow principals to dinner with the producer, director, head writer and a couple of studio executives so that everyone would have a better opportunity to get to know each other.

Following the initial reading of the full script, the next few weeks would be filled with scene readings and then rehearsals as Ben determined how he wanted to shoot the film. Painstaking detail about camera placement, lighting and other adjustments would happen during this time until Ben felt ready to shoot the first scene. In the mist of this, I had an extensive list of trainings, which included: Working out with a personal trainer, flight instruction and exploration of zero gravity environments with Astronauts from NASA, and basic combat skill training for some of the fight scenes in the movie. Lastly, James and I had to do zip lining and bungee jumping in preparation for two scenes in the movie, which I was not happy about. In fact, I was totally FREAKED and SICK to my stomach thinking about it. Maybe I could ask for a stunt double? But I didn't want to be a chicken about it … perhaps it would be fun? *Or not!*

I was the first to arrive at the read-through the next morning at Pinnacle Sage Movies Studio in Culver City, the studio responsible for developing and distributing *Galaxy Drifters*. I enjoyed the peacefulness of the early hour, and grabbed a cup of coffee that the catering crew was just putting out. A large u-shaped table was set-up with name signs indicating where we would sit. I took my seat, grabbing the script that was waiting for me and started to read it. I was so absorbed, that I didn't notice that the room was slowly starting to fill up.

"Surprise!" Audrey Hampton, my friend and former co-star, yelled excitedly, wrapping her arms around me from behind. "Hey lovely!"

Startled, I knocked my coffee cup over. "What the fuck?" I immediately jumped up to clean the coffee spill with my napkin before it ruined my script. Once I determined that the coffee mess was under control, I turned to Audrey and laughed. "Geeeezzzzzzzzz what the hey!!!"

"Sorry if I scared the living crap out of you!" Audrey laughed. "I told Ben that I wanted to surprise you.

"Man *oh* Man…you practically put me into cardiac arrest! What are you doing here?"

"It was a last minute decision, but I'm going to play the role of Candice!" Audrey blurted out ecstatically.

"That's great Audrey, but what happened to Lucy? I thought she was scheduled to play the role?"

"I dunno." Audrey answered. "Ben said the actress had to drop out last minute, so he asked me if I was interested in the role. I had some availability and although the part is small, it will be fun to work with you again. Plus, I'm dating Mark Andrews, and I thought it would be exciting to be part of all the buzz."

"Buzz?" I inquired with a raised eyebrow. "Mark Andrews?"

Mark Andrews was playing the part of my eldest brother in the Blake Family, but I had no idea that they were dating. With those two hooking up, I guess things would definitely be, um, colorful on the set.

"Yeah, buzz!! This movie could be, like, the next big thing! If it does even half as well as expected it could be HUGE!" Audrey chirped enthusiastically. "Where have you been living…under a rock?"

Before I could reply, Lydia, my manager, arrived and joined our conversation.

"No she hasn't been under a rock," Lydia exclaimed, "just on *Cloud Nine* in New York."

"*Why?* What *happened* in New York?" Audrey asked with sudden interest.

"I want *all* the details," Lydia chimed in.

I could tell that my cheeks were turning crimson from all the attention, but I didn't want to discuss it, at least not in a room full of cast and crew.

"I-I'll tell you about my trip *later.*" I said abruptly changing the topic of conversation. "Lydia how was your meeting with Toby yesterday?"

Toby Sawyer was my talent agent with the Gauthier Group entertainment agency.

"It was a good meeting Alex and we have a lot to discuss. You've been offered several projects, and Toby has sent us a number of scripts. I plan to review them this week and if anything look's promising I'll give them to you."

I was about to answer Lydia when I noticed the arrival of James. As he moved around the room, we all stared at him blatantly, like he was a tall glass of water in a room full of thirsty people.

"My oh my...he really is shockingly gorgeous! I think he is even better looking in person than in the magazines and commercials," Audrey commented with a low quiet whistle.

"What type of modeling?" I asked curiously.

"You really are living under a rock aren't you?" joked Audrey. "James Prescott has done a lot of big time fashion modeling; you must have seen him in one of the advertisements for Calvin Klein, Dolce & Gabanna, Gucci, Versace or Guess?"

My eyes widened in recognition. "Oh, that's why he looked so familiar the first time I met him."

Ben who had taken a spot at the head of the table interrupted our conversation and started to speak.

"Could everyone please take their seats," he paused for a moment as cast and crew did as he asked.

Lydia took a seat in the back of the room with the other managers and agents, and Audrey took a seat at the opposite end of the table from me. I was still watching James who was slowly making his way over to his seat, which was just on my right. As he approached, he mouthed "Hi," and smiled at me. It literally made me want to melt. Just as we were about to say hello, the actor, Andrew Mitchell, who was playing the fictional role of my dad, Dr. Daniel Blake, came over to us.

"Hello Miss Brown, Mr. Prescott," he said shaking both our hands.

"Please call me Alex," I started to say as he took the seat next to James.

Before James could say anything, Ben interrupted and started to speak to the group again.

"Hello, for those of you who do not know me, I'm Ben Avery, the director and co-producer for this film. I would like to start with introductions so when we get to you please introduce yourselves to the group by both name and job title," Ben said and then he looked to his left. "Jonathan, I believe you're next..."

After that, Jonathan Banks, the illustrious producer for the film introduced himself. Followed by introductions from the other department heads, financiers, studio executives, writers and so forth. Then it was the actor's turn to begin. It started with me, and then James on my right, followed by Andrew Mitchell and continued on until the last actor had spoken.

When the introductions were finally complete, Ben addressed the group again.

"It gives me great pleasure to welcome all of you onto the set of *Galaxy Drifters*. We have gone to great lengths to find the perfect cast and crew, and each one of you bring your own unique strength and talent to this project. My gut tells me that as we gather and work together we will make this film magical. I encourage each of you to make suggestions and to communicate with me regularly. Let's get started folks..."

When the reading was complete, a hush fell over the room. It was quickly replaced by the babble of voices and everyone seemed overly excited. No one verbalized it, but there was a sense that this was going to be an overwhelming hit.

I sat in stunned silence basking from the afterglow until James stood snapping me to attention. He offered me his hand. "Alex," he smiled. "Nice job!"

"Um, thanks." I mumbled. "You too."

Our eyes met and lingered and my stomach fluttered at his nearness.

"Well done," Ben said as he came over to James and I, causing me to jump slightly from the interruption. "I want you to meet Jonathan Banks, the producer, *now*, because he has to fly out this evening. Also, it would be good if you met a few of the studio execs..."

It continued like that for a few hours as James and I were ushered from one person to the next. Quite frankly it was boring and Jonathan and the other head honchos fit the terrible cliché of suits in Hollywood. You know the type ... overly expensive designer suits, red, stuffy noses from snorting too much coke, and blonde trophy wives with surgically enhanced breasts hanging all over them. Finally we were given a break for a few minutes before the dinner with the department heads and other cast members that was being held at a local gastropub three blocks from the studio.

James talked first. "It's good to see you again. How have you been?"

"Um, I'm good, just a little tired, wish I could duck out of the dinner."

"If you do it, I'll do it too," he dared playfully.

"Could you imagine if we did? Unfortunately, I think Ben would have our heads," I stated with a frown.

"Oh well, it was a nice thought," he said with a wistful smile.

Lydia interrupted us and I introduced her to James.

"James, this is Lydia my manager, organizer and all around best bud! Lydia, this is James, my extremely elegant, sophisticated, and absurdly good-looking co-star." *Oh no…did I actually say that out loud?*

"Nice to meet you Lydia," he said. Then he turned to me. "Elegant and sophisticated, eh? Not sexy?" he questioned with a raised eyebrow.

I turned beet red, but happily Lydia saved me so that I didn't have to reply.

"Nice to meet you James. Alex, could we have a few minutes together before dinner to discuss a few items?" she asked.

"Um, yeah, Lydia, that's a good idea." I mumbled, fiddling with my hands. "Ah, alright then. I better go James. See you at dinner."

"I'll save you a seat," he said smoothly, winking at me. "See you later ladies."

After he left, Lydia turned to me. "*Wow*, you could cut the sexual tension in here with a knife."

I gave her a sheepish grin and looked over my shoulder. "*Shh* Lydia, someone will hear you!"

"I don't think I've ever seen you this rattled before," she whispered with a smirk.

I nervously twisted a strand of hair around my finger. "Stop smirking Lydia," I stammered. "And for the record, I'm not rattled. Come on, let's go work."

\*\*\*

During the dinner, James and I fulfilled our duty well, talking with several of the financial and creative heads. After that, we were free to mingle, but both of us chose to stay together as we met the rest of the cast.

First, we talked with the actors and actresses playing the characters of our parents. Andrew Mitchell and Kelly Wayland were talented and seasoned actors and they were playing the role of my parents, Daniel and Katherine Blake. After that we talked for quite awhile with Owen Stevenson who was playing the character of Christian Samuel, head of the Samuel family, and actress Sally Clark playing the role of his wife, Diane Samuel.

It was getting late when we finally made it over to the table where the younger cast members were seated. I had met all of them before during the audition process, but this was my first real opportunity to get to know them as people. Audrey jumped up first and said that she wanted to introduce me to her boyfriend, actor Mark Andrews, playing the character of my eldest brother Trevor Blake.

"Hi Mark, it's really nice to see you again," I said with a smile in my voice.

"Likewise. I think you're a really talented actress," he said with enthusiasm.

Mark had his arm casually draped over Audrey's shoulder, and I could see how happy they were together. James was casually talking to Sean Ames and Ellie Hawthorne who were playing my brother, and his sister. I turned to them so that we could all be introduced. After the introductions, everyone started to chat and it was a lively animated group. Everyone got along well and it was fun from the start. The only minor irritation I felt was with Ellie Hawthorne who shamelessly flirted with James all night. She kept flipping back her hair and giggling at all of his jokes. Throughout the night she stood by him like glue and was constantly touching him, a caress here, a stroke there. I knew that I was unjustified with my jealousy and that I was acting irrational. After all, I had a boyfriend. James was free to date whoever he wanted. But it still bugged the crap out of me. He could do better than Ellie Hawthorne.

My brooding was interrupted when Sean Ames came over to chat. "It's really good to see you again Alex, I was bummed that I wasn't chosen for the role of Matt Samuel opposite you," he stated.

"You did really well during the audition, I know that it was a difficult choice," I said trying to be comforting.

"It's not so much about losing the job. That did hurt, but I'm over it now. I meant I was hoping to play opposite you so that I could kiss you again," he stated boldly.

I wasn't sure how to respond? *Ugh.*

"Are you dating anyone?" he questioned.

"Yes," I stated firmly.

"How serious?" he continued. "Do you have a boyfriend?"

I was about to say *the relationship was very serious* when I hesitated as I realized that James was watching us and seemed to be listening intently to our conversation.

"Earth to Alex...you didn't answer my question?" prompted Sean.

"Yes, I have a boyfriend," I finally told Sean.

Then I quickly took a peek at James, but I couldn't tell if he was listening or not as he was nodding his head to something that Ellie had just said. Happily my conversation with Sean was interrupted by Audrey and Mark who wanted me to solve a debate they were having over some cinematic trivia from the film that Audrey and I had worked on together. I answered their questions, and then I told the group that I was going home, as I was tired.

"I'll go with you Alex," James said quickly and he grasped my hand and we walked companionably out together.

"Thanks, you saved me from Ellie," he told me conspiratorially with a sly smile on his face.

"You mean you don't want a 'fuck buddy' tonight as she seems a very eager and willing partner?"

"She's not really my type."

"What is your type?" I asked before I could stop myself.

He leaned forward and gave me a playfully seductive look. "I'll tell you one day," he said in a low voice, his eyes roaming over me. I swallowed and found it hard to break my gaze from his.

Something in his promise, the sound of his voice, and the way he looked at me, made me shiver and I trembled slightly. James noticed my reaction and mistakenly thought it was from the cold temperature. He pulled his jacket off and wrapped it around my shoulders.

"Thank you, but you must be freezing." I objected.

"No, I'm fine really. Please wear it as we walk to our cars," he insisted.

"Um, ok, thanks...but tell me if you get cold?"

"Alex, would you like to rehearse lines together on Friday afternoon after we bungee jump?"

"WHAT?" I asked anxiously. "I thought bungee jumping wasn't on the schedule for two weeks?"

James was staring at me intently, a mixture of concern and amusement in his expression. "It got moved to Friday on the new schedule."

"Oh?" I tried to hide my unease, but I could tell that I wasn't fooling him.

"Are you nervous Alex? Don't be it will be fun and I promise I'll distract you as long as you promise not to throw up on me!"

"Throw up on you? Is it a tandem jump?" I asked with a quiver in my voice.

This was getting worse by the second. My head was throbbing and my palms were sweaty thinking about it.

"You'll be fine," he whispered in my ear as we arrived at my car, gently putting his hand on my shoulder to reassure me.

"Thanks for the jacket," I said as I handed it back to him.

"Good night Alex," he said as he waited for me to get into my car and drive away.

*** 

The next few weeks went by in a blur of activity and I was lucky, because bungee jumping preparation got eliminated from the schedule, but I would still have to face my fears of jumping during the actual filming of it. Every moment was packed with training, rehearsals, and workouts. During my first real break, I had lunch with Lydia and Audrey together.

"Ok spill?" said Lydia.

"About what?" I asked innocently.

"You promised us the details about your trip to New York. What happened with Lance? Come on, fess up?" she prodded.

They both stared at me waiting for answers and I shyly looked down while playing with my hair.

"Did you have sex with him?" Audrey finally blurted out.

I nodded my head.

"Was this your first-time?" Audrey asked.

"How was it?" Lydia implored.

They continued to assault me with rapid-fire questions until silence filled the air.

"It was really good. At least, I think it was really good as I have nothing to compare it to." I said bashfully.

"Well...did he make you come?" Audrey asked bluntly to my great embarrassment.

Audrey didn't have a shy bone in her body. No topic was off limits.

"Orally, yes," I said with a big goofy grin.

"What about through intercourse?" Lydia asked.

My brow furrowed at this intimate line of questioning.

"I'm not sure, " I confessed with uncertainty.

"What do you mean you're unsure?" questioned Audrey.

"Well, I know I didn't the first few times, but then it got better and better, and I think I did that very last time, but I'm not totally sure?" I confessed awkwardly.

"You'll know it when it happens." Audrey said with great confidence.

After that, they both told me their first time sex experiences. Which were horrific and hilarious at the same time. We laughed and enjoyed girl chat for the next hour, but right before I got up, Audrey said something that made me pause.

"We all thought you and James were dating. It's been the *buzz* around the set," she told me with a big smile.

"What?" I questioned.

"Well, the chemistry between you both during the first reading was so obvious and then your body language that evening at dinner started to make people wonder," she answered. "Then we witnessed it again during the second reading and throughout rehearsals, and you've both been spending a lot of time together. Yesterday, James asked Mark if he knew how serious the relationship with your boyfriend was?"

"He did? How did Mark respond?" I asked with curiosity.

"Mark told James that he didn't know, and Mark said that James dropped it, and they haven't talked about it since," answered Audrey.

The rest of the afternoon Ben and the crew had James and I, with fellow actors, reading scenes through to determine how Ben wanted to position the scene. I was self-conscious after what Audrey told me, so I purposely tried to mingle with the other actors and crew members during breaks rather than spending it alone with James. Sean seemed overly pleased by my attention, and before I knew it we were wrapping up for the day. Ben told me later that evening that right now he just wanted to get a feel for everyone to see how we were feeding off one another, but that everything was going well and according to schedule. He felt confident that we would be ready to transition from rehearsal to shooting the first scene in Vancouver in a few short weeks.

***

The nonstop flight from LAX to Vancouver, British Columbia, otherwise known as "Hollywood North," took approximately three hours. Vancouver got its nickname, because it has a thriving film production industry and is now the third-largest film production center in North America and the second-largest location for television production outside of LA.

When Lydia and I arrived, it was a wet, but mild and pleasant day in April. We hailed a cab that took us to our furnished short-term apartment rental on W Georgia St. in downtown Vancouver, where the cast and crew were staying. This location would be our primary residence for the next ten to twelve weeks, but we would also go away for a few days to shoot some of the outdoor adventure sequences at other locations. Lydia and I had been to Vancouver on a previous film shoot, thus we knew the breathtaking city well and loved it. The downtown apartment was located at the crossroads of the business and shopping district and it was just a short walk away from The Seawall, a path that lined the city's scenic waterfront and was one of my favorite running routes - maybe 13 or 14 miles in length. We were also close to Stanley Park that bordered downtown and was almost entirely surrounded by waters of the Pacific Ocean. When I had time, I liked to explore the park's forest trails, beaches, and lakes.

There was a gentle knock on my door early the next morning.

"Who is it?" I asked

"It's me, James."

"Just a second!"

I was still in my ratty tank top and pajama pants but in an effort to look presentable I quickly brushed my hair and teeth.

"Hey," I said as I opened the door.

"Sorry did I wake you?"

How could he look *so* good this early in the morning? My heart skipped a beat just looking at him.

"No, I was in bed reviewing the script and some notes that Ben gave me," I answered suddenly shy.

"Well, this is for you," he said handing me a sterling silver pilot wings pin. "It's for good luck today. Jumping isn't as bad as you may fear and you might surprise yourself and have fun doing it. "

Today was the filming of our bungee jump scene and I already felt *sick* to my stomach thinking about it.

"Thank you so much, James. This is…" I started to choke up. "Really sweet. I-I'll definitely wear it, but I'm still going to be scared shitless until it's over."

He scooted closer to me, leaving almost no space between us. "You'll be totally fine, I promise."

"Thanks." I said glancing at the clock. "Um, Christ! Is that the time? I better take a shower now."

He reluctantly pulled away. "Alright, see you soon. No wimping out!"

"Yes sir!"

James and I, along with one of the assistant directors, and a camera crew left soon after for the one and a half hour's drive to Whistler. We were told that we would be jumping 160 feet off a bridge over the glacier fed Cheakamus River, which was regarded as one of the most scenic bungee jumping sites in the world. It was a unique setting, surrounded by cliffs and forest with the breathtaking peak of Black Tusk in the background. The crew had to determine the camera position for filming it. Once that was all set, James and I would do the tandem jump.

During the drive in the van, I asked James to distract me.

"How would you like me to distract you?" he asked wickedly.

"Are you flirting with me James?" I asked innocently.

He leaned in closer. "If I was, you would know it!" he promised with a devilish grin.

Wow, I couldn't stop smiling! When he sat this close to me and so good-naturedly joked with me, he was irresistible. A few times we accidently brushed up against each other in the van, and each time it literally took my breath away. I felt like a burning hot branding iron had scorched me and I was suddenly wet between my legs. I looked away flustered and embarrassed. I loved Lance, and I needed to keep some distance between James and I, but how was I going to do it?

We made it to the bridge quicker than I would have liked as I was still trying to find the courage to *psych myself up* for the jump. The instructor was giving us a safety briefing and told us that we had to leap out as far as possible with our arms outstretched like a bird of prey, otherwise we would spin like a corkscrew on the way down and I definitely didn't want that to happen. Next, the instructor strapped us into a full body harness, and yes, I could feel every delectable inch of him.

James smirked. "Hmm, I rather like this," he whispered.

Our ankles were snugly strapped together with various tight ropes and since we were jumping tandem, the operators tethered us face-to-face. We were on the platform, and the director yelled "ACTION!" We raised our hands in the bird of prey position together and just as we jumped, James started to kiss me passionately.

His kiss took me by surprise, the ultimate diversion and it worked perfectly. I kept my eyes shut for the first 50 feet and by the time I opened them and realized what was happening we were already in a free fall and it was thrilling, terrifying and exhilarating all at once. We flew upwards again on the rebound, and there was no denying the adrenaline rush. When the cord had stopped moving and we stopped bouncing we were slowly lowered down by the operator onto a boat below. I had a feeling of elation after the jump and I turned to James and smiled.

My heart was pounding, and I wanted to launch myself into his arms and press my lips to his, but instead, I just thanked him. "Thank you so much, James. Um, I couldn't have done it without you."

"You're welcome Alex. I'm happy to distract you anytime."

On the ride back, I asked him about himself and his family. He grew up in the Boston area and attended a private school about 30 minutes away in the town of Milton. He loved the East Coast and it sounded like he came from a prominent family, but he didn't like to talk about it so I didn't ask. His dad was a well-known conductor and his British born mother a music professor and pianist. They had a great love of art and music, and tried to instill it in James and his younger sister Rachel. James attended Julliard majoring in both music and drama. He was the lead vocalist in a local Boston band and had written a few songs, and was also adept on the piano and guitar. His parents had hoped he would pursue music permanently, as they were less enthusiastic about his acting career. When James decided to drop out of Julliard to pursue acting full-time it caused a rift with his parents, as they did not approve. His younger sister who was about my age seemed to share the musical talent of her family, and was planning to attend Berklee School of Music next year as a freshman.

James started acting at a young age in school productions and in a local theatre company. He found he was good at acting, and he received positive accolades from peers and audiences alike. His first break came not through acting, but when a modeling agent spotted him. He became a child model, getting a steady stream of work, which he found helped open doors into the acting world that he loved.

At seventeen, he received his first break by getting a minor movie role in what would later become a huge blockbuster. Although his role was small, he received positive reviews and due to the popularity of the movie, he was suddenly getting sought after for both film and modeling work. It was with great difficulty that James tried to balance the work he loved with being a student. It continued that way for another two years, until he decided to quit Julliard causing friction with his family.

"Your quiet," James commented when he finished talking.

"Sorry, I was trying to figure out your age," I told him truthfully.

He cocked his head to one side and looked amused.

"I'll be twenty-two in May. You know what that mean's don't you?" he asked with raised eyebrow. "You need to respect your elders," he finished with a grin.

I started to giggle and rolled my eyes. "Nuh-uh."

"UH HUH." He returned. "When do you turn eighteen?"

"In July."

"Good…you'll be legal," he joked. "Now that I've told you about me. I want to hear about you?"

"What do you want to know?"

"Everything!"

"Everything? That's an awful tall order, man!" I said with a smile, wiggling my eyebrows playfully at him. "Well, I grew up in LA in a zany loving family and we're all close. My parents are avid gardeners and they like to hike. They have, um, really eclectic taste and eat, like, lots of soy and berries.

"Eclectic?"

"Yeah, they were into tofu and stuff like that way before it became popular."

"What do they do for work?"

My mom is a stage manager, and my dad is a script supervisor. They both work in Hollywood and love it.

"Are they supportive of your career?" James asked with interest.

"Are you kidding? My parents are my biggest fans!"

"You're lucky," James muttered.

"Doesn't your family support your acting career?"

"Halfheartedly."

"Oh...I'm sorry." I said feeling awkward. I wanted to ask James to explain further, but I didn't want to seem nosy, so I let it drop.

"Do you have any brothers or sisters?" he asked.

"Yes, I have two older brothers; Zach is twenty at UCLA studying theatre and writing. My eldest brother, Pete, he got the brains in the family and is studying medicine at Stanford."

"...And you got the beauty and talent," James finished with an irresistible smile.

I knew that I shouldn't be so pleased by his complement, but I was, and I had a stupid looking grin on my face because of it.

"What about you James? Are you close with your family?"

"Yeah...but it's challenging." He sighed. "My parent's have really high expectations for my sister and I, and at times it get's exhausting trying to live up to their standards. But, yeah, overall, I would say that we're close."

When we returned back to the set, we spent the rest of the day rehearsing lines together, but often we would take breaks and talk about favorite music, theatre, cinema, sports, food, and activities we liked. I got him to promise to let me hear him sing sometime. I found out that he loved the ocean, something we had in common, and that he was an avid sailor. He also liked to play tennis, hike, bike, and run so we shared a lot of the same interests.

Over the next several weeks, James and I fell into a pattern of waking up early and running together at The Seawall and then rehearsing. We found ourselves staying up into the wee hours of the morning talking and confiding in each other about every topic and insignificant detail from our lives. I told James everything about me from the most trivial and mundane facts, like how I was scared of my fourth grade science teacher and would pretend to be sick in an effort to miss the weekly field trip, to deeper, more serious topics, like my insecurities as an actress and the death of my grandmother. James did the same. He told me how controlling and cold his father could be and his discomfort about the phony shallowness of Hollywood and of his being stared at all the time and treated like a pretty face and piece of meat. I shared intimate details with him that I had never shared with anyone else in my life and I felt like I could tell him anything and he would understand.

I thought back to the very first time I met James and the strong affect he had on me. The same butterfly "fluttery" feeling was in my belly now, in fact, it was even more powerful. During the last few weeks my feelings for him had grown far beyond physical attraction. James was kind, considerate, extremely intelligent, good humored and likeable. I enjoyed spending time with him, and found myself drawn to him. He was a natural born leader who radiated vigor and a sense of seriousness and competence. I liked him, and he was quickly becoming a trusted friend that I could count on.

I didn't need Audrey to tell me that people were speculating about us, because I knew they were. In an effort to create some distance, I tried to mingle, rehearse and socialize with our fellow actors as much as possible. But James and I had such a natural relationship, that we invariably ended up spending the lion share of our time together.

With Ben, each day of shooting the film was a very organic experience. I would come to the set at the studio well-briefed, but often after a first take Ben would talk to me or to another actor to tweak a performance, and we would do another take and then another. He was a perfectionist who knew exactly what he wanted and he was a genius at knowing when all the elements of the scene – actors, camera, sound, stunts, effects etc. – were ready to come together in perfect harmony. This process was repeated with meticulous detail until everyone was satisfied with a scene and then Ben would shoot it several more times until he got what he was looking for. Then we would do it all over again with another scene.

Things were going well and Ben commented that visually and technically the film was "looking great." In the days and weeks that followed, it became a kind of magic to watch the project come together. The whole cast got along famously and the chemistry between James and I and the other principals were palpable. We were riding the crest of a wave from the very first day. No one verbalized it, but it just felt right and you could almost smell it. We all felt it and experienced it and were convinced of it.

## Chapter 6: Drinking Games

It was a Friday night in mid-May when we arrived at the Shawnigan
Lake Resort & Cottages for a six-day shoot across Vancouver Island,
from Shawnigan Lake to the harbor city of Nanaimo and the town of
Ladysmith.

Lydia had flown back to LA to take care of business matters. I
talked with her daily, but I didn't think I would see her again until
filming wrapped up and I flew back to LA the following month.

I also spoke with Lance if not daily, then a few times per week.
The play was not doing well and was scheduled to end its run in a
few weeks. Although he was disappointed that the "Cat" revival had
not been successful, his performance of Brick had received favorable
reviews and he had several new projects lined up. Once the show
wrapped up, he was going to fly out and visit me. After that he had
business and auditions in LA, thus we would meet up again when I
returned home. I was excited to see my family, friends, and Lance
when filming concluded, but the break would be relatively short, as I
was expected with my fellow principals in late August to go on an
extensive press tour throughout the fall until the big Premiere slated
for mid-November in California.

I had plans that evening for dinner and drinks with James, Audrey,
Mark, Sean, and Ellie. Everyone was in high spirits, because we had
a day off from filming the next day. We had an Italian feast. The
legal drinking age in British Columbia was 19, so Ellie and I were
the only underage drinkers at the table, but that didn't prevent us
from joining in, and I was a little intoxicated from all of the red wine.
We surprised James with a birthday cake and he seemed embarrassed,
not liking the attention. After dinner, we all went back to the resort
on the lake, and were planning to hang out together in Sean's cottage.
As we walked there, I handed James a birthday gift.

"You shouldn't have bought me anything," he said with a smile
on his face. "Do you want me to open it now?"

"If you want to."

I had given him a pair of sneakers with a note that said: "Thought these *might* help you to keep up with me!" I also gave him some music journals as he said that he liked to write songs when he had quiet moments on the set. Lastly, I had given him an iPod Nano with some of my favorite songs downloaded on it.

"No way! This is great. Thank you." He said, while scrolling through the playlist. James seemed genuinely pleased by my gifts and I was happy that he liked it. Then he took a step closer and I felt a 'flip-flop' sensation in my chest. "Alex?" his voice was hoarse with emotion and for one brief moment, I thought he was going to kiss me. I freaked out, abruptly pulling away and breaking the mood. I'm sure James noticed my reaction, but he was too much of a gentleman to point it out, so instead we just quietly walked together, both preoccupied with our own thoughts.

We joined the others in Sean's cottage where our friends had apparently started to play drinking games before our arrival. *Uh oh* – I had to be careful, as I was already tipsy from too much wine at dinner.

The group was playing a modified version of the game of *Truth or Dare*. Apparently, the last person who drank got to ask the next question. The person receiving the question, got to hear the question before deciding to choose truth or dare, but if they decided to take the dare, they had to drink two Kamikaze shots.

About an hour later, there was a dull ache in my head when Sean banged his beer on the table, "Time for round four!"

Soon after, Mark smirked while finishing off the last bit of potting soil, completing his third dare of the night. He chuckled and turned to the group, "yummy!" Then he went on to lick the inside of the plant container.

"Gross!" Ellie muttered. "I think I'm gonna be sick from watching you eat dirt."

"It was soil not dirt!" Mark boasted with glee.

We were getting rowdy and drunker as the night progressed. It was in this festive, but inebriated state, when I heard Mark call my name.

"Alex is it true that you lost your *virginity*, right before coming here?" he asked.

I couldn't believe he asked me that! The blood drained from my face and I felt humiliated. Did he really say that in front of everybody? Anger took over, and I felt bitterly betrayed by Audrey who at least had the decency to look embarrassed.

"You don't have to answer that Alex," Audrey interrupted. "Mark you're an asshole," she said as she elbowed him in the rib cage looking furious at him.

I couldn't look at anyone, least of all James. Suddenly, I decided it would be best to move on quickly and make a joke of it.

"No, it's fine. I'll take the dare. Come on Mark give me your best shot?" I teased boldly to hide my discomfort.

Sean handed me two Kamikaze shots, and I downed them one after another. They tasted awful and burned my throat, but I didn't care, better that, then to think about Mark's words. I was mortified.

"Ok Alex…go outside and run a lap around the lake," Mark said.

*That didn't seem so bad.*

"And Alex, you have to strip down first and run in your bra and underwear," he challenged smugly.

*What an asshole.* He wanted a show; I would give him a show. Before I lost my nerve, I got up as gracefully as I could. *Whoa* – I was feeling off balance from all of the alcohol. Without another thought, I discarded my shirt and jeans trying to look as seductive as possible. I stood in front of the group for a moment and then went outside and started to sprint. It was unseasonably cold, and my head and throat were sore. I was feeling unsteady, but the brisk air helped as I focused on putting one foot in front of the other. From the distance, I thought I heard loud voices, and something clattered, and then there was silence. Moments later, I felt James arms around me. I stopped running and looked up at him as he lifted his sweater off over his head and put it on me.

"Come on. I'm taking you home," he said with authority.

I thought he sounded angry, but I was so tired and drunk that I didn't argue. I was feeling wobbly and suddenly I was off the ground. It took me a minute to realize that James was carrying me.

"What are you doing? I'm fine. Put me down," I yelled.

He ignored me and carried me to the doorstep of my cottage. It was the second time tonight that I was humiliated and I hoped that no one had seen it.

He gently put me down and leaned me against the doorframe so that he could fetch the key. Then I heard him curse as he realized that my clothes, purse and room key were back in Sean's cabin. He turned to me and grabbed my hand and led me to his cottage instead. I was sick and dizzy when we walked in his room and I took a seat on his bed feeling droopy.

"I think I'm going to be sick," I said and ran to the bathroom.

He followed me in and pulled my hair back as I vomited in the toilet. I continued to hurl the contents of dinner for the next ten minutes and then abruptly it was over.

When he was certain that I was no longer going to be sick, he took a damp cloth and washed my face. Then he helped me to the bed. I was mortified; truly this was the worse night of my life.

"Here drink the entire glass of water and the aspirin," he ordered.

"Thanks," I said feebly and then I curled up in a ball on his bed and fell asleep.

I awoke abruptly the next morning and was momentarily confused about where I was until memories of the humiliating events of the previous night came flooding back. I slowly sat up. I had a headache and still felt off kilter, but other then that, I was better than I expected. What I really wanted was a long hot shower. When I looked up, James was staring at me from across the room where he sat in an armchair reading what looked like a script.

"What time is it? I asked.

"A little after Nine. How are you feeling?" he asked.

"Better than I should, but I need a shower and more aspirin," I replied.

"I left you water and aspirin on the bedside table. Also, I went to Sean's cabin this morning to get your stuff. It's over there," he indicated with his hand.

"Thanks. I owe you."

"Don't worry about it," he said graciously. "I'll give you some privacy for a few minutes and I'll grab us some food."

"I'm not very hungry."

"It's not a question Alex. You're eating," he said with authority.

"I never realized you were so bossy," I responded haughtily.

"After the stunt last night, someone needs to take command. Go take a shower," he ordered grumpily.

He didn't wait for my response as he got up and left. I was ticked off by his bossiness, but on some level, I knew he was right. When I got up, I realized that I was wearing his t-shirt with my bra and underwear. I didn't remember putting it on which only led to further embarrassment.

When I got out of the shower I put on my clothes from yesterday minus the grimy bra and underwear that I had slept in. I put toothpaste on my finger and brushed my hair with his comb. I was feeling significantly better.

James came in with bagels, muffins, coffee and juice. To appease him I took a bagel and started munching on it.

"Are you happy that I'm eating?" I questioned.

"Ecstatic," he replied sarcastically looking pissed.

"What's your problem James? Are you mad at me?"

Silence filled the room as I waited for his reply.

"I'm more mad at myself," he finally responded.

"I don't understand. Why?"

"Well, for one I punched Mark in the face last night. Don't get me wrong, the guy had it coming, but I'm still feeling a little bad about it."

"When did this happen?" I asked with interest.

"When you were running. I told him the game was over, then he said something obnoxious which ticked me off, so I punched him."

"What did he say?" I asked burning with curiosity.

"Nothing worth repeating, but in the light of day, I realized part of what Mark said is true."

"Which Is?"

James started to pace and I had the impression that he was struggling with something. Then he turned to me and with determined steps came closer until we were facing each other.

"I've known this whole time that you have a boyfriend, but I was hoping that it was not a significant relationship. Last night, I realized that I was wrong and it is tearing me up inside. The thought of you with any other man is making me sick. I want you to break up with him Alex."

I suddenly felt very tired and I put my hands on the table for support. I slumped into the open chair next to me and put my face down in shame.

"I don't know what to say James?" I told him sincerely.

"Tell me that you feel the same way and that you'll break up with him?" he implored.

"I'm confused," I whispered.

I could tell he was hurt by my hesitation. He moved away from me then and his facial impression became hard.

"If you're confused, I think you should leave my room now."

"Please don't be angry," I begged. "I just need some time."

"I'm not angry, but I think we should keep our distance, until you figure things out," he answered without emotion.

Tears blinded my eyes. I nodded and left.

## Chapter 7: Ultimatum

I went back to my room and threw myself on the bed and started to sob. I felt like someone had sucker punched me in the gut and that I couldn't breath. I stayed like that for hours, certainly not how I imagined spending my day off.

There was a light knock on my door and I fervently hoped it was James changing his mind. I just wanted it to go back to the way it was before. When I opened the door my hopes were squashed. It was Mark and Audrey.

"Can we come in?" Mark asked.

I opened the door to let them come in and I noted that they looked embarrassed and Mark's face was ashen. He also had a large bruise under his right eye.

"Alex I'm really sorry for my behavior last night," he said quickly trying to get the words out in a jumbled rush. "I was really drunk and stupid, and I know I acted like an obnoxious dick. Can you forgive me?"

"Well, you were an obnoxious dick," I stated flatly. "But you're forgiven. Just no repeat performances, ok?"

Relief flooded his face.

"I promise. I'll be a boy scout from now on," he declared.

"You a boy scout? I highly doubt that!" I joked. "But I would like you to reconcile with James? I'm not sure what happened last night between you two, but you need to sort it out. Especially before tomorrow when filming resumes," I stated seriously.

"I know. I'm going to make amends with him now. I'll leave you and Audrey alone to talk," he said glumly like a little boy, then he turned and left.

An awkward silence filled the room as neither Audrey nor I spoke.

"I'm so very sorry," she finally said with a catch in her voice. "I value our friendship and I never meant to betray your trust."

"How could you tell Mark something so personal about me?" I questioned angrily.

"I didn't mean to tell him it just sort of slipped out one day and Mark promised that he wouldn't say anything," she said with a shaky voice.

"How does something like that just slip out?" I accused bitterly.

Her face was drained of color and she didn't look me in the eye. Finally she said, "Everyone on the set had a bet that you and James were secretly dating. Mark was sure of it and he had a lot of money riding on it. Of course, I didn't agree with them, because I knew you were serious with Lance. Mark kept pushing and prodding asking me why I thought you were serious with Lance and then I let it slip that you had taken your relationship to a new level. I'm so very sorry Alex. Can you ever forgive me?"

Moments passed as I processed the information. I was undecided about if I wanted to forgive her or not, but I was the one who shared the intimate details, and if I didn't want anyone to know, I shouldn't have shared it to began with.

"I will try to forgive you," I said with hesitation. "You hurt me and it's going to take me awhile to trust you again."

"I understand," she said.

"Can you tell me what happened between James and Mark last night? What did Mark say to provoke James to hit him?" I asked.

Audrey's cheeks were red and she looked embarrassed.

"Are you sure you want to know Alex?" she asked gently.

"Yes, I want to know," I responded.

"After you accepted the dare and went running, the mood in the cabin had shifted from festive to arctic in seconds. James was pissed and everyone else was disgusted with Mark. James took command and told everyone that the game was over. He was about to leave when Mark approached him, stinking drunk. They were face-to-face and Mark said: *You're just mad, because you wanted to deflower her yourself.* Then boom, James hit Mark in the face and Mark went down on the floor. I think James wanted to tear Mark's head off, but Sean broke up the fight and James left seconds later. So now you know everything that happened," she concluded.

As I reflected on Audrey's description of the events from the previous night, I kept repeating in my head what James had said to me only a few hours before –

*A part of what Mark said is true...I've known this whole time that you have a boyfriend, but I was hoping that it was not a significant relationship. Last night, I realized that I was wrong and it is tearing me up inside. The thought of you with any other man is making me sick. I want you to break up with him Alex.*

Over and over again the scene from last night and this morning repeated in my head. Minutes passed, but one question remained in my head.

"Audrey, why does everyone think that James and I have been secretly dating?"

"Isn't it obvious Alex?"

"Not to me."

"Let me think about it for a sec." I waited patiently for Audrey to collect her thoughts. Then she turned to me and started to talk. "Unlike everyone else here, I've known you and Lance for awhile and I always thought that you and Lance were like a nice couple together. You know pleasant, comfortable and stuff like that. I thought you guys were cute, until I saw you with James. But when I see you and James together it just blows me away! I know it sounds cheesy, but um...it's like magical to see you guys together...on-screen and off-screen."

"What?" I interrupted, scowling at her. "I'm like, not following you?"

"Do you really need me to spell it out for you? The connection and chemistry you have with James is just so noticeable – come on, everyone sees it! I've never seen two people more in love in my life."

"So Aud...are you telling me that I should break up with Lance?"

"Of course not Alex, but can you deny you have feelings for James?"

"Dude, I have no idea! Yeah, I want to jump his bones and I have feelings for him, intense friggin cheesy feelings...but I'm much too young to even know what that means? Maybe its just lust?" I said with uncertainty.

"If you say so..." Audrey acknowledged in her cynical, know-it-all voice.

I was never a good poker player and I could tell that Audrey knew that I was full of crap and making excuses.

"What are you scared of?" she asked gently.

"I've always tried to be fully in control of my emotions and with James I'm not." I stated simply. "I'm already in so deep. If I go down that road, he has the power to hurt me and I'm scared that I'll lose myself in him."

"Why do you think he will hurt you?" she questioned.

"I don't think James would intentionally hurt me, it's just we are so young and it is so intense so fast, that I'm scared as fuck." I admitted. "Also, I thought that I was in love with Lance and now I'm so confused. I don't know what to do. I don't want to hurt anyone."

"I think you should take it one day at a time and don't rush into anything. Just have fun for now," she said soothingly.

"I guess." I swallowed. "Um. Hypothetically, what would you do if someone gave you an ultimatum?"

"I would tell them to *go to hell*, hypothetically of course," she grinned. "Now get some rest, we have a busy day tomorrow."

With that, she gave me a hug and said goodbye.

***

That first week after the incident at the lake was torture. James was always professional and polite, but otherwise he kept his distance and didn't acknowledge me at all. In front of the cameras, no one would know, as I have to admit that we were good actors and the production was coming together at a rapid pace. When I was off camera that's when the depression set in. The days dragged and I was miserable and lonely. I tried to bury myself in work, and when I wasn't working, I went running, or to the gym, but every time I came up for air, the stinging slap of reality hit me in the face. I had lost my appetite and I knew that I was being a recluse and that I had to snap out of it.

Lance was wrapping up the play and he would be coming to see me later next week. My emotions were twisted. One part of me desperately wanted to see Lance. He was always fun, easy, and uncomplicated. I was feeling lonely and it would be nice to be with him. On the other hand, I had terrible guilt and I was afraid that I would not be able to look Lance in the eye. I was confused about my feelings. If I loved Lance, how could I have these intense emotions toward James? I kept trying to tell myself that I hadn't done anything wrong. James and I were just friends, and it was the close proximity and intimate nature of our job that kept throwing us together. I repeated the lie to myself multiple times until I almost believed it.

I didn't think it could get worse, but I was wrong. I was running really early one morning when I saw the pretty blonde production assistant; I think her name was Julie, leave James hotel room. It was clear from the choice of clothes and 'just fucked' hair that she had spent the night with him. I shouldn't care. He had every right to date or sleep with whatever girl he wanted.

That same day, I had just finished with wardrobe and makeup, when I saw Ellie step down from James trailer with the biggest shit-eating grin on her face. Later, during a break in filming, Ellie was shamelessly flirting with James like she had the very first night at dinner after the read-through. She would touch or stroke him, and he would let her. In fact, he seemed to encourage it. Were they dating? Well, he was certainly wasting no time *playing the field.*

On Monday of the following week, I heard through the grapevine that the guys had gone to a hip downtown bar on Saturday night where James had introduced Sean and Mark to his model friends who were in Vancouver for a photo shoot. Mark told Audrey that James had hooked up with a stunning model.

I pretended that I didn't care, but I was fuming mad. If James had truly had genuine feelings for me, how could he act this way? I told myself that he had done me a favor, as I was no longer feeling guilty. Any feelings that I thought I had for James were dead and buried and I looked forward with anticipation to Lance's arrival on Friday.

It was Tuesday morning and we were having a group lesson with a renowned Hollywood Gun Coach. I had listened to his instructions with care, but I was having trouble. I needed to learn how to shoot the gun if I was going to look credible on screen. As usual I noticed that James had picked it up flawlessly and the coach was commending him. It infuriated me how good James was at everything. He was one of those people who spent five minutes learning something and then he was exceptional at it. James was skilled and competent and exuded confidence in whatever he tried while the rest of us, spent hours and perhaps days on a task, only to do it with mediocre results.

I was surprised when James came over to me.

"You're holding it wrong. You need to hold it more like this," he tried to show me, but I moved out of reach. If he noticed, he didn't say anything. "When you shoot, focus on the target. Remember to keep your eye on the target at all times Alex," he said with authority.

"How kind of you to take a break from your carnal activities and actually address me James. This must be my lucky day!" I said sarcastically.

"I hadn't realized you noticed anything that I've been up to as you haven't looked me in the eye for a week," he said rudely matching my tone.

We sneered at each other like that for what seemed like a long moment. I was about to move away when he grabbed my hand. "Is it true your boyfriend is coming this weekend?" he asked.

"Yes, Lance is coming," I replied. "Maybe you would like to double date with one of your ladies? Who is the lucky girl this week James? Is it the model, the PA, Ellie, or perhaps there is a new flavor of the week that I'm not aware of?"

Before he could answer. I walked out. I was really mad and was sick up to my eyeballs with it. I was just outside the shooting range when he caught up.

"Could you hold on for a minute?" he asked.

"What?" I yelled.

"I'm sorry, I know that I've been rude Alex, but what do you expect?" he asked.

"I thought we were friends James, and I didn't expect for you to shut me out so completely?"

"I'm sorry Alex, but nothing has changed for me unless you plan to break up with your boyfriend this weekend."

I didn't say anything and just looked at the ground.

"That's what I figured. Goodbye Alex," he yelled.

He turned on his boot leaving a muddy trail of wet rocks and roots in his wake. Again, I was confounded, and alone with my thoughts.

***

Wednesday morning James and I arrived for the filming of the zip line scene, which would require an overnight stay, as we had to first drive and then take a helicopter to our final destination. We had already done our zip lining preparation training a few weeks before and it was piece of cake compared to the bungee jump, so I wasn't so much nervous about the activity, more about the close proximity of James and I all day and night long.

"Good morning," I said crisply to James, and the crew when I arrived at the van.

"Look's like everyone is here," yelled the assistant director. "Let's get rolling folks as the film crew is already set up on location and waiting for us."

We climbed on board the van, which was going to take us to the helicopter that would fly us to Vancouver Island to film the scene, set in a coastal forest. Ben and the crew got there late yesterday by ferry.

"Can I join you?" James questioned when we boarded the van.

I was surprised that he wanted to sit together after our recent squabble.

"Sure."

"Listen I know that I've been impolite and distant, but I'm just protecting myself," he said in a hushed tone so that we wouldn't be overheard. "I'm trying to accept your *choice* and with time I'm sure that things will go back to normal with us."

"What *choice* James? I'm not following you?" I asked confused.

"Well, obviously your boyfriend is coming into town on Friday, so you've made your feelings perfectly clear," he stated.

I looked into his eyes and for a moment I saw the sadness. Then quickly his wounded look was replaced with a mask of false bravado. I could have let him believe the lie; it might be easier if he continued to believe that I didn't share the same feelings.

"I've made *no* decisions James."

He looked at me quizzically. His intense gaze smoldering. "What does that mean Alex?"

I went out on a ledge, but only slightly. "I never said that I didn't have feelings for you James. You've come up with that hypothesis all on your own. Of course, the parade of pretty girls in your company lately hasn't endeared you to me."

"So you *do* have feelings, but not deep enough to break up with your boyfriend for me?"

"If I break up with Lance, I have to do it for me, and for no other reason. Can you understand that James?"

"I think so," he acknowledged, begrudgingly. "Does that mean you are thinking of breaking up with him?" he asked, sounding hopeful.

"It...it means I'm *mixed up* James," I stammered. "In this business, I've had to grow up fast. Real fast. And I guess...well...I guess, I've seen a lot of shit and I thought that made me wise. I have felt like an adult since like age ten. But...um...when it comes to relationships and stuff...I don't know much. Since, I've met you, my life has, like, suddenly been turned upside down..." I trailed off and I could feel my cheeks redden. I couldn't meet his eyes. "I...I don't know what I'm doing anymore. Could you give me some time to figure things out?"

"How much time?" he questioned.

"I don't know," I answered truthfully.

"You know that we could be great together. Give it a chance," he said, his expression intense.

"How can you be certain? Maybe it's just an intense physical attraction?" I said, embarrassed, with a catch in my voice.

James ran a hand through his hair and smiled wolfishly at me. Slowly he took my hand and stroked it gently. Then he cupped my chin until we were gazing intently into each other's eyes. "I'm not going to deny it. I would like to rip your clothes off right here, right now. I've wanted you since the first day that I laid eyes on you," he whispered huskily. "But it's much more than just physical attraction, when I'm with you, it just feels right. I like your laugh, your mannerism, and your spirit. I even like your damn stubborn temper and your clumsiness. I'm crazy about you Alex and I don't want to stop how I feel, just because you're too scared to try."

I didn't know what to say. My heart was beating wildly and desire coursed through my body. I was stunned by his words and for once in my life I was speechless.

"Please James," I begged. "I need time to process this and figure it all out. Can you give me some time?"

He nodded his head and started to read his script. I did the same and we sat in companionable silence for the rest of the trip.

From the van we boarded a helicopter for the thirty-five minute ride to the island. The last time we were on the island, we had taken the ferry over with the crew, but due to a scheduling conflict with the gun coach and time restraints, they wanted us to take a helicopter. I was both nervous and excited. I knew it would be fun, but I also knew that I was a big chicken, thus a little uneasy about my first helicopter ride.

"It will be fine, just sit back and enjoy the beautiful scenery," James whispered in my ear and took my hand.

I knew that I was encouraging him by holding his hand. It felt good, and I was a little anxious. James exuded confidence and his touch was reassuring, so I sat back and let myself enjoy the ride. The scenery was breathtaking, and I felt exhilarated by the ride.

When we arrived at the rainforest location, it was a nice temperature, perfect for shooting the scene, and the cameras, microphones, props, and equipment were ready to go. Ben had already been there for hours with the director of photography, camera and sound crew, and several of the assistant directors. The team came over to us to discuss the live action shot. In the scene, the bad guys were chasing us. In an effort to get away, we take a zip line and travel deeper into the forest to escape our pursuers.

The day was long and physically demanding, but Ben thought he got what he needed. We would do a few minor shots in the morning, and then after that, we could probably pack up and head out. We were still dressed in the clothes from the shoot, which were tattered, wet, and muddy. I said my goodbyes in search of a hot shower and change of clothes. We were staying in cute little bright colored cottages, all with covered porches and outdoor showers. I remembered fondly summers on vacation in Pismo Beach with my family and coming back to spray the sand off in our outdoor shower at the house we rented each year. It had always been a hedonistic pleasure of mine. I was just about to get in the shower when I saw that James was in his shower in the cottage next door. His towel was hanging up on the outside hook, and it was just to tempting to pass up, so I took it. I knew that he was going to get me back for stealing his towel, but I was in a mischievous mood, so I decided it might be worth the price.

When I got out of my own shower, tightly wrapped in my fluffy towel, I looked over my shoulder, but I didn't see James, thus I smirked imagining his surprise at finding no towel. I was about to enter my cottage and there he was, fully dressed, sitting on the front porch waiting for me.

"Alex, you have been forewarned that payback is a bitch," he threatened pleasantly. "When you least expect it...*I'll be waiting.*"

He came over to me then and stood very close. I tightened the towel around me as he came within inches of my face. I could feel his breath on my face and I thought in that instant that he was going to kiss me, but instead he gave me a peck on my forehead and left, leaving me flustered and anxious.

That evening we had dinner with Ben and the rest of the crew. Everyone was in jovial spirits, and I felt like a kid at summer camp. Ben told us that the project was close to completion and he felt that we would wrap up filming in the next three to four weeks. After that, we had about seven week's off, and then we would be back on the road for the promo tour.

James and I walked back to our cottages together and suddenly I was nervous to be alone with him, especially since I was going to see

Lance in two days, and I needed a clear head. As we approached my cottage, I turned to James and started to say goodnight.

"You can't go to bed this early," he protested. "How about one game of scrabble or backgammon?"

I knew the safe thing would be to say good night, but it had been such a good day and I wanted to hang out. "Ok, I'll play one game, but then I'm going to turn in."

One game turned into several games and then we started to talk and before I knew it I had fallen asleep. I woke up in the middle of the night and found myself curled up against James. I didn't want to wake him, so I tip toed gently out the door and returned to my cottage. I was feeling guilty, I knew that I had technically not done anything wrong, and that I continued to be a faithful girlfriend to Lance, but if the roles were reversed and it was Lance spending so much time with his co-star, I knew that I would feel betrayed. It was with a heavy heart that I went to sleep alone in my bed tossing and turning for the rest of the night.

Thursday morning, Ben knocked on my door.

"Hey what's up early bird," I greeted.

"We are ahead of schedule Alex. I looked over yesterday's material last night and it look's good, so I would like to move on and film the tent scene this morning. Do you think you could be ready?" Ben inquired.

I got a strange feeling in the pit of my stomach. I knew the scene well, it was a pivotal love scene between Matt Samuel and Amanda Blake and we were not supposed to shoot it for another two weeks. I did not relish filming it today. It was one day before Lance's arrival. *How was I going to keep a clear head now?* I was a professional, so I pushed my personal concerns to the background and told Ben that I could be ready.

"Have you spoken to James yet?" I questioned. "Can he be ready today?"

"Yes, I just spoke with him and he is ok with it," Ben confirmed. "Can you prepare for it now while the technical crew sets up? After you've had time to review the latest script changes, you need to get over to makeup and wardrobe. Then come over to the set. You and

James can do a quick rehearsal and then we are going to shoot it," he stated decisively.

Of all days to film the sex scene, why did it have to be today? I felt like this was some cosmic joke. I dragged myself into the shower and tried to psyche myself up for the day ahead.

Wardrobe dressed me in the same outfit as the day before…ripped jeans and tank top with a buttoned down plaid shirt that I wore open. James walked in then.

"Good morning," he said to everyone. "Did you sleep well," he whispered in my ear.

"Fine," I said, avoiding eye contact and nervously tapping my foot.

"Are you ready for today? Personally, it's my *favorite* scene," he said playfully, emphasizing the word *favorite*.

I just nodded my head. I knew that I wasn't fooling him and that he could detect my distress. If I had hoped for understanding or sympathy, I wasn't going to get it from him. He was enjoying my discomfort too much. It wouldn't surprise me if I found out that he had bribed Ben to film this scene today. I knew that didn't happen, but I wouldn't put it past him to try. Especially after I took his towel yesterday…

The makeup artist covered us in mud. We would also be sprayed down with water, but not until right before filming began.

Due to the nudity and intimate nature of the scene, it was a *closed set* with essential personnel only. My agent had negotiated detailed language in all my contracts saying what could and could not be shown and no *private parts* could be shown on film, however the scene required that James and I strip down to our underwear. We would be in a sleeping bag, so we would be covered up for the most part, but there was an intimate moment when the sleeping bag gathers down around his waist and his hand is draped over my breasts, with me leaning against his bare chest. After that we are turned to each other kissing, more or less, hidden in the depths of the sleeping bag. For me, it was incredibly uncomfortable and I was freaked.

Ben started to give us step-by-step instructions for the scene.

"Are we ready to roll?" he asked.

"Yes," we answered in unison.

"Ok, and "I want crazy sex kissing!" he yelled. "Quiet on the set. Let's roll..."

We were soaking wet. *Matt* came over to me and started to undress me. "Put your hands up over you head *Amanda*," he whispered. I did what he said. *Matt* quickly pulled the wet tank top off me. I shivered. With trembling hands, I tentatively started to unbutton his shirt until I had removed it from his bare chest. He stood before me Adonis-like. I then put my hands on the button of his jeans, but I was clumsy and nervous. He caught my wrist and stopped me and he quickly removed his jeans. When he was through, he put his hands on my waist and with swift deliberate action he removed the remains of my wet clothes. I stood before him in my bra and underwear and then he grabbed me and started to kiss me. He kissed me passionately and greedily and I returned the kisses with equal strength, matching his fervor. He led me over to the sleeping bag and with one swift move; he zipped us securely in it. My back was against him and he unhooked my bra and quickly discarded it. I leaned against him, and he cupped my breasts letting his outstretched arm linger there. Then he flipped me over until we were pressed together, hungrily kissing and devouring each other.

"Cut," yelled Ben. "That was great, but let's do it again."

After the ninth take, the shoot was finally completed, but we continued to kiss each other like we had the first time during James audition. Abruptly, we both stopped and pulled away as we realized with embarrassment that Ben had yelled cut and that we were being observed. We lingered longer than necessary in an attempt to return our breathing to normal. I was handed a robe and I quickly made my exit. I knew that James couldn't follow, as he had to recover from his *arousal*, thus I smirked that he was probably still in the sleeping bag.

The rest of the day and evening went by quickly in a flurry of commotion and travel. James and I remained friendly, but it was awkward. I kept recalling the many sex scenes and the feeling of his kisses on my lips, his hand on my breasts, and our naked bodies pressed against each other. Lust spiked through me, and I longed for his touch, but I willed myself to forget. I had never felt like this before, and I was scared by the intensity of my feelings. I could no longer deny that I was *falling* for James, but the question was how much? I knew that I needed space and distance away from him, but I wasn't sure *if* I could stay away?

I was lost and it was obvious that I was not being fair to either Lance or James. I reminded myself that I had only technically kissed James on-screen, unless I counted his attempt to distract me during bungee jumping, which I did not. I had not crossed over any boundaries...so far. Yet I knew deep down, that with every day that went by, I was getting closer to James, and I felt disloyal to them both. It was clear that it could not continue this way and that I had to make a decision soon.

When the van finally dropped us back late Thursday night I turned to James and was about to say good night when he asked me to walk with him. He walked me to my door and asked to come in for a minute.

He steered me into the hotel room and blurted out, "I'm trying to respect your wishes Alex, so I'll give you some time to figure things out, but this weekend is going to kill me. This dance can't go on for much longer," he cautioned. "Do you understand?"

I gave him a sad look. "Yeah, I'm sorry James. I feel like I'm letting everyone down. I don't want to hurt anyone."

James shrugged. "Don't think so much." He gave me one last look and said, "Just follow your heart Alex."

Right before he closed the door, I nodded my head to let him know that I got the message.

## Chapter 8: The Visit

I was finishing up filming a scene with Kelly Wayland and Andrew Mitchell on Friday afternoon when Lance arrived on the set. He was watching us and smiled at me, but I could tell that he didn't want to interrupt. I didn't know how it would feel to see him, but it was nice and I was relieved. When I spoke to Lance during the week, I had told him that I really needed to get away, so he promised that we would escape somewhere for the weekend. I wanted to be far away from James and the movie set, otherwise I knew that I would be a tense bundle of nerves. I was looking forward to getting away, and we were planning to leave when I was done with the scene.

Happily the scene did not involve James, so I didn't have to introduce them, which I was thankful for. When Ben called cut, Lance stepped up then and grabbed me and twirled me in his arms giving me a big hug and kiss.

"It's so good to see you baby," Lance said with a big grin on his face.

"You too," I said with genuine warmth. "Let me introduce you to the director. Ben, I would like you to meet Lance Smith. Lance, this is Ben Avery, the legend himself."

"Flattery will get you everywhere Alex," Ben joked and then he shook Lance's hand. "Lance so nice to finally meet you. Sorry about the play, but I've heard your performance was very strong and favorable. What are you up to next?"

Lance started talking with Ben about some upcoming projects, but I wasn't listening, because I saw that James had arrived for what appeared to be a re-shoot. I was going to have to introduce them I realized. *Damn it.* My heart started to beat erratically, and I was feeling faint. James started to approach us and with each step, my trepidation increased. James and I locked eyes, *if looks could kill* I thought. Maybe it was something in my expression, but in those last few steps, I looked at Ben for help, and thank goodness the ever astute and charming director saved me.

"Ah James, so good that you're here. I need you over there by the staircase as we've made some changes and we are going to need to change the camera angle and your position," Ben instructed. He turned to Lance. "It was nice meeting you, but you better get going already as this young lady really needs a break."

"Thank you Ben," I answered with gratitude. "Come on Lance, you heard the man, let's go," I said grabbing him as quickly as possible.

I knew I was a coward as I practically sprinted away from them without a backward glance.

"*Wow*...you must really want to get me alone," Lance joked as we left the studio. We quickly grabbed my bags from my dressing room and headed out to his rental car. "So do you want to know where we are going this weekend?"

"Surprise me!" I said.

I shut my eyes and relaxed in the car as Lance chatted telling me funny stories about his former cast members, life in New York and Laguna Beach, and mutual friends that we shared. He then talked to me about upcoming projects and auditions. When I finally opened my eyes, I realized that our car was approaching the ferry terminal and I cringed. It looked like I was going back to Vancouver Island, not the best way to help me forget about James.

I was pleasantly surprised getting off the ferry when we drove to the West Coast as I had not been to that part of the island yet and was looking forward to exploring it. We drove to the Wickaninnish Inn located in the lovely town of Tofino in the Pacific Rim region of Canada. The area was beautiful as was the Inn. Our guest room had a balcony, fireplace and soaker tub. When we entered the room, I walked onto the deck admiring the panoramic ocean views while Lance took care of the bags. I started to take deep calming breaths to try to squelch my nerves. I was uptight and tried to will myself to relax. Lance approached and put his arms around me.

"I've missed you babe," he whispered and started to kiss me. The kiss was nice, but I felt detached and I couldn't seem to relax.

When the kiss was over, I pulled away and walked into the room.

"Let's explore," I suggested overly enthusiastic.

"I rather explore you," he said suggestively.

"I'm just really keyed up and I think I need some exercise first," I lied.

"Alright, if you insist, we could walk around the grounds first," he agreed grumpily.

I knew I was disappointing him, but I needed more time and a drink or two would be nice to calm my nerves. We walked the Chesterman Beach, which was beautiful and should have been very romantic, but I was too anxious to appreciate it. After we had strolled, I knew Lance wanted to go back to the room.

"Can we get a bottle of wine?" I asked.

"That's a great idea, I'll get one and meet you up in the room. Why don't you draw us a bath?" he suggested seductively.

I ran a bubble bath as he suggested, but I couldn't seem to chill out and unwind. *Crap*...maybe I had made a mistake coming here with Lance? I started to pace back and forth, and I knew that I was panicking. I forced myself to calm down, because I needed to figure out my true feelings for Lance away from the outside world. I reminded myself that Lance was my boyfriend and I thought about all of his good qualities and that helped me to loosen up. *I can do this*...I repeated over and over again in my head. I quickly decided to undress myself, rather than the alternative, and then I went into the tub. The water felt nice, but I was still uneasy.

When he got back to the room, he looked pleased that I was in the tub.

"You in the tub is the best view I've seen in a long time," he said admiringly. "Now you should start to relax babe."

He poured us glasses of wine and then got into the tub with me. I drank two glasses quickly, quicker than I should, but I needed liquid courage and something to calm me down. I wasn't really into it, but I forced myself to try, as I had to give this weekend with Lance a real shot. He started to kiss me and before I knew it we were having sex. When it was over, Lance seemed happy. But I was far away with my thoughts, thinking of James, and feeling like a heel. I knew that I hadn't done anything *technically* wrong; Lance was my boyfriend, not James. But I was feeling guilty. We had dinner in the romantic restaurant at the Inn and I should have enjoyed it, but I felt like I was acting more than anything else and I drank too much in an effort to relax. The alcohol helped, and when we returned to the room, we had sex again, but it wasn't very good. I never climaxed, but I wasn't sure why? Was it the alcohol, my uptightness or a lack of compatibility? Lance fell asleep easily, but I was up for hours berating myself and feeling terribly guilty.

We woke up early Saturday morning and went hiking for the day. I had a hangover from the night before, but the physical activity felt good and I pushed myself to go further and further until I was exhausted. On the return trip, I stumbled on some rocks and twisted my ankle. Due to my injury, we had to take it very slow and it was becoming painful. We didn't get back to the Inn until nightfall and I was totally spent. I took some painkillers and fell fast asleep.

On our last morning at the Inn, we went to the spa for massages, which was really nice and although my ankle was still a bit sore, I was starting to feel better. Lance suggested that we go into town for a few hours if my ankle was up to it, grab lunch, and then we could check out and take the last ferry back for the long drive back. I thought my ankle could handle it and I wanted to see the picturesque town so I agreed.

"It's a beautiful town, baby, glad we came," he said taking my hand as we walked on a waterfront bluff overlooking Tofino Harbor after lunch.

"Me too, Lance," I said, sounding more positive than I felt.

"Are you?" he said, agitated. "You've been far away all weekend."

I looked at him, my head filled with doubts. I was about to broach the subject of our relationship and my uncertainties, but then he moaned, and I quickly backed down.

"Lance, are you okay?"

"I'm not sure," he choked. "I think I'm going to be sick from the clams I ate during lunch."

Lance was violently ill for the rest of the afternoon and evening, so I extended our stay by a day and called Ben to tell him that I wouldn't be back until Monday evening. He understood, but needed me back no later.

On Monday morning, Lance was feeling better and he kept apologizing for ruining our weekend, but deep in my heart, I knew that neither food poisoning nor sprained ankles were the cause of our troubles. I wanted to bring up my concerns to Lance, but instead, I chickened out.

"Don't apologize for getting sick Lance. It was klutzy me who sprained my ankle."

He dropped me back late Monday afternoon with promises and kisses for when we would be reunited together again next month in California.

## Chapter 9: The Decision

After Lance left my room, the first thing that I did was take a long hot shower in an effort to wash off the weekend. I was feeling guilty and I knew that as much as I cared for Lance, I was going to break his heart. I did love him, but not in the all-consuming passionate way that girls dream about. It was more friendship than anything else. The weekend had been a terrible mistake and I was angry with myself for leading Lance on and for my disloyalty to both of them. I was really disgusted and I only had myself to blame.

Later that evening, there was a knock on my door, but I didn't answer it, because I didn't want to see anyone. I was feeling guilty and ashamed, and I just wanted to be alone. I kept the lights off so that if anyone passed by, they would think I hadn't returned from the weekend yet.

The next morning I awoke at dawn. I had a lot of pent up energy and I paced my room anxiously in anticipation of the day ahead. I got to the set early, eager to preoccupy myself with work. The actors and crew started to slowly filter in, and when I looked up James was looking at me. He looked angry and remained aloof and distant all day. I knew that I had to talk with him, but I was putting it off for as long as possible as I felt mentally drained and I didn't feel like a confrontation.

When we were done filming, I caught up to James and asked to speak to him alone.

"Are you limping?" he asked.

"Yeah. I hurt my ankle hiking over the weekend."

"Is that why you were not here yesterday?" he accused. "I was worried. You could have called."

"I'm sorry...you're right. I told Ben that I would miss Monday. Um, Lance got food poisoning and he became really sick. We had to extend and I...I should have called you...I'm sorry...it was just really weird and I never thought..." I finished tongue-tied.

Suddenly, James had a huge grin on his face.

"Why *are* you smiling James?"

"Well, I was thinking you extended, because you had an amazing time, glad to hear I was wrong." He cleared his throat. "So how *was* the weekend?"

"Could we talk somewhere more private?' I suggested, nervously fiddling with my hands.

We walked to James's room, just casually shooting the breeze. He told me what the group had done over the weekend and what I missed on the set.

When we arrived at his room, he resumed his earlier line of questioning. "So how was it Alex? Did you break up with him this weekend?"

"No, I didn't break up with him."

He sighed, running his hands through his hair. "So, what did you want to talk about?" he frowned, clearly irritated with me.

He started to pull away and I could tell he was frustrated, so I quickly started to talk. "I told you that I needed to figure things out, and I have James. I needed this weekend to be sure about my feelings. When we wrap up filming and I go home, I...I will talk to Lance, I promise."

"And what *exactly* will you say to him?"

"The truth."

"Which is?"

I looked up at him briefly from the corner of my eye. "You *already* know."

"I want to hear it Alex?" he whispered.

I mustered up my courage and looked him straight in the eye. "I will break up with Lance, because I'm...I'm in love with you."

With those words, James was beside me and he took my face in his hands and kissed me good and hard. I mean really kissed me...really fucking good...really fucking hard. The kiss was sensual and raw, and oh...so mind-blowing...that my entire body trembled from his hot mouth. James pressed his firm body against me, his hands buried in my hair, and I parted my lips letting his tongue explore my mouth. I pulled him closer begging for more and his lips came down on me again...slow, soft and maddening. It was hotter and more intimate than anything I'd ever imagined.

Abruptly he ended the kiss and released me. I was panting like an animal, so I took a sharp intake of air... "Hey, what's wrong?"

A ragged breath escaped his mouth and he sighed, taking a step back. "You are still his girlfriend and if I keep kissing you like this, I'm going to want to rip your clothes off. That's not happening until you end it with Lance."

I contemplated begging, but James was a determined guy with a moral compass and I could tell from the finality in his voice that my quest was futile. I was disappointed, and wanted to protest, but deep down I knew that waiting was the right thing to do.

"Ok," I said sulkily like a little child who doesn't get her way. "You realize that we are here for like, three more weeks, and then we will be apart for, another seven weeks, so that's um, two and a half months to wait?"

"My, my Alexandra, you seem suddenly very eager," he teased, grinning from ear to ear. "Where is your willpower?"

I shot him an icy glare. "I bet my willpower is stronger than yours!"

He leaned back and started to laugh. "You think so?" he challenged, his eyes shining with mirth and he was grinning like a crazy lunatic.

I scowled at him and turned to go. "I think I better leave, because I would hate to embarrass you by breaking your resolve on the very first night..."

James grabbed my waist and spun me around in his arms to face him. "You're not going anywhere...I'm not done kissing you yet." He pulled me close to him and trailed kisses down my ear to my throat. "I'd really like you to stay...please, Alex," he murmured, sounding seductive and irresistible.

"I...I want to stay," I admitted, trembling slightly.

"Good." He smiled mischievously and I flushed from head to toe. "And just because we're waiting, doesn't mean that we can't do any basic training."

***

The final weeks of filming were some of the happiest in my life. James and I were inseparable and we didn't care if people gossiped.

We tried to be as discreet as possible, but if people caught us holding hands or gazing into each other's eyes, then so be it. We were young and in love, and it was an idyllic time for us. The only gray cloud hanging above us was that I still had to talk with Lance, which I was dreading, but I knew that it had to be done.

During the last week of filming, James presented me with an invitation.

"I've been thinking…"

"Oh, no, that's dangerous," I teased.

He swatted me on the butt, but ignored me, and continued to talk, "I don't think I can stay away from you for seven weeks and I would like you to meet me in Maine for a few weeks."

"What's in Maine?" I asked.

"My family owns a vacation house on a small island off the coast. It's beautiful and tranquil there. I thought it would be nice if we went there to relax for a few weeks before the insanity of the tour begins."

"Would we be alone James or would your family be there?"

"I would like to introduce you to my family, but not *now*. This trip, I want you *all* to myself," he murmured softly, a naughty gleam in his eyes. My breath became quick and excited just imagining spending a few weeks with James. "If you tell me what dates work for you Alex, I'll take care of the logistics…you just need to show up."

Something in the tone of his voice and the look in his eyes made me hot and bothered all over. We still hadn't had sex, and the build up was torment. The thought of a vacation for just the two of us was extremely appealing. I knew that once the tour began in September it would mean a sea of people, places, interviews, cameras, and public appearances. Our schedules would be stuffed until the movie premiere and *if* the movie did well, the insanity would increase exponentially into the foreseeable future.

"Yeah, let's do it."

"Really?"

"Yup, but I need to figure out how to pull it off. My parents are going to be disappointed, you know, and they haven't met you yet, so um, they will definitely not be pleased about it. My brothers are coming home for my birthday in July, so I need to be home, um, at least until the party. And...oh, god, oh god...Toby, that's my agent and Lydia, my manger who you've met, are going to go ape-shit on me!

"Why?"

"Are you kidding, James?" I asked disbelieving, cocking my eyebrow at him. "Do you know how many work and publicity kind of things I'll have to blow off to go to Maine? And I still need to talk with Lance..." I trailed off.

"I know it won't be easy, especially the Lance part, but when will we have an opportunity to escape like this again?" he gently persuaded. "Also, I won't see you on your *actual* birthday so I want to celebrate it with you in Maine."

I nodded. "Okay James, make the travel arrangements." I wasn't sure how I was going to shorten my stay in California, but I would find a way, as I wanted nothing more than to be with him.

***

It was the last week of June and our last night in Vancouver. There was no official wrap up party, so the cast and crew threw our own little wrap up celebration. Although the *Galaxy Drifter* books were huge hits, the fate of the movie was unknown, so we didn't know if the sequels would be made. The entire cast and crew worked extremely well together and we would gladly work together again if given the opportunity. It had been a great experience and it was emotional to say goodbye to everyone.

Ben gathered the group together for a toast before everyone departed. "First and foremost, I want to say how much I've enjoyed working with all of you. It's been one of my most positive experiences on a movie set. When we first gathered together in February, most of us were strangers, but today I look around and see good friends. I told you that first day that if we all worked hard together we would make this film magical. Well, folk's my gut instinct has been proven right again. *Whatever* happens at the box office, please know that you've all done an amazing job!"

James and I walked out together and I remember the satisfaction we felt and shared at a job well done. The excitement of the group, combined with the prospects for the movie, and our young love was a powerful drug. From the very first day we were riding the crest of a high, and that momentum continued to carry us forward with great force.

I felt like Cinderella and James was my Prince Charming. It was the beginning of our fairytale. I was flying out in the morning to LA, and he was going home to Boston. We would reunite in Maine in one month.

## Chapter 10: California

My mom and dad insisted on picking me up at LAX and met me at the luggage carousels.

"Alex!" my mom yelled.

"Mom! Dad!" I shouted above the noise. "Over here!"

It was so great to see them. My mom or dad had always accompanied me when I was on a movie location. Now that I was almost eighteen, they had respected my wishes and let me film *Galaxy Drifters* without a chaperone. I was surprised that they hadn't insisted on coming for at least a visit, but both of them had successful careers of their own and with me away and my brothers at college, they took the opportunity to travel and went on an African Safari during their time off.

"We've missed you honey," they said in unison.

My dad took my luggage while my mom started to tell me about their trip to Africa and then she filled me in on the local gossip and all that I had missed while away. I in turn, regaled them with stories about the movie set, the Hollywood executives and department heads that I had met, cast and crew. They couldn't believe that I had actually gone bungee jumping and zip lining, joking about my lack of athletic coordination. The traffic to Brentwood was awful, and the drive seemed to take forever, but at least I was able to bide my time, as I was waiting until we got home before I brought up the subject of my relationship with James, and my decision to break up with Lance. My family adored Lance, so I wasn't sure how they were going to react to the news. I also hadn't told them that I was leaving early to go to Maine, a tidbit that I'm sure they were not going to be happy about.

Finally, we arrived home and I unpacked my luggage and took a shower. After that, I spent hours pouring over emails, mail, scripts and assorted business matters. Although *Galaxy Drifters* had a conservative budget, as the star of the film I had earned my first-ever seven-digit paycheck, and I knew that I had to meet with my accountant while Lydia was interviewing potential financial managers to help handle my business affairs that were growing more complicated by the day.

That evening I had a quiet dinner at home with my parents, as my brothers were not coming home to visit until the weekend. After dinner we went into the living room for coffee and I knew that I couldn't prolong the conversation any longer.

"Mom, Dad, I have some things that I would like to talk with you about," I said. "During the filming of *Galaxy Drifters*, I got very close with my co-star James Prescott whom I would like you to meet when he is in Los Angeles."

"Of course, we would like to meet all of your friends," my dad replied.

"Well, he's more than just a friend. He has become an important person in my life and I'm *in love* with him," I blurted out.

Both my parents were momentarily stunned by the news. Finally, my dad spoke. "What about Lance?"

"Yes, what about Lance?" my mom prodded. "And how can you be certain that you are in love with this actor, it's only been a few months."

"It's been five months and we've spent more time together then most people spend together in a year," I said defensively.

"You don't have to get defensive honey, we are just surprised by the news," my mom said in a soothing tone.

"Have you told Lance?" my dad questioned.

"I'm seeing him Wednesday after I meet with Lydia and Toby," I told them. "I'm not looking forward to the conversation, the last thing I wanted to do was hurt Lance," I said sadly.

"Are you sure this is what you want?" my dad asked.

"I've never been more certain of anything in my life," I told them sincerely.

"Tell us about him?" my mom asked.

"Well, um, at first glance, you'll be struck by how ridiculously handsome he is." I cleared my throat. "But um, there is so much more to him then just his looks. James is witty, brilliant, kind and considerate. He is also very confident and self-assured.

Professionally speaking, he is a natural and gifted actor, and musician."

"Does he walk on water too?" my dad chuckled.

"Pretty close," I confirmed. "James seems to excel at everything."

"No one is perfect," my dad warned.

"Where did he grow up?" my mom asked. "Did he go to college?"

"He grew up in Boston, and he spent two years at Julliard studying drama and music before quitting to pursue acting and music full-time."

"How old is he? Is he close to his family?" my mother asked.

"James is twenty-two and yeah he's close to his family, but um, they have sort of high expectations." I said with a slight scowl, recalling everything that James had told me about them. "Uh, his dad is Michael Prescott, the famous conductor, and his mom, Stephanie Prescott is a professional pianist and music professor at Harvard. Ooh, his sister, Rachel, is around my age and she will be a freshman at Berklee School of Music in the fall. It's intimidating – it's like the whole family is brilliant and super talented."

"Sounds like you are smitten!" My mom joked.

"Smitten doesn't cover it…" I said, fiddling with a loose strand of my hair.

"Just be careful, honey. You sound very serious about him and you are very young, it's better to be carefree at this age," my mom emphasized, giving me a stern look.

"This isn't just some fling! He's really important to me. I'm not going to change my mind."

"Even so, you have your career to think about. You need to stay disciplined and focused," my dad warned gently.

"I can do both." I promised. "There is just one more thing and I don't think you are going to like it, but I hope you won't argue with me about it."

"What?" my dad asked.

"Well, James's family owns a vacation home in Maine and he has invited me to go there with him prior to the start of the tour, and I said yes. I'm leaving on August first."

"You just got home," my mother said, raising her voice. "That's in four weeks."

"I know and I'm sorry. But I'll be eighteen in a few weeks. I'm an adult and you need to respect my decision."

"Well, that's disappointing," my dad said. "But it sounds like your mind is made up. Just be careful honey and take it *slow*."

***

Wednesday morning was stuffed with meetings. First, Lydia and I were meeting with Toby to discuss scripts and potential new projects as well as a discussion about the potential for future *Galaxy Drifters* movies depending on how it would do at the box office.

Toby Sawyer had been my talent agent for several years. At times she could be aggressive and irritable, but she always came through on finding me good jobs and promoting my interests. Lydia and I were sitting in her office discussing several projects.

"It's a good script, refreshing and I think you would be perfect for the part," said Toby.

"Lydia, what do you think?" I asked.

"I like it, but my only concern is that it look's like they want to start filming it in the spring," Lydia trailed off.

"And that's a problem…why?" I asked Lydia.

Toby interrupted. "It's not a problem, but we are hoping with the buzz around town that if *Galaxy Drifters* does well, the studio will want to quickly exercise it's option and go into production on the second movie in the series as early as this spring."

"How likely is that to happen?" I asked.

"Ask me again after the release when the box office results are in?" Toby smirked.

"Can we see how flexible the producer of the new project is on production dates?" I asked.

"Planning on it." Toby gruffly replied. "Moving on, your publicist hasn't sent me the latest publicity schedule for *Galaxy*. What's happening with that?"

"We are meeting with her tomorrow and I can give you an update later this week," Lydia announced.

After that, we discussed a few other potential projects and Toby handed us four new scripts.

"*Wow* … four more scripts," I commented, a little bowled over from the recent spike in attention I was getting.

"Don't be surprised your name is coming up a lot lately and I've received several inquiries," Toby stated. "Your star is rising,"

After our meeting with Toby, Lydia and I went for coffee to discuss business matters.

"Was it just me or was Toby more bad-tempered than usual?" I asked.

"She's afraid that she will lose you as a client," Lydia answered.

"Leave Toby? I've never thought about it. Why would she think that?"

"Because she was right when she said your star is rising. With fame, there are a lot of new opportunities. At some point, you may have to think about it," Lydia told me honestly.

"Maybe," I said without committal.

"How is the hunt going for financial managers?" I asked.

"I have several people I would like you to meet next week," Lydia answered. "I'm hoping we could make a final decision at the end of next week. How does that sound?"

"That should be fine, but it definitely needs to be wrapped up by the end of the month, because I'll be traveling in August."

"What Alex? This is news to me…*why*?"

"Well, it's part of a longer discussion, because it might, um, have an impact on my public image. I'll fill you in tomorrow before our meeting with the publicist."

"Ok, *now* I'm really curious. Can you tell me?"

"I can't. I'm meeting Lance at his place in Laguna Beach and I, um, really need to hit the road soon," I told her avoiding eye contact.

"I bet I can guess," she whispered with a sly look on her face.

"What?" I asked surprised.

"Does it have anything to do with a certain James Prescott?" she said with raised eyebrow.

"What? Did my mother say something to you?" I asked haughtily.

"Ha! I knew I was right. Your mother hasn't said a word, but you know I'm not blind and I was there. Not to mention, that there has been gossip linking the two of you…"

"Gossip?" I asked. "Why hasn't it been brought to my attention?"

"It's just been idle chitchat, not on the internet or tabloids yet," she answered.

I looked at her seriously and I couldn't hide the distress from my face.

"Anything that Lance would hear?" I asked anxiously.

"I don't think so," she replied honestly and took my hand. "It's going to be *ok* Alex. Go to him. It's best to have the conversation as soon as possible."

"Ok," I replied softly.

In an effort to lighten the mood, we changed subjects. "I bought myself a present for the work on *Galaxy Drifters* and I paid cash. Want to see it?" I teased.

"*Hell*, yes," she smirked.

"My mother really cannot keep a secret," I said with playful disgust.

"It was your dad!" Lydia confirmed.

Outside the coffee shop were my shiny new wheels that I had picked up that morning from the Audi dealership. I had bought a black convertible. Lydia let out a long admiring whistle.

"I'm jealous that you'll be driving that to Laguna Beach. I want a rain check on the next ride! Good luck today."

***

When I arrived at Lance's place in Laguna Beach, I sat in my car for a long time willing myself to find the courage to face him. I scrolled through messages on my phone as a distraction, but I knew that I was just prolonging the inevitable so I shut off my phone and got out of the car. My head was hurting and my feet felt heavy like I was dragging a ton of bricks. I wish I could just send Lance an email. I had never been good at confrontation, the written words were so much easier, but Lance deserved better. I forced myself to be courageous and I rang the doorbell. His roommate Carlos answered.

"Hey Brown, looking good," Carlos purred.

"Hey Carlos, you too. What's new?"

Before he answered a bikini-clad woman with a surfboard walked in.

"Come on Carlos," the bikini chic said.

"Coming sweets," he uttered softly. "Lance!" he yelled, "Alex is waiting."

Carlos started to walk out the back door with his friend, but then he turned to me and whistled, "You really are fine. Wish I had met you before Lance." Then he waved farewell and blew me a kiss.

Lance came in then. His hair was wet from a recent shower. He was wearing blue jeans and a t-shirt and I admired him for one last time as I thought about all of his good qualities. He had such a sunny disposition; I think that's what attracted me to him originally.

"Hey babe," he said coming over and greeting me with a hug and kiss on the lips. "I've missed you."

I was speechless and I didn't know how to begin. I pulled away from his embrace and I started to pace.

"Lance, I need to talk to you," I said softly with a catch in my voice.

I saw his smile fade away. "What's wrong?" he asked immediately.

I didn't know what to say and I looked down at the floor.

"Lance, you know that I think you're wonderful. My family adores you and so do I, but..."

"Are you breaking up with me?" he interrupted, shooting me a shocked look.

"Um...I just think that my schedule doesn't allow for a relationship right now," I started to mumble.

"That's bullshit Alex," he said loudly. "I knew something was up that weekend in Vancouver. You were uptight and distant the whole time."

"I'm so sorry Lance, I-I never meant to hurt you, but during the filming of the movie, I developed feelings for someone else, and I've been confused."

"Have you cheated on me Alex?" His voice was barely audible.

"No, I've been faithful."

"Is it your co-star…what's his name, James, isn't it? You couldn't wait to get me off the movie set that afternoon in Vancouver."

"I'm sorry Lance. I never meant to hurt you. You are a great guy and you deserve better. I-I never intended for any of this to happen," I said, unable to fight back sobs.

"You still haven't answered my question Alex?" he asked, sounding angry.

"Yes, it's him." I whispered.

He was disappointed, but not surprised. "Have you had sex with him?"

"I've already told you that I've been faithful."

Lance walked over to me then and grasped my wrist. "It's not too late then, don't throw it away Alex."

I looked up at him to protest, but before I could utter a word, his lips came down on me urgent and desperate.

"Don't," I said, pulling away. "You deserve better than I can give you."

I was so ashamed by my actions and for hurting Lance, but I had to be honest with him. My feelings for him had changed and it wasn't fair to pretend otherwise.

"Do you love him?" he asked, emotion heavy in his voice.

"I…I do," I stammered unable to look Lance in the face. "I'm sorry Lance."

I tried giving him a hug, but he shrugged me away. I kept waiting for Lance to say something, but he didn't. He looked so dejected and I wanted to reach out to him again, but I knew that my touch was unwelcome. *What could I say to ease his pain?*

Minutes passed and Lance refused to look at me. When he finally spoke his voice was hard. "I think you should leave Alex."

I turned to go, but I didn't leave. Instead, I stood sadly at the door deliberating for what seemed like an extremely long time. I finally whispered a pathetic, "I'm so sorry I hurt you, Lance. Don't hate me."

I closed the door and I was assaulted with fresh feelings of shame for hurting Lance. I casted about for a few more seconds, but I knew there was no turning back. So I left his place and silently said good-bye to my first love.

## Chapter 11: Maine

The Portland International Jetport is small and compact, so upon arrival it took me only moments to get to baggage claim. Four weeks without James felt like an eternity and I felt like an addict who needed her *fix*. I looked around the airport, but didn't see him immediately, and then from behind, I felt his strong arms wrap around me.

"Alex," he whispered in my ear and handed me two-dozen long stemmed red roses.

I turned to face him and for a long moment we stared into each other's eyes.

"They're beautiful." I said grinning like a lovesick fool.

Excitedly we started kissing each other and the kisses grew more impatient until we were practically clawing each other in the middle of the airport. I heard a passerby yell, "Get a room!" and I pulled back embarrassed and flushed from our hungry embrace.

"Come on," James said and took my hand, while grabbing my bags. He led me to the parking lot to a Range Rover and opened the door for me. As I got in, he leaned over and gave me a gentle kiss.

"A Range Rover, eh?" I smirked

"What were you expecting?" James asked with a grin.

"Well, I knew it had to be something nice, but not to flashy, and um, possibly good for the environment. Considering that we aren't in a Prius, I see the man style preppy side won out!" I winked at him with a playful smile.

"You have such a smart mouth," he said sarcastically. "For your information smarty pants, I have my name on a waiting list for a Tesla."

"A Tesla?" I questioned.

"It's an electric car. The company was founded in 2003 by a group of Silicon Valley engineers and they make an emissions-free roadster that I want. You'll see it soon enough when I get it in California," he replied. "How was your flight?"

"The flight from LA to New York was good, but we hit turbulence from New York to Maine, but otherwise fine," I replied. "How was the drive up from Boston?

"Good, but I think my family wants to meet you. They asked me a million questions, and it was good to finally escape and get on the road," he said.

"Well, I hope your family didn't give you any lectures, 'cause I received like a ton from my folks. Even my brothers who are usually laid-back were getting on my nerves," I said exasperated.

"About what?" he questioned.

"It's weird – it's like they still think of me as a little girl or something. It's getting so old." I huffed with a scowl.

James laughed and quickly gave me a small peck while we waited at a traffic light. "They're just concerned and being protective. I think that's good. I'm sure I'm the same way with my sister," he told me honestly.

"Whatever." I said rolling my eyes.

He patted my thigh and told me that we were almost at our destination. After about a fifteen-minute drive, we pulled into the Portland Yacht Club.

"A yacht club? Are we staying here?" I asked with raised eyebrow.

"No, just passing through," he said playfully and took my hand and the luggage.

We walked over to the marina and boarded a small motorboat. I knew nothing about boats, but it looked sleek.

"How big is this?" I asked James

"It's 21 feet," he exclaimed excitedly. He looked like a kid in a candy store as he described the features of the motorboat. I heard words like "lightweight, performance, powerful," and I sat back and enjoyed the fresh air as we zoomed away from shore. He handled the boat expertly and I was struck again by his self-assurance and competence. "We should be there in about twenty minutes," he yelled through the wind and pointed to nearby Cove Island. He told me that the clusters of islands off the coast of Portland were in Casco Bay and he described the history for the rest of the ride. Cove Island was a wealthy coastal village on Casco Bay, technically the island was part of Portland, but the similarities ended there, and the island enjoyed a slower pace of life. As we started to pull in to shore, I saw a stunning residence come into view.

"Is that your family's vacation house?" I asked shocked. "I was expecting a little beach cottage."

He seemed embarrassed and nodded his head in affirmation. No wonder he never seemed to care about Hollywood or making lots of money. He didn't need to worry. My attention was sidetracked by a classic wooden sailboat moored to the dock.

"Does that sailboat belong to your family?" I questioned.

"Do you like it?" he asked with a big smile on his face. "We can go sailing tomorrow."

His enthusiasm was contagious and I could see how much he loved it here. I smiled back at him and he took my hand helping me off the boat. We made our way up a stone walkway to the exquisite house, which was surrounded by Casco Bay and the Gulf of Maine. There were westerly and southern views with Portland skyline in the distance. The beautifully maintained grounds offered sloping lawns to the water's edge consisting of private coves, beaches and ledge outcroppings. It was breathtaking and I was speechless.

"Let me show you around the house?" he offered.

The house was spectacular. There were water views from most rooms, seven en suite bedrooms, a gourmet kitchen and wine cellar, a fitness area, Jacuzzi and an infinity pool.

"I may never leave!" I joked.

"Promises, promises," he muttered. Then he twirled me into his arms and started to kiss me passionately. He broke the kiss first and told me to follow him as he grabbed our luggage. "This is our bedroom and the bathroom and linen closet are over there," he pointed.

As he put the luggage away, I wandered aimlessly around the room. There was a fireplace and floor to ceiling windows surrounded by water views, which made me feel like I was on a ship in the middle of the ocean. I opened the glass doors and I walked out on the balcony that had expansive views of the bay. Suddenly, I was feeling a little overwhelmed. Everything about James was already so perfect and now this too? But I tried to remember my dad's point that *no one walks on water* and that helped me stay grounded, a little.

He came up to me then and started to nuzzle my neck.

"Are you tired?" he questioned.

"No, I'm good," I replied shakily as desire raged through me.

"Do you want something to eat or drink?" he asked while trailing little hot wet kisses behind my ear and down my neck.

I had butterflies in my stomach and I nodded my head no, unable to talk as yearning for him overtook my senses. I was hot all over and wet between my legs. His kisses became more persistent and I was practically mad with longing.

"What would you like to do?" he asked calmly.

I didn't respond, instead I turned to him and started to kiss him hungrily almost ferociously. He responded matching my intensity and took a bite of my lip. We greedily begin to rip each others clothes off right there on the balcony. When he removed my bra, it was freeing. I knew I was aching for him and my nipples were hard and erect under his gaze. He started to cup my breasts and then he squeezed my erect nipples. He put one in his mouth and started to suck on it and I thought I was going to climax right there in front of him. I blushed from embarrassment and he whispered in my ear: "Let go Alex," and I did as I started to convulse, receiving the most exquisite orgasm. He picked me up and carried me to the bed. Quickly he took off my skirt and underwear and then he discarded his clothes on the floor. "You are so beautiful," he whispered.

He continued to torment me with hot wet kisses from by belly button down to the inside of my thighs. Suddenly he fingered me, "you are so wet," he said admiringly and then he pulled out his finger and replaced it with his tongue. Again I was so embarrassed, that I momentarily froze, but the craving for him was so intense that it overcame all my other senses and I gave into it completely. He buried his head deeply between my thighs and expertly tongued me back and forth until I was writhing and convulsing on the brink of another orgasm. Suddenly he stopped, and withdrew his tongue. I was panting and disorientated.

"Are you on birth control?" he asked softly.

I nodded my head yes.

"Good," he said with a smile and then he entered me. He didn't move for a moment, as he let me adjust to the weight and feel of him, and then he slammed inside me, hard. We moved in unison in a frenzied pace back and forth until we both climaxed to a shattering conclusion.

We laid in each other's arms for a long time spent and exhausted, until the craving built again and then we greedily made love several more times. Sometimes our lovemaking was slow and gentle and other times it was fierce and extreme. We made love in the bed, on the floor, in the shower, the bathtub, against the railing of the balcony and finally one last time in the bed. We fell asleep with our bodies wrapped around each other and as I drifted off to sleep I was overwhelmed by the intensity and love I felt for this man. With him at my side, I felt complete, nurtured, and fulfilled.

***

The next morning I awoke to the aroma of coffee. On a bedside table was a note, "Follow the Trail" and I saw rose petals scattered on the floor making a path to the door. I smiled with giddy pleasure, but instead of following it, I decided to go to the bathroom first and take a quick shower. After cleaning up, I hastily threw on a sundress and underwear not bothering with a bra. I brushed my teeth and quickly combed my wet hair and braided it into pigtails. From there, I followed the rose petals in the bedroom, through the door, and down the steps to the kitchen. On the table, was a muffin with a birthday candle and gift-wrapped presents that said "OPEN ME?" I smiled to myself, but instead of opening presents, I poured myself coffee and walked out on to the deck. The view was beautiful and I was lost in thought thinking about the night before. James was an unbelievable lover, and my reaction to him was beyond anything that I had ever experienced. It was overpowering and all consuming and my cheeks reddened as memories of the night before flooded my thoughts.

"Penny for your thoughts?" he called as he walked up the grassy slope with a contented smile.

"Hey," I called. "Are you trying to spoil me?"

He jumped over the railing like a lithe panther and grabbed me in his arms. I was breathless with anticipation waiting for him to kiss me. But instead he bended his head slowly down to meet my gaze and whispered in my ear "Yes." He led me back into the kitchen and sang me a solo version of *Happy Birthday*. "Come on Alex, you have to open your presents now!" he said enthusiastically like a little boy.

"You bought me too much." I scolded tenderly eyeing the table loaded with presents.

"It was fun shopping for you," he said handing me a gift-wrapped box. The first gift was a pair of new running shoes with a note that said: "Your turn to keep up with me. Better start training!"

I playfully hit him in the arm. "You know I'm going to crush you the next time we go running."

"I would like to see you try," he challenged. "Here open this one next," he said handing me a beautifully gift wrapped present.

It was a beautiful black halter dress and in the same box was the most exquisite lingerie.

"*Wow*…it's gorgeous, thank you James," I said admiringly.

"It will look gorgeous on you Alex. I want a fashion show later," he murmured huskily.

"Okay last one," he said handing me a small box.

Inside were a stunning blue topaz necklace, ring and earrings.

"I love it James, but you've gone overboard," I admonished lightly.

"No I haven't and it matches your eyes. Let's put it on now," he said as he took it from the box and started to help me put it on.

"Thank you. I love it James."

"And I love you," he said with passion in his voice.

We started to kiss hot and heavily against the kitchen counter and before I knew it, he lifted me on top of the counter and I wrapped my legs around his waist pulling him closer to me. He pushed the gifts off the table and pulled his khaki shorts to his ankles. He pulled my underwear off, ripping them in half and plunged himself deeply inside me as I screamed his name. The rhythm was intense and he brought me to climax quickly and then he followed swiftly behind me. After making love, we laid in a crumpled mess for a few minutes panting until our breathing returned to normal.

"If this keeps up, I'm going to need a nap later, " he joked happily. "Do you want to go swimming, hiking, sailing, exploring town or back to bed?"

"It's a difficult choice James, but let's go sailing."

It was a sunny clear day and the ocean air was salty and pungent. The name of the mahogany wood sailboat was the *Crescendo*, which seemed a suitable boat name for the musical family. James was in his natural environment on the open ocean and I could see how much he loved it. He told me that the wooden sailboat was a replica of an Olympic class racing boat that his father loved, called the *International Dragon*, but that his dad had it built for more cruising purposes with a longer cabin trunk and a couple of small berths. James was a skilled and competent sailor as I had expected and he handled it smoothly. I was still waiting to see if there was anything that he did not excel at. So far he was exceptional at everything.

We sailed to Westchester, the largest island in Casco Bay to stock up on supplies. The island had unparalleled ocean views and access. We walked hand and hand into the small town of Westchester.

"How about breakfast," he asked.

"Sure, I'm starving." I told him eagerly as I realized that I hardly had eaten a thing for the past twenty-four hours.

He smirked. "We have worked up quite an appetite, haven't we?"

I smiled recalling our extracurricular activities. He put his hand in my back pocket and started to stroke my buttocks. "Behave yourself!" I warned playfully through clenched teeth.

James laughed and I tried to ignore him as we strolled along into the center of town. I smelled fresh cinnamon buns and coffee, and my stomach began to growl.

"Okay, its time I fed you," he joked.

The town was really quaint with a general store, post office, bakery, wine shop, a fresh fish market, a couple of restaurants, and a number of gift shops. James told me the island had a thriving artist colony with several local art exhibits and galleries.

"The town is so cute James, I love it," I exclaimed excitedly.

"Have you noticed anything missing in the town?" he asked with a smirk.

I started to examine my surroundings more closely; I saw children playing, bicyclists, people walking and then someone in a golf cart tooted his horn and waved as he passed us by.

"Where are the cars? I questioned.

"Very good, Alex," he laughed.

"Are cars allowed? I asked curiously.

"Yes, cars are allowed, but most people walk, bicycle or use golf carts for transportation," he answered happily.

We walked into a charming little diner and I was assaulted by the wonderful smell of bacon, fried eggs and coffee.

The waitress came over and gave James a hearty hello. "How are you James? How is your family?"

"They're good Jean. How is Paul?" he asked good-naturedly.

"He's good, but he put out his back again," she complained.

"I'm sorry to hear that," James said genuinely.

"Are you going to introduce me to your lovely friend?" she questioned.

"I'm sorry. Alex, this is Jean she owns the place and I've been coming here every summer since I was a little boy. Jean, this is my girlfriend Alexandra."

"Beautiful name, for a beautiful girl," she said brightly. "What can I get you today?"

James told me that everything was homemade and delicious. He ordered a farmer's omelet and I ordered waffles with strawberries. We both got iced coffees and chatted with the locals and tourists who came in. If anyone recognized that we were actors, they didn't seem to care, which put us at ease immediately. After breakfast we spent the afternoon exploring around the island and again I was struck that no one had bothered us.

"Do you realize James, that not one person has stared at us or asked for an autograph today? It's liberating," I said lightheartedly.

"Oh, believe me they stare at you," he said, but his tone was cheerful.

"Maybe it's you they are staring at?" I lightly challenged.

Just then a grandmotherly woman passed by and said to her friend loudly: "What a striking couple. Isn't young love grand."

"I guess that settles that, " James teased and took my hand giving me a gentle kiss.

Later, after our leisurely afternoon, we stocked up on groceries and supplies and headed back to the boat. The heat had risen and it had become hot, hazy and humid, but it felt nice on the water. When we arrived back it was early evening and James suggested a swim before dinner to cool us off. I changed into my bikini and went out to the pool, but he wasn't there so I walked down to the beach. When I arrived, he was swimming and I watched his powerful stroke from the shore. He had an easy, fluid, smooth and fast motion. After a few minutes of swimming above surface, he dove underwater and I could see how much he enjoyed it. When he popped back up, I saw him looking for me and then he spotted me.

He whistled. "Nice bikini Miss Brown! Are you coming in or do I have to come and get you," he teased mischievously.

"I'm coming, keep your hands to yourself!"

I reached for a football that was on the sand and whipped it over to him, but he jumped out of the water and caught it easily.

"Is that the best you can do?" he teased heartily.

I walked into the water and it was really cold, but the air was hot and sticky, so I continued moving forward until the water reached my waist. He threw the football back to me and we began to throw it back and forth to each other in the water. The sky was an intense fiery reddish pink and it was a perfect moment. We were smiling and laughing and it was the most relaxed I had been in years which I knew sounded odd for someone so young, but that was how I felt. Suddenly, a summer storm was upon us, and it started to rain, but we ignored it, and James and I continued to toss the football undisturbed by nature's fury. We played like that for a long time, and in those untroubled carefree moments, they were among the happiest in my life. The intensity of the rain picked up and James came closer until he stood next to me. We should have run in the house to dry off and find shelter, but instead we passionately kissed each other. Our kisses become more demanding and untamed and like wild animals we clawed and pulled at each other until we were on the sand rolling around and making love.

Later we went inside and washed off. He tenderly wrapped me in a big fluffy towel after we got out of the shower and then I pulled on a tank top and shorts and dried my hair. We prepared dinner together and opened a bottle of wine. We talked and laughed about everything and I had never felt closer to anyone in my life. The physical and mental connection with James was beyond anything I had ever experienced and the intensity both thrilled and scared me.

After dinner, we went into the living room where there was a baby grand piano and he played for me and started to sing. His talent blew me away. He had a beautiful, deep; rich melodic singing voice which astonished me. When he played the piano his fingers flew over the keyboard effortlessly and it was amazing to watch. I was not familiar with the melody, it was captivatingly beautiful, almost haunting, and when I asked him what piece it was; he admitted that he had recently wrote it.

After the rain had stopped, we went back outside, but the brief storm had not ridden us of the heat. It was a sultry night and we walked down to the dock to dip our feet in an effort to cool off. We started to talk late into the summer night until we both were groggy and fell asleep next to each other on the dock holding hands. I woke up unexpectedly in the middle of the night and I was momentarily confused by my surroundings. The sky had turned the shade of dark blue.

"James, wake up," I cooed softly in his ear.

He made a grunting sound, but didn't move.

I straddled him and yelled louder in his ear "Wake up."

His heavy lids opened. "You have my attention," he said sleepily and then suddenly he rolled me underneath him. We sat there looking at each other like that for a long time until he slowly and gradually undressed me. My body was on fire from his touch, but I resisted in an effort to stay focused while I leisurely undressed him too. When he was naked, I crouched down and put his erect penis in my mouth. I started to lick him like a Popsicle and boldly sucked him up and down until he was panting with desire. I knew that he was close to coming, but then I felt his mouth between my legs and he buried his head and nose deep inside me. I was mad with desire and on the brink of collapse, but I held back and continued to focus on pleasuring him until we shuddered and climaxed together.

"I never knew it could be so intimate." I told him sincerely.

"I feel the same way," he said looking seriously in my eyes.

"Is it always like this?" I questioned.

"I've never experienced this with anyone, but you Alex," he told me tenderly.

"I love you James," I whispered.

"I love you Alex," he whispered back.

The rest of the trip went by in a blur of activity. We fell into a pattern of making love, playing tennis, exploring the coast, hiking, swimming, and sailing, and before we knew it, it was our last day and evening together, until we packed up and headed out in the morning.

We sailed to the town of Cumberland for their annual Homecoming event. It was a perfect summer day and we ate ice cream strolling through town. The town center was packed with locals and tourists. There was face painting, balloons, a clambake and Maine lobster fest. We stayed there for hours watching the local parade with a grand march for all children in attendance. Finally, we escaped the crowds and found a private grassy nook on a beautiful oceanfront park where we leisurely picnicked. From the distance, we heard music from an outdoor concert. My head was on his lap as he softly read to me.

"We will come back again soon," he promised placing a gentle kiss on my forehead.

We were both pensive knowing that this was our last night in Maine. Neither one of us really wanting to go, but knowing that it was time to return to reality.

"If asked about our relationship, what do you want to say?" I asked.

We both hated this part of show business. As much as we loved what we did, we both valued our privacy, and we didn't relish being the subject of attention and gossip. But we knew that we had to be prepared for questions.

"As little as possible," he joked.

"Sounds good," I said.

"May I have this dance, Miss Brown?" he asked reaching down to take my hand.

We danced for hours from sunlight to dusk wrapped in each other's loving embrace listening to the big band music from another era playing in the background.

The weeks in Maine were among the best and most carefree days of my life, and it was with mixed emotions that we departed Maine and boarded a plane to New York the next morning.

## Chapter 12: On the Road

The promotional tour for *Galaxy Drifters* was packed full with multiple photo shoots, interviews, *meet and greet* events, and mall tours scheduled all over the country. I was starting to feel a little ragged from the whirlwind agenda, constant travel, and screaming fans. In the last seven days alone, I had been to LA, Miami, Minneapolis and Seattle. I was scheduled to make a mall appearance tomorrow in DC, and the next day in New Jersey. I had not seen James since we did a photo shoot together for *Vanity Fair* and *Entertainment Weekly* two weeks ago. Since then, he had been in San Francisco, Dallas, Chicago, Philadelphia, and he was now on his way to Boston. Finally, after his trip to Boston, and my trip to New Jersey, we would be flying separately to Rome to meet up with Ben for the *Galaxy Drifters* Italian movie premiere during the Rome Film Festival.

After Rome, we would fly back to LA for last minute interviews and promotional events until the big star-studded LA premiere, where we would be reunited with the full cast. A few days later, was the highly anticipated worldwide release of the film.

"Miss, you need to get off your cell phone and buckle in," the flight attendant said to Lydia who was seated next to me.

"Getting us in trouble again Lydia?" I joked.

"Sorry, that was the publicist giving me the latest update. Alex, this thing is getting bigger and bigger by the second," she said enthusiastically. "Advance ticket sales in the United States just opened yesterday and shows are starting to sell out, causing some theaters to add additional showings already."

"Are you pulling my leg Lydia?" I questioned skeptically.

"I'm telling you the truth Alex. This is bananas! The soundtrack, which was released just five days ago, has already hit #1, and sold something like 200,000 copies. Can you believe it? It's amazing…"

The news flabbergasted me. "This thing is like over the top crazy! When I spoke to James yesterday, he said his appearance at the mall in Philadelphia was like totally nuts and that there were, like, actually a thousand screaming fans or some obscene number like that."

"Mostly teenage girls, I bet!" teased Lydia.

I cringed. "Don't remind me," I said rolling my eyes at her.

"Oh come on now. Don't tell me you're insecure about it?"

"I'm not insecure Lydia, but it's not fun having thousands of attractive girls throwing themselves at your boyfriend."

"Um, considering that you are fucking gorgeous, I don't think you need to worry. Not to mention, that I see how he *looks* at you. No one can even stand to be in the same room with the both of you … it's disgusting!" said Lydia.

"*Puh-lease*, Lydia. I think you need glasses. As for disgusting, I remember when you dated that British guy, it was pretty hot and heavy for awhile, but you never saw me leave a room."

"Maybe so, but it's beyond hot and heavy with you guys, and neither one of you can keep your fucking hands off each other. I could deal with the touchy feely stuff, but the way you guys giggle like school children and the lovey-dovey smoldering looks that pass between you guys make me want to cringe. You move, he moves, he sits, and you sit. Pretty soon you'll be finishing each others sentences." Lydia said dryly. "You guys are nauseating to be around."

"We are not!" I said unconvincingly. "Anyway, with this crazy shit schedule who even has time to think about romance?"

"Does that mean that when we arrive in Rome, that you would have some quality time to spend alone with me before running to see James?" Lydia questioned with feigned innocence.

"Of course Lydia! I'm not going to run to see James the split second my feet hit Italian soil."

"If you say so." Lydia said dryly, sounding like a mother scolding her child for stealing cookies from the cookie jar. "Hey, Alex…moving on…things are happening so fast that it's definitely new territory for us and we need to discuss next steps…"

"Like what?"

"Well, the studio just signed a film deal for the rights to the second, third, and fourth books in the series and Toby said that they have commissioned the screenwriter to adapt the screenplay for the second book immediately."

"Wow…that was fast!"

"Yeah, exactly. I've also been told that the author just completed book five, which will be published in March and that the final book in the series, book six, has a tentative publishing date for the following spring."

"Oh my God! Already?"

"Yeah. And, um, if this tour is any indication, this movie is going to be BIG. The studio is fully aware that they likely have a blockbuster on their hands and with it comes a massive franchise opportunity. If this comes to fruition, the studio will want to bring the next installment to the big screen as soon as possible. This puts you, in a powerful position at the negotiation table and we need to be smart about our next move."

"Okay." I replied. "What do you suggest?"

"Well…I've started to receive several calls from some of the biggest talent agents in the industry. I think you need to determine if you want to stay with Toby or if we should consider changing teams?"

"I'm not sure. I just feel torn about it Lydia. Toby helped me to get me where I am today, and I-I think she is good, but she is not the best in the industry, nor is she a power broker. Is that what you think I need?"

"Don't get me wrong Alex, I have nothing against Toby. It's just that you've worked hard since childhood, and suddenly your work as an actress is paying off earlier and greater than any of us could have predicted. If this thing takes off like I think it will, I just want you to have the best possible representation." She cleared her throat and continued. "You'll need someone who will fight for you and get you where you should be…"

"I know. When we get back to LA, pick two or three of the best agencies that are wooing us, and let's meet with them quietly," I told Lydia in confidence.

"Good." Lydia said. "Also, you should talk with James about it. Whatever future deals are made on *Galaxy Drifters,* it would be good if you two were united in negotiations."

"I'm not sure what his thoughts are about his agent and if he would consider switching, but I'll discuss it with him and let you know."

"Ok, I'll make some calls," she said. "Let's explore the options."

\*\*\*

It was a hot and humid October day when we arrived in D.C. and the shopping mall was swarming with hundreds of teenage fans. I signed posters for over seven hundred fans that persevered to wait in the outrageously long line and then took photographs with an additional forty fans that had won a *Galaxy Drifters* radio contest. The boys fell into three categories: sci-fi nerds who asked lots of outer space questions, shy ones who trembled nervously around me, and a few macho overconfident shits who tried shamelessly to flirt with me. But the boys were in the minority. The majority of fans were teenage girls, and they were usually really loud. Most of them swooned about the movie and talked incessantly about the heartthrob male characters in the film, especially James character, Matt Samuel, and asked me what it was like to kiss him?

The experience in New Jersey, except for the weather, which was cool and drizzly, was almost a carbon copy of the day before in D.C. with hundreds of teenage fans jammed in the mall waiting for me to sign posters, several freaking out or fainting as they waited to see me.

One aggressive teenage girl and her friend who also seemed to be an avid fan bounded up to me, "Oh my god! It's Amanda! We need to ask you a question, are you still a virgin or did you and Matt have sex in the tent?" they asked in unison.

I was speechless. Were they kidding? I guess they wanted the character of Amanda, and not the actress playing the role. So I answered them in character, "Yes, I'm still a virgin everything was above the waist."

"He's so dreamy, you're so lucky!" they exclaimed as they happily left with their autographed posters.

It continued like that for hours until I was about ready to drop from fatigue. As we left, Lydia wrapped up conversation with some of the executives in charge of the publicity campaign as well as representatives from Fandango for advanced ticket sales, and various sponsors of the in-store events for the movie. She kept smirking at me with a super-sized shit-eating grin on her face, while I examined the indentation marks caused by the pen on my right hand after signing so many autographs. "Ok…what gives?" I questioned warily. "You look like the cat who ate the canary!"

"*Galaxy Drifters* is being compared to the likes of *Star Wars* and *Harry Potter*, and you and James are being called the modern day *Romeo and Juliet*," she smirked. "This just keeps getting better and better."

I rolled my eyes at her. "Oh, brother!" And this was just the beginning…

***

Lydia was right about one thing. The moment my feet hit Italian soil, the only thing I wanted to do was see James. It was extremely early in the morning when I arrived in Italy, and I was exhausted and should have slept, but the only thing I wanted to do was to be with him. I knew that we would have only a few hours of privacy and then I would be meeting with a team of stylists who would help me get ready for the *Galaxy* Premiere that evening, followed by a Q&A fan event and then a private dinner for the big suits and foreign investors that we were scheduled to attend. My fashion stylist from LA had sent the clothes ahead of time to Rome; I would be wearing an all-white Dior outfit for the Italian Premiere. James would be wearing a black Gucci suit, which he looked striking in. We both would fly back together to LA tomorrow, where we would stay until the LA Premiere which was now only a week away.

James and I tried to be as discreet as possible with our romance, as neither one of us wanted a media circus. Our hotel rooms were next to each other with a connecting door that James had left open when he arrived the night before. I tiptoed quietly into his room, as it was very early in the morning. I undressed quickly and slipped into bed next to him. He was sound asleep. I listened to the shallow sound of his breathing and admired his beauty as he peacefully slept. In such a short time, he had grown so dear to me. Aside from acting, he was the most important thing. Suddenly, the physical toll from the demanding travel schedule hit me like a ton of bricks, and before long I had drifted into a heavy sleep by his side.

I woke up confused and groggy. I looked at the clock and it was almost noon. *Damn it*, I had overslept and was meeting with the stylist and hairdresser in an hour. Where was James? I looked at the bedside table and there was a note…

> *Alex,*
> *You are beautiful when you sleep.*
> *Ken and I are meeting in the living room.*
> *There is a robe in the bathroom when you wake.*
> *xo James*

I quickly got out of bed and jumped in the shower. I was still feeling disoriented and slightly weary. James was meeting with Ken, his manager. I wondered if James was suddenly getting inundated with scripts and various offers the way I was? I imagined like Lydia and I, that there was a lot to discuss. I couldn't keep my head in the sand any longer; I knew that the business side of things was getting more complicated and that I needed a power broker in the entertainment business who could represent me well. I wanted to discuss it with James, but there would be little private time today.

When I got out of the shower I quickly towel dried and put on the plush white cotton hotel robe. I wish that I had brought my luggage into James room, but I didn't so I guess I was going to have to go out there in my robe.

"Hey, sleepy head," said James crossing the room and giving me a kiss. "Do you remember Ken, my manager?"

"Sure, hi Ken," I said awkwardly really wishing that I was fully dressed. "Sorry to interrupt, I'm going to get dressed now."

"Hey not so quick," James said catching my arm. "Ken could you give us a few minutes alone?"

"Sure thing James. I'll be back at one. Nice seeing you again Ms. Brown," he said.

"Please call me Alex," I mumbled to Ken as he made his way to the exit.

When Ken left, I turned to James, "that was awkward."

"Probably more for Ken, then for you," he said with a grin on his face. "I've missed you."

He took me in his arms and started to kiss me passionately until we were both panting, hard. God, how I had missed this man! I was like some wild insatiable creature ripping at his clothes as we stumbled into the bedroom. James tugged at the strap of my robe and slipped his fingers inside. My body ached desperately for his touch and we had the most unbelievable mind-blowing hard, sweaty sex. It was fucking intense.

After we made love, we lay naked on the scrunched up sheets, our legs and arms entwined. "That was unbelievable!" I told him.

He shot me a slow lazy smile. "When I saw you come out in your robe, all I could think about was getting you naked and underneath me. It's torture being away from you for so long. I hope I wasn't to rough with you?"

"Are you kidding? I feel great! Um, that thing you did with your finger and uh, my backside, I never thought, um, it could feel so good." I admitted sheepishly.

"You're so innocent Alex," he laughed softly and kissed me sweetly. "It's really endearing."

I knew I was turning beet red. "I…I am not." I stammered trying to object.

He just laughed and tenderly kissed me again. "You really are so cute…did you sleep well?"

"Yeah."

"Good, because I plan to make love to you all night long…"

Hearing his words, I could feel the stirring of desire deep inside and a fluttering sensation in my stomach. We just made love … how could I want him again so soon? I tried pushing James and those delicious thoughts of him aside, as I had to be focused on the busy day and evening ahead.

"I'll hold you to that promise!" I teased as I swatted his behind and got up from the bed.

"If we had time now...I wouldn't wait until tonight," he playfully bantered.

"Talking about time, I need to move it. I'm late as it is," I told him hastily as I realized the late hour.

"You better get going while you still can, otherwise I might not be able to control myself and we may need to have another quickie!"

"Don't even try James!" I warned playfully. "I'm leaving, but when we have time, I would like to talk with you about some business matters."

"Everything ok?"

"Yeah, everything is fine, but I'm thinking of switching talent agents and I also think that we should be unified in any future negotiation talks with the studio about the next installments in the franchise."

"Agreed. Ken and I were just discussing this. After being on the road meeting thousands of impassioned fans, I'm convinced that this thing is going to be a blockbuster," James said. "Ken and I were going over the advanced ticket sales data and Internet search statistics, and it's mind-boggling. I'm overwhelmed by the amount of calls and offers coming in, that I haven't been able to process it yet. Let's discuss this at length on the plane ride back tomorrow and we can start to come up with a strategy. How does that sound Alex?"

"It sounds very, *very* good Mr. Prescott." I purred as I scooted out of his bedroom.

"You better run Alex, before I drag you back *in* here," he yelled good-naturedly.

***

The rest of the day in Rome flew by quickly, and before I knew it I was stepping out of the limo and onto the red carpet. Screams and cheers greeted my arrival as I waved to the fans. I still wasn't used to this type of adoration, and I was at a loss of how to act toward all the fanfare. I spotted Ben, and made my way over to him.

"You look beautiful Alex," he said and kissed my cheek.

"This is so crazy." I whispered in his ear. "Did you expect this kind of reaction?"

"I don't think anyone could have predicted this, least of all me," replied Ben.

Just then the car with James pulled up and Ben whispered in my ear, "we should have brought ear plugs!"

Literally before my eyes, the crowd went wild when James got out of the car. The screams and cheers I received were nothing compared to his. It was crazy fuckin' mayhem!

"You would think he was John Lennon back from the dead!" exclaimed Ben in awe as he shrugged his shoulders.

James waved to the crowd, smiling and signing autographs to those fans who got close enough to the red carpet. When he finally made his way over to us, he seemed embarrassed almost sheepish from all of the attention.

"This is nuts!" James exclaimed bewildered that he was the reason for hundreds of women aggressively catcalling, whistling, and screaming his name.

The announcer called out our names and James and I walked out together. The crowd went wild and started to chant, "Kiss! Kiss! Kiss!"

"Should we give them what they want?" James whispered in my ear. Before I could respond, James dramatically swept me into his arms, playing up to the crowd, and they loved it. The chant became louder and James paused for a few seconds and then he gave me a heart-stopping sexy kiss. I thought pandemonium would erupt as the crowd exploded. When the kiss was over, we were quietly and quickly ushered into the auditorium for the show.

I knew that the *Galaxy Drifters* screenplay was incredibly good, and that's what led me to want to act in it. So when I saw all of the elements come together in perfect harmony on the big screen, I was amazed. The scenes, one by one, were riveting, especially towards the climax. It struck me right away that you had this intense fast-paced thriller, and then, in equal measure, a really beautiful and romantic love story. After the première, we were escorted to a smaller more intimate auditorium where Ben, James and I were seated on stage for a Q & A session with the media and fans. The questions were in Italian and translated back and forth into English.

**Is it true that at one time you had almost 1000 actors vying for the role of Matt Samuel? Was there anyone else close to getting the role?**

**Ben Avery:** "Yes it's true we searched for what seemed like a very long time for the perfect Matt, but he kept alluding us. We finally put together a semifinalist list of like five or six guys, and while each one had some of the qualities, they were not Matt."

**So what made James Prescott the perfect Matt?**

**Ben Avery:** "Well for one, James and Alexandra had killer chemistry together which was clear from the start. As for finding the perfect Matt, we were looking for an actor who could bring the character to life so he needed to be very handsome, intellectually deep, and dangerous. A lot of the actors were good looking, so they had the looks, but it was that combination of beauty, danger, and emotional depth that made it ridiculously clear that James was the one.

**What about Alexandra Brown? Is it true that you knew right away that she was the perfect Amanda Blake?**

**Ben Avery:** "Amanda is the heart and sole of the story. The moment I met Alex, I knew she was the one. I couldn't imagine any other actress in the role."

**Alexandra, did you think this film was such a big deal when you were first cast as Amanda?**

**Alex Brown:** "I knew that there was a fan base, because of the books. But I had no idea how large it was until recently. During production I started to get a better idea that this could be something big, but it wasn't until I was on the road promoting the film that I became fully aware of the weight of it."

**Talking about weight, I imagine all of this attention must put a lot of weight on you and James Prescott?**

**Alex Brown:** "It's funny, because I've been making movies since I was ten years old and no one really cared who I was, and now suddenly I'm being followed around and strangers are screaming my name. My family keeps sending me articles on the Internet about me and it's weird. Like I don't understand why people care where I buy my coffee and trivial stuff like that? It's really a strange feeling. I also think the tabloids and the stuff written can get downright nasty. Like if I'm not dressed stylish one day, they will tear me down and write about how awful I looked. And if I don't smile, then I'm a bitch. I'm trying to ignore it, but it gets challenging.

**That is really difficult. What about you James?**

**James Prescott:** "It's totally taken me by surprise and I think I'm still in a daze from it. It's the oddest sensation to get out of a car or to go somewhere in public and to have a flock of teenage girls yelling your name, or a stranger asking to take a photo with me. One day you're invisible, and then suddenly you're not. I thought the worst of it would be an LA, but since traveling to several major cities, it's wider than I expected.

**Talking about screaming women, how does it feel to know thousands adore you?**

**James Prescott:** "Again, it's really an odd sensation. I mean a year ago, I could hardly get a date and now this..."

**I find it hard to believe that you ever had trouble getting a date with those ridiculously good looks?**

**James Prescott:** "I don't know what to say to that? [*Laughing*]."

**What do you think about so many of the opening weekend screenings already being sold out in advance?**

**Ben Avery:** "Hope I can get a ticket."

**Do you think there will be a sequel?**

**Ben Avery:** "It's very likely, but the film business is a business after all, so in the end it will depend on how much the movie makes."

**Well good luck with it. We sure love it here in Rome!**

\*\*\*

When we landed in LA the next afternoon, James and I were exhausted, but happy to be together again. During the flight, we discussed business strategies and agreed that after the LA premiere and worldwide opening of *Galaxy Drifters* we would start meeting with potential new agents to represent us.

Those final days leading up to the Premiere included interviews with Jay Leno, David Letterman, Conan O'Brien, and Jimmy Kimmel. The questions were all remarkably similar to the ones in Rome, with the addition of several questions about the chemistry between James and I. Repeatedly, I was asked if I had broken up with actor Lance Smith and if I was dating my co-star, James Prescott? He was getting the same questions about me. The clip of us kissing on the red carpet in Rome was shown constantly during interviews, by the press, in tabloids, and on the Internet. Speculation about our off-screen romance almost surpassed the publicity for the film.

The Vanity Fair cover with James and I had been a huge hit and bestseller, and they wanted us to do another cover and full-length feature article with the cast about the movie. In addition, James was doing a photo shoot with GQ and I had one lined up with Vogue, and we were asked to do one together for Harper's Bazaar. The studio was thrilled with the publicity.

It was one day until the LA Premiere and five days until the worldwide release. All eyes were on us to sink or swim.

## Chapter 13: Fame

When I got out of the car to walk the red carpet for the big LA premiere, I was self-conscious and nervous in my Gucci tight fitted black open back dress and high-heeled Yves Saint Laurent shoes. The lights from the flashing cameras momentarily blinded me. I stood rooted in my spot as my ears adjusted to the sound of the high pitched screams, coming from thousands of fans, some of whom had camped there for hours, and perhaps even days as rumored by some media outlets, in the hope of catching a glimpse of us on the red carpet. The experience in Rome and at all of the fan events was nothing compared to this. If I had any lingering doubts about *Galaxy Drifters* becoming a smash hit, they were quickly discarded during the riot-inducing evening that screamed success.

After the premiere, the entire cast was reunited at the after-party. Spirits were high and champagne was flowing. I was standing with Audrey catching up on the latest gossip.

"*Wow*...You look hot!" Audrey joked. "That dress is sexy."

"Thanks," I said. "You look beautiful Audrey. Who designed your dress?"

"Thanks. It's Chanel!" said Audrey enthusiastically. "We may look hot, but the guys are stealing the show tonight!"

"Yup, they certainly got a lot of cat calls and whistles!" I said rolling my eyes. "Those screams were deafening. Does it bother you that Mark is now considered a sex symbol?"

"Nah, let him bask in the glory while he can. It doesn't bug me." Audrey said confidently. "Anyway our attention is nothing compared to you guys. We're on the sidelines; the real scrutiny *is* on you and James. How are you taking it?"

"I try to ignore it." I confided honestly.

"You guys are together now, like as a couple, right?"

Suddenly, I felt James gaze on me and I smiled at him from across the room. He continued to stare at me with a hint of mischief in his eyes. I stood there transfixed unable to register anything else around me.

"Umm Alex?" Audrey said clearing her throat as she waited for my response. "Um-um."

I reluctantly slid my gaze back to Audrey and tried to refocus my attention on her question. "I'm sorry, could you repeat that?"

"I asked if you were dating James, but I already know the answer so don't bother denying it," she huffed crossing her arms.

"Is it that obvious Miss Know-it-all?"

"Is water wet?" Audrey replied drolly, raising an eyebrow. "Like I said to you before, since day one we all noticed the, ah...powerful connection that you shared. Everyone knew it was only a matter of time before you both hooked up."

"Do you think everyone knows?"

"Well, it's certainly the source of gossip and speculation," said Audrey. "Don't worry everyone from the film will be happy for you guys. Well, almost everyone..."

"What does that mean?" I questioned defensively.

"Come on, you know that Ellie and half of the female crew had big time crushes on James. Also, if I recall, Sean had a thing for you."

"Whatever." I anxiously rubbed my hands together and smoothed the non-existent wrinkles out of my dress. "Um...changing subjects...have you spoken to Lance lately?" I questioned softly, a slight tremor in my voice.

"Don't worry Alex. Lance is ok and he will get over it with time." Audrey said tenderly, giving my hand a gentle squeeze.

"I just feel like the biggest shit for hurting him."

"Don't keep beating yourself up about it. You couldn't stay with Lance out of some misplaced guilt. You fell in love with James, and with time Lance will heal and move on."

"Ok," I stammered quietly not meeting her gaze.

Just then Lydia came over and joined our conversation.

"Can you believe all of the stars, producers, directors and agents that are here tonight? It's like the *who's who* of Hollywood," Lydia bubbled enthusiastically.

"Yeah, fucking film people...there everywhere tonight!" Audrey said dryly, rolling her eyes dramatically at us. "If I get one more air kiss from some wannabe kiss ass I might have to puke."

"I know I hate these events!" I agreed vehemently, nodding my head.

Ben and Mark joined us at that moment and we started to talk about the evening and expectations for the release of the movie. Then, Jonathan Banks, the Armani clad, coke-snorting, producer for *Galaxy Drifters* and Valerie Sims, the surgically-enhanced voluptuous blonde VP of marketing for Pinnacle Sage Movies, the studio responsible for developing and distributing *Galaxy Drifters*, joined us and updated us on advanced ticket sales, soundtrack earnings, and fan counts. The numbers were staggering and expectations were high.

After Jonathan and Valerie left, James came over and joined the group. James and I had purposely circulated among other people trying not to spend too much time together as we didn't want to be at the center of intense public attention and gossip. Fuck...who were we kidding? We tried to repel questions about our relationship, but the more we deflected, it seemed like it left the crowd fuckin' foaming at the mouths for more. It was pretty obvious that we were hot news, at least for the moment.

"Does anyone know Diane Wilkes, she is a senior talent agent and partner at William Morris Agency?" James asked the group.

"Why are you thinking of switching talent agents?" Ben asked with interest.

"It's a possibility," James said.

"Diane is good. She is smart and a shrewd operator, and is respected in the industry. But if you want a real scrappy power player I would go for someone younger and quick thinking like Tom Hunter or Curt Westcott at Hunter Westcott, or Bradley Stevenson at Creative Artists Agency," replied Ben. "Don't get me wrong, Diane is great, and you should give her a fair chance, but the other three agents I mentioned are proving themselves to be the dominant players in town. Especially Hunter, he has a reputation for ferocity and a keen business head and his clients seem to love him."

"Funny you should mention Hunter Westcott and Creative Artists Agency as both have been persistent trying to acquire Alex as a client," replied Lydia.

"That doesn't surprise me, the agents I mentioned have barely veiled ambition," responded Ben. "I'm sure that they would love to acquire Alex and James as clients."

"Do you prefer one over another Ben?" asked Lydia.

"Well, Creative Artists Agency is the dominant player, but if I was a betting man, I would probably go with Hunter Westcott," said Ben.

"Why?" James questioned.

"Well, Hunter Westcott is one of the fastest-growing Hollywood talent agencies and represents some of the world's most successful actors," replied Ben, "but it's probably because of Hunter that I would recommend them. You might think he is a *dick* when you first meet him, but if he believes in you, he will fight tooth and nail until the death for you."

"I'm not sure if I want to deal with a *money hungry arrogant dick*," James protested.

"He's an acquired taste that's for sure, but definitely worth meeting him," said Ben with a chuckle. "When he was your age he was an agent trainee at Creative, and quickly rose to one of the youngest and most powerful agents in Hollywood by his mid to late twenties. He started Hunter Westcott before the age of thirty a few years ago with his business partner, Curt Westcott, and it has done tremendously well becoming a major player and influencer in Hollywood."

"If you haven't convinced James to meet Tom Hunter, you've convinced me Ben," I said with a wink.

"Me too," said Audrey, "but he's not exactly breaking down my door. Can you put in a good word for me as I want someone like that representing me."

"I'll see what I can do," I promised.

"In that case, put in a good word for me too," requested Mark.

"So James, what do you think?" I asked with raised eyebrow.

James just rolled his eyes and turned to Lydia. "Lydia, could you speak with Ken and coordinate the meetings with Diane Wilkes, Bradley Stevenson, Hunter and Westcott?"

"Sure thing," she replied, "consider it a done deal."

*Galaxy Drifters* worldwide release followed four nights later surpassing projections and breaking all records with an opening weekend of just under $150 million. It was estimated that the film would likely finish just above $700 million solidifying it's part in pop culture and assuring that the next film's in the series would be developed as soon as possible to capitalize on it's popularity and enormous profit-making potential.

In the days and weeks that followed, it became a kind of bizarre thing to suddenly be recognized everywhere I went. I didn't know what to think of this near-instant fame. I had always been proud of my previous work as an actress, but now this one little niche was suddenly defining me. People couldn't get enough of Amanda Blake in *Galaxy Drifters* and it was up to me to continually promote that fantasy. It seemed like nothing else mattered. People were obsessed with the books and movie, and now they seemed equally obsessed with James and me. I tried acting natural and to ignore it as best as I could, but it was unsettling when I realized that people were watching me a lot more than they ever were before.

I knew that James felt it to and that it was worse for him. Everywhere he went it seemed like hundreds of teenage girls would follow him and call his name. He played this heroic supernatural figure in the movie, and he had the tousled hair, the piercing green eyes, the ridiculously good looks and sexy smile, and women went wild for it. If anything, they were angry with me for taking him *off the market*.

James and I thought that the attention from fans and media would be short-lived, but instead it seemed to gain momentum every day. Fueling the fire was speculation about our off-screen romance. At times our personal lives seemed to overshadow the beloved characters and romance in the story. Why people were interested in our personal relationship, I couldn't fathom, but they were, and that interest became all consuming and pervasive.

## Chapter 14: Tom Hunter

James, Ken, Lydia and I arrived for what was now our second visit to the Hunter Westcott offices in Beverly Hills. The building was architecturally sleek and sophisticated, a showcase of modern design, but with an element of calm. We followed a perky young intern from the main reception area up a cantilevered raw wood staircase that led to an elevated glass conference room and a row of glass-fronted offices on the second floor.

We had been to the offices last week to meet with Curt Westcott. Tom Hunter had been out of town and could not join us, so we were back today to meet with him. Hunter Westcott was an exciting agency filled with a lot of energy and movement. During the initial meeting, Curt Westcott and a handful of top agents had done their best to impress us. Curt was a shrewd businessman who knew the *ins and outs* of the entertainment industry well. I had no doubts about Curt's ability, but I wasn't sure if I felt a connection with him, and neither had James, so we were still undecided. Since that meeting we had met with Diane Wilkes and Bradley Stevenson. Both were likeable and solid, but as Ben had described, Bradley was younger and quick thinking, and we felt that he might be better suited for us then Diane. However, we wanted to meet with Tom Hunter first before we made our final decision.

The intern handed us off and we were ushered into Tom Hunter's office by his assistant, Scarlett, who was a very attractive woman in her twenties with short-cropped dark hair. She said that Mr. Hunter was on his way from another meeting, but would be here in five minutes.

Hunter's office had style. It was all glass, and had views overlooking Wilshire Boulevard in Beverly Hills. The room was divided into two zones. The first was dominated by an imposing but minimalist designed Scandinavian-modern desk, piled high with scripts, while floor-to-ceiling shelves held more scripts and photos of Hunter with colleagues and family. Then the second zone had a seating area with two sofas, armchairs, and a massive white and chrome coffee table. On one wall, was a TV screen, and on the other, bright pieces of modern art. Overall the look was simple, but it exuded warmth and exoticism.

We sat down and Scarlett came in with coffee and assorted cold beverages, followed moments later by a tall man with a powerful booming voice who I assumed to be Tom Hunter. He was ending a phone conversation, but another phone was ringing from his pocket, which he ignored with utter confidence as he focused his attention on us.

"Hello, I'm Tom Hunter," he said with gusto. "Sorry that I'm late, but my last meeting ran over and traffic was fuckin' brutal."

Before anyone could speak he continued talking, "Scarlett, you call these refreshments? Where are those good cookies...you know the chocolate covered ones that came in yesterday from Belgium?"

"I think there gone," answered Scarlett.

"GONE ALREADY? Damn! Ok, bring us an assortment of artisan cheese, fruit and crackers. And oh ... I'd like some Red Bull too."

In the middle of this, an agent popped his head in, but Tom told him to come back later.

"It's pretty important Tom." The agent came over and whispered something in Hunter's ear.

"It can wait." Hunter replied with authority. "Tell him to go get laid or something and I'll call him back when I can."

James and I exchanged a look. Tom Hunter had a big personality and radiated a certain eclectic magnetism that I couldn't describe. He was highly energetic and a fast talker. In the background, multiple phones kept ringing, which he ignored and so did we.

"It's so good to finally meet you," he said warmly shaking my hand, and then introduced himself to James, Lydia, and Ken with high-octane enthusiasm.

Watching Tom Hunter in action, I recalled Ben's words. Yes, *scrappy* was certainly a good adjective to describe Tom Hunter. What I wasn't prepared for were his good looks and charm. He was in his early thirties and he was athletic looking with broad shoulders, brown hair, and blue eyes. Tall, dark and handsome was a fitting description for Mr. Hunter.

Tom took a seat and stared the four of us down, regarding us shrewdly with his intense blue eyes. There was a pause as we waited for him to talk. Then he leaned forward, and captured our attention with his loud voice.

"I know you were here last week and met with Curt and some of our top people, they gave you a formal presentation, a tour, etc., so I'm not going to try to sell you anymore on us. Instead let's talk casually for a few minutes and get to know each other without any bullshit!"

"Ok." I chimed in. "If we were to sign on with Hunter Wescott which agent would represent us?"

"Whoever you want!"

"If I want you, do you have the time to dedicate to represent me well?" I asked bluntly.

Tom smiled. "I do everything well Alex...can I call you Alex?"

I nodded my head.

"If you or James...can I call you James?" he said looking at James for affirmation and when he received it he continued, "...were to sign on with me, you will get so much personal attention, that you won't know what to do with it. I will practically become a family member and if you don't believe me, ask any of my clients?" he warned. "If I rep you, I can be reached at all times and that's not bullshit! I eat, drink, and sleep this business, and I work harder than anyone I know."

With a flourish, Tom dramatically pulled out one of his cell phones from his suit jacket and started scrolling and reciting *Galaxy Drifters* stats to us verbatim. When he was finished he looked up and intently stared at us.

"Jesus Christ, people! *Galaxy Drifters* mania is sweeping the country! Fuck...we all know that this thing is the hottest deal around town and you two are on FIRE! I'm happy to continue to sit here and recite the book and movie revenue projections all friggin' afternoon, but you already know this shit has lit up the movie box office! What I want to know is how are you going to cash in?"

"We've done our homework and we know the break-even numbers for the film," said Ken smugly. "When the time comes, we'll be ready!"

"I certainly hope so hot shot, because the folks at Pinnacle can be stingy bastards. They paid you peanuts on the first movie, because Alex & James were relatively unknown. The power equation has changed, but that doesn't mean the studio will roll over and make it easy for you in future negotiations."

"We will be prepared," said Lydia confidently.

"How?" questioned Tom arrogantly, "because you can never be too prepared, not when this much money and power rests on the table?"

He paused and stared at us closely for a few minutes. Everyone was quiet, as the question remained unanswered.

"Ok, you say you know the break-even points for the last film. How are you gonna figure out what is an attainable number for the sequel so that you're not exploited again especially when it comes to upfront pay, backend compensation, and box office bonuses?" asked Tom looking around at the group.

"Well, obviously that's why we're here," stated Ken.

"You get an 'A' hot shot!" Tom smirked. "Let's back up for a sec. Anyone know the most used Internet search phrases related to *Galaxy Drifters*?"

"Probably their names," stated Ken.

"You get another 'A', what else?" Tom asked, waiting for a response.

Tom looked at the group, but no one said anything.

"It might interest you to know that these are among the most popular search phrases: *Alex Brown and James Prescott in Galaxy Drifters, Alex Brown and James Prescott a couple, Alex Brown and James Prescott Dating, Alex Brown and James Prescott kissing, Alex Brown and James Prescott living together, James Prescott modeling, James Prescott abs, Alex Brown legs,* "I would continue, but I think you've got the idea."

"Ok Tom, you've done a nice job doing your homework. So what does it all mean?" questioned James.

"It mean's for one, you've hit the big times kid, and life as you and Alex have known it is over!" snapped Tom. "Your 'name commodity' and 'Q score' is suddenly off the charts!"

"Which mean's exactly what?" pressed James.

"Think about the fascination and love affair that fans had with Kate Winslet and Leonardo DiCaprio after *Titantic*? Now take that and multiple it by...*six*. Yeah, that's right, I said six. At the end of *Titantic*, DiCaprio is dead and the ship sinks, but *Galaxy Drifters* is going to be a total of six movies. Now I don't know if each movie is going to do what the first one did, but if the books are any indication, it will sky rocket and be hugely successful. Additionally, you have a few other factors to consider. When *Titanic* came out it wasn't the era of penetrating Internet paparazzi that we have now. Get ready; because I can smell these things, the fans and the media are obsessed with you and your relationship status. The only thing the world finds more entertaining then a great book or movie, is the idea of *true love*, and all that other *fairy tale crap*, and you've given it to them on a silver platter and they are eating it up."

There was silence in the room and James and I just stared at each other. Finally, I said, "For argument sake, let's say everything you just said is correct, what now?"

"First, what I said is true," Tom answered with assurance, "second, you and James will need to learn how to separate your true selves from the public image."

"I'm not clear on what you're saying," Ken interrupted.

"What I'm saying is that the name Alex Brown or James Prescott is now a household brand and you have to treat it that way. You are now selling an image of Alex Brown and James Prescott, like a company selling a product," replied Tom with authority. He paused for dramatic effect and looked closely at James and I, "Alex, James, you no longer own your names," Tom declared boldly, "from now on, your actions are no longer your own, and you need to be prepared."

"Are you trying to depress us or scare us?" James questioned mockingly.

"Not deliberately, and I haven't talked about the good stuff," said Tom. "Most people in the world would do anything to trade places with you right now. You're young, beautiful, and talented and you will be able to do work you love, and get paid millions of dollars for it, that's something that eludes most of us. As you prove yourself, your power, stature, and wealth will increase, and with it the ability to do the type of projects you want with people you admire and respect. You will have the opportunity to travel to exotic places, and meet interesting people. Your lives will be glamorous and exciting. BUT, and I *stress* my earlier point, the quicker you both understand what it means to be *FAMOUS*, the better off you'll be. You want to *CONTROL* the fame and *NOT* allow it to control you. You're both young, which makes it a greater challenge, because you're just learning whom you are, and now you have to learn it in front of the whole world," Tom uttered.

"So if we sign with you, what would be your strategy moving forward?" I questioned.

"Well, regarding *Galaxy Drifters*, like I said before, they paid you next to nothing on the first one, that's not going to happen again. By the time I'm through with them, you both could buy your very own small countries. The opportunity with the franchise extends beyond the film, sound track, and DVD's; it goes to merchandise, video games, action figures and Barbie dolls. Obviously, if I represent both of you, I can represent a united front at the negotiation table. What else do you want?" Tom asked appearing to pay close attention.

"I don't want to be defined by *Galaxy Drifters*, it's important to me that I broaden my range by playing a variety of dramatic roles that can bring out my best performance. I want to be able to do projects that I'm passionate about even if they are not big budget commercial projects," I replied earnestly.

"I hear what you're saying independent films, blah, blah, blah," Tom said dryly rolling his eyes.

"I saw you roll your eyes Tom, can you be supportive of those goals, otherwise I'm leaving," I threatened.

"You are certainly feisty and direct," Tom replied, "I'm sure we can make it happen. What about you James, what do you want?"

"Well, like Alex, I want the ability to work on other projects. It we are committed to six movies, plus promoting it, that's doesn't leave a lot of room for other things, but it's essential that we have the freedom and ability to select and work on other projects during breaks in filming," said James.

"What about your music career. I hear you're very talented. Would you be interested in doing some music for *Galaxy Drifters*?" Tom questioned.

James looked up with sudden interest and I could see the gleam in his eyes. "Could you make that happen Tom?"

"I would like to learn more about your long-term musical interests and hear you perform, but yes we can make it happen, and if you're as good as I hear, it will give you the exposure that you need and then the sky is the limit!"

There was a pause in conversation and everyone seemed deep in thought.

"You've given us a lot to think about. Could we have a few days?" asked Lydia.

"Of course, as you know we would like a five year exclusive contract. If you go with one of our top agents, it's a 10% commission for each of you. If you prefer to go with Curt, or me, we charge a 15% commission. If we get both of you, Curt and I are willing to drop it to 12.5% each. Remember, we don't get paid, unless you get paid, so it's in our best interest to get the best deals for you."

"12.5% is too much. We have better offers from competing firms," said Ken.

Tom got up and started to pace the room and then he gave us a disarming smile. "I'm sorry, but you get what you pay for, and that's my price. It might seem like a lot, but I guarantee you that no one will not be disappointed if you select me to represent you," Tom said with a cocky swagger.

It was clear that negotiations were over, and I thought that we were about to wrap up when I felt Tom's scrutinizing gaze on me.

"Before we wrap up, there is one more thing…"

I raised my eyebrows, uncomfortable being the focus of his attention.

"It isn't often that I'm caught off guard, but Alex you're not what I expected?"

"What were you expecting?"

"A moody unfriendly teenage Bitch." Tom stated matter-of-factly.
I was flustered. *Why – the fucking nerve!*

"Are you always this fucking rude?" James interrupted, putting a
protective arm around my shoulders. "Alex is a private person and
doesn't like the attention, that doesn't make her a bitch."

"Hey, I'm sorry, but if you want someone to blow smoke up your
asses then go to another agent, because I'm not your enemy and I'm
trying to help." Tom said, unflinching. "So Alex, what do *you* have
to say for yourself?"

"It's ok James," I said looking at him with an adoring smile and
then answering Tom. "I've read the scornful blogs and comments,
and I know that I can seem awkward at times and that I get uptight in
interviews. It um, stresses me out and I get tense and don't know
how to respond."

"My question was not intended to be insulting Alex, but I'm not
often surprised so I'm amazed at how wrong my image was of you
until we met. You need to fire your publicity person and we need the
world to see the real you so that they can fall in love with you as
much as they have with James. Also, you need to smile and be more
open with your body language at public events and during interviews.
You need to work on loosening up and being more approachable in
public."

Then Tom fixed his attention on James.

James sighed. "What?"

"How often are you working out with a personal trainer?" Tom
inquired.

"Three times per a week...why?"

"James you're very social and friendly, so nothing needs to
change on that front. But you need to buff up for the camera for
shirtless scenes, so you will need to increase work out time with a
trainer and change your diet to build extra muscle," Tom said with
authority, almost sounding like a drill sergeant.

"Excuse me?" James snapped as he stiffened his back and
scowled at Tom. I could sense his annoyance and irritation.

"He already is a wall of muscle. He has washboard abs, and is chiseled," I replied to Tom, equally annoyed, "what else could he possibly do?"

"I'm not trying to offend, obviously James is absurdly handsome. I'm straight as an arrow and I got to tell you, whether you're male or female, anyone would stop to look," Tom explained with a wink. "James, whether you like it or not you are now a sex symbol and you also happen to be the *hottest thing on two legs* right now. That mean's you are going to be put into comprising positions on camera and expected to take your shirt off a lot. In this role, you're supposed to be this supernatural incredibly strong hero, and the folk's at Pinnacle will expect you to fulfill that role and live up to that heroic fantasy. That will require building more muscle, I'm sorry, but it's reality."

"I'll think about it," James answered begrudgingly, recognizing the truth of Tom's words.

"We need to be at a photo shoot in one hour," Lydia interrupted, as Tom's phone started to ring again. Then there was a knock at the door, and Scarlett told Hunter that his next appointment had arrived.

"We're not finished here, Scarlett. Please give us five more minutes."

"I know that you have to go, but we haven't talked about your relationship yet. Obviously, you're a couple, and that will require a publicity strategy moving forward," Tom stated.

"We are both very private people," James spoke firmly and his tone was stern. "No strategy is needed, because our relationship will never be discussed publicly."

"Yeah, it's off limits." I added. "People can speculate all they want, but we both feel adamant about not disclosing our relationship to the public."

"If that's how you both feel, I won't bring it up again, but if you hire me to represent you, there may become a time when it's necessary to discuss it," said Tom sounding and looking serious.

"We need to run or we will be late," Ken told the group.

"Tom." James held his hand out, his look unreadable.

"James." Tom said returning his handshake.

Then Tom turned to me and shook my hand. "Alex, you are a stunning, talented, and very pleasant young woman, and I'm sorry if I offended you earlier."

"No worries." I replied, "You've given us a lot to think about…we will be in touch."

***

After leaving the offices of Hunter Westcott in James's SUV with Ken and Lydia, I replayed the conversation in my mind. I felt wonderfully energized after the meeting. Tom Hunter had presence and bravado and I enjoyed talking with him. I knew he was arrogant, and I certainly knew about his reputation for ferocity and unbridled ambition, but I found him gregarious and charming. I expected someone cold, but I actually thought he was warm and refreshingly straightforward, and that he was the perfect agent to represent us. I just hoped that James felt the same way as I did.

"Ben was right, he is an *arrogant dick*," James said.

"Does that mean you don't like him?" I questioned.

"I wouldn't say that. He definitely knows how to perform for an audience. I found him highly entertaining," James murmured, making it difficult for me to concentrate as he nuzzled on my ear.

"I liked him," I said honestly.

"He liked you too," James replied.

"How could you tell?" I asked.

"Well, for one he could hardly take his eyes off you, it was starting to piss me off," James admitted.

"Don't tell me you're jealous?" I smirked. "Didn't you see all of the photographs of his wife and little girl?"

"I hear that he is happily married," Ken interjected into the conversation.

"Hunter's wife is pregnant with their second child," Lydia added.

"Whatever." James said rolling his eyes. "But I did feel like he really listened to us when we talked, and he was clever, and quick witted. All in all, my impression is positive."

"What did you think Lydia, Ken?" I asked from the back seat.

"I think he has a big personality that might drive me crazy," chuckled Ken, "but there is no doubt, the man is sharp as a whip."

"I found myself drawn to him effortlessly," Lydia replied, "and I think he is a mover and a shaker who will provide both of you with great opportunities if you let him represent you."

"Then it's unanimous, Tom Hunter is our man!" I declared as we all nodded our affirmation.

## Chapter 15: Meeting the Browns

"Peter! Zach! Mom! Dad!" I yelled as James and I entered the house, but no one seemed to be there.

"They must be in the back yard," I said leading James over to the glass door at the rear of the house.

Through the window I could see my mom and dad drinking white wine on the far side of the patio. My brothers were playing football on the grass.

"They are going to love you!" I told James.

He grinned at me, flashing me his playful, sexy smile that made me weak in the knees, and I grinned back at him like an idiot unable to hide my giddiness. I was still holding onto James's hand, as I opened the door wide.

"Hey," I called waving to my family.

"Keep your eye on the ball!" Zach yelled.

Suddenly, a football was flying at me with high speed. James let go of my hand, and gently pushed me out of the way and effortlessly caught it.

My brothers ran over, "nice catch," exclaimed Peter shaking James's hand, followed by Zach.

"Did you play football in school?" Zach asked.

"No, not really, but I would pick up a casual game every once in awhile. Between school, acting and music, it didn't leave a lot of time for sports," James answered.

"Not to mention modeling and sailing!" I added proudly, a cheesy grin on my face.

James looked embarrassed so I stopped listing his extracurricular activities.

"Alex told us about the sailboat in Maine, it sounded awesome man!" Zach said.

"Have you ever sailed competitively?" Peter asked.

"I've done the *Figawi* Race three times and a few other smaller competitions," James answered.

"I didn't know that James?" I replied.

He smirked and winked at me and stood very close, stroking my back. "One of my many hidden talents," he quietly whispered in my ear.

"What is the *Figawi?*" asked Zach.

"You are such a Californian!" exclaimed James sounding amused as he rolled his eyes. "It's a sailing event with 200 plus sailboats competing annually from Hyannis Port on Cape Cod, to be the first one to reach Nantucket."

"Cool, but I rather hear about the hot female models that you've worked with..." Zach interrupted with a sly smile, "...can you introduce us?"

"Zach!" I exclaimed, elbowing him in his rib cage.

"Ouch!" he exclaimed.

"Sorry guys, but not in front of your sister." James laughed.

"Do you want me to elbow you too?" I said to James with raised eyebrow.

My parents came over then, "Guys do you think you could stop monopolizing our guest so that we could be introduced?"

"Mom, Dad ... this is James Prescott. James...these our my parents, David and Jennifer Brown."

"Please call me Jennifer," my mom said warmly hugging James, "I feel like I know you from all that Alex has told us."

"Don't believe everything you hear!" James joked. "Jennifer it is so nice to finally meet you, now I see where Alex get's her natural beauty from."

My mother flushed and I could tell that she liked him.

"Mom, James brought you flowers and wine, but we left it in the kitchen," I said.

"Oh that's very thoughtful," she said brightly sounding girlish.

James Prescott *strikes* again I thought. My mom was looking at him like a lovesick teenager with a crush. *Uh oh.*

"Please call me David," my dad said pleasantly while he coolly accessed James.

"Sir, it's so nice to finally meet you," James said giving my dad a firm handshake and a broad smile.

The dinner was going well. It was a beautiful evening and we ate al fresco style on the patio. My dad was serving us swordfish hot off the grill accompanied by his homemade mango chutney and couscous salad. My mother had decorated the table with candles in hurricanes, fresh-from-the-garden California poppy and black-eyed Susan flowers, and brightly colored dishes. There was plenty of cold beer and white wine on ice and my mom had concocted a new fruit drink fresh from her juicer. Conversation was flowing easily and everyone seemed to be having a great time. My dad was regaling us with a funny story from his most recent television project. The show had a complicated time traveling storyline and it was my dad's job as a script supervisor to avoid continuity errors.

"How do you maintain continuity when the storyline is so convoluted like that?" James asked with interest.

"It's not easy, I keep a lot of notes," my dad chuckled.

"What about you Jennifer, how do you like being a stage manager?" James asked.

"I love it, especially the ability to control the chaos."

"What type of chaos?" James questioned quizzically.

"The chaos of a live TV broadcast. It's like air traffic control, both terrifying and exhilarating at the same time," my mom exclaimed excitedly. "Both you and Alex haven't done many live performances yet, but you probably remember when you've done live interviews or gone to an award show that there was a stage manager who helped you to get more comfortable, and signaled you on when and where to move, that's what I do."

"Well, after hearing you describe it with so much enthusiasm, I have a new found appreciation for what stage managers do." James said.

"Thank you, but that's enough about me; let's talk about *Galaxy Drifters* and your performances. I thought the action scenes were nail biting and the romance between your characters is the best onscreen romance that I've seen in a longtime. You both did tremendously well and I couldn't take my eyes off either of you. I cannot wait until the sequel!" my mom gushed proudly.

"I agree. Your performances were spot on and you proved yourself to be talented lead actors. I wasn't expecting much from the movie, but I have to admit after the first five minutes, I was hooked. The only disappointment is that with the success of the movie, we feel like we never get to see our daughter, *the big star*, anymore," my dad said half joking, half serious.

"Huh! Dad. So not funny!"

"Alex, when do you leave for Vancouver, as I forgot to mark it in my calendar," my mom asked.

"I'm going with James to Boston for Easter in two weeks to meet his family and then from there we will fly to Vancouver to start filming *Galaxy Drifters 2: Paradise Lost*," I told my family.

"*Holy Crap*...the studio and producers certainly haven't wasted anytime, talk about fast!" Peter commented wryly.

"Numbers don't lie Peter, where there is money, there is action," my dad answered.

"*Ugh*, Dad. You sound like our new agent." I said dryly.

"Good, I hear he is a brilliant guy, so I like the comparison," my dad joked. "Tom Hunter certainly has done well for you kids, if this keeps up you can retire in a few years."

James smiled a wicked grin. "Talking about the deal for *Galaxy Drifters*, Hunter was able to get a housing allowance for Alex and I."

My eyes widened and I looked warily at James. He looked pleased with himself as he gave me a huge grin, innocently shrugging his shoulders. He knew I was hoping to avoid this conversation tonight, especially in front of my brothers. He was one frustrating male.

"Housing allowance?" my parents questioned in unison.

"Yeah, it's true. I'm not sure how Tom pulled it off, but he was able to roll in a housing allowance for James and I during the time that we are under contract for the *Galaxy Drifters* movies.

"*No way!*" Zach exclaimed, "You're already making a boat load of money and now you both get to live rent free for the next few years on top of it?

"How much do you get?" Peter asked curiously.

"It's no big deal guys and anyway, I've already told you that I'll take care of your rent and tuition bills, so butt out!" I hissed.

"Oh come on now, just tell us?" Zach asked sweetly.

I knew they wouldn't stop bugging me until I answered their pleas.

"Fifteen thousand," I mumbled softly.

"*A month?*" exclaimed Zach.

"Yes," I confirmed.

"For *each* of you?" asked Peter.

"Yes," I replied.

"Is this your way of telling us that you're moving out?" my dad asked sternly and suddenly the dinner party didn't seem so festive anymore.

"Um, well, yeah...but not until after filming in Vancouver and the next promo tour is finished," I mumbled. "*We* still have to look for places, so it could take months, maybe even a year with our crazy schedules."

"*We?*" my dad frowned, examining me.

"I think you're a little young to be moving in together," my mom added, sounding angry.

At that moment my brothers interrupted helping to diffuse the tension that now filled the space.

"Hey James it was nice meeting you, but Zach and I have plans with some friends so we are going to take off now," Peter exclaimed while putting his hand out to give James a farewell handshake.

"Mom, dad, great dinner," he said while kissing my mom's cheek. "I'll see you next Sunday and then I'll be back for Easter, and I'll pick Zach up on the way."

Zach followed Peter's lead and said his farewell.

"Sis, could you walk us out?" Zach questioned.

I looked at Zach with relief, thankful for the opportunity to escape for a few minutes. I shrugged my shoulders at James and left him alone with my unhappy parents. It served him right for bringing up the *moving out* topic. *Let him stew*, I thought.

I was standing at the front door with my brothers biding time before having to face my parents.

"Thanks Zach for saving me," I said.

"No problem sis," Zach said sweetly.

"So guys what did you think of James, and I want your honest opinion?" I asked.

"He's great." Zach answered enthusiastically.

"Thanks Zach," I said happily.

Zach was easy-going and friendly, and tended to like everyone immediately so I wasn't surprised that he liked James and was welcoming. Then I looked at Peter, my eldest brother who was at Stanford Medical School. Peter was friendly too, but he was more serious and reserved then Zach so it usually took him longer to warm up to new people.

"I agree with Zach, James is approachable, friendly, and smart, and for an actor I was surprised at how authentic and real he was. It's clear that he is in love with you Alex and you with him. I've never seen you like this before about a guy, you're in deep." Peter smirked.

"Is that bad?" I asked my brothers.

"Well, you're really young to be in such a serious relationship, but I saw how good you guys were together, so just enjoy it and be happy Alex," Peter said seriously while kissing my cheek.

"Ditto what Pete said," Zach replied while giving me the thumbs up sign of approval and a big bear hug.

After saying farewell to my brothers I slowly made my way out to the back yard to save James from my parents wrath. When I approached the table, I braced myself for my parents' anger, but instead I was confronted with smiles and laughter. Everyone looked unbelievably relaxed. *How the heck did James charm my parents -- and so quickly?*

"There you are sweetie," my mother said smiling at me. "Help me get dessert, I've made strawberry short cake so everyone has to try it, especially since Zach and Peter already left."

I started clearing off the patio table and followed my mother into the kitchen. We busied ourselves in the kitchen for a few minutes and worked together in companionable silence.

"So Mom. Do you like him?" I asked, feeling anxious.

"He's very nice," she said. "Your father and I both like him."

"But?"

She looked at me seriously and took me into her arms. "I still think you're too young, but it's clear that boy loves you and I would be foolish to think we could stop you. Our concern is not so much about James, it's that you are doing grown-up stuff and you're only a teenager. It's a lot of pressure to handle for someone so young..."

"Mom, I know I'm young, but we can't pretend that I've led a normal life or that I'm a typical teenager, because I'm not. Don't worry, you and dad have given me a good foundation...I know what I'm doing and I'm not going to cave to the pressure."

"We know honey, its just things are moving so *fast* for you now, and for James, and there is so much public interest in you as a couple. I just don't want to see you lose your sense of self and neither does your father," she said hugging me.

"I know mom, I promise that I won't," I said hugging her back.

## Chapter 16: Meeting the Prescott's

We walked through Boston Logan International Airport escorted by a bodyguard that Tom insisted we hire. His name was Jeff Clark and he was a former Navy Seal. He worked for his older brother David Clark, who was also a former Navy Seal, and his business partner, Adam Cohen, a veteran of Israeli special operations, who operated *Flash Security*, an elite Los Angeles based private security firm. The firm was known for helping Hollywood stars fend off stalkers and paparazzi.

James sister, Rachel Prescott, was scheduled to pick us up in front of the airport. We both wore sunglasses, hats and hoodies, in an effort to disguise our identities as we walked quickly through the terminal with Jeff escorting us. I caught a few whispers and stares...we had been spotted...fuck. Behind me I heard the eager, high-pitched squeal of a young girl, "James Prescott and Alexandra Brown!" A group of people approached us and asked for autographs. James chatted and engaged with several fans amicably for a few minutes while I signed autographs. After signing my last autograph, I looked up and realized that the small number of fans had quickly multiplied into an enormous crowd...Fuck.Fuck.Fuck. I was about to put my hand on James shoulder to alert him to the growing mob scene, when I felt someone grab me and awkwardly try to hug me. "Oh My God...You're Alexandra Brown! I love you! Can I get a picture?"

In the middle of the confusion, the flash of cameras from the paparazzi started. "Alex and James, are you dating?" "Smile Alex!" "Smile James!" "Hey, hey, did you get them?" "I got them. I got them!"

Jeff exuded the calm confidence of an experienced fighter; he took control and removed the groping freak that had grabbed me, pushing him away. Then, Jeff opened a large umbrella to ward off the paparazzi camera lenses and quickly told us to follow him. Several people screamed that they were being trampled, pushed, and elbowed, and the security staff at the Boston airport was forced to get involved. Security officers started to clear fans out of the way to make a path for us. I didn't look up. I kept my head down, and didn't look or speak as we made our way through the mob of screaming fans and paparazzi. We were taken to a private side exit, where James called his sister on his mobile. He handed a security officer his phone so that the officer could provide Rachel with directions for picking us up.

"Are you ok?" James whispered in my ear.

I was still shaken and realized that my fists were in my pockets, but I tried putting the tumultuous start of our trip behind me and gave James an encouraging half smile.

"I'm…I'm okay," I stuttered. "Where did Jeff go?"

"He went to get the car rental. He is going to follow behind us and make sure we get to my parents house safely, then he will check into his hotel," James said staring at me intently for the first time since the havoc erupted. He put his forehead against mine and whispered, "Alex, it's going to be alright."

James phone rang and he quickly took the call.

"Rachel is here, and so is Jeff, let's go!" he said.

Security escorted us through the side exit to her waiting car.

"That was scary." James said to Rachel and I, and then we zoomed away. Rachel drove fast, way above the legal speed limit. For a few minutes, we drove in silence and then James introduced me to his sister Rachel.

"Hi, it's great to finally meet you," I said awkwardly from the back seat.

"You too, loved the movie," she said as she expertly weaved the car through late Friday afternoon traffic.

James and Rachel started to chat. As they were talking, I started to scan the headlines from my iPhone and within minutes the following headlines appeared …

CHAOS AT BOSTON AIRPORT! ALEX BROWN & JAMES PRESCOTT ARRIVES AT BOSTON AIRPORT CAUSING HAVOC! ALEX BROWN & JAMES PRESCOTT LOVE COUPLE! BROWN & PRESCOTT IN BOSTON TOGETHER –

ARE THEY OR AREN'T THEY? *GALAXY DRIFTERS* STARS IN
BOSTON – IS IT BUSINESS OR PLEASURE?

My phone started to ring - "Hello," I answered. It was Sandy
Doyle, the new publicist that I hired recommended by Tom. "Yes,
I've seen the headlines," I told her as I rolled my eyes and smiled at
James who took my hand in his. I accounted the details of what
happened and told her that this was a vacation and that we wanted as
much privacy as possible.

"What did she say?" James asked when our conversation had
ended.

"That she would try to do damage control, whatever that means?"
I said dryly while looking out the window at the passing scenery.

It was a sunny Friday afternoon in late March, but the trees didn't
have any leaves yet, thus I thought it looked depressing. We were
driving along Storrow Drive, which Rachel said was a major cross-
town parkway in Boston that ran along the Charles River. We took a
right into Cambridge, crossing the river and I saw several crew teams
rowing as well as a few recreational rowers. James pointed to the
Harvard Kennedy School of Government and told me that we were
entering Harvard Square and that Harvard Yard would be further up
on our right, which was the historic heart of Harvard University. We
passed beautiful old buildings, stores, restaurants, coffee houses, and
an eclectic mix of students, business people, and residents. It was
crowded and traffic was heavy, so our progress was slow. To distract
myself, I started counting the number of North Face jackets that I
saw people wearing. I was up to *fourteen* and counting...

The Prescott's lived in an affluent neighborhood next to Harvard
Square that was close to Harvard University where Mrs. Prescott was
a Professor of Music. Rachel pulled into the driveway and my first
impression was that the house was very grand. James told me that his
parents had painstakingly restored it, and that the restoration project
had taken almost five years to complete. When we entered the house,
I saw that it was both luxurious and comfortable at the same time.
Rachel told us that their parents were running late, so James said that
he would give me a tour and get us situated first. Then we would
meet up with them for dinner. The house was detailed and intricate.

It had coffered and cove ceilings, built-in bookcases, six fireplaces, large windows and beautiful light. James led me up the ornate staircase to the second floor and then up another flight of stairs that led to his bedroom on the third floor. His bedroom was enormous with an en-suite bath and fireplace.

"Nice digs! Is this the room you grew up in?" I asked playfully.

"When I wasn't at boarding school," he answered dryly.

"What's wrong with you?" I asked suddenly sensing his bad mood.

"Your family is so warm and lively, and everyone is so down to earth and accepting. My family isn't like that, and I'm just afraid that you will not like them," he answered sourly.

"James, they had you, so obviously they did something right," I said coming over and putting my hand on his shoulder. "Plus, your sister Rachel was very welcoming."

"Rachel's great, it's my parents. They can be cool and stiff," James warned.

"Don't worry, I think I can handle it. After all, it's only for one weekend."

James didn't answer and unexpectedly he took a step closer and took off my baseball hat and unsnapped my hair tie, releasing my hair. He brushed his fingers through my hair, and gently caressed my cheek. Then he tipped my head back. "I want you," he groaned.

Desire exploded in my body, all the tension from the melee at the airport, seeking an outlet, I strained against him, wanting more.

He pressed his forehead against mine, "Alex, I love you."

I pressed my forehead back against him, "I love you more."

Then his lips were on me and there was a desperate, fiery quality to it. I kissed him back deeply, matching his ardor. We were all tongues and hands, panting, in a vain attempt to rip our clothes off as quickly as possible. He pulled my jeans down to my ankles, and his hand caressed my hips and squeezed my buttocks. I felt like I was going to come, I was so wet with the urgent need to feel him inside me. He frantically removed the remains of my jeans from my ankles and ripped my underwear off in the process. He pushed us against the wall and pulled my leg over his shoulder so that I was standing on one foot and he was supporting my weight. I heard him unzip the fly on his pants, and he looked wildly at me and then I felt him inside me. He held me up against the wall, where he started to thrust, I mean really thrust, each pull and push taking me to the brink of the most pleasurable sensation that I had ever experienced, and just when I thought it couldn't get any more intense, it did. I was groaning his name, panting and begging for release and then I experienced the most unbelievable earth-shattering orgasm. James quickly followed and we held each other in a tight embrace trying to steady our breathing.

He smiled a lopsided grin and his green eyes were twinkling. "You are an amazing lover Alex," he said grabbing me and kissing me passionately.

"Surely, I should be saying that to you," I said still trying to re-gain my composure. "You know you take my breath away James – always have, always will."

He gave me a shy smile, "Forever," he whispered.

***

I got out of the shower and dressed quickly. I could hear voices downstairs and suddenly I was very nervous to meet his parents. James was already down there, so I made my entrance solo.

I walked into a large country kitchen with glass pantry cabinets and a fabulous center island with a butcher-block top that dominated the room with eight stools. On the island there was an assortment of cheeses, breads, fruits, nuts, and olives. Behind the island there were doors that led to a flower adorned back patio.

I heard a male voice saying, "he is horrible, he can't play to save his own life, and he thinks he is this tremendous talent." When he finished speaking, I heard hearty laughter. As I walked in, he turned to me and it was clear by the resemblance that this was James father. He was a tall man with a lean athletic build, intense green eyes, a strong jaw, and dark-brown hair slightly gray at the temples. He wore an elegant suit and was extraordinarily handsome like his son.

Next to Mr. Prescott was a beautiful woman who appeared to be in her late forties who was obviously James mother. She had sandy hair that was severely pulled back into a knotted bun in the back and wore glasses that covered clear intelligent green eyes. She had a beautiful long neck, high cheekbones, and a dimple when she smiled. She was dressed in a tailored fitted suit and was drinking a glass of white wine, munching on olives.

"There she is now," yelled Rachel excitedly. "Come over and meet our parents while I get you something to drink. What would you like?"

It looked like Mr. Prescott was drinking a vodka martini and James and his mother were drinking wine.

"A glass of wine would be lovely," I answered Rachel with a smile.

"Red or white?"

"Whatever is opened is fine," I answered.

"Are you *old* enough to drink dear?" questioned Mrs. Prescott.

Before I could answer, Rachel interrupted. "I'll get you a tonic with lime, that's what I'm drinking," she said rolling her eyes.

"Sure, that would be great!" I said with embarrassed relief.

James gave me an apologetic look and came over to me. "They can act like puritans," he whispered softly.

"Mom, Dad, I would like you to meet Alexandra," he said proudly and there was such affection in his voice that it felt like my heart had expanded to the size of a balloon. I loved him so much that it scared me at times.

"Mr. and Mrs. Prescott, it's a pleasure to finally meet you," I said shaking their hands.

"It's lovely to meet you as well. We've never seen our son so enamored before," said Mr. Prescott.

"Doesn't she look like the actress Evangeline Lilly from *Lost*?" Rachel said bouncing over with my drink.

"Who dear?" Mrs. Prescott asked. "I've never heard of her. I think she looks like a young Jaclyn Smith," she said studying my face.

I guess *that* was a complement, after all wasn't Jaclyn Smith one of the original *Charlie's Angels*? At least she thought I was pretty if nothing else.

"You're embarrassing the girl," Mr. Prescott interrupted. "Shall we go into dinner?" he asked the group.

Rachel started recounting the details of our tumultuous arrival as we went into the dining room, "you should have seen the crowds and all the cameras, total pandemonium, it was nuts! By the way James, your bodyguard is hot, is he single?"

"How would I know Rachel," he said rolling his eyes at his sister.

"Bodyguard?" Mr. Prescott asked with raised eyebrow.

"You didn't tell us you had hired a bodyguard?" Mrs. Prescott repeated sounding concerned as she walked in carrying a platter of food.

"Can I help you Mrs. Prescott?"

"Thank you dear, but you're the guest. Rachel, James can you get the rest of the food?" she ordered sweetly.

After Rachel and James left, there was an uncomfortable silence that followed. *Great! Left alone with the firing squad,* I thought.

"You're home is lovely. When was it built?" I asked trying to engage in conversation with The Prescott's.

"It was originally built in 1833 by a Sea Captain and restored by previous owners in 1920, 1965, and 1980. We bought it in 1996 and the restoration project lasted almost five years," Mr. Prescott answered.

"Architecture is a passion for my husband," Mrs. Prescott added tenderly.

Just then James and Rachel returned with the rest of the food saving me from having to make idle chitchat. James was right, The Prescott's were tough and it would take time to build a relationship with them. However, Mrs. Prescott could cook, the food was scrumptious. There was roast prime ribs of beef with pink and green peppercorn crust and red-wine sauce, grilled asparagus, red bliss potatoes, and baby carrots in a garlic butter sauce. Red wine was flowing for The Prescott's and James, but Rachel and I, being under twenty-one, sipped sparkling water throughout the evening. It was unfortunate, as a glass of wine would have relaxed me.

So began the inquisition…"What was that about a bodyguard? Is it necessary James?" asked Mr. Prescott.

"We didn't want to get one, but our agent insisted on it and after experiences like today at the airport, I think he was right. Dad, it's hard to articulate, but you have to understand the crazy attention we've received since the release of *Galaxy Drifters*. The movie has made us household names almost overnight and our faces have been put on every magazine around the world. We have *no* privacy anymore and often there are over-zealous fans that attempt to get too close or worse, the paparazzi!"

"Why is the paparazzi worse?" questioned Mrs. Prescott. "Don't you think you're exaggerating darling?"

"He's not Mrs. Prescott," I said. "It's awful having cameras shoved in our faces all of the time and untrue stories written about us."

James took my hand from underneath the table and gave me a reassuring squeeze.

"I don't think you can understand it until you live it." James said. "Sometimes Alex and I can't believe this is our lives. Everyone thinks it's so glamorous and wonderful, and part of it is, but another part, is truly nasty. The constant attention and intrusive questions from the press are exhausting."

"Do you expect our sympathy?" questioned Mr. Prescott rudely. "You never should have gone into acting James, we never approved. It's an artificial lifestyle…plastic and phony."

"But how can you say that Mr. Prescott? James lights up the screen. He is a natural and gifted actor," I said calmly, but irritated. "This is his calling."

"If you think acting is his calling, you obviously haven't heard his music," Mr. Prescott said bitterly.

"You're wrong, I have heard him and he is amazing, but that doesn't mean he can't do both. Has James told you that he will be working on several musical arrangements for the next *Galaxy Drifters* soundtrack and film score?" I questioned.

"Why didn't you tell us James, that's wonderful," his mother praised.

"Have you even seen the movie yet?" James accused.

Was he joking? Of course they saw it – *didn't they*?

"I loved it! It was totally addictive and I can't wait to see the next one. You guys rocked it! I'm so proud of my big brother," Rachel said with affection trying to lighten the mood.

An awkward silence followed, and finally his mother spoke. "We had planned to see it darling, we've just been so busy with your fathers tour schedule, my teaching schedule, and the pianist concert in Vienna, that we haven't had a chance. But of course we are going to see it," she trailed off seemingly embarrassed.

I was personally offended for James and I really wanted to tell off his parents, but I held back my tongue until I couldn't take it anymore. Finally, I spoke. "I'm shocked you haven't seen it. Obviously, you don't approve of James career choice, but he is your son and he is an extremely talented actor with a very bright future ahead. Please go see the movie and support your son."

His father stared, blatantly accessing me and seemed to be weighing his words. "You're frank and honest, and very spirited Alexandra, I like that. Clearly you care for our son and you're right we've been incredibly rude and selfish." He turned his head toward James. "I'm sorry son, we will go see it this weekend. Changing the subject to less heavy matters, who wants dessert and a game of billiards?" his father asked pleasantly lightening the mood.

The change at the table was immediate. His father had a smooth and commanding personality and with his sudden change in attitude, everyone seemed to relax. The rest of the evening was fairly light-hearted with conversations about Rachel's school, the symphony and mutual friends and colleagues. The Prescott's were a highly educated and affluent family, and it was clear being around them that they valued cultural, intellectual and educational pursuits above all other activities.

Through my occupation as an actress, I had been exposed to varied activities and people. I was well traveled, often went to fine restaurants, the opera, lectures and recitals. I was a voracious reader, and had participated in a range of dancing and music classes and I considered myself an enlightened, open-minded and cultural savvy person. Yet despite my accomplishments, I knew that my education did not meet the Prescott's high standards, and I felt terribly insecure among them.

The remainder of the weekend, James played tour guide showing me around Harvard Square, the Back Bay, Faneuil Hall Market Place, and several other Boston highlights. Jeff was always close by, as were the constant cameras, and screaming fans. Easter brunch with James family went off without a hitch, and overall the experience was positive, but I was happy for it's conclusion. I breathed a sigh of relief that I had survived my first visit with The Prescott's.

## Chapter 17: Blissful Times

"How can a nineteen year old girl...even a famous one...have accumulated this much crap?" complained Zach as he pulled another moving box from the van.

"I'm a woman, not a girl and I'm almost twenty!" I said defensively.

It had been over a year and a half since I had the conversation with my parents about moving in with James and finally the big day was here. James and I had wanted to move in together sooner, but with *Galaxy Drifters 2* filming and all the fucking madness that went along with it who had time? It was weird - - I was so never the person who had to set aside time to see friends and family, but for the last two years my life was crazy assed pandemonium.

"Your not twenty until July..." my brother pointed out.

"*Wow* Zach...you know my birthday and you can count!"

"Zach! Are you going to whine the whole time?" Peter questioned, "Time is money...tick, tick, tick...start moving will you already!"

"Talking about money, you and James have so much of it, why didn't you hire a moving company?"

"Are you kidding Zach? I can see the headlines now...TAKE A TOUR OF THE BEDROOM WHERE ALEX BROWN GREW UP!" I huffed in an irritated tone. "Why do you think the house we are renting is so *secluded* Sherlock?

"Well, I didn't think about that." Zach said.

"Do you ever think?" Peter questioned sarcastically.

"Will you stop acting like children," I said to my brothers.

"Where is James anyway?" Zach complained.

"He was needed for post-production music editing for *Galaxy Drifters 3*," I said. "The worldwide release is in November and we will be busy filming number four starting this summer."

"What does post-production music editing mean?" Zach griped, but sounded interested.

"It's compiling and mixing the music in the film to provide an optimal sound experience."

"He has to do that?" Zach questioned quizzically.

"No it's not a requirement, but he is learning about it and loves to do sound and music editing and the sound engineer was recording the musical score today, part of which James wrote and composed."

"Cool! I can't believe you guys are already half-way thru the film series."

"Are you still talking Zach?" asked Peter coming in to get another box from my parent's house. "Or are you going to actually help move some boxes now?"

"I'm coming," Zach said defensively lugging another heavy box.

The house that James and I decided to rent was in Bel Air with dramatic reservoir and canyon views, and the entire property was secured and gated. I would have preferred to rent a beach house, as that was more my style, but in the end, we decided it would make more sense to go with something in a private setting. Plus, it was only minutes from Beverly Hills and Brentwood, where my parents lived, which was really convenient. The house was an exceptional property, and I still couldn't believe that I was going to live in it? I had never aspired to great wealth; I mean I liked nice things, but for the most part, my tastes were simple, and I still had to pinch myself that this was really happening.

"This view is amazing!" Peter whistled appreciatively. "Where is my room?" he joked.

We were outside on the large terrace enjoying the million-dollar view. There was an area for entertaining and barbecuing, a pool and spa, and a gazebo for watching sunsets.

"There *is* a guest house," I said with a grin.

"Sign me up!" Zach said enthusiastically. "You guys better throw a huge party, and tell James to invite some of his single female model friends."

James came in then and I smiled. My pulse started to race and I wondered if I would ever get enough? Often he was dressed in suits for photo shoots and events, which made him look urban and sophisticated, and somehow intimidating and untouchable, but today he was dressed casually in blue jeans and a t-shirt, which is what I preferred. He had a tan and his hair was tousled, he looked darkly sexy.

He came over to me, "If you keep looking at me like that, I might need to undress you right now," he threatened seductively.

I responded with a sexy grin, and planted a tender kiss on his lips, but then my brothers interrupted breaking the mood.

"Don't you guys ever get enough?" Zach questioned.

James let go of my hand. "Hey guys, thanks for helping with the move. What can I do?" he asked as he walked over to the truck in the driveway. "How can there still be so many boxes? Have you guys been hanging by the pool all day?"

"As I said to Zach, stop complaining and start lifting," Peter challenged.

With that, James lifted a heavy box and followed Peter into the new house.

When my brothers had left and we had finally unpacked, James and I sat back on the couch in the living room curled up together happily drinking white wine.

"How did it go at the studio today?" I asked.

"It was awesome," he exclaimed excitedly. "It's been an amazing process to watch what happens from when we decided where the score would be, to where the source music would be needed and then actually syncing the score to the final cut. The music brings the film to life and it's extremely satisfying," he beamed enthusiastically.

His excitement was contagious and I could see how happy it made him, which in turn, made me very happy.

"What's new with you?" he asked.

"Well, I'm meeting with Tom on Monday about a new script," I answered.

"Anything interesting?"

"Don't laugh," I warned, "but you might be looking at the new Jane for a big new studio production of *The Adventures of Tarzan & Jane*."

"Tell me it isn't so!" James chuckled with mirth. "This is going to be hilarious," he roared. "Although come to think of it, I will look forward to seeing you dressed as a jungle woman, that will be hot!"

"Whatever James!" I grumbled somewhat irritated.

"I'm just joking, Alex. Don't be so serious." he said. "Please tell me all about it?" he continued sweetly, his voice sounding sincere.

I sighed. "Fine, I'll tell you as long as you promise *not* to laugh?" I said hesitantly.

"I promise, scouts honor," he said raising his hand in a pledge and smiling earnestly at me, waiting for me to speak.

"Well," I began uncertainly. "As you know, I've done a couple of independent films during the breaks from *Galaxy Drifters*, and they have been rewarding experiences, and I'm proud of them, but only a handful of people have actually seen them. Tom feels that it would be beneficial for my career if I would consider doing another studio project. You know some big commercial project that will likely attract a large audience, and be a big hit, so when *Galaxy* finally wraps up, I will be known for some other big projects, to prevent being type cast in Amanda Blake only roles."

"He is feeding you a *line* Alex." Heavy sarcasm. "Tom doesn't like any of the films that fall into the art house domain that you like. You should do the roles that interest you, don't be deceived by Tom, who is *only* thinking about dollar signs!" he said, his voice raised and challenging.

"But the role *does* interest me," I said defensively. "Plus, I think Tom is right that the more commercial hits that I can make, the more likely that I'll be able to establish myself as a star who earns both critical and commercial respect."

He was quietly processing my words. "That's a better reason for doing it. At least, I understand your motivation. I guess it is an end to a means, jungle woman!" he said calmly breaking into a sly, sexy smile.

"Enough about work. I have a *surprise* for you," I said hardly able to contain my excitement. I got up from the couch. "I'll be back in a minute."

I came back carrying a large box. "This is for you."

He smiled shyly, and then his face became serious.

"You really shouldn't have bought me anything. You're present enough," he said, but sounded delighted and started to tear it open eagerly like a little boy digging into Christmas presents.

"Here," I said handing him scissors. "Be careful."

Inside the box was a painting of The Prescott's beloved mahogany wood racing sailboat the *Crescendo*. I had found a local artist whose work I had admired and asked her to paint a mixed media original on stretched canvas. The boat was the focus of the print, but using a palette knife to apply paint, she provided an abstract view of Casco Bay in deep-sea blue in the background. I thought it was stunning and I hoped he would like it.

"I'm speechless Alex, thank you. This is amazing, I love it!" he said hugging and kissing me. "How did you do it?"

"I hired an artist, her name is E.R. Winick," I said proudly.

"How did she capture it so well? Is she an artist in Maine?" he asked tenderly studying the print.

"No, she is local. She painted it from copying photographs I took of our trip," I answered with a grin, pleased by his reaction.

He walked over to the fireplace. "I think we should hang it here," he said eagerly pointing above the fireplace.

"Sure, that would be great."

For the next fifteen minutes or so, James busied himself with measuring the wall to determine the best place to hammer in the nail. "Does it look center and at the right height to you?" he asked.

"I think it look's perfect!"

"Good," he said, marking the spot, and driving the nail in. After he hung up the painting, and admired it, he turned abruptly and walked back over to me with a big grin. "You're not the only one with a surprise." I felt a thrill go through me as he took my hand and told me to follow him.

He led me to the garage. "Are you ready?" he asked eagerly.

I nodded with gleeful anticipation.

He opened the door to the garage and switched the light on. Inside, was the most magnificent shiny red sports car that I had ever seen…"This is for me?" I asked with wonder in my voice.

He nodded his head. "Do you like it?"

"I love it James...what kind of car is it?"

"You're such a *girl*," he said sweetly giving me a kiss. "It's a Mercedes SLS AMG in Cherry Red, but if you don't like the color we can switch it."

"Are you kidding, I love it!" I said excitedly. "Can I take it for a spin now?"

It was a beautiful night and the dark sky was a vibrant deep purple color, making you want to tilt your head up and admire it. We had the top down as we zoomed through the Santa Monica Mountains above the Stone Canyon to Mulholland Drive and then back up again. We passed lush landscapes and environs in a wild blur as I pushed the car faster and faster past the speed limit. It was thrilling!

"Are you trying to kill us or just get a speeding ticket?" James asked lightly.

"Sorry," I said and I removed my foot from the accelerator slowing down.

I pulled into a secluded spot above the reservoir where we could admire the view and star-filled sky. "I love it James, thank you," I said my voice filled with emotion.

He looked at me intently and I felt that familiar tug of my heart whenever we were close together like this.

"Perhaps we should *christen* the car?" James asked, his voice smoldering.

I flushed with desire and felt the current between us. It was electrifying.

"What did you have in mind?" I asked innocently.

"Why don't you come closer and find out?" he challenged mischievously.

I lifted my leg teasing him and moved over until I sat astride him in the passenger seat and let him feel me. When we were close like this, I lost all control, forgetting the outside world completely. I put my hands on the back of his head, but we didn't kiss, instead we just stared intently at each other savoring the moment. I could feel his arousal and I was so turned on. I arched my back and started to move playfully in a slow torturous rhythm backwards and forward on his lap. He started to kiss me, and I kissed him back with abandonment.

"Ok," I whispered, "let's *christen* the car, and we did.

***

*Zap! Great...another fuckin' camera flash!* The drive to Tom's office on Monday morning was unpleasant and I was irritable. The moment Lydia and I had left the gated security of the house behind; we were followed by aggressive paparazzi trying to get photos and screaming questions at me. I was really getting sick and tired of the relentless scrutiny by the press, but I didn't see how to avoid it. I took the side entrance into Tom's office, which provided more privacy, while Lydia parked the car. I looked behind and sideways to see if anyone had followed me, but the coast seemed clear for *now*. Shit...I was getting paranoid. Really, really fuckin' paranoid. When I got off the private elevator, Tom was there saying good-bye to some big, tall, muscular guy who looked vaguely familiar.

"Alex!" Tom beamed at me, his booming voice echoing through the lobby. "Let me introduce you to one of my clients, before he leaves."

"Alex, this is Mark, he is the quarterback for the Jets. Mark, please meet the lovely and talented actress Alexandra Brown."

"Nice to meet you Mark." I smiled pleasantly, but my tone was dismissive. I was in a pissy mood from my encounter with the paps, and I really just wanted to get the hell out of Dodge and escape to the privacy of Tom's office.

Mark gave me a slow sexy smile. "It's nice to meet you." He said, kissing my hand and leaning in close to me, too close. "I'm a big fan."

*Not gonna happen buddy.* "Thanks." I said. Then I abruptly turned to Tom. "It's been a bad morning, could I wait in your office?"

Tom frowned. "Of course, where is your bodyguard Alex?"

"I didn't think I needed one for a meeting in your office. I'm getting sick of the babysitter, Tom!" I huffed and walked away. I knew I was being rude, but I didn't care.

Tom came in a few minutes later and closed the door.

"Listen Alex, I know you don't give a shit, but you could have been fuckin' nicer to Mark, he's one of my top clients."

"Yeah…I'm sorry about that Tom, but it's been a rough morning. Plus, I don't know the first thing about football anyway."

Tom laughed and rolled his eyes. "I don't think Mark was *interested* in your football knowledge!"

I rolled my eyes in return. "Whatever, Tom. Anyway, I thought it was public knowledge by now that James and I are together, together."

"Well, I guess *not* everyone reads the gossip rags." Tom replied dryly. "Is Lydia joining us?"

"Yeah. She was parking the car, and should be here any minute."

"Good. Before we get down to business…are you ok Alex?"

I looked down at my clenched hands in my lap. Then I stood up and started to pace. "It's just so damn oppressive Tom."

"What *is*?"

I slowed my pace to gaze out his office window. "Everything you said Tom when I first met you is true. I *am* a living brand and so is James. I think we probably get more attention than the President! Is that crazy shit or what? It really, really sucks and it *is* freaking me the fuck out. I know that I should stop whining and that I should be grateful for making a fortune doing what I love, but the cost has been my freedom and it's getting to me…*sometimes* I feel like James and I are living in a god damn prison. When will the insanity stop?"

"Alex, I get that the constant personal scrutiny *is* tough, but you have to learn to ignore it. For Chrissake, you've been given a life that most people would trade their souls for. It's not perfect, and it comes with challenges, but I'm not going to be sorry for you nor is the public. You will only sound like a spoiled little rich girl! You need to rise above it and ignore it. It's the only way to survive."

Scarlett knocked on the door then and Lydia entered Tom's office. It was time to get down to business and discuss the role of Jane in the upcoming production of *The Adventures of Tarzan & Jane*. Lydia and Tom exchanged pleasantries and then they got down to details about film production schedules, locations, and money.

"She cannot start in January…that's impossible Tom," Lydia frowned. "Filming for the fourth installment of *Galaxy Drifters* starts next month, from June to September, and then Alex will have to immediately travel and promote *Galaxy Drifters 3* which will be released world-wide in November. After that, she will need a break. Do you think you can get the studio to agree to move the start date out to February or March?"

"Yeah, I can do that, but we don't want to delay it too much or we will have the same scheduling nightmares on the back-end when filming starts back up for the final two *Galaxy Drifters* installments in the series," Tom pointed out.

"So it's true that Pinnacle is planning to have us shoot the last two *Galaxy Drifters* films back to back?" I asked.

"That's the plan," Tom agreed.

"How long do you think that's going to take?" I asked.

"Anywhere from six to nine months would be my guess," Tom said, raking his hand through his dark hair. He started to pace the floor and talked fast so that I had to listen attentively to catch every word. "Listen, I know it's a full plate for the next year or two, but it will be worth it when it's done. You can take a break after that."

"Where will production be based for *Tarzan & Jane*?" Lydia asked.

"Tunisia, Hawaii and California," Tom said. "I think something like February to May would be doable. What do you think?"

"What happens if it goes over that timeline?" Lydia worried.

"I'll tell them that it absolutely has to wrap up by June at the latest." Tom said firmly, sounding exasperated. "Don't worry so much Lydia and we haven't discussed the best part yet, the money. I can get Alex $10 million for *Tarzan & Jane*. Add that to the *Galaxy Drifters* salary and the shares that Alex will take of the films' total profits and she may well become one of, if not the top, wealthiest leading ladies in Hollywood."

"Can you both stop talking like I'm not in the room," I said sullenly.

"What's wrong with you?" Lydia asked miffed.

"Nothing, I'm just sick of talking about money. It's not what *drives* me," I said getting angry.

"It may not be what drives you sweetheart, but believe me, it's what drives everyone else!" Tom said arrogantly sounding superior.

"It doesn't *drive* James," I said petulantly.

"That's why you're the *perfect* couple," he said mockingly, emphasizing the word *perfect*.

"Will you do the role of Jane?" Tom asked me directly, suddenly serious.

"Yes, I'll do it," I said. "Are we done here?" I asked to no one in particular.

"There is just one more thing." Tom said frowning, his voice sounding concerned. "I'm hearing that the role of *Tarzan* will likely go to the actor Jon Hanley. Do you know him?"

"Is he that cute Aussie film hunk?" Lydia asked.

Tom rolled his eyes and looked annoyed. "Yeah, I guess you could describe him that way. Listen I don't know him personally, but I thought you should know that he has a reputation for being a shit."

"A shit? Like how so?" I asked.

"The usual…sex, drugs, women, alcohol."

"Thanks for the heads up Tom, but don't worry, I can take care of myself."

"Ok then…you've been warned." Tom said wrapping up the meeting. "I'll give you a call when the contracts are ready."

***

The water balloon landed directly on James. "Bulls Eye!" I yelled to my brothers laughing. "I told you that I had good aim!" I boasted giving them high-fives.

James looked up at us drenched, we were standing on the balcony playfully assembling and launching the balloons. I could see the competitive gleam in his eye. "You guys are like fourth graders," he called. "Alex, be prepared for my wrath when you come down here," he joked.

James and I were leaving on Tuesday to go on location for the fourth installment in the series. We were hosting my family for an impromptu barbeque and Tom was going to come by for a drink as he had some paperwork he wanted to drop off. James was manning the barbeque, and my parents were sitting in the gazebo reading and drinking margaritas. I came down from the balcony and took the tomato and mozzarella salad out of the refrigerator as well as another pitcher of margarita. I took the food outside and the moment I placed it on the table, James lifted me off the ground and threw me over his shoulder. He started to carry me to the pool.

"I'm wearing a sundress, you wouldn't dare?" I shrieked. "Please! Please! I will not throw a balloon at you again!"

But my pleas fell on deaf ears and James lifted me in the air and threw me in the swimming pool. James, Peter and Zach were laughing their butts off, practically rolling on the ground.

"Hilarious." I said sarcastically getting out of the pool to search for a towel.

"I believe you want this…" Tom said as he entered the backyard and threw me a towel.

"Thanks." I said peeling my wet dress off my head. I wore a white string bikini and I looked up to find Tom staring at me. His gaze lingered a fraction too long and I was suddenly flustered. I wrapped the towel around my body self-consciously and turned to leave. I felt rather than saw James scowl. Huh, he was jealous! Served him right for throwing me in the pool.

"Hey boys and girls! If the water fight is over can I have your attention?" Tom addressed the crowd.

Just then, I saw James, Peter and Zach exchange mischievous glances and they came over and dragged Tom to the edge of the pool. Tom was a strong athletic man, but so were James and my brothers.

"I'm wearing my Italian loafers," Tom protested.

Those words were his undoing and James, Peter, and Zach pushed him in.

"I'll get another towel!" I snickered.

Sometime later, we all sat around the table drinking margaritas and laughing.

"I'm just about dry, and need to leave soon, but wanted to drop these off." Tom said getting his briefcase and pulling out *Galaxy Drifters* Amanda Blake and Matt Samuel action hero dolls.

"These are terrific!" Zach laughed, "and look at the resemblance," he said putting the doll next to my face.

"Whatever." I said rolling my eyes.

"Don't knock it." Tom warned. "You and James will get a share of the profits from the sales, and I'm happy to report that DVD and Blu-ray sales have been brisk for the second film. In fact, the earnings for it have already far surpassed the first film and reflect the strength of the *Galaxy Drifters* franchise. I'm going to leave you the dolls, sales data figures, and final signed contracts; the originals are with your attorneys and Ken and Lydia have copies."

"Is that everything?" James asked.

"Two more items," Tom said talking fast. "First, James, I want you to take a look at these two scripts and let me know what you think? One is about James Dean, and the other Elvis Presley. You would be perfect for both roles if the projects go forward."

"I'll take a look." James acknowledged.

"Good." Tom nodded. "So, Alex," he said turning his chair and looking at me. "This envelope contains the final contract for *Tarzan & Jane*, as well as a detailed schedule of dates and locations. If you or Lydia has any concerns, let me know?

"Don't worry, I will." I said winking, "Thanks Tom."

***

After everyone had gone home, James and I lingered by the pool and skimmed through the scripts.

"You would make a great Elvis Presley."

"You think?"

"Absolutely!"

"Both projects sound intriguing," he said, his interest clearly piqued. "I'll review the scripts in greater detail on the plane or when we get to our hotel in Vancouver."

I rolled my eyes at him and frowned. "Well, you'll definitely have plenty of time for reading!"

"What's that supposed to mean sarcastic girl?"

"It's just so hard to leave our hotel room that sometimes I think of it as a prison."

"I could always fuck you on the balcony like last time!" he teased. "Um, seriously, I thought you liked staying in the suite and just hanging out?" He asked kindly, giving me a concerned smile.

"I do like it, but only because I'm with you. Sometimes it would be nice to go out for a walk or grab a drink with our friends and I feel like it's not worth the hassle to do it anymore. It kind of gets to me after awhile."

"If you want to go out more, we will figure out a way to do it." James promised coming over to me and taking me in his arms. "Remember last time, when we snuck out the back entrance through the kitchen into the alley to avoid the paparazzi?"

"Yeah. I remember." I smiled fondly recalling the memory. "Those disguises were great and we got to go out without security. But come on James, it's getting harder and harder to do that ... practically impossible. It's not worth the trouble."

"Of course it's worth the trouble. Otherwise, you'll feel bitter. The hotel is not meant to be a prison." James said firmly. "We will go out more."

"Ok." I said giving him a half smile.

"I want to see a real smile Alex," he replied seriously. "It pains me to see you unhappy."

"I'm always happy when I'm with you James," I replied honestly, giving him a tender kiss. Aside from my struggles to cope with the public and media attention, my life was perfect. With James at my side, the last two years had been the most fulfilling and happiest in my life. Sometimes I had to *pinch* myself to remind myself that it was real.

"I love you Alex," James whispered in my ear, "Come on, let's go for a swim."

"I'll race you," I challenged affectionately, swiftly stepping away from him and diving into to the pool.

James laughed and quickly cannon balled after me into the pool. We started splashing each other, messing around in the middle of the pool. Then without warning James stopped and gave me an intense look.

"I didn't like the way Tom was looking at you today, I think he has a crush on you," James commented.

"Tom is happily married with two kids," I said defensively. "I can't help it if he admires *great beauty*," I joked trying to lighten the mood. "Plus, every woman we meet looks at you that way…"

He didn't say anything and we just stood in the middle of the pool looking at each other. Then James took a step closer and smoothly undid the strings of my bikini top slowly pulling it off and letting it fall. I gasped and bit my lip. We started to grope and kiss each other and before I knew it we were having the most unbelievable sex. We clung on to each other contented and happy. Life was good.

## Chapter 18: *Tarzan & Jane*

I arrived on location in Hawaii during the second week in March. Pre-production had begun six week's earlier in California and we had filmed several scenes already.

*The Adventures of Tarzan & Jane* was a big budget picture. It had a strong cast and crew led by an experienced director, Preston Foley, who had worked on numerous big budget Hollywood adventure films as well as a skilled team of creative and business producers.

"Hey beautiful!" Jon boomed loudly as he came onto the set where I was reading my script.

Jon Hanley was an Australian film hunk and he was my co-star. I had to commend the casting crew and director on a well-chosen *Tarzan*. Jon visually fit the role perfectly. He was very tall with thick shoulders, blonde hair, and blue eyes, and a ripped body. I mean this guy had herculean muscles!

"I'm shocked, that you're here so early. It's a miracle!" I joked sarcastically giving Jon a hard time.

"I'm not always late," Jon smirked.

*Yeah right!* Late was an *understatement*. Jon was notoriously late and almost always stoned for every scene we filmed. In the six weeks that I had worked with him, it was a guarantee that he would walk onto the set ten or fifteen minutes late. Usually his lack of professionalism was over-looked, as his violations were never severe. He seemed to know instinctively what he could and couldn't get away with and professional boundaries were never actually crossed by him. Personally, I think he enjoyed the reputation of being a bad boy and thrived on pushing the envelope as much as he could without causing any real harm.

"So why the early arrival?" I asked with curiosity. This was the first-time that I had seen him arrive on the set early; it must be a special day.

"Well, I get to see your hot, tight body in a bikini and I most definitely plan to jerk off to it," he flirted giving me a sexy slow grin, while exposing his straight white teeth and dimples.

"You're a disgusting pig!"

"Oink, oink." He smirked. "How about coming to my trailer and I'll show you just how disgusting I can be?"

"No thanks."

"Your loss baby, but you know where to find me if you change your mind." He winked. "It's an open invitation with no expiration..."

*I wanted to vomit.* I rolled my eyes dramatically at him and shuddered. "Lucky Me!"

"Are you ready for the waterfall rappelling adventure scene?"

"Not really," I grimaced.

"Are you scared? Don't be *Tarzan* will protect you," he said playfully, while mimicking an ape pounding his chest loudly.

Jon liked to play around and have a good time – in essence he was the epiphany of a frat boy. On the set, he pulled a lot of pranks and was always joking around. At times he could be irresponsible and it irritated me when he wasn't prepared, but for the most part he was easy to work with and we got along fine. He was cocky and there was *not* a lot of substance to him, but he was harmless and fun to be around. When he wasn't acting, Jon was a party boy who liked to go on the town and hit the trendiest spots he could find. He drank and got high a lot and often bragged that he had done just about every drug possible. Tom was absolutely right about Jon's reputation as a *male whore.* He had fucked so many different chicks in the short time since we had worked together that I had lost count. At the beginning, Jon constantly flirted with me and made several sexual advances, which I always rebuffed. When his attempts to seduce me failed, Jon became persistent and asked me out daily for two weeks, even though I clearly told him that I was not interested and that I was in love with my boyfriend. Jon did not take *no* easily, and he continued to send me gifts and flowers in the hopes of changing my mind. For the moment, he was spending his nights with a new woman, thus his sexual advances toward me had slowed to a crawl. I was relieved that he finally seemed to be giving up on making me his conquest.

The scene we were scheduled to film was an action sequence followed by a love scene in which *Tarzan & Jane* escape hunters by rappelling down a waterfall off a cliff. The location was spectacular in Puohokamoa Valley, a Maui rain forest with stunning waterfalls and canyons, including a dramatic 230-foot waterfall where the film crew was set up. Jon and I would not do the actual descent down the cliff as that would be done by our stunt doubles. The activity was considered dangerous for amateurs without the proper harness, helmets, and flotation devices. Jon and I would film are scenes at the top of the cliff above the waterfall and again at the bottom of the rappel. We would then come back the next day to film the love scene beneath the waterfall.

It was a long day of physical activity in rugged terrain. We had been filming for several hours in the hot sun covered in mud and debris, and everyone was tired. I was eager to wrap up for the day, but Preston really wanted to film as much as possible, so we continued shooting. We had finally wrapped up the scene at the top of the cliff, and were now ready to film the scene at the bottom. The rope was disguised as vine and Jon was told to hang onto it with one arm while holding me in another as we floated in mid-air just above our destination, the pool below. Once we reached the pool, he would lower me into it and then he would join me, and then we would be done for the day.

The scene was physically demanding and it took several attempts to get it right. On one of our final shots, Jon slid his hand on my bikini bottom and started to caress my ass. I was just about to confront him, and tell him to remove his hand, but then he quickly removed it, so I wasn't sure if it was an accident? Through the next several shots, he kept brushing up against me or touching me intimately and I knew it was intentional. I was sort of flabbergasted by his boldness, but didn't want to say anything in front of the entire film crew. During the final shot, when he lowered me in the pool, Preston yelled, "cut," but instead of letting me go, Jon put his hand under my bikini top and started to fondle my breast and then he started to kiss me.

I took a step backwards ending the kiss and then I slapped his face hard. "What the hell are you doing?" I yelled through gritted teeth. "If you ever touch me like that again, I'm gonna rip your balls off! Do you understand?"

Everyone was watching us and I saw the flash of cameras from the distance. *Oh no way*! It was the perfect end to the perfect day, I thought with great sarcasm.

"I'm sorry," he said embarrassed, "but you can't blame a guy for trying, can you? It's not my fault you're so delectable Alex."

I gave him a frosty look and excited the pool with the help and assistance of some of the staff. I was really ticked off and angry. "Stay away from me Jon!" I warned.

***

Did paps or tourists take the photos? I knew it wouldn't be long before the story was breaking news, thus I quickly spoke with Lydia, Sandy, and Tom via Skype filling them in on the details of what transpired. Sandy and the PR Team were going to coordinate with Jon's PR Team, and the studio execs, and they would come up with a plan of action to deal with the situation. I was told that Jon was going to send out an apology statement immediately, and then my team would respond with a prepared statement to minimize the damage from the incident. I could hear Sandy's words in my head like a mantra, *tell it all, tell it fast and tell the truth.*

"Have you spoken to James yet?" Sandy asked crisp and business-like. "He needs to be prepared, because I'm sure the media with swarm around him too. I'm working on a statement for him if he wants it, but it might be best for him to remain silent. What does everyone think?"

"He will probably want to remain silent Sandy, but why don't you talk it through with Ken first and then James," Tom said, his authority calmly taking over the discussion.

My mind drifted away from the conversation and I suddenly felt exhausted. I heard a knock on my door, and Jon quietly called out my name, but I just ignored him. That was the *sixth time* this evening that he had knocked on my door in an attempt to see me. No doubt he was trying to make some *lame* apology. After the incident occurred, Preston Foley came to see me and he told me that he would handle it. Preston was livid and I'm sure that he had ripped Jon a new one for touching me and potentially causing a media firestorm.

"I'll call James soon. Does anyone know what time it is in Italy?" I questioned.

"Italy is twelve hours ahead of Hawaii, so it would be morning there," Lydia said softly.

"Ok, I'll call him now. Bye." I said hanging up before anyone could respond.

Originally, James had planned to do the James Dean and Elvis Presley projects, but neither one had received funding or the green light yet, so in the meantime he had accepted a new project. He was filming a period piece on the early life of Vivaldi and he was fairly excited about it, as were his parents. He had been working on location in Italy and England for almost a month now and I missed him terribly.

"Hey sleepy head," I said forcing my voice to sound cheerful. "Did I wake you?"

"It's not that early. I've already gone for a run and taken a shower. How are things in Hawaii Alex?" he said sounding genuinely happy to hear from me. My heart skipped a beat just hearing his voice. I missed him so much.

"It's fine, but there was a little mishap on location today," I mumbled. "You might get contacted by the media for a statement about it. Sandy is going to give you a call soon…"

"What happened Alex?" he asked concern creeping into his voice.

"It's nothing really, but you know how the media blows everything out of proportion," I said, a catch in my throat. I knew I was hesitating, and that it would be best to just spill it, so I started talking quickly, trying to get the words out fast. "I had to film a scene with Jon climbing down a waterfall into a pool and he got a little frisky and I had to slap him and it was caught on camera. But it's no big deal."

There was a pause in conversation. "James are you there?"

"I'm looking for it on the internet now," he answered. His voice trailed off. "Are you alright?"

"My hand stings a little, but otherwise I'm fine," I said calmly wanting to change the subject. The whole situation was embarrassing and frustrating, and I wanted to forget it.

"How frisky…do I need to fly over there and break his neck?" he said suddenly sounding angry. *What miserable shit was he reading on the Internet?*

"Of course not. Don't worry I can take care of myself," I answered trying to project confidence.

"You're still avoiding my question, what exactly did the cocky asshole do?"

"Nothing really James, it's been blown out of proportion by the paparazzi, otherwise I wouldn't even be troubling you with this *nonsense*."

"I still want to know what happened?" James said steadfastly.

"He kissed me without my permission," I stammered.

"Anything else…"

"What do you want the whole *play by play* James?" I asked, my voice rising.

"Did he hurt you?" he asked softly, tenderly.

"Of course not, or he would be in an ambulance by now?" I said deadly serious.

"Do you want me to see if I can take a break from filming and visit for a few days?"

"James there is nothing more that I want in the world then to see you, but it can wait until we are back in California. You're busy and I'm busy. I'll only be in Hawaii for another week and then I fly to Tunisia. Honestly, don't worry, I'm fine."

I heard his phone ring.

"*Fuck*, Sandy is calling," he swore sounding frustrated, not ready to end the conversation.

"Take the call James…I'm fine…I love you."

"I love you too," he sighed. "I miss you Alex," he said huskily and hung up, ending the conversation.

Several media outlets got hold of the photographs of me slapping Jon, which soon appeared with the story over the Internet. The headlines were abundant… TARZAN GETTING FRIENDLY

WITH JANE! A BIG HAWAIIAN SLAP FOR JON HANLEY'S
TARZAN! ALEX *BROWN HITS CO-STAR IN FACE AFTER HE
GETS TOO FRIENDLY! ALEX BROWN SLAPS BAD BOY HANLEY
IN THE FACE!*

The next morning Preston came to see me. He told me that we
were going to reshoot some scenes from yesterday and that the love
scene beneath the waterfall was postponed for two days.

"How are you doing?" Preston inquired gently.

"I'm fine Preston. Don't worry."

"Have you spoken to Jon yet?" Preston questioned. "I know he
wants to apologize."

"I'll speak to him soon."

"Good," Preston said, starting to leave. "I just want you to know
that Jon knows that I can make *shit* real uncomfortable around here
for him, and that's what we're going to do if he doesn't behave. He
is on thin ice and if he even lifts one finger the wrong way, his ass is
cooked...*capiche?*"

"Thanks Preston," I said with a smile, shutting my door.

A few minutes later there was a knock on my door. I knew Jon
was going to have his tail between his legs and I was going to enjoy
every minute of his apology. Let him *sweat it* I thought wickedly.
*Maybe I would pretend to cry?* It would serve him right to have to
grovel for a while.

I opened the door. "What Jon?" I said coldly.

"Can I come in?" he said softly, sounding unhappy.

I opened the door wider, letting him in. "What?"

"I know I was totally out of line yesterday Alex and I'm sorry.
Can you please forgive me?"

"What are you exactly sorry about? Are you sorry that you put
your hands all over me and groped and kissed me?" I said through
gritted teeth and then I continued my assault. "Or perhaps you're just
sorry, because you did it in front of an audience and got busted? Do
you always harass women who have repeatedly told you no?"

"I wasn't thinking Alex. I'm sorry."

Was that the best apology I was going to get?

"Jon, I know you think you're irresistible to women, but you need to grow up and learn to show respect."

"I know," he said sounding like a disgruntled little boy accepting his punishment.

"If you act unprofessional again on this movie set, Preston is going to have your ass, and I'll walk off the set. Do you understand?"

"Yes, it won't happen again," he promised.

Jon Hanley kept his word and never showed up late nor acted unprofessional on the set again. Off the set, he continued to party, but during filming, he remained sober and alert, and begrudgingly I thought he did a decent job of playing *Tarzan*. I was surprised to realize that Jon had talent and could be a good actor when he was focused. The rest of the project ran smoothly and an unlikely alliance formed between us. By the end of filming we parted as friends.

*** 

I paced the floor of our house for what seemed like the thousandth time, eager and impatient for James to arrive home from Europe. This had been our longest separation. We had seen each other twice during film breaks, but the visits were never long enough, and I was lonely without him. It was the beginning of Memorial Day weekend, and we had been apart from each other since February. Although we talked every day by phone, email or text, the distance was difficult and we both missed each other terribly.

When James walked in the house, I was filled with emotion and I became all choked up. I saw him looking for me and when he spotted me, a huge grin spread over his perfect features. He moved smoothly toward me with quick determination, and held me close, burying his face in my hair.

"I've missed you," he whispered.

I nodded, flushed and happy. It hit me how empty I had felt without him, and I suddenly couldn't speak, afraid that I would cry. Did he know how much I loved him?

He started to kiss me insistently all over and then he started to laugh, radiating joy. He grabbed me and swung me around happily, looking lovingly at me.

"Oh, James," I stammered kissing him hard.

He returned my kisses with ardor and we quickly made our way to the bedroom not coming up for air for several hours. That weekend we had been invited to a number of parties and Memorial Day BBQ's, but we skipped them choosing to spend the weekend alone and in bed.

The rest of the summer went by in a joyous haze. I turned twenty-one that July and for once we had the luxury of time on our hands, having no work obligations until late August. We spent an entire month in Maine on vacation, two weeks with his family, who seemed to be warming up to me, and two weeks alone on a romantic holiday. Our separation became a distant memory as our bond became stronger.

At the end of the summer, James and I traveled together during the extensive promo tour for *Galaxy Drifters 4* from late August until mid-November. Each sequel seemed to get bigger and bigger. The excitement from the fans was contagious and we were blown away once again by the staggering amount of attention, enthusiasm and dedication that the films, and us as actors, received. I kept thinking that the media frenzy and public interest in our relationship would start to decline, but it never did. The crest of the wave that we had been riding from the very first day continued on its upward climb and it was anyone's guesses where it would end? The debut weekend for *Galaxy Drifters 4* set new box office records and the film raked in more than $155 million at North American box offices during it's first four day's alone ensuring it's place as one of the top box office hits of all times. It was an incredibly busy and exciting time for us.

In January, we returned to Vancouver to film the final installment in the *Galaxy Drifters* series. We were three quarters of the way through filming *Galaxy Drifters 5 & 6*, when we took a hiatus so that James and I could both do publicity for *The Adventures of Tarzan & Jane* and *Vivaldi*, prior to their premieres and worldwide releases.

We drove together to the airport on our way to separate destinations. James was scheduled to fly to Europe for promotional activities for *Vivaldi* and I was on my way to New York for the start of a busy promo tour through various domestic and international cities for *Tarzan & Jane*. James and I were both anxious to fulfill our obligations to the films as quickly as possible and then complete the final months of filming and publicity for the *Galaxy Drifters* wrap-up.

During the car ride to the airport, I looked up at James, and I could see him scowling. He seemed far away.

"Is anything wrong?" I asked concerned.

"I'm not happy that you have to be around Jon Hanley again." he said, unflinching.

*Oh that again*. Jon Hanley was a sore subject around James, even though I had repeatedly told him that we were friends and that Jon was harmless. Jon was more bark than bite, but James didn't view it that way.

"You have nothing to be concerned about James," I reassured him. I was scheduled to do most of the touring and promo activities for *The Adventures of Tarzan & Jane* with the director, Preston Foley, and his beautiful wife Sylvia, while Jon and a few co-stars visited other locales on the publicity tour. I got along splendidly with the Foley's and I thought it would be an enjoyable experience. "I've already told you that my travel schedule is primarily with the Foley's. I won't even see Jon again until the premiere and after-party in New York which I'm hoping that you will still be able to make."

"It's not likely that I'll make it with my schedule," James said gloomily.

"Will you snap out of it?" I said trying to coax a smile from him.

"I think the guy is bad news," James warned.

"I can take care of myself James. Don't you trust me?" I questioned unable to hide my hurt feelings.

"Of course I trust you, its Jon Hanley that I don't trust," he said in his authoritative voice.

"God, you sound like Tom," I said dryly rolling my eyes.

"Tom is an astute man and you're naive Alex. I may not always see things eye to eye with Tom, but on this issue, we have the same view."

We pulled up to the airport and the driver started to get our bags out.

"Let's not argue about this, ok?" I said, but before James could answer, I was in his lap, kissing him passionately. We stayed in the car kissing for a few minutes murmuring our good-byes until I was escorted away first, then James, by our separate bodyguards through the airport.

***

Jon greeted me with a huge bear hug as we posed for photos on the red carpet for the New York City première of *The Adventures of Tarzan & Jane* at the SVA Theater in Chelsea. Legions of fans snapped pictures, and it was crowded and glamorous, but it lacked the excitement and fanfare of the *Galaxy Drifters* premieres.

"*Wow* Jon, I'm speechless to see you in a suit," I joked.

"Nice legs," he whistled admiringly. He narrowed his eyes at me and let them linger longer than necessary. "You look stunning."

"Thank you," I said; suddenly feeling uncomfortable and wishing that James could have made it for the evening's events.

After the red carpet rolled up, we made our way with the cast to an after-party at the retro modern Standard Hotel in the heart of downtown Manhattan's meatpacking district. The party was located in the Boom Boom Room, which was an exclusive club at the top of the Standard on the 18th floor. Following the after party was a smaller party in the VIP section of the club that lasted until 5am. Throughout the fun festive evening I had only three or four drinks, but during the last hour I was suddenly feeling super spacey and extremely tired. *Oh, shit, I felt dizzy!* While I was not totally inebriated, I did not feel right and knew that I had to leave. I put my hand against the wall for support, but the room started to spin, so I shut my eyes.

"Are you ok?" Jon asked.

The next thing I knew we were in the elevator, and I could not remember how we got there. Then I felt his lips on mine, and I thought I saw the flash of cameras, but I was so disorientated that I wasn't sure if it was really happening or if I was imagining it?

"Where are we going," I slurred.

"To the hotel room."

When I awoke the next morning, I had the worst hang over of my life and a splitting headache. I ran to the bathroom leaned over the toilet and emptied the contents of my stomach. After a few minutes, when I was sure that I was done vomiting, I washed my face and drank a large cup of water from the bathroom sink. That's when I realized that I was naked, and with sudden clarity, I was sure that I wasn't alone. I leaned against the bathroom wall and slowly slid down to a sitting position on the floor feeling miserable and utterly dejected trying to recall the events of the previous evening. Fragments of the night before flashed before me, but it was fuzzy, nothing concrete. It didn't make sense ... *how could I have gotten so drunk? Could my drink have been laced with something? If someone had put something in my drink, wouldn't I be able to tell?* Tears streamed down my face and I sat there alone and depressed for a long time. Then I took a hot shower and wrapped myself in the hotel robe. I entered the room determined to deal with whatever lay before me.

Jon Hanley was there, naked and snoring in the bed.
*Damn what had I done?*

## Chapter 19: Aftermath of a Scandal

TARZAN & JANE'S BOOTY CALL! ALEX BROWN CAUGHT CHEATING! BAD BOY HANLEY CAUGHT IN THE ACT WITH CO-STAR! IS IT QUITS FOR BROWN & PRESCOTT? HANLEY & BROWN HOTEL HOOKUP!

I sat motionless in my hotel room in New York re-reading the headlines from my red puffy eyes swollen from so many tears. The pain was raw and I was devastated and despondent. What had I done? I heard the beep of another text and I knew that my voice mailbox was filled with messages that I had not listened too. I didn't care; I didn't want to face the world, especially James. I knew that I had to get it together, but I didn't know where to began. Obviously, James, our families, Lydia, Sandy, Tom, the Studio execs and the never-ending teams of PR folks for *Galaxy Drifters* and *The Adventures of Tarzan & Jane* had to be dealt with. I was overwhelmed thinking about it.

Finally, I got off the floor. I knew that I had to face the music. I wiped away the tears and took a few calming breaths before reaching for the phone and calling James. It went straight to voicemail. I cleared my throat trying to sound normal.

"James, it's Alex." My voice was hoarse and shaking. "I know it look's bad, but please call me; it's not what you think."

I sent him texts and email messages obsessively throughout the day begging him to call me, but the hours passed and I received no responses. My unease turned to dread. What if he doesn't forgive me? My head throbbed and I listlessly returned to bed broken and depressed shutting out the world for another day.

The next morning there was a loud knock on the hotel room door, and for one brief moment I absurdly hoped it was James.

"Alex, it's Lydia! Open the door."

I limply opened the door unable to hide my disappointment.

"Are you ok?" Lydia asked, concern thick in her voice, as she gave me a hug.

"I've been better," I said attempting to make light of the situation, but without much success.

"What happened?" Lydia asked intently.

"I think someone slipped a *roofie* in my drink, as I have absolutely no memory of the last hour of the party and what transpired after it."

"Nothing?" Lydia probed.

"A few flashes of lucidity, but not enough to really piece anything together." I said frustrated while resting my forehead in my hands.

"What has Hanley said about it?" Lydia said not disguising her distaste at saying his name.

"He said that we exchanged a few kisses here and there, but that when he took me to his hotel room, I passed out on his bed, and that nothing happened."

"Do you believe him or do you think he's lying?" Lydia questioned.

"Why would he lie? If we slept together why not admit it and tell me," I questioned with despair.

"Because than the fucker would be admitting to being a rapist," Lydia shouted coldly.

I was full of anguish, as Lydia had verbalized my deepest fears. Minutes ticked by and neither one of us said anything, both deep in thought. What a nightmare.

"Jon is a lot of things, and I would venture to call him a cocky asshole, but he's not a rapist," I said in a low monotone, but I didn't sound convincing -- *not* even to my own ears.

"How can you be certain?" Lydia continued to probe gently, but with force behind her words.

"I'm not." I admitted. "But I need it to be true for my own sanity Lydia. Can you understand that?"

"Ok, let's say Jon is telling the truth, and there was no sex. How can you be certain that he wasn't the person responsible for slipping the *roofie* into your drink?"

Again, Lydia was expressing my deepest fears, and I just didn't want to explore them. Perhaps I was in denial or perhaps I didn't want to know the truth. Did it matter anymore? I needed this conversation to come to an end.

"Lydia, I don't want to discuss it anymore. Do you understand?" I said with artificial steely resolve. "Can we talk about something else? I haven't heard back from James. He is ignoring my calls. Have you spoken with him?"

I couldn't stand the look of pity on her face, as she nodded no. I tried hiding my despair, but I knew that she could see right through me. I wasn't fooling her.

"Ken has been trying to reach James, but James seems to be off the grid for the moment. Like you, he is ignoring everyone," Lydia stated.

"How bad is it?" I asked.

"I'm not going to lie to you, it's bad," she said pacing the floor. "I don't want to sound overdramatic, but we have a real PR nightmare on our hands, and you're at the center of it. Since the moment this story was released, it has become a full-blown scandal with you being labeled as a slut, whore, and cheater. We have everyone up our ass from the studio execs to the devastated fan-base mourning over their beloved virginal Amanda Blake. And don't even get me started about the paparazzi camping outside this hotel, James hotel in London, Tom's office, your house, and your parent's house."

"My parent's house? James hotel?" I repeated horrified.

"Sandy is waiting for a call from us to explain our side of what happened," Lydia explained. "From there, Sandy and the crisis communication team will develop a plan of action to deal with the scandal. We've also hired the PR consultant team that Tiger Wood's used after his cheating calamity. In the meantime, Tom is putting together a strategy meeting with all the stakeholders involved. You and James will need to attend the meeting once James returns from Europe."

"What I told you about my suspicion of something being slipped in my drink *is* private and not to be shared. The subject is forbidden. Do you understand Lydia?" I said mustering up all my strength and resolve.

"I understand." Lydia said sounding frustrated and unhappy.

I glowered at her until she turned away and walked over to the desk pulling out her cell phone. I listened with half an ear as she made dozens of calls to deal with the situation. Her face was serious, as she talked quietly with a subdued voice. I admired how she calmly took charge and how she juggled and coordinated everyone with skill and diplomacy.

While Lydia dealt with the fallout from the scandal, I finally listened to my overflowing voice box. There were hysterical messages from my parents, and brothers, Sandy, Tom, Lydia, Ken, Jon, Ben, Preston, and countless studio execs. There were even messages from members of the press who wanted exclusive interviews. *How did they get my cell phone number?* The list of callers was endless, but I noted, no messages from James. His silence tormented me and I felt the stirrings of unease in the pit of my stomach. I had lost my appetite and was having trouble sleeping. I was distraught with worry and despair. *Where was James? His silence was killing me.*

Tom had insisted on a fairly large squad of bodyguards to escort Lydia and I from the Standard Hotel to JFK Airport. At first, I thought it was a bit much, but I did not want to argue with Tom. As we emerged from the hotel, I wore sunglasses in an attempt to hide my red puffy swollen eyes and I couldn't believe what I saw! There was a sea of jostling fans and paparazzi screaming at me and taking photographs. The crowd was aggressive, and I was jostled and touched several times. Disgruntled photographers shouted questions at me. IS IT TRUE YOU HAD AN AFFAIR WITH JON HANLEY? HAVE YOU & JAMES PRESCOTT BROKEN UP? WHAT'S THE FUTURE OF THE GALAXY DRIFTERS FRANCHISE? WILL YOU & JAMES PRESCOTT WALK THE RED CARPET TOGETHER IN NOVEMBER? From others I heard...HOW COULD YOU? SLUT! CHEATER! YOU DON'T DESERVE JAMES PRESCOTT YOU SELFISH WHORE! The bodyguards quickly covered me and several pulled out umbrella's to shield the camera lenses. Something was thrown at us? Eggs? Dog Feces? Jeff maneuvered us through the chaos into a waiting SUV with tinted dark windows. My heart beat erratically with fear laced with adrenaline as we quickly drove away from the commotion.

"Are you alright?" Jeff asked Lydia and I, concern etched on his strong features.

"That was scary, I mean really scary," Lydia said her voice shaky.

"I'm ok," I said distracted as I heard my phone beep.

I opened a text from James:

***Got your messages. Need space. I will be home next week. We can talk then. -J***

I responded:

***Ok. -A***

Twenty-Four hours later Jon Hanley released a statement of apology, saying, "I had too much to drink at the after-party for *The Adventures of Tarzan & Jane,* and I acted inappropriately kissing my co-star Alexandra Brown. While we did share a hotel room together, nothing happened and we did not have sexual intercourse. That is the end of the story. I'm sorry for any hurt or embarrassment that I have caused to Alexandra Brown, James Prescott, our beloved fans, friends, and families."

In response to Hanley's apology, I issued the following statement, "I would like to sincerely apologize to everyone that has been affected by this, especially my friends and family. I'm ashamed by my lapse in judgment and I'm so sorry for the hurt and embarrassment that I have caused."

***

The opening weekend box office numbers for *The Adventures of Tarzan & Jane* in North America were good. I breathed a sigh of relief and thanked my lucky stars. It had earned a very respectable $64 million for its debut weekend. Projected total domestic and international estimates were roughly expected to reach $400 million. At least that would be one studio off my back. In fact, many believed that the free publicity from the coverage of the scandal had helped *Tarzan & Jane* to do great business and attract a wider audience. Whatever the reason for its success, I was happy to have it behind me, so that I could concentrate my full attention on James.

Hungrily, I read any news and articles that I could find about the *Vivaldi* première in London. James received very favorable reviews for his performance, but there was little written about it. Instead, I was troubled to see that everyone's focus seemed less about the actual movie and more about the real life drama unfolding between James and I. The one silver lining was that *Vivaldi*, which was a small artsy independent flick with a total production budget of only $11 million, opened with positive numbers with a three-day box office total slightly above $12 million.

I noted that reporters continually harassed James with questions about our relationship on the red carpet and during interviews for *Vivaldi*. To my great relief, James remained dignified, poised and articulate in front of the camera without saying anything concrete. When asked about the scandal, he usually cracked a joke, but otherwise remained silent, declining to comment, trying his best to focus attention back on *Vivaldi*. James was adept at side stepping issues with tact and diplomacy. He had been raised as a gentleman with perfect manners, and whatever lay underneath the surface; he was skilled at hiding it with charm and grace.

The constant attention riveted on James and I was getting to me. I couldn't leave the house unless I had an army of bodyguards with me. I was scrutinized like never before, the butt of every joke for late night talk show hosts and the subject of countless unflattering and untrue news stories. During this time, I started to receive boatloads of hate mail and saw an increase in nasty untruthful stories written about me. James was seen as the victim while I was crucified constantly as a CHEATER or SLUT. The public fascination was relentless and scary at times and I wasn't sure if I could handle it for much longer.

For the first time in almost a week, I left my house on Wednesday to attend an all day strategy meeting at Hunter Wescott. It was a grueling day and I was exhausted. Contributing to my fatigue was my anxiety at knowing that I would see James the next day. I missed him desperately and was heart sick from his silence. It was getting late when I arrived home, and I was bone tired. I took a quick shower and pulled on a tank top and pajama pants. As I walked through the bedroom on the way to the kitchen, I caught a small movement and glanced up. Sitting in an armchair in the corner of the room, with scotch in hand was James watching me intently.

"Hello Alexandra." His voice lacked his usual warmth, and his expression was the one I recognized when he played poker with my brothers...blank and unreadable. He took a sip of his drink, not saying anything further.

"I...I didn't expect you until tomorrow," I stammered stumbling over my words. "You're sitting in the dark, let me put on a light?"

"Leave it," he ordered.

I was nervous. He wasn't going to make this easy. My throat was dry and I decided to get a drink to distract me from my anxiety.

"Do you want anything from the kitchen?" I asked.

"No," he replied morosely, sitting statue-like in the dark. I had never seen him like this before and it both saddened and terrified me. I wanted to say something comforting, but words escaped me.

I quickly drank a large glass of water. I took my time in the kitchen and decided to pour myself a glass of wine. I was going to need something a hell of a lot stronger than water to face him again. When, I returned to the bedroom, I noted that he hadn't moved a muscle, but that his scotch glass had been emptied. I took a large gulp of wine, and put my glass down. With an assurance that I didn't feel, I crossed the room until I was standing in front of him and then I crumpled before him down to my knees desperate for his forgiveness. I put my chin on his knees, and placed my hands on his thighs, tipping my head up to look at him. Our eyes locked, and we stared at each other, unblinking, until tears rolled down my cheeks. He took his hand, and gently wiped the tears away, still not saying anything.

"I'm sorry James," I whispered, putting my tear stained face in his lap. I continued, my voice steady and quiet. "I know that you've been publically humiliated and that you've been badly hurt, but you have to believe me when I tell you that nothing happened."

"Nothing?" he questioned, sounding incredulous. "How can I believe that? Do you take me for a fool? How could anyone believe that after seeing those photos?"

"I know it look's incriminating, but it's not what it seems. Please let me explain?" I begged.

"You and Hanley looked drunk off your asses, totally reckless Alex," he hissed, sounding angry.

"Would you just let me explain?" I yelled.

"No, I really don't want to hear how his tongue incidentally found its way inside your mouth," he said with vehemence, and I was surprised by the hardness in his voice. His face was close to me and I could smell the alcohol on his breath. "If you want reckless, I'll show you reckless."

Suddenly, he started kissing me hard or maybe I was kissing him. I didn't remember how it happened, but it was like a tidal wave washing over both of us. With one fell swoop, he pulled me on his lap, and we kissed each other roughly. Before I knew it, he turned me abruptly over on his knees and pulled down my pajama pants and panties. Before I could react or be embarrassed, he started to spank me with one hand while fingering me with the other. It was a combination of hot, naughty and hedonistic pleasure, and I climaxed wildly in his lap. We both were breathing hard and then he turned me over again so that I was sitting in his lap facing him. I wrapped my legs around his waist and leaned into him holding him tightly. We started to kiss passionately with the same intensity as before. He unzipped his pants and we made love on the armchair. The experience was incredible. Afterwards, neither of us spoke or moved. We dozed off entwined in each other's arms postponing our unfinished conversation.

I woke up sore and stiff from my position on the armchair, and I quietly got up trying not to wake James. It was the middle of the night, and my throat felt dry and I needed to go to the bathroom. When I returned to the bedroom, James was awake.

"What time is it?" he groggily asked.

"A little after two in the morning. Do you want to talk now or in the morning?"

"Morning," he said stifling a yawn. He stripped off his clothes and went into bed. "Are you coming?" he asked reaching for me.

"Yes," I said with my first smile of contentment since the night of the after-party. I reached for him with the false confidence that we would be ok and I quickly fell asleep in his arms.

***

The next morning, I awoke to the smell of coffee and fried eggs. I was ravenous and I quickly threw on my clothes and made my way to the kitchen.

"Good morning," I said suddenly nervous for our conversation. I wasn't good at confrontation and I went a long way to avoid it.

"Good morning," he said pleasantly enough, but there was still a hint of something wrong in the sound of his voice. "Are you hungry?"

"Starving," I said eagerly.

We ate breakfast in strained silence. Both of us seemed weary, uncertain of what to say to break the tension between us.

"That was great James, thanks for cooking," I said clearing the dishes.

After the kitchen was sparkling clean, conversation could no longer be avoided. We moved to the great room and James took a seat on the couch.

"Okay Alex, start from the beginning and tell me what happened?" James said sounding open-minded.

I took a deep breath and launched into the same story that I told Lydia while pacing the floor with nervous energy unwilling to look at him. When I was finished recounting the details, I finally stopped pacing and looked at James.

His expression changed from anger to sorrow to something that I couldn't quite identify. I waited patiently for him to respond.

He cleared his voice to speak, but it came out in a whisper. "How can you be certain it wasn't Hanley who slipped you the *roofie* to began with?"

"I know you think I'm naïve, but I don't think Jon did this," I said trying to project strength and confidence.

"Why?" he asked.

"Why not?" I replied shrugging my shoulders. "Does it matter?"

"It matters to me and it should matter to you," he said firmly.

"James I cannot change what happened that night, and I don't want to revisit it ever again. I just want to know that you forgive me and that we are going to be ok? I love you and I've been desperately unhappy since you cut off communication. I understand that you were humiliated and hurt, and you probably felt that I betrayed you. But I didn't, and I felt like you deserted me in my hour of greatest need."

James covered his face with his hands, and I didn't understand his reaction.

"Say something," I implored.

He looked up and his lashes were wet. "Of course I forgive you, it's me that I can't forgive," he stated.

"Don't be silly, you have nothing to feel guilty about," I said crossing over to the couch and sitting next to him. "I understand why you were angry with me and why you needed space, I just wish that you would have let me explain first. But I get it; I saw the photos and read the news stories. It was horrible and I'm so sorry that you were publically humiliated," I cringed recalling the ugliness.

"It's not that," he said his tone flat and lifeless.

The color drained from my face. I couldn't understand a word he was saying.

"What do you mean?" I asked with my first inkling of dread. I felt the hair stand up on the back of my neck and a shiver ran down my spine.

"When the story was released, all hell broke loose and I was hounded relentlessly by reporters. Everywhere I went, I was pestered and pitied and I just wanted to escape it. The pain was intense and I was in shock, and then I just wanted to forget. That's when I got drunk. I mean really plastered. I was drunk for days. I'm sorry Alex, I met someone at a bar and I slept with her. I hope you'll find it in your heart to forgive me…I'm so sorry."

His words sliced through me like a knife and I felt like I couldn't breath. He had *sex* with someone else. He reached for my hand, but I quickly pulled away. I couldn't look at him. He started to say something, but I could no longer hear the words. My ears were ringing and the heartache was intense, like nothing I had ever experienced before. I fixed a blank expression on my face and calmly nodded my head in a response to something he said, but I didn't know what. In an effort to pull myself together, I tried taking calming breaths.

"Please say something Alex?" he begged hanging his head with guilt.

I knew I had to say something, but what could I possibly say? Should I shout at him? Hit him? Cry? We sat in an uncomfortable silence and the minutes ticked by. Finally I found my voice, and I was surprised by its hardness.

"I want to be alone. I think you should leave the house James," I said coldly and then I walked out of the room.

A few minutes later I heard the door close, and it was my undoing. The façade that I had held together, fell apart and the floodgates opened. I was shocked and confused and completely hysterical. My heart and spirit were broken, and I succumbed to the grief as it swept over me taking me down.

## Chapter 20: Ups and Downs

Tom continued his tirade pacing his office floor like he was in a road race. His words were fast and furious and I stopped listening.

"Tom, could you stop yelling at me," I hissed.

"I'll stop yelling when you start showing some professionalism," he ranted. "Remember that first day when I feared that you were a brat, well now you're acting like one."

I opened my mouth to speak, but then I shut it again. Did he just call me a brat? He had some nerve. I sat there scowling at him and he scowled back.

"You can scowl at me all day Alex, and I'll scowl back. If this is a staring contest, I guarantee you that I'll win," he said arrogantly.

"Do you speak sweetly like this to all of your clients or am I just the lucky one today?" I inquired sarcastically with a raised eyebrow.

"When someone needs a swift kick in the butt, client or not, they will receive it," he warned sounding cocky as ever.

I didn't answer Tom and suddenly I wished that I had not blown off Lydia. If she were here today she would defend me.

"Where is Lydia today?" Tom asked like he could read my mind. It was uncanny.

"I blew her off. I was sick of her looks of pity and hovering over me like a babysitter," I answered honestly.

"Maybe you need a babysitter!" he snapped. "You should thank your lucky stars to have such a fine manager and friend. She really cares about you, you know."

"I know Tom. I might not always show it, but I know," I admitted seriously, my voice heavy with emotion. "I'm sorry about blowing off the meeting yesterday, and I promise that I will never do something like that again. I know that it's a poor excuse Tom, but it's been a rough couple of weeks."

"I know it's been rough Alex, but it took a lot of effort to get everyone in the same room yesterday. These are powerful people and you can't just blow them off, because you're depressed and don't want to deal with it," Tom said gently, but firmly.

"I swear to you that it will not happen again Tom. Could you tell me what I missed?"

"The studio is freaking out since the scandal and they want to lock in your personal appearance dates with James as well as secure a commitment from the both of you that the final three months of filming will go smoothly?" Tom said, his tone serious. "Do you realize that in less than five weeks, you and James are scheduled to travel to Madrid, London, and Tokyo to promote the next film? This is very last minute and everyone is up in arms about it."

"If I wanted to travel separately on the promo tour, is there still time to make those changes?" I asked quietly, not looking Tom in the face.

"I don't understand Alex?" Tom questioned. "James was here yesterday, and he will do the dates with you, and he seemed very eager for a reconciliation. What the hell is going on?"

"It's complicated," I stammered.

"How so? James must have forgiven you for the situation with asshole Hanley, so what gives?" Tom asked sounding confused.

"We have issues that extend beyond the scandal and I'm not sure that I can travel and promote the film with him," I said quietly.

"Like what?" he asked with interest.

"It's none of your business," I hissed.

Tom started to pace the floor again and then he ran his hand through his hair and sighed loudly.

"As your agent, I could give a fuck if you guys breakup or not. But I have to warn you that you have contractual obligations to Pinnacle. Do you realize that you and James have to work together closely and intimately for the foreseeable future until the release of the final film in the series? Whatever is happening with respect to your relationship, it is still in your best interest to present a united front and fulfill those obligations," he said sounding crisp and business-like. "But as your friend," he said softening his tone and coming closer to sit next to me, "if the plans for the promo tour need to change to accommodate separate schedules, we will make it happen. It won't be good for publicity, and the studio and fans won't

like it, but we can do it. I just want you to really think it over before
you make a final decision?"

"Thanks Tom." I said relieved. "Can you give me a few more
days and then I'll let you know?"

"Yeah, I can give you a few more days, but I'm going to have the
studio breathing down my neck the whole time, so you need to make
a decision fast. Also, I'm sorry to hear that you and James are having
problems. I usually don't admit these things, but the two of you were
good together. I hope you guys can work it out."

When I arrived home from Tom's office, James was waiting on
the front steps for me. It had been six long days of agony since he
had told me about his fling. It was ironic, because I was desperately
unhappy when I was away from him, but on the other hand, I
couldn't stand being near him as it brought back the pain of the
betrayal and all of my insecurities and complex feelings surrounding
it.

"Can we talk?" he asked tentatively.

I sat down next to James on the porch. I was weary and I didn't
feel like fighting. In ten days, I would turn twenty-two, but I felt
more like an old hag ready to be put out to pasture. *When had my life
gotten so complicated?* I yearned for a more simple existence. If only
I could return to innocence? If I couldn't have that, I wished for
ignorance. I was tired of thinking and analyzing. Why couldn't I be
like every other soon to be twenty-two year old and just hang out
with friends, go to clubs and parties, fill out grad school applications
and have an uncomplicated life.

"Did you get my flowers?" James asked, looking rather sheepish.

"Are you kidding?" I said with a half smile. "It look's like a
florist shop in there. You need to stop sending flowers James."

"Ok, no more flowers. How about if I get down on one knee
instead?" he said pleasantly enough, but his tone was serious and he
was looking earnestly at me.

"Will you be serious James?" I gently scolded ignoring the
reference to the proposal. It was left hanging between us awkwardly.

"I'm deadly serious Alex. I know that I fucked up royally, but I don't want to live my life without you. Please forgive me?" he pleaded.

"I understand how it happened," I whispered in a small voice and it was painful to get the words out. "But it's already hard enough to watch women throw themselves at you all of the time and now I don't know how I'm going to trust you again?"

"It was a drunken stupid mistake. You have to believe that Alex? Please forgive me and with time I promise that I'll earn your trust back?"

"It's not just the infidelity James. I thought I could always count on you, and when I really needed you, you turned your back on me and didn't give me an opportunity to explain. I need to know that you'll be there in the future? If we are faced with adversity again, I need to know that you will stay open-minded and communicate with me rather than flee?" I said steadily.

"You have my word," he pledged and then he tentatively kissed me. The kiss was emotional and I felt vulnerable.

He stood up and took my hand and started leading me into the house.

"Where are we going?" I stammered.

"To have *make up* sex," he said giving me a lascivious grin.

My emotions were at war. I wasn't sure that I was ready? The pain was still so raw, but my body betrayed me. Even under duress, the chemistry between us was palpable and I longed for his touch. James knew this and he used it to his advantage. He picked me up and carried me to the bed and murmured his love. The lovemaking was incredible, so I forgot our troubles, and let myself go.

***

Months went by, four to be exact, and life resumed to almost, normal...well, as normal as one could expect under the circumstances. James and I were back together again, but the hurt and anger while pushed aside, was still very much present. It would take time to put it behind us.

The worldwide release of *Galaxy Drifters 5* ruled the box office its opening weekend taking in $162.3 million domestically, and $178 million abroad for a total earning of $340.3 million word-wide, proving its phenomenal popularity with audiences. The studio was initially concerned that the scandal with Hanley, and James and I brief, but real-life relationship drama, might erode attendance, but fans turned out in record numbers.

The opening success of the fifth film boded well for the final title in the franchise, which would be released next fall. After the New Year holiday, we would join the rest of the cast in Vancouver to resume filming of the final installment in the *Galaxy Drifters* film series.

I had mixed feelings about the franchise coming to an end. It had been both a blessing and a curse to be part of such a phenomenon, but overall I felt incredibly lucky for the experience. *Galaxy Drifters* was a huge part of my life and I had grown up during each film. I considered the cast and crew to be among my closest friends and I would miss them very much when the film series finally wrapped up. In one way, it was liberating to know that the commitment would be over so that I could move on to other projects and activities, and have more free time to spend with friends and family. James and I could finally travel where we wanted, when we wanted, without the pressure of knowing that we had to shoot or promote another *Galaxy* film. On the other hand, I would be terribly sad to see it all end and I wondered if I would feel at loose ends without it being a constant in my life.

Lastly, and it was my biggest fear, when the franchise came to an end, what would that mean for James and I? I never articulated my fear to anyone, but on a particularly bad day or in a dark moment, I would ponder it relentlessly. The film series had brought us together, and kept us together when we had problems. Without the film series in our life...would we have separated? That worry caused me many sleepless nights and I feared a future without *Galaxy Drifters* in it.

Five months later, on a warm, but rainy April afternoon, the day of reckoning was *finally* here...filming of the last *Galaxy* movie was over. I was free to walk away from the "Hurricane" that had ruled every second of my life for the last five years. It was a very emotional and bittersweet experience as filming came to an end and I said farewell with tears in my eyes to cast, crew, and the character of Amanda Blake forever. I knew that I would see the actors and crew later at the wrap up party, and at several events during the promotional tour, première and after-party, so technically I wasn't free yet, but never again would we *all* be together like this again. It had been a remarkable, exciting, and scary experience, and I would miss it.

Pinnacle had rented a hip three-story bar and grill located in the heart of downtown Vancouver to host the private wrap up party that evening. It was a cool place made up of several bars and dining rooms decorated like living rooms. Some of the rooms had their own fireplaces, and the top floor was a wide-open space with a considerable dance floor. When James and I arrived we decided to start on the top level and make our way down throughout the evening. The music was blaring and lights were flashing, and the bar was crowded with all the people involved with the production. Wait staff walked around with food, but everybody seemed more interested in partying hard and letting off steam. James and I were having a lot of fun together dancing, but then we begin socializing with coworkers, and I lost track of him.

I was in the sushi room on the second floor with Audrey devouring my fifth avocado roll, when Mark and Sean came in with a plate full of shots.

"Come on ladies, it's time to drink!"

We each took a shot, and I grimaced as the alcohol burned down my throat.

"Where's James?" Mark questioned.

"I don't know?" I yelled over the music.

"Let's go find the man." Mark bellowed loudly. "I'm going to make him drink tonight!"

Mark and Audrey starting to lead our group into the next living room space, this one filled with a huge assortment of cheeses, fruits, meats, and breads.

"Look at the size of that ham!" Mark exclaimed with glee pulling Audrey over to the buffet with him.

While they were getting food, I chatted with Sean who had become a good friend over the years. Sean put his hand on my shoulder and asked me if I wanted to get some air. I nodded my head and we made our way to an outside deck off the room.

When we got to the deck, I noticed that James was there. I was about to call his name when I saw that he was in a heated conversation with Julie Blaine, the blonde production assistant that he had slept with five years ago after he gave me the ultimatum to break up with Lance. I had never liked Julie, as I had always caught her looking at me with undisguised dislike and envy. I thought on an unconscious level, that I was probably jealous of her for having slept with James and it was clear that she had a crush on him. I was irritated that they were talking. *Why were they talking and why was it so heated?* I was upset, and wanted to confront him about it, but I knew that this wasn't the time or place. I didn't want to stand there gawking at them awkwardly, but at the same time, I hesitated going over there.

"Sean, would you mind if we went somewhere else?" I asked, hoping that I didn't look or sound upset.

"Sure Alex, lead the way," Sean said smoothly. If he noticed that I was distressed, he didn't say anything.

Sean and I made our way down to the lower level, which had a calmer vibe. There was a lounge with exposed brick and a massive bar stocked with every kind of alcohol imaginable and a table full of various desserts and chocolates. The lounge was set up like a living room with multiple flat screen televisions, each projecting a gallery of photos of the cast and crew from the last five years of *Galaxy Drifters* films. There was a bookshelf of board games, and various plush couches and comfy chairs to relax and hangout. The atmosphere was soothing and a great place to have a few drinks and mellow conversation. Sean and I sat on a couch that was so damn comfy I thought I might fall asleep. I briefly shut my eyes and stretch my legs out on the coffee table.

"Do you want to talk about what is troubling you?" Sean asked.

I open my eyes and look at him. "Is it that obvious?"

"You don't have to be jealous of Julie Blaine. I know it must be irritating for you to watch Julie follow James around the movie set for five years like a puppy dog, but James only has eyes for you."

"Do you think so Sean, because lately I've been worried?" I replied honestly and I hated admitting that out loud. I knew that since the scandal, that I had been uptight and insecure. Part of it was the pressure from the constant media attention. I felt like I had become paranoid and that I was continually looking over my shoulder to see if someone was watching, photographing or taking a video of me. I was afraid that if I didn't appear perfect or look a certain way that I would have to read a nasty story about it the next day. But it wasn't just the media attention that was making me crazy. I was still reeling from the shock of James infidelity and I knew that it contributed to my paranoia, especially with other women. I was jealous and I hated myself for acting this way. I knew that for our relationship to work, that I had to trust him. I was trying to re-establish trust, but it was difficult, especially in moments like these, when I saw James having a private heated conversation with a woman that he used to fuck.

"Worried about what?" he asked gently taking his hand and stroking my cheek.

"I don't know, it's hard to explain," I said softly, hesitantly.

"You don't have to explain to me if you don't want to," Sean said kindly. "But if you and James are having problems, you should know that there is a long line of men, starting with me, who would be very happy if you were single and obtainable."

I was uncomfortable by his admission. I had certainly known early on that Sean had harbored some feelings toward me, but then he started to date a beautiful exotic actress and it was quickly forgotten.

"I thought you were dating Sophia?" I asked changing the subject.

"I was, but we split up about two months ago. So I'm free and available…" he said with a wink.

*Oh my*…how to respond? This was tricky. To my dismay, I found myself tongue tied as I desperately tried to come up with something clever to say to try make the moment less awkward.

To make matters worse, James entered the room at that very moment, and I saw him scowl as he took in the intimate scene of Sean and I sitting together on the couch while his hand was stroking my cheek. I knew that Sean had meant it as a reassuring and sympathetic gesture, but with the cold glare that James was giving us, I didn't think that's how he had interpreted it. James made his way over to us, and his mouth was settled into a hard line. I thought he seemed angry....*shit.*

"Alex, could I speak to you for a moment...*privately?*" he said tightly, glaring at me.

Well, at least that got me out of an awkward conversation with Sean, even if it took me *from the frying pan into the fire.*

"Excuse me Sean," I said getting up from the couch.

"No problem. Bye Alex, James," he said and I couldn't ignore the disappointment in his voice.

James took my hand, practically dragging me, and led me to an outside patio that wasn't very busy, considering the late night hour and cold temperature. I broke his grasp and walked over to a fire pit that dominated the space, trying to get warm.

I felt his hand on my elbow. "What the hell was that?" he whispered, his expression dark.

I glared at him. "Don't use that tone with me!" I said turning on him with anger. "Sean was just being a good friend, because I was upset after seeing you with your old fuck buddy. What the hell was that about?"

"You mean Julie?" he said the color draining from his face.

"Why? Are there others here tonight that I should be aware of?" I said coldly and I detested myself for acting juvenile and jealous, but I couldn't help it.

"Of course not," he said calmly. "I'm sorry that you had to witness my altercation with Julie."

"What was it about?" I asked softly.

James was quiet, apprehensive even. He ran his hand roughly through his hair, as I waited for his next words.

"I told Julie to stop harassing me with phone calls, emails, and texts...I made it clear that she was to stop contacting me."

"I didn't realize she was?" I asked confused. "Could you explain?"

"She was a production coordinator on *Vivaldi* Alex," he said hanging his head with guilt and looking down on the ground.

I was about to say who cares, when it hit me. *Shit...*Julie was the woman he had the drunken fling with. *Oh no...*

## Chapter 21: Last Trip to Maine

As reality set in, an on-and-off relationship ensued between James
and I. At times, things seemed perfectly normal and we would be
happy again. But then we would be faced with a new obstacle to
overcome. The obstacles ranged from petty jealousy, negative
publicity and media attention, demanding work schedules, and
separate travel. It didn't really matter what the root cause of the
adversity was, what mattered was how we handled it and we did not
handle it well.

I silently fumed about James drunken fling with Julie. He swore
to me that he had only slept with her twice. Once before we were
together, and again in Europe during the filming of *Vivaldi* when he
was drunk and despondent over the scandal with Hanley and I. I
wanted to believe him, but I was consumed with jealousy, doubt, and
insecurity about it.

It was during this tense period in our relationship, that we would
spend what would later become, our last trip to Maine together.
James had turned twenty-seven that spring, and I had just celebrated
twenty-three. I eagerly awaited our trip to Maine, but unfortunately
we would not be alone, instead his family and a house full of guests
would be there to celebrate his grandparent's 50th wedding
anniversary. I was nervous about seeing his parents, especially after
the negative publicity about me. In the aftermath of the scandal the
previous summer, we had skipped our annual trip to Maine, and I
had not joined James for his brief trips to see his family during
Thanksgiving and Christmas, hence it had been almost a year and a
half since I had last seen the Prescott family. While I liked his sister
Rachel, and adored his grandparents, my relationship with his
parents continued to be formal and strained.

When we arrived at the house it was almost dusk, and everyone
was hustling and bustling with activity in preparation for the big
party that evening. I knew that due to our late arrival that I had to
quickly get ready, as guests were scheduled to arrive in less than an
hour, but I stopped to admire the view, while James searched for his

family to say hello. I inhaled the fresh sea air, mingled with an intoxicating smell of fragrant white flowers and summertime. Soft white lights twinkled from the canopy of century-old trees that lined the vast garden, and perimeter. Tea lights in hand blown jars illuminated the pathways, the dock, and the edges of flowerbeds. Fresh cut Gardenias were floating in the pool and pond, and in water along side candles in stunning centerpieces, casting a warm glow everywhere. An outside dance floor had been erected on the lawn and an impressive 16-piece jazz orchestra was setting up. The Prescott's certainly knew how to throw a party…it looked to be a magical evening ahead of us.

I successfully made it to the bedroom without having to engage in small talk with anyone. When I entered the room, I saw that James had already brought up our luggage, but that he wasn't there, so I quickly took a shower and got dressed for the party. I opted for a sleek one-shoulder spaghetti strap white gown by Valentino with a high slit that revealed my legs. I wore my hair tousled and wavy down my back with minimal make-up and accessories. Overall, I thought the look was simple, but pretty.

When I was finished getting ready, I went down to the party in search of James. The smooth sounds of jazz filled the air and echoed through the house and gardens. It was a perfect summer evening. I'd been to a lot of standout parties, but this was among the grandest, most enchanting I'd ever been too. It was starting to get crowded with guests as I made my way outdoors to the lawn. Servers walked around with trays of mouth-watering appetizers, sophisticated cocktails and champagne. I didn't see James among the crowd, so I decided to get a gin and tonic, before continuing my search for him.

As I weaved through the crowd, I received numerous admiring glances and I was happy that I had selected the white dress for the evening, at least I thought so, until I found myself staring into the disapproving eyes of Mrs. Prescott.

"Mrs. Prescott…um, so nice to see you," I said while fidgeting with my dress. "I haven't seen you since your 50th birthday party, you look amazing!"

I tried to hug her, but she barely returned the embrace, giving me a cool side hug instead – it was awkward! *What an utter bitch.*

"Thank you dear, so good to see you too. It seems like none of the guests can take their eyes off you..." she said sharply while gesturing towards the crowd of guests.

I blushed. Embarrassed by her comments. I wasn't sure if she meant it as an insult or not, but her tone was polite enough, thus I hoped she intended it as friendly chatter.

"I'm sure that's not true Mrs. Prescott," I said trying to squelch my unease. "This is a lovely party."

"Oh no dear, you are definitely the center of attention, but you must be used to that by now?" she asked, again sounding polite, but there was an edge to her voice and an undercurrent of hostility in her question.

Before I could answer, Mrs. Prescott continued to talk. "You're right Alexandra, this is a lovely party, and hopefully it will not be in tomorrow's news for any reason?"

I was tongue-tied and didn't know how to answer her rude question? It dawned on me that no matter how much I tried to make her like me, it was a fruitless effort. I was depressed to realize that Stephanie Prescott would never approve of me for her son.

Richard Prescott, James grandfather, saved me from my unhappy thoughts as he interrupted our conversation and rescued me, taking me away from Mrs. Prescott. He was a tall man, suave and elegant in a suit, with pushed-back silver hair, intense green eyes, and a strong jaw. The resemblance to James and his father, Michael Prescott was obvious and striking. Even in his seventies, Richard Prescott was a handsome, vibrant and energetic man.

"Well, aren't you a lovely sight for these old eyes!" he said warmly, grabbing me and twirling me around.

"Thank you Mr. Prescott, but there is nothing old about you," I said laughing as he placed me back on the ground. "Congratulations on your anniversary!"

"Please call me Richard or grandpa, no Mr. Prescott, ok? It makes me sound like my stuffy up-tight son the conductor," he said wrinkling his nose with laughter.

"Ok, it's a deal." I said delighted by his humor. "Where is your better-half?"

"Elizabeth will be excited to see you. She is here someplace, chatting with god knows who, but you'll find her eventually," he said with a warm chuckle.

"Thanks grandpa Richard," I said kissing him affectionately on the cheek and excusing myself to go find James and Elizabeth.

As I made my away across the lawn, I heard someone call my name and I turned to see Rachel Prescott coming toward me with what looked to be her date.

"Alex! Alex!" Rachel shouted over the music. When she reached me she gave me a huge bear hug. "It's so good to see you, it's been forever!"

I was delighted by the enormity of her warmhearted greeting, especially after the less than cordial greeting from her mother.

"I know, how have you been?" I asked returning her hug.

"Really good. Can you believe that I'll be entering my last year of graduate school?"

"Already? Wow…that seems fast. What is your focus?"

"It's a Master of Music in Contemporary Performance Careers," Rachel replied enthusiastically.

"What exactly does that mean?"

"It allows you to hone your concert performance skills while at the same time studying the music business, technology and production end of things. I also have a sub-specialization in jazz studies."

"Cool, maybe you and James will collaborate on a project one day."

"I would love that." Rachel replied and then she turned excitedly to her date. "Alex, I would like to introduce you to my boyfriend. This is Timothy Diamond," she said beaming at him with obvious affection. "Tim is studying medicine at Harvard," she added proudly.

I had never seen Rachel look this smitten about a guy before. It was nice to see her so happy. She almost looked giddy which was not a description that came to my mind easily when I thought about the Prescott family.

"Tim, this is the *one and only* Alexandra Brown in the flesh!" Rachel exclaimed brightly.

His mouth was hanging open and he was staring at me with puppy dog eyes. "Wow! Ms. Brown...I'm a big, big fan! I can't believe I'm actually talking to you in-person!"

I smiled and shook his hand. "It's nice to meet you Tim. Please call me Alex."

Tim was handsome in a bookish sort of way. He was tall with jet-black hair and he sported back tortoise framed glasses that gave him a geek chic look.

"T-thank you," he stammered politely, blushing a deep shade of red.

I raised my eyebrow in surprise. His admiration was cute, but a little dorky. "What year of medical school are you in?"

"My second," he answered nervously.

"Do you know what you want to specialize in?"

"No, not yet, but next year I'll start clinical rotations. I'm hoping it will give me a better idea of what I want to pursue."

"Yeah, I remember. My brother Peter graduated Medical School last year and just started his residency."

"Where? What is he specializing in?" Tim asked with interest seeming to forget his earlier nervousness.

"Peter graduated from Stanford and is now doing his general surgery residency at UCLA," I replied proudly whenever I thought of my intelligent big brother.

"Nice! That's a great training program. If I decide on a surgical track, do you think your brother would be willing to talk to me about it?" Tim asked.

"I'm sure he would be happy too," I said warmly. "Have either of you seen James? I think I've *lost* him?"

Rachel pointed toward the bar. "He's over there!"

My eyes were immediately drawn to him. James was leaning casually against the bar talking to an elderly couple. He was wearing a Dior black suit and white linen shirt that fit his toned body like a glove. As usual, his hair was tousled and he looked absurdly handsome. I sighed and wondered if there would ever be a time when

I would feel adequate in his company? I saw the hint of a smile on his perfect features as he talked intently to the couple. He glanced in my direction and stilled when he saw me. I was pleased by his admiring assessment as I saw his eyes travel over me. His face broke out into a brilliant grin and I saw him excuse himself as he gracefully walked toward me.

"You look dazzling!" he said giving me a passionate kiss on the lips.

When James released me, it took me a few minutes to gain my composure. I half listened as he hugged his sister and chatted with an awe-struck Tim. Tim asked us about what it was like being a "movie star?" After we answered him, he eagerly followed up, bombarding us with several more questions about other famous actors and directors that we knew in Hollywood? It was tiresome in the beginning, but after awhile Tim got over his initial anxiety of talking to us, and I found myself enjoying Rachel and Tim's company. They were warm, wry, and intelligent, and we all got along well, discussing a range of topics from travel to politics.

The orchestra started to play a waltz. "May I have this dance?" James whispered to me. I nodded and he took my hand. "Excuse us," James said to Rachel and Tim, "but I'm going to dance with my lady now."

I followed him to the dance floor. James put his hands on my waist and I put my hands on his shoulders and soon we were twirling around the dance floor. We were really enjoying the moment. James was a good dancer, strong and confident, and he led me around the floor gracefully as we waltzed, tangoed, and shimmied to one cool tune after another. Finally the music slowed, and he pulled me into him as I put my head on his chest. He wrapped his arms around me and we swayed slowly and contently to soft jazz music.

We let go of our intimate embrace when dinner was announced. The night was surpassing all my expectations, and I was truly happy. We sat with Rachel and Tim, and two other young couples. Conversation flowed easily, and it was turning out to be a really fun evening. The trepidation I had about his parents was quickly forgotten as I let myself forget it and enjoy the party. It was the most relaxed and loving that James and I had been with each other in a very long time, and I was hopeful that the worst was behind us. The future looked bright and promising.

After dinner, everyone toasted Elizabeth and Richard, and a giant 50th Anniversary cake was rolled onto the dance floor, which the happy couple cut, similar to the traditional cutting of a wedding cake. Elizabeth and Richard asked James to come up to the dance floor to sing their favorite Frank Sinatra song, "Fly Me to the Moon." The orchestra played in the background, while James crooned their beloved song with his deep, melodic voice. It was captivating and amazing to watch.

After the solo, Rachel got up from our table to dance with her grandfather, while James danced with his grandmother. It was beautiful to observe, but soon the floor was crowded with other guests dancing that I lost sight of them. I excused myself from the table and made my way down to the gazebo on the far end of the property to enjoy a moment of fresh air and privacy. The view from the gazebo of Casco Bay and the Gulf of Maine was breathtaking under the dark skies and twinkling lights.

I thought I was alone until I heard James father, Michael Prescott's voice. "It's beautiful tonight. Isn't it?"

"That it is, sir."

"Are you having a good time tonight Alexandra?"

"Very much so. It's a beautiful party," I commented with pleasure. "Your parents are inspirational. They seem so much in love, even after all this time."

"Yes, they make it look simple," he said dryly. "But it's rarely ever simple Alexandra."

His words were left hanging between us. *Shit.* I knew a lecture was coming.

"I know that you think that Mrs. Prescott and I don't like you, but that isn't the case," he said his tone serious.

"Isn't it?" I accused unable to hide the hurt from my voice.

"Of course we like you. What isn't there to like? You're talented, kind, intelligent and clearly in love with our son. It's not that we don't like you, we dislike what you represent."

"Which is?" I prodded.

"I know my son," he said his voice thick with emotion. "I know he has a commanding presence, and because of it, one can jump to the false conclusion that he is made of steel, and that nothing can hurt him, but that assumption would be incorrect."

"I'm not sure I'm following you, sir?" I asked bewildered. I was unclear as to the point he was trying to make.

"James *is* a very private man. I know that the scandal last year wasn't your fault, because James confided in me, but that doesn't negate the fact, that he was humiliated in front of the world. The attention that each of you receive individually is bad enough, but put the two of you together, and it's obsessive, almost terrifying how fascinated people are with the status of your relationship and this idea of *true love* which you guys embody. The public and media cannot seem to get enough. It is relentless and I don't see an end in sight."

"What are you trying to say Mr. Prescott? Please just spit it out?" I asked projecting a confidence that I didn't truly feel. I feared Michael Prescott's next words.

"You are both still young, but there is a time when you both will grow up and reality will set in, and the fantasy will end," he said coldly.

"What fantasy is that?" I asked unable to hide my bitterness at the hardness I heard in his voice.

"There is no way that your relationship can possibly sustain itself," he said without emotion, his face impassive. "My son will not be able to live in this fishbowl forever, and if you stay together, that's the life you'll lead. You will never truly have freedom together. You will have to be surrounded by bodyguards. Is that the family life you envision for the future? At least if you have separate lives, and you select mates wisely outside the public eye, eventually the fascination will diminish and you can have a crack at normalcy."

In my gut, I knew that some of what he said was truthful and it hurt acutely to hear it verbalized, more so than I ever could have imagined. I turned my back on him and a tear ran down my cheek. I wiped it away quickly trying to show some semblance of dignity before I turned around and responded. I wasn't going to show this man how deeply his words had affected me.

"That's enough Michael!" scolded his mother with authority. "Your wife is looking for you, so why don't you go back to the party now. If anyone is looking for us, please let them know that Alex and I are together and that we will join the party shortly."

"Ok mother," he acquiesced and I heard his footsteps retreat up the path until we were alone. I felt her hand on my shoulder and I turned around to gaze into the compassionate eyes of Elizabeth Prescott, James grandmother. She saw my tear stained face and handed me her handkerchief.

Elizabeth Prescott was a lovely lady and I knew that James loved her very much and I could see why. She was smart, shrewd, and feisty, with a sharp mind, and a keen wit. Although older, you could still see glimpses of her natural beauty. She had been considered a great beauty for her time, but the beauty extended far beyond her exterior. She was warm and loving, and kind and generous, it was easy to see why Richard Prescott had fallen madly in love with her.

"I hope you're not going to let my pompous, self-righteous son ruin your evening? I've never seen two people more in love or well suited for each other than you and my grandson. What does Michael possibly know about love anyway?" Elizabeth declared with brazen indignation.

I cleared my throat and gave Elizabeth a small smile. "I appreciate you trying to cheer me up, but I'm ok," I lied.

"I don't believe you," she said gently.

"It's just painful to hear the truth," I admitted, sounding hoarse, my voice shaky.

"What truth? It's a guess. Don't listen to naysayers, like Michael. He doesn't know. None of us can predict the future," Elizabeth said with conviction.

"I hope you're right," I said trying to sound more positive than I felt, because I didn't want Elizabeth to worry. This was her evening and she should go back to the party and celebrate. I blew my nose and wiped away the last of my tears. "Um, Elizabeth, before we go back to the party…" I cleared my throat. "Promise me that you won't tell James about this? He's gotten closer with his parents again, especially since the *Vivaldi* role, and if he knew, well, it would set back relations and he would be hurt and angry."

"For good reason," she huffed.

"Please Elizabeth…"

"Fine. But on the condition that you also make me a promise?" Elizabeth said shrewdly raising her eyebrow at me. "I feel like you've given me the brush off and that your answers have been what you think I want to hear. You don't have to tell me if I'm right or wrong, but I don't want you to brood about this when you're alone later. Promise me that you will not listen to Michael and that when it comes to *matters of the heart*, that you follow *only* your heart and gut, and nothing else. Do you understand?"

"Yeah, I understand. Do we have a deal?"

"Alright," she sighed and gave me a motherly hug, which was almost my undoing. But I quickly masked it, and pushed any negative thoughts to the background. Tonight was about a celebration, and nothing else.

Elizabeth and I walked companionably back to the party. We found James and we chatted and laughed together late into the evening under the warm glow of melting candles. Soon the rest of his family joined us, and I listened as they recounted funny heartwarming stories. I was spent from the emotional conversation with Michael Prescott and I felt sleepy. I rested my head against James shoulder, and must have dozed, because I suddenly felt James carrying me in his arms.

I opened my heavy lids. "Put me down," I protested, but it came out as a soft whisper.

"Shh," James whispered, kissing the top of my head. He carried me to our room, and tenderly undressed me, putting me under the cool sheets where I fell into a sound sleep.

## Chapter 22: Another Party, Another Fight

Like all vacations, the trip to Maine went by too fast; as did the rest of the summer, and before we knew it James and I were thrown back into a promotional circus as we embarked on the highly anticipated global tour for the final *Galaxy Drifters* film. When we returned from the dizzying array of international cities, our schedules were packed full with a worldwide press junket in Los Angeles followed by national press and talk shows, then the premier tour in LA, London, Madrid, and Berlin. In the closing days leading to the release, I was nervous as we waited with high expectations for the results of the final film in the franchise.

*Galaxy Drifters 6* did not disappoint and the final installment continued its box office reign drawing in massive audiences and taking in a whopping $348.9 million in global ticket sales during its debut weekend, making it the franchise's best opening worldwide. It was projected that the final film would bring in a total of $800 million. When all was said and done, and the ticket, soundtrack, DVD, video game, and merchandise sales were calculated, the *Galaxy Drifters* franchise was worth an estimated $5 billion.

Due to the phenomenal success of the *Galaxy Drifters* films as well as *The Adventures of Tarzan & Jane,* and various other films, modeling, and paid endorsements, I had become a wealthy young woman and I now topped the list of highest paid actresses.

James had an impressive net worth of his own and together we were named as one of the world's highest grossing celebrity couples. *Galaxy Drifters* had catapulted us to fame, fortune, and superstardom.

Saying goodbye to *Galaxy Drifters*, the character of Amanda Blake, and the much-loved cast and crew had been a very emotional event for me, more than I had anticipated, and I was sad to see it conclude. It had been an extraordinary experience one that had altered my life forever and I would sorely miss it. However, I didn't have time to ponder the loss of it, nor did James, as we were kept very busy reviewing scripts for potential new projects and fielding a number of new offers.

With stardom, came popularity. We were invited to exclusive A-list parties and the hottest events from some of the most interesting and glamorous people from around the world including celebrities, politicians, world-class athletes and CEO's. We were sought after and adored. People we hardly knew schmoozed, flirted, and lied for the chance to meet us. It was a plethora of leeches. They had an image of us and they wanted to ride that crest of success with us. It didn't matter to these people that they didn't know us. What mattered to them was being seen with us.

In addition to the lavish parties, and trendiest events, we were offered an array of social spoils and celebrity endorsements. It became commonplace for a designer or company to send us luxury gifts in the hopes that we would wear it or promote it.

It was against this backdrop, that we happily accepted an invitation from actual friends. Ben and Sue Avery were throwing a lavish 20th anniversary party at their Bel-Air Mansion. I was excited, because I knew Audrey and Mark would be there as well as a few other mutual friends. I was also looking forward to it, because I loved Ben, he was a dear friend and father figure who I looked up too. I liked his wife Sue very much and it was nice to see them celebrating twenty years together which for Hollywood standards was huge.

I had visited Ben's house on numerous occasions, but it was usually during the daytime for work, thus seeing it at nighttime gave it an entirely different look. An enormous brick driveway led to the grand front entrance comprised of formal gardens, a fountain, and four garage doors. Their home was a gorgeous ivy-covered brick two-story that sat on a hill and conjured up all kinds of romantic imagery for me. I recalled the first time that I had been there to audition for the part of Amanda Blake, and how nervous I had been to meet him.

The inside of The Avery's house and grounds were as magical and beautiful as the exterior. As we walked through the grand house, James and I peeked into the lovely atrium where we had filmed our first love scene together during his audition. I still blushed at the memory of our heated kiss and falling off the couch in front of the camera crew.

The party was in full swing indoors and outdoors and I recognized a lot of familiar faces. We were on the patio having drinks and snacks with Audrey and Mark, and it was like a mini-reunion seeing so many people that we had worked with in the industry.

"Have you accepted any new roles yet?" Audrey asked.

"No, nothing yet, but I'm looking at a lot of scripts and I have a meeting with Tom and Lydia next week to discuss it," I replied. "Same with James. I think he is weighing his options at this point."

"Isn't that right James," I called over to him trying to hide my amusement as Ben showed James and Mark his new set of golf clubs. All three of them were handling the clubs and talking about them excitedly.

"I see the smirk ladies. Don't tell me that you don't behave the same way when you talk about clothes, shoes and jewelry," James replied rolling his eyes and coming over to me to put his hand lightly on my shoulder. "Could you repeat the question?"

Before I could respond George Wally, the famous director and his much younger date interrupted us.

"Twenty-years Ben, eh? Congratulations!" George Wally shouted.

"Thanks," Ben said coming over to where James stood behind my chair with George Wally and his date.

"I don't believe I've met your date? Hello, I'm Ben Avery," he said to the woman.

"I'm sorry, this is Olga Pavlos," George boomed.

"Pleased to meet you Ben," Olga purred embracing Ben's hand.

I noticed her eyes roamed over to our group and then stopped with James.

"James!" Olga murmured, removing her hand from Ben and giving James a lingering hug.

If James seemed a little surprised or embarrassed from her overly warm greeting, he didn't show it. *How did he know her?*

"Olga, so good to see you," James replied smoothly. "Let me introduce you and Mr. Wally to the rest of the group. You've met

Ben already, and over there with the golf club is the actor Mark Andrews.

"Hey!" Mark acknowledged with a hand wave.

James pointed to Audrey next. "This is the lovely and talented actress, Audrey Hampton, and she also happens to be Mark's girlfriend."

"Hello," Audrey greeted from across the patio, not getting up from her chair.

"And last, but certainly not least, this is the beautiful and gifted actress who also happens to be the love of my life, Alexandra Brown," James murmured proudly.

"It's nice to meet you," I said getting up from my chair to stand next to James where I shook hands with George Wally and then Olga Pavlos. "Olga, how do you know James?"

"We modeled together years ago, and I used to have the biggest crush on him," she said laughing with a slight edge to her voice.

There was something in the sound of her voice and in the aggressive way that she looked and admired James that irritated me, but I couldn't put my finger on what it was exactly. I frowned and realized that I was probably overreacting, because I was jealous. I seriously needed to get over it.

I shook my head and turned to George Wally. "Mr. Wally, I'm a huge fan of your work," I said admiringly.

"Thank you Alex and I would like to return the complement as I'm a fan of yours as well. I think you are an exceptional young actress and maybe we will have the good fortune to work together down the line." George said kindly.

Then George turned to the rest of the group, and he proceeded to complement everyone on their work in *Galaxy Drifters*. I listened with half an ear as I heard George and Ben discuss upcoming projects, but I was more intent on trying to listen to Olga, who kept trying to engage James in conversation. I caught her staring at me and I had the uncomfortable feeling that she was checking me out so I did the same with her. I could see why Olga Pavlos was a model. She was tall and slim with long, dark hair, big almond-shaped eyes, and exotic beauty. What I couldn't understand was why she was with a man more than double her age? I knew that George Wally was known as a creative and outspoken genius, and I'm sure that he was fascinating to be around, but still the age gap was enormous. I wondered if she truly cared for him or if she was with him for his prestige and connections? The way she kept looking at James, made it disturbingly clear to me that it was the latter. This woman was *trouble*.

I forgot about Olga Pavlos and decided to enjoy the evening. It was a fun party filled with people and former colleagues that we hadn't seen in ages. We danced and socialized for hours and I was on my fourth Sangria when we were asked to toast the happy couple and then the cake was cut. After that some guests went swimming, while others went in the hot tub.

"Come on let's go in the hot tub?" Mark bellowed to James, Audrey and me.

"No way, I don't have my swim suit," I protested with laughter.

"Alex is a chicken! Bock! Bock! Bock! Begowwwwk!" joked Mark. "Go in with your bra and underwear. It's not like we've never seen it before?"

"No thanks, but you children have fun," I teased leaving a giggling Mark, Audrey and James behind. "I'm going to grab coffee, I'll catch up with you guys later."

Inside the Atrium, was a vast buffet filled with scrumptious desserts and a lovely tiffany box designed anniversary cake. I avoided it, instead making my way to the coffee bar in preparation for the drive home. It was getting late, and I thought that James had too much to drink, so I would probably be the designated driver for the evening. While at the coffee bar, I ran into a very happy and tipsy Sue Avery.

"Are you having a good time?" she asked cheerfully.

"It's been a wonderful night and I'm so happy for you and Ben. We were recently at James grandparent's 50th anniversary and I was struck by their love and adoration for each other. They looked so truly happy together. Well, you and Ben also make it look that way," I said genuinely.

"You are very sweet to say that Alex," she exclaimed, patting me on the back.

"The house looks wonderful. Did you do something different since the last time I was here?"

"We made some changes upstairs and have a new master bath and balcony off the master bedroom. Do you want to see it Alex?" Sue said eagerly grasping my hand and leading me up the stairs.

The new master bath was spacious and beautiful. It felt like a vacation retreat with an extra large glass shower, a sunken bathtub, vaulted ceilings and hand-made marble tiles on the floors. However, what really made it outstanding were the floor-to-ceiling windows and the expansive balcony that extended from the bedroom to the bath with staggering, unobstructed city to ocean views.

We stepped on the balcony as Sue told me about the architect and designer responsible for the new addition. It was a very beautiful and serene night and we sat together chatting, listening to the sound of the muted voices from the party below. It was getting late, and I noticed that the crowd had thinned out, with only a few guests still remaining.

"I should probably find James, as it's getting late, but before I leave, may I take a look through the telescope?" I asked gesturing toward it.

"Of course, the view is amazing with it," replied Sue.

Sue was right the view was breathtaking. With the telescope I could see a commanding view of downtown Los Angeles, Santa Monica, the Pacific Ocean, and Catalina Island. I was about to go, when I decided to scan the crowd to see if I could find James, and I got the unexpected shock of my life. I could not believe what I was seeing? I had to do a double take and catch my breath as a flood of emotion washed over me. I shut my eyes and willed myself to calm down. James was holding a towel out to a dripping wet Olga who was half naked wearing nothing but a bikini bottom. She took the towel and wrapped it around her head, like a turban. Obviously she wasn't modest as she exposed her naked breasts and I watched with mounting horror as she kissed James fully on the lips in a passionate embrace.

"Fuck." I swallowed and bit my lip. "I need to leave," I said, my voice shaky.

*Oh no...*I felt like I was going to cry...Instead I squeezed my eyes shut resisting the urge to fall apart. *Get it under control Alex.*

As I stalked down the steps and through the house to find James, my sadness quickly turned to anger, and suddenly I was furious. I didn't have to look for long as I saw James coming toward me.

"We're leaving," he hissed, sounding angry.

"Correction, I'm leaving. You can find your own way home!" I snapped back at him angrily.

"What's your problem?" he yelled.

"It's not me with the problem as I wasn't the one lip locking a half naked woman five minutes ago!" I yelled and stormed out of the room, quickly making my way to the car.

"Will you wait?" I heard James shout, but it was too late. I quickly got in the car, started the ignition and pressed my foot firmly on the gas. I skidded out of there like a bat out of hell.

I was out of control and driving way to fast. My heart beat wildly as I pressed my foot firmer on the gas pedal and increased the volume on the radio. I knew I was driving like a maniac, and that it was totally reckless, but at that moment I didn't care. I saw something move, and I swerved at the last second to avoid it. It was dark, and I was tired, so I pulled to the side of the road to get my bearings and calm down.

I heard my phone beep and saw that I had several missed texts from James and Audrey.

I opened the texts from James first:

*Nothing happened. Will u come back here? - J*

*Where r u? -J*

*I'm going to stay at Mark and Audrey's tonight. See u tomorrow. -J*

Then I read the texts from Audrey:

*I saw the whole thing. Olga made a pass at James and he told her to go F*** herself. Don't be mad at him. -A*

*James is going to stay at our place tonight. We will drive him home tomorrow. -A*

I responded to both texts:

*Ok.*

After I read James and Audrey's messages, my anger dissipated and I felt foolish. I flushed with embarrassment as I recalled storming out of The Avery's home. I knew it had been childish and that I had been impetuous. It dawned on me that I had behaved with the same knee jerk reaction as James following the scandal. I was so hurt when James wouldn't communicate with me after the situation with Hanley and now I had acted in the same irresponsible manner. I would try to keep an open-mind and give James an opportunity in the morning to explain what happened. I owed him that. I only prayed that I didn't read about our quarrel in the news tomorrow.

The next morning I sat on my bed and quickly grabbed my laptop while scanning the headlines:

RUMORS OF FIGHT BETWEEN ALEX BROWN & JAMES PRESCOTT DURING LAVISH PARTY AT BEN AVERY'S BEL AIR MANSION! MODEL OLGA PAVLOS RUMORED TO HAVE KISSED JAMES PRESCOTT! WILD PARTY RUMORS AT DIRECTORS HOME!

On the bright side, at least there were no photos I thought glumly as I picked up the phone to call Ben and apologize.

"Ben Avery," he answered, his tone was business like.

"Ben, it's Alex. I'm really sorry … about last night," I stammered.

"Alex! Don't be silly; you're not responsible for this. Plus, I haven't had this much fun in years," he chuckled. "My teenage kids think I'm cool. There is nothing to worry about on this end … we're fine."

"That's a relief as I felt truly awful about storming out last night. And then when I read the headlines, well…I…I'm sorry again," I stuttered.

"Stop apologizing. Maybe George Wally will choose his dates more *wisely* now," Ben said, emphasizing the word *wisely*.

"Are you ok?" His voice became lower and sounded serious.

Before I could answer Ben's question, I heard the front door open, and then I heard James call my name. He entered the room and stared at me, his expression unreadable.

I gestured to James that I was on the phone. "Ben," I said, my tone anxious. "James just walked in, so I should probably go."

"Be easy on him," Ben said kindly.

"I will, bye." I said hanging up the phone.

"Before you yell at me," James said sounding nervous. "Nothing happened."

"I know," I admitted quietly.

"If you know, then why did you storm out?" he asked exasperated.

"Well, I didn't know last night, but Audrey texted me…and well…I realized," I stammered, clearing my throat. "I realized that I acted in anger…and…haste…and I should have let you explain first."

James began to pace the floor and I started to feel uneasy. He had a frown on his face and seemed far away.

"James?"

"If Audrey hadn't texted you, would you still believe that nothing happened?" he asked, his tone quiet, but serious.

I watched him pace the floor as he waited for my answer. My hands were sweaty and my mouth was dry. *Would I have believed him?* "I don't know." I answered truthfully.

"I see," he said, his tone clipped. He suddenly looked exhausted or perhaps defeated as he took a seat on the bed. "Is that the way you're going to be?" he muttered, rubbing his temples with his eyes closed.

"What does that mean?" I asked defensively.

"It means that I had to deal with that nutcase Olga pouncing on me all night, and now I have to deal with your insecurity and trust issues."

"That's not fair," I said raising my voice. "If the roles were reversed and you had seen me kissing a half naked man, I don't think you would have stayed calm, cool, and collected."

"I suppose not," he agreed.

After a long moment, he stiffened and said very quietly. "If we don't learn to trust each other again, our relationship will not survive."

My head started to pound and my heart was racing. "I know," I whispered in despair.

I couldn't stand to see us like this. What happened to make us so broken? I swore that I would learn to trust James again. I loved him and a life without him was unthinkable.

I went to him then and murmured sweet promises in his ear. We hugged and kissed and held each other tightly. Surely, this was just a bump in the road for us? We would navigate over it together...we had too.

## Chapter 23: End of a Fairytale

The following week, Lydia and I were in Tom's office to discuss new projects.

"Hey ladies," Tom said gesturing to us to come in as he talked on the phone.

"I have to go," he was saying into the phone, "but tell them no dice, unless they increase the offer substantially."

"How are my two favorite, most beautiful ladies doing?" he said hanging up the phone on his desk and getting up to greet us.

"What would your wife and daughter say?" Lydia joked with false indignation.

"Ok, I will amend that to my second favorite, most beautiful ladies," he chuckled pleasantly. Then, Tom quickly switched gears and his tone became sharp and businesslike. "So we have a lot of interesting projects to discuss, but before we get to that, I got an offer for you this morning, that we need to discuss *first*."

"You've got my attention Tom, what's up?" I said plopping down on his office couch.

He came very close to me sitting on the edge of his coffee table and looked me squarely in the eye. "Keep an open mind, ok?"

"Ok, now you've gotten my attention too," Lydia, said, taking the seat next to me.

"The studio is planning a sequel for *The Adventures of Tarzan & Jane,*" Tom said quickly, the words flying out of his mouth at torpedo speed. "They are offering you $10 million to reprise your role Alex, but I feel that I could probably get them up to $12M. The screenplay is almost complete, they are going to send it this week and I'll forward it to you for your review. Filming is tentatively scheduled to begin this March. What do you think?"

There was an awkward silence as Lydia and I took in the news about the upcoming sequel. What an unexpected *surprise*.

Lydia spoke first. "Is Hanley reprising his role as *Tarzan*?" she asked icily.

"Yes, they want the same cast and director," Tom answered. "Listen, I obviously understand the concerns. After the studio called, I had conversations with Preston Foley and Jon Hanley's agent and manager. All of them have assured me that Jon has cleaned up his act and will be a perfect gentleman on and off camera in Alex's presence. After that, I spoke with Jon directly and I read him the *riot act*, he assures me that he will be professional and respectful at all times. We all know that he's no boy scout, but he knows that he cannot afford to get out of line again. I'm not telling you what to do, but in my professional opinion, you won't have any trouble from Hanley if you decide to take on the role."

"Do you think I should take on the role?" I asked Tom and Lydia seriously.

"Well, let's examine the reason why you took it to begin with," Tom said. "We felt at that time the more commercial hits that you could make, the more likely that you would be able to establish yourself as a star that earns both critical and commercial respect. It was also an opportunity for you to be known by the general public for something other than *Galaxy Drifters*. Although you've accomplished that goal nicely so far, you never know when the well is going to dry up, so sometimes you need to strike when the iron is hot. I don't have to remind you, but I will, money and success talks, especially in this town."

"Tom, can't you just give me a yes or no without the bullshit?" I snapped.

Tom stared at me and I stared back. Then he broke the stare and ran his hand through his hair. There was a pause as he pondered my question and then he spoke strongly. "It's likely that the sequel will be a hit again, especially with the public interest in you guys since the scandal. Hanley will behave himself, or he is a dead man," Tom hissed. "So, yes, if I was you, I would do it."

"Lydia, what do you think?" I asked turning to her.

"To be honest, I'm not sure. Clearly, there are pros and cons, but ultimately only you can make the final decision," Lydia stated soberly. "You know that I will support whatever you decide to do, but James will never agree to you doing a sequel, so isn't this conversation a moot point?"

My feathers were ruffled. "It's not James's decision to make," I said quietly, but assertively.

"Isn't it?" Lydia said seriously. "Are you really going to go *toe to toe* with him over this? Does it mean that much?"

"It isn't about the movie so much…" I said, my voice trailing off. *How could I say this clearly so that they would understand?* "It's more a trust thing."

"James trusts you," Lydia murmured sweetly. "He just probably doesn't trust Hanley."

"Well, obviously he doesn't trust Hanley and it's a sore subject for me to even bring up his name," I told them honestly.

"Then why do it?" Tom interrupted.

I stared at them both. Why do it? The question reverberated in my head. Was it worth an argument with James?

I cleared my throat to speak. "I don't know if I'm going to do it," I told them truthfully. "Let me have a few day to consider it and then we can re-group next week."

"Fair enough," Tom said, "let's move on to other business…"

***

It was almost dinnertime when I arrived home, and James was outside cooking on the grill.

"How was your day?" I asked greeting him with a kiss.

"It was really good. I was in the sound studio, recording an album for almost six hours today, but we made a lot of good progress, and it's coming together nicely," James said. "How was your meeting with Tom and Lydia?"

"It was good, but long. We discussed a lot of potential projects, and there was one independent film that I would really like to do, but it doesn't have financing yet, so it's up in the air."

"Anything else of interest?" James asked, sounding mildly curious.

"There is one thing, and I do want to discuss it with you, but let me get a glass of wine first," I said trying to push the conversation about the *Tarzan & Jane* sequel off for as long as possible. "Do you want a glass?

"Sure," James replied.

I was nervous to broach the subject with him. My hands were sweaty, and I washed them under the cool water in an effort to dry them off. I knew that Hanley had been a hot button issue with us for sometime, and I was debating on how to bring up the topic without causing a confrontation.

"Here you go," I said while bringing out a bottle of wine and pouring it into our glasses. "What can I do to help?"

"Nothing, just sit and relax, while I serve," he said pleasantly.

James had grilled swordfish and asparagus and had made a spinach salad. It looked terrific, and I knew that I would ruin dinner if I brought up the sequel, so I pushed it off for as long as I could. I distracted him with stories of my brother's white rafting trip, which led to other conversations. It was a nice night, and we were finishing off the bottle of wine, when James brought up the subject again.

"What was the potential project that you wanted to discuss?" James asked.

The color drained from my face and I steeled myself with a deep breath. This was it! "Tom received a call this morning. The studio has green lit a sequel for *The Adventures of Tarzan & Jane.*"

James stilled and his body tensed. "If Hanley is in it, then you are not doing it Alex," he said sternly.

My anger flared. I did not appreciate being treated like an errant child. "I didn't ask for your permission James," I stated quietly.

Our eyes locked and we looked at each other impassively, neither of us yielding. "Why would you want to do it?" he said after a long while.

I tried to back paddle. "I...I haven't decided anything. I...I just want to have a rational discussion about it," I stammered.

"What is there possibly to discuss? Why would you even consider doing the sequel?" he asked again stiffly.

"Why wouldn't I? They want to start filming in March, and I'm available. It's practically a guaranteed commercial hit. Plus, the offer is very good."

"We don't need the money Alex and you can find another project. These arguments are weak," he said. "You're not doing it. I forbid it!"

"You *forbid* it?" I yelled. "How dare you!"

"Use any word you would like, it's not going to change my mind Alex. You are not working with that asshole again. Do you understand?" he shouted and stalked away from me.

I washed the dinner dishes methodically, thinking about the argument with James. I was brimming with anger. Who the hell did James think he was, my father? *He forbids me?* Even my dad knew better than to talk to me that way. James was usually such a rational, clear-headed, thinking man, but when it came to Jon Hanley you could *not* reason with him. I was torn. I didn't want to antagonize James, but this was my career, and my decision to make. I felt James was being totally unfair to me, but what really troubled me was his hostility. I didn't do anything wrong, and I should be able to talk to him about it without walking on eggshells.

An awkward silence developed between us for the rest of the night. A few times I opened my mouth to say something, but I was not in the mood for round two, so I remained silent. We went to bed angry at each other, and the next morning, there was a note on the bed that he went to the recording studio.

The day dragged. I busied myself with exercise and reading scripts, but it wasn't enough to distract me from my fears. I couldn't stop thinking about James and I started to panic. *Is James still angry with me? Will he forgive me? Should I call him and apologize?* But then my panic turned to anger. I did not do anything wrong and I resented his tone and bossiness with me yesterday. *Who did he think he was?* I was seriously annoyed and irritated with him and I expected an apology. My emotions warred like this throughout the day until I couldn't think straight anymore. But from somewhere deep inside, was a nagging, gnawing feeling. It shouldn't be this difficult? Why couldn't we talk about this? If I was truthful with myself, I already knew the painful answer. The truth was that James and I had *not* forgiven each other over what happened with Jon

Hanley and Julie Blaine. We loved each other, so we tried to forget it, but it was slowly ripping us apart.

Acknowledging that simple truth was somehow liberating, and for one glorious moment I felt oddly healed. But then the heartbreak came. If we couldn't get past it, and honestly trust each other again, what type of future could we possibly have together?

I heard him come into the house. He came up behind me and wrapped his arms around me. "I'm sorry about yesterday," he said softly in my ear. "I shouldn't have lost my cool like that, but you took me by surprise and I wasn't prepared."

I was relieved by his words and that he was communicating with me again. I started to relax and felt some of the tension disappear from my body. "Thank you James," I said hugging him. I was scared to ask my next question, but I needed to know. "Do you trust me James?"

He paused and my panic resurfaced. I pulled away from him, taking a step back.

"I'm trying," he admitted refusing to look up.

"So all this time, I thought you just didn't trust Hanley," I said bitterly. "You don't trust me!"

"I don't know Alex. I'm confused and I can't just give you a black and white answer, it's not that simple. Our life *is* not simple..." he said shooting me an apologetic look.

My hands were sweaty and my heart was racing. I felt like my legs had turned to rubber so I took a seat and waited for him to continue with trepidation. If only I hadn't brought up the subject of the sequel, perhaps this all could have been avoided? But I knew deep down that this was building, and that sooner or later we would have to confront it.

"I was really hurt last year by the news of your affair with Hanley, and although I understood intellectually what happened, it still eats away at me," he admitted. "I also have awful guilt about what I did to you. I see how I've undermined your self-confidence and how you look at me differently now. You are guarded and less trusting." He looked away from me and cleared his throat. "*But* if that wasn't painful enough, to have to live it so publically has been humiliating and excruciating -- I wouldn't wish it on my worse enemy!"

"What are you saying James?" I asked unable to hide the building hysteria from surfacing in my voice.

"I have never loved anyone the way I love you," he said fiercely. "But I need a break. The strain of the media attention and negative stories have been mentally draining and I'm exhausted by it."

I couldn't breath. I felt like someone had punched me in the stomach. Was he breaking up with me? "Do you want a break from me?" I whispered horrified.

"No. But something needs to change," he said coming closer and crouching down to where I sat so that we were eye level with each other. "I'm asking you to please decline the role of Jane in the sequel? I want us to take a break for awhile and to escape somewhere far, far away where there are no cameras."

I felt my breathing return to normal as I absorbed what he had said. An escape for two somewhere far away from cameras would be very good for us and it was very tempting.

He continued, "Just think about it Alex? It would be a good time for us to leave. The lease on our house will end shortly and we will be forced to move soon. We could put our stuff in storage or rent a temporary place, while we travel and enjoy life out of the public eye for a while. I think it would help us gain perspective and rebuild trust again if we could get away from the constant pressure of living under the microscope."

I didn't have to think about it. *Of course*, I would go with him. "Yes." I replied, and my voice was strong and determined as happy thoughts of exotic locales swirled in my head.

***

The conversation with Tom was not going well. I pulled the phone away from my ear for a moment to 're-charge' and gain my composure.

"I think this is a *rash* decision Alex!" I heard him say again.

"We've given it a lot of thought Tom, and we both need a break," I repeated for what seemed like the tenth time during our five-minute phone conversation.

"I'm scheduled to meet with James later this week and I guarantee you that he is going to change his mind on the time table for your break," Tom said with his usual cocky arrogance.

"Why?" I asked with curiosity.

"You'll have to wait until I meet with James, but can you just hold off on saying 'no' to the sequel, until after that?" Tom persisted.

"Come on Tom, give me something?" I cajoled.

"Ok, and you didn't hear it from me, but a film that James has been *very interested* in has been green lit and I have an offer to discuss with him. It so happens, that the timing could work out perfectly for you both so that each of you could be away on location at the same time. Then after that, if you both still want to take off, I'll be the first to say bon voyage. How does that sound?" Tom asked.

"Interesting. Ok, I'll wait until after your discussion with James before making a final decision about the sequel. How does that sound?"

"Perfect. Bye Alex," he said and I could almost imagine his self-satisfied grin as we hung up the phone.

***

I was jogging when I heard someone whistle. "Hey beautiful, want a ride?" James called as he passed by me in his sleek and sporty white Tesla Roadster.

He pulled over to the side of the road and I jogged up to his window, trying to catch my breath.

"Hey," I said while jogging in place next to his car. "How was your meeting with Tom?"

"Unexpected," he yelled from his car.

"Unexpected good or bad?" I asked.

"Good I think, but it would change our plans. Are you headed back to the house now?"

"Yup. I'll see you there!" I called over my shoulder as I started to hit my stride again. Tom predicted this one right, I thought with a smirk. Although James was a bit drained, it looked like our break from acting might be put on hold for the moment? It was ok with me, as I was looking forward to the thought of working on the sequel for *Tarzan & Jane*, especially the opportunity to work with Preston again. Although I had a few reservations of working with Jon, for the most part, they were minor qualms, thus nothing significant enough to prevent me from moving forward with it.

"Hey, I'm home." I yelled from the kitchen as I quickly drank two glasses of water in an effort to hydrate and cool off. "I'm going to take a shower and then we can talk."

After my shower, I quickly dressed and then went searching for James. I found him in his office, and he looked *pissed*.

"What's wrong?" I asked as the color drained from my face.

"This!" he shouted as he scowled at me and pointed with frustration to a headline from *Variety:* HANLEY'S TARZAN & BROWN'S JANE – TAKE 2! "I thought we agreed that you were declining the role of Jane in the sequel?"

I heard the hurt and anger in his voice and I felt bad, but thought he was making a mountain out of a molehill. "Obviously, the story is not accurate James. No contracts have been signed, but I guess news of the sequel is out." I answered shrugging my shoulders.

"Have you or have you not turned down the role?" he asked bristling with anger.

I hesitated. How had this conversation turned so unexpectedly into another confrontation where I was on the defensive again?

I answered truthfully, "I notified Tom, but he asked me to wait until after you met with him today, before I officially turned down the offer. Why is that James?"

"I see," he said in a low tone, his voice quiet. "What happens if we push off our travel plans for a few months? Will this story suddenly come true?"

"I...I don't know," I hesitated. "Do you want to change our plans?"

"I don't know," he said his voice trailing off. "Financing has finally been secured for the biographical film focusing on the life of Elvis Presley. I've been offered the role of Elvis and they want to start shooting it this spring."

"That's great, you've wanted to do the project for several years," I said enthusiastically.

"Is it?" he asked bitterly.

"What's wrong? You've been so eager for this project and now you're completely morose about it. Surely, this dark mood cannot be the result of some stupid news story?"

"I thought you had already said *no* to the role and now I find out that you didn't. So if I decide to do Elvis…Will you *DO* Hanley?" he accused rudely, his expression dark.

"You're shitting me, right?" I hissed, suddenly angry. "That was totally uncalled for, especially from the guy who *fucked* Julie Blaine, and who knows who the hell else?"

"I have *not* been with anyone else and I'm getting sick of your jealousy and paranoia. I told you what happened with Julie was a drunken mistake, and at least I remember it, you have no clue what you did or didn't do that evening with Hanley," he snarled.

I could tell he was furious, but so was I.

"Go to hell James!" I snapped.

I turned on my heel and started to leave the room, but James blocked my exit. He took my hand, practically dragging me back into the office.

"You are not leaving until we sort this out!" he yelled.

I glared at him. "Let go of my hand!" I spat.

He let go and I walked to the other end of the office. I flushed with anger and watched him from the corner of my eye as he glared back at me. Neither one of us took a step forward, as we both stood there defensively, letting time pass.

"Don't you see how unfair and contradictory you're being?" I asked unable to hide the hurt from my voice. "If I give up the role, while you're on location, what am I supposed to be doing and how is that reasonable?"

"You could come with me while I'm on location," he said gently.

"Sounds like a ton of fun, to sit around, while you're working." I said dryly with sarcasm.

"Alright. Stay here and look for new houses for us instead," he said quietly unable to look me straight in the eye. "Listen, I know that my request seems like a double standard, and it probably is. The alternative is unacceptable for me. You *cannot* do that movie!"

"Why?" I implored. "Stop using the movie as an excuse when the truth is you cannot forgive me for what happened last year. You haven't gotten past it!"

"That's not entirely true," he said defensively. "Nonetheless, don't you understand that if you do another movie with Hanley it would be like pouring salt into the wound?"

"James, the issue *is* about TRUST, it's *not* about the movie or Jon." I pleaded. "If I don't do the film, what does that say about our relationship and your ability to trust me?"

I closed my eyes and rubbed my throbbing temples. A feeling of dread overpowered me and I feared his next words before he even said them.

"Maybe that's true Alex, but if you do the movie, you kill any chance of us getting through this." James stated, his voice intense. "I will *not* standby and watch you accept the role. Do you understand what I'm saying to you? At least by declining it, you give us a chance to solve our problems."

Neither one of us said anything as I digested his ultimatum. It was time to *sink or swim*? That horrific reality swirled around my brain and I felt sick. A life without James was unthinkable. The thought tortured me. The only sensible conclusion would be to turn down the movie role...*right*?

I remained silent, still processing his words and my jumbled irrational thought patterns. How did we get here I thought sadly? Was this a bad dream? If I gave up the movie would I feel bitter toward him? He was the one who cheated on me, so why was I the one being punished again? My emotions were at war. I stood there with paralyzing indecision – I did not know what to do?

"I don't know what to say?" I whispered with tears running down my cheeks.

He recoiled as I spoke and then he took a few steps back, broadening the divide between us. I saw fear and sadness flicker across his handsome face and then it was quickly replaced with a cold hard expression.

"I think you just said it. Good bye Alex!" James said fiercely, the anguish apparent in his voice as he walked out of the room and away from me.

"Wait James!" I yelled running after him.

We were in the hallway near the front entrance and I touched his shoulder, but he shrugged me off.

"*Please* don't leave…I love you." I cried panicked.

He shook his head sadly and turned to me. His voice was heavy with emotion. "I will always love you Alex…I'm sorry…so sorry."

His voice trailed off and James covered his face with his hands. When he looked up again, the look of intense sorrow was so painful for me to see, that I had to look away.

"I thought after the trip to Maine, that we would be ok," he whispered, and I could hear his anguish. "It was like old times, but then we came back, and the incident with Olga made you so untrusting and anxious again. I caught you one day going through my messages on my phone, but you didn't see me and I didn't say anything about it. I don't think you've realized how tense you've been since the scandal? Anyway, it's been tough on both of us. Then when I heard your news about the sequel, it threw me over the edge and I'm sorry about that."

I felt sick and wanted to cover my ears like a child. It was true that I still felt raw and hurt from his unfaithfulness, and in a moment of weakness, I had become that "insecure woman" going through his personal stuff. I despised myself for it and did my best not to think about it and get past it. I thought I was doing ok? Yet the reality was that I was struggling to cope with James unfaithfulness and the constant attention from the paparazzi and other women. I tried my best to hide my mistrust, but I guess I had not fooled James. As I admitted these troubling truths to myself, I felt slightly faint and unsteady so I concentrated on breathing in and out. James started to talk again, but I couldn't process his words. I tried focusing on what he said, but my mind was blank and distracted. I kept thinking of what his dad had said to me in Maine. It was a bitter pill to swallow to realize that James father was right that a high-profile relationship like ours was unlikely to result in a happy ending. I shook my head to clear away those unhappy thoughts and tried to re-focus on what James was saying...

"It shouldn't be this complicated Alex...It's not healthy for us to continue to live this way...I'm going to stay at a hotel for the rest of the week...When I find a place to live, I'll be in touch to get my stuff..."

He took a step closer and stroked my cheek. "I'll always love you, but right now, we cannot make each other happy. I need time and space to clear my head," he said gently and then he pulled away. "Take care of yourself."

"Wait James! I won't do the movie!" I pleaded with desperation as the tears rolled unbridled down my face. "Please don't go?"

I reached out to touch him, but he shook me off. "It's too late Alex. I just can't live this way anymore. I'm sorry."

I watched him walk away, and close the door behind him. James was gone.

## Chapter 24: Wild & Depressed

My eyes were glossy and my head foggy from so much alcohol. The music was loud and I pulsated my body to the tempo while the stripper grinded her body against me while doing a lap dance. Jon was obviously 'turned on' as he hollered and hooted uncontrollably while watching us. After the dance, we staggered out of the club and back to our hotel room.

It had been 14 months since the split with James. I was currently traveling mindlessly through Australia with Jon Hanley and his friends in an effort to have fun and mend my broken heart. *My efforts were not working well.* I was restless and not feeling better. I put up a good front for everyone so that they thought I was getting better, but I wasn't, not really. I was just a very good actress who spent my days pretending that I was having a good time – *but* I was full of shit!

In the days following the split with James, I fell into a deep depression and my family and friends were profoundly worried. I tried not to think of those days, as they were simply agonizing *to* remember. After the break up, I constantly checked my phone and email messages waiting to hear from James, but I heard nothing. I composed dozens of unsent emails and regularly picked up the phone to call him, but then I would hang up knowing that somehow I had to stay strong and hold on to the last shreds of dignity that I had left. I hated weakness almost as much as I hated silence. And his silence was the worst form of torture that I had ever experienced in my life. Damn James. Damn him. The pain was so acute that sometimes I thought I could feel the hole in my heart. I was despondent, I couldn't eat, I couldn't sleep, and after a while I couldn't even cry anymore. That's when the nightmares started. The same awful dream night after night after night.

In my dream I was always desperately searching for James. It was dark and cold and he was walking down a pier, away from me. I kept moving in a trance like haze following him, but he never turned around no matter how much I screamed out his name. I didn't see the loose floorboard. My foot got caught on it and the next thing I knew I was falling, seemingly flying in air, in what felt like a continuous free fall. Then I hit the icy cold, pitch-black water. I couldn't swim, I couldn't move, I froze, feeling my throat close and my body shut down as I drifted deeper and deeper into infinite darkness.

I would wake up screaming. The dream felt so terrifyingly real that my head would be pounding and I would be sweating. My heartbeat was erratic, almost wild, and I would fear a heart attack, but it was most likely a panic attack. I reminded myself that it was just a nightmare and I learned to breath in and out slowly in an effort to calm down. My mother insisted that I speak to a professional, and although I cringed at the thought of seeing a therapist, after weeks of sleep deprivation and overwhelming despair, I finally caved in. The doctor prescribed an antidepressant and although I was vehemently against prescription drugs because I thought they only masked the problem without fixing it, I filled the prescription anyway.

The drugs helped and I slowly settled into a routine…eat, sleep, exercise…eat, sleep, exercise. I was mechanical in my actions, and my spirits were still low, but at least I was no longer in the depths of despair.

During this period, I moved out of the house that I shared with James for almost four years, and Lydia found me a private townhouse in a gated community to rent with a two-car garage. I told her to take the Mercedes, as I knew she loved it and I couldn't stand to look at it anymore as it reminded me of him.

With each passing week, it became painfully obvious that James was not coming back and that we were done. My sorrow turned to anger and I "put the nail in the coffin" and signed the contract for *The Adventures of Tarzan & Jane 2*. Filming for the sequel began in LA in March, and while work was a good diversion, I desperately wanted to get far away from LA and all reminders of James and our life together. I counted the days anxiously until I could leave on location for Hawaii and Tunisia. I urgently needed distance and distraction.

It was during filming in Hawaii when my fling with Jon started. To be fair, he had been a perfect gentleman; it was me who made the first move. I was lonely and sad, and Jon was entertaining and amusing. I had invited myself to go out with him and members of the film crew who were going to a local bar. That night I drank a lot and when Jon and I went back to our hotel, I told him to make love to me and he did. Jon was fun and uncomplicated, and the perfect rebound to help me try to forget.

After filming wrapped up that summer, I decided to take a break from acting as I dreaded the thought of returning home. I was not ready to be back in LA, as I wanted to be far away from any reminders of my life with James. I bummed around Europe with Jon and his buddies, and then we went to New Zealand and Australia irresponsibly partying and carousing wherever we went.

I knew that my family as well as Tom and Lydia were not pleased by my actions. I was the focus of countless negative news stories and gossip, and Tom, Lydia, and Sandy in particular were concerned with my increasing party girl image and the impact that it would have on my career. I listened to all their lectures, but I carelessly ignored their advice, and continued to party on. I did not give a rat's ass what the paps printed or reported. I just didn't care anymore.

It was with a mixture of dread and longing that I planned to return home in a little over a week's time. In the morning, I was flying to Paris for a photo shoot with Marie Claire and then I would attend a fashion show later during the week. After that, I was scheduled to fly home to LA. My family was thrilled that I was finally coming home and Lydia had my schedule packed full with work meetings and social engagements that I had pushed off and ignored for months. Tom was the first on the list, followed by my publicist, accountant and so forth. I was also scheduled to meet with my therapist, Dr. Weiner, which I was not looking forward too. When I first started taking antidepressants, it was to be for a very brief period of time, but because of my travel schedule, and fear of discontinuing the drugs, I kept cancelling appointments and found excuses to extend usage. Finally, Dr. Weiner threatened to stop the prescription abruptly if we didn't come up with a plan for slowly reducing each dose in small increments. And so my current dose had been cut down to 20% the original strength. Still, I clung to it like a crutch. The rational side of me, wanted to discontinue it, but I feared going 'cold turkey' especially with the anxiety of returning home.

The airport was crowded as I walked to the gate to board my flight from Sydney to Paris the next morning. Jon was sad to see me, his, "fuck buddy," leave, but I would see him shortly at the LA première for the sequel. And if truth were told, it was the right time for me to go. Jon had been an entertaining diversion, but I did not suffer fools lightly, and I was getting sick of the 'empty' lifestyle and the endless parties, sex, booze and drugs.

***

"Darling!" I heard someone yell to me. It was Mimi Salinger, a model and 'Fashionista' who I knew, but not very well. She always attended the fashion shows in Europe and New York and loved to gossip and cling to famous people.

"Hello, how are you?" I exclaimed with false delight.

"Very good, where have you been hiding lately?" she inquired.

I knew that anything I told her would be gossiped about and shared, so I kept the conversation light and casual.

"I've been traveling. How about you?" I asked turning the topic of conversation away from me.

"I've been up to *no* good!" she smirked with a wink. "After the fashion show, are you going to the party tonight?"

"What party?" I asked.

"On board Gabriel Dumont's yacht. It's going to be great! You must come as my guest. I simply will not take no for an answer!" declared Mimi.

The next few weeks were going to be busy with work in LA and then I would have to do the promo tour for *Tarzan & Jane 2*, so it was tempting to have one last hurrah before leaving Paris in the morning. Especially when I thought about returning alone to that empty lonely townhouse in LA. I grimaced thinking about that gloomy reality and panic set in. I suddenly did not want to go back home.

"Alright. I'll join you. Is it at the Paris Yacht Marina at the *Port de Grenelle*?"

"No, no," she chuckled. "We are going to Monte Carlo darling!"

"I can't," I said with dismay. "I have to fly back to LA tomorrow."

"So miss the flight and grab one the following day. Does it really matter?" Mimi asked.

Did it really matter? My mind was blank, as I couldn't come up with a valid reason for rushing back to LA. Of course, there were lots of reasons for going home, and I had a packed schedule full of business and personal obligations that I had to deal with, but suddenly that didn't seem so important to me anymore.

"Ok, Monte Carlo, here I come!" I exclaimed happily.

The flight from Paris to Nice took less than an hour, and then Mimi had chartered a helicopter that took us to Monaco where we met her friends and boarded the yacht. It was a lavish party aboard a $65 million yacht. The owner, Gabriel Dumont, was a charming French business tycoon who had decided to dabble in films and had successfully acquired controlling shares in one of the largest independent film companies.

We slipped on boat shoes and were given a tour of the impressive yacht that included six suites, a gym and a screening room. After that, we sipped champagne and danced the night away.

"More champagne?" Mimi yelled over the loud pulsating music.

I giggled. "Sure!" guzzling it down and gyrating my hips to the music.

Several hours and drinks later, I slipped away from Mimi and her friends in search of a bathroom. My ears were buzzing from the loud music, and my head was spinning from so much alcohol. *Holy Cow...I was drunk!* My feet were wobbly as I weaved my way unsteadily through the crowd. I stumbled awkwardly and someone caught me...

"Are you having a good time Alexandra?" the handsome stranger asked keeping his arms around me to prevent me from falling.

"Very much so," I slurred. "However, I'm at a disadvantage as you obviously know my name and I do not know yours?" I flirted emboldened by all the champagne that I had consumed.

"I am Gabriel Dumont," he answered with his sexy French accent.

Gabriel Dumont was a charismatic flirt and I enjoyed his company so much that when he asked me to spend the night I said "yes."

The next morning, I woke up naked and alone in Gabriel Dumont's bed feeling sick and nauseated. My head was sore, my hands were shaky and I felt like the room was rotating. *Damn...was the boat moving?* I got off the bed and teetered over to what I thought was the bathroom, but it was a closet. I held on to the door of the closet to balance myself before changing direction to find the bathroom.

When I entered the bathroom, I looked at my reflection in the mirror. Mascara and lipstick were smudged down my face and my hair was clumped together like straw. I looked like a poster child for a bad hangover and I hung my head in shame as I recalled my lack of control from the wild night before. *Christ, why did I keep doing this?* I washed my face rigorously in an attempt to forget the evening and I slowly started to feel better. Like so many times before it, I began making excuses for my actions until I convinced myself that my behavior wasn't so bad. By the end of my shower, I had absolved myself entirely of any wrongdoing. It was a rite of passage in one's twenties to be wild and fancy free and if I wanted to get drunk every night and hook up with different men, then that was my prerogative.

I made my way up to the upper boat deck and noticed that we were indeed cruising.

"Alexandra!" Gabriel called. "I want you to meet my friends."

I walked unevenly over to Gabriel and his stylish group of friends who were playing poker, smoking weed and snorting coke -- and just about everything else (it was like a box of chocolates with just about every selection possible: cocaine, ecstasy, LSD, heroin etc.), and drinking what appeared to be Bloody Marys. After the introductions were completed, Gabriel gently pulled me onto his lap and gave me a passionate kiss.

"How are you feeling?" Gabriel asked.

"Like crap!" I exclaimed.

"You need a *Hair of the Dog*! Walter will you please get Alexandra a Bloody Mary, water, aspirin, and some crackers or toast."

"Yes sir, coming right up," replied Walter, a member of the yacht crew.

"What is a *Hair of the Dog*?" I asked Gabriel wrinkling my nose at the unappetizing image that the name conjured up.

"*Hair of the Dog* roughly translated means the best cure for what ails you is to have more of it. Drink up, darling!" he answered while trailing kisses along the arch of my neck.

"You don't really believe in that old wives tale do you?" I asked raising an eyebrow.

"Trust me, because I know it works." Gabriel countered as he continued to trail kisses from my ear down to the side of my face. "You are now partying with the *pros* Alexandra so get ready for one wild ride."

"Umm…yeah about that. I noticed that we were cruising, but I have to get back to LA."

"When?" he murmured seductively while pressing a tiny kiss to my lips.

"S-soon." I stammered unconvincingly.

My protests were feeble and lacked conviction, thus one "wild ride" on Gabriel Dumont's yacht extended into a two-week cruise along the French and Italian Riviera until I couldn't put off returning to LA any longer. Everyone was angry with me, especially Lydia and Tom for dropping my obligations. They called me "immature" and "irresponsible" and I knew that they were right and that I had to face them, thus it was time to go home.

***

"You better tell me that your *ass* is in LA, otherwise I'm hanging up the phone now," Tom hissed.

"Yeah, I'm back. I got home yesterday and had dinner with my family last night. I'm meeting with Lydia today and then I'm free to meet with you at your convenience Tom," I said sweetly trying to smooth his ruffled feathers, as I knew he was mad at me for blowing him off.

"Ok Alex, I'll expect to see you in my office Monday morning, 9 am sharp. Got it?" he growled into the phone.

"Got it, Tom." I said about to hang up.

"And I strongly recommend that you meet with Sandy soon. We have a lot of image cleaning up to do."

"Yeah Tom. I know." I conceded sweetly.

"Good, that's real good. No more partying Alex…ok?" Tom said with authority and I heard the warning in his voice.

"I know." I whispered quietly. "See you Monday."

"Glad to see you are starting to make amends," Lydia said standing in the doorway.

I looked up from my desk. "Amends is my middle name Lydia," I said dryly. "I'm ready for the firing squad, so give it your best shot!"

Lydia walked in and gave me a serious look. I knew that she had been worried about me and I could see the concern written all over her face. I did not want her concern and I certainly did not want her sympathy or a *heart to heart* talk. Dinner with my family had been bad enough; I really didn't want a pity fest with Lydia too.

"I think I'll leave the firing squad to Tom. He's so much better at it then me." she replied.

I nodded my head. "I can't argue with that!"

"How are you doing?"

"I'm fine Lydia. Truly…I'm fine," I said. "How are things with you?"

She didn't answer my question. Instead, Lydia came over and scrutinized my face. "How are you really?" she asked, her voice filled with kindness and concern.

I hesitated. I really wanted to keep it light and casual, and focused on business, but somehow I didn't think she was going to let me get away that easily. I knew I owed her something. She had been a loyal friend and manager for years, and I knew that I had been a tough client and "bad girl" for the past year.

"I have good days and bad days, but I'm slowly getting better," I said with honesty. "I know it's been a rough year to work with me and witness my shenanigans, and I'm truly sorry for putting you through that."

"Does that mean I can count on you to be responsible again?" Lydia asked.

"I'm working on it." I answered truthfully.

"What about acting? Are you ready to start work again?" Lydia prodded gently.

"Yeah, I would like to get back to work. Any interesting scripts?" I asked.

"I think that's the topic of conversation to have with Tom," Lydia said not looking me in the eye and I could tell she was troubled. "Listen Alex, I'll give you a preview of what you can expect when you talk with Tom so that you're prepared for it. You're talented so people do want to work with you again, but only if they can be assured that you are clean and sober. Your party girl reputation has tarnished your image and it didn't help when you extended your trip and blew off the MTV sketch and Vogue thing not to mention the work dinner related to the script we sent you. If you want to be treated as a serious actress, you need to show everyone that you can be reliable and counted on."

"I-I can do that," I stammered. "I've been acting since childhood, and I'm not going to throw it away Lydia-it's who I am." I said with a sudden overwhelming conviction as it dawned on me how much trouble I had caused.

"Good. I'm happy to hear you say that," Lydia said. "Before we get down to business, there was something else I wanted to discuss."

"Shoot! What's up?"

"I saw Ken and we caught up about things."

"Stop." I muttered panicked that she was about to bring up *his* name. "Please don't."

Lydia met my gaze and saw my fearful expression.

"I don't want to hear his name, not ever." I choked, my voice raw with hurt and emotion. "Do you understand?"

"Yeah," she whispered and she did not bring up the subject again.

We spent the next several hours discussing projects and strategies for rebuilding my image and it was a productive day. When Lydia left, she seemed satisfied and optimistic that we would fix my problems. It was Saturday night, and I didn't have any plans so I was feeling lonely. I asked Lydia if she wanted to go out to dinner, or do something fun, but she had a date with a "new boyfriend" who she had been dating for almost three months. I asked her why she never told me about him and she seemed embarrassed by her omission, and gave me some vague excuse that she had forgotten. However, I knew the real reason why she hadn't told me. For one, I had been a poor friend since the break up. I was so damn preoccupied with myself that I neglected Lydia and everyone else close to me. Second, Lydia treated me like a fragile flower and walked on eggshells when it came to the topic of romance. My brothers were the same way. Both Peter and Zach were "in love," but they attended the family dinner solo and did not bring up the topic of their relationships. I knew that they were trying to "protect" me and I wish I could have told Lydia, Peter, and Zach, that I was fine and wanted to meet their mates. Secretly, I was relieved, as I wasn't sure if I could "stomach" being surrounded by a bunch of adoring couples. I didn't want to be selfish, as I was glad for all of them, but I still found it hard to be surrounded by such happiness.

The minutes ticked by slowly and I was feeling restless and bored. I was half way through drinking a second bottle of Pinot when I heard the message from Audrey about a beach party at a famous actor's house in Malibu that evening. I was sitting around feeling sorry for myself, and the thought of getting out and seeing friends was very appealing. But Tom's words haunted me and I knew that I had promised to keep a low profile. On the other hand, it was Saturday night, and I was young and single, so why not go out? What was the harm in going to one party with friends?

The drive from my townhouse to Malibu usually took a half hour with no traffic, but because I had been drinking, it took a very long time. I stopped at traffic signs longer than necessary and stayed under the speed limit the entire drive. I was feeling giddy and had a big grin on my face. God, it felt great to be out! I was humming to the music and I promised myself that there was no way I was going to be front page news tonight. I was proud of myself for being so "cautious" and I arrived in Malibu in one hour and ten minutes. By this time, the alcohol "high" was diminishing and I was starting to feel guilty for driving when I was under the influence, but I pushed those negative thoughts aside as I walked through the enchanting courtyard and entered the beach house in search of Mark and Audrey.

Riley Scott hosted the star-studded beach party. He was a young hot television actor who was currently on a hit show, but I had never actually met him or viewed his work, so it was my first time going to his house. He lived in a fabulous Spanish villa on one of the best sections of sandy beach in coveted Malibu Colony. There were beautiful finishes including wide oak plank floors, terra cotta pavers and decorative tiles throughout the spacious living area that led to a lovely beachfront patio with a pool.

The party was in full swing and filled with current young Hollywood stars that I recognized, but that I didn't actually know, thus I was feeling a little out of place. I made my way up to the large rooftop viewing deck with spa tub and mood lights and lingered there as I admired the breathtaking view of the Pacific Ocean. I was stopped several times by over eager guests who hovered around me and wanted to talk or take a picture or some crap like that, but I didn't feel like faking it tonight. What I really wanted was to hang out with friends and people that I truly cared about.

I wandered aimlessly through the house hoping to find Audrey, Mark, or someone that I knew. But instead of finding my friends, I walked into one of the bedrooms, and awkwardly interrupted Riley Scott, who I recognized, with a group of people who were snorting and shooting up Heroin. They invited me to join them, but I declined and quickly moved on. I had no idea where I was going, or who I was any longer, but doing Heroin *definitely* wasn't my scene.

Although I'd banged myself around a bit, something held me back from completely going over the edge. Growing up in the industry, I'd seen a lot of shit, and it made me think twice about ever getting involved in it. On a couple of occasions, I had *drank the bong water*, but even in my darkest hours of despair, I never allowed myself to get involved in it in a dangerous way. Instinctively I knew that I had been lucky so far, but I knew that I would be lost if I continued on this destructive path for much longer.

I continued to roam around the party, but didn't see any familiar faces. I texted Audrey:

*I'm at Riley Scott's party. Where r u guys? -A*

Audrey responded:

*Hurt ankle-playing tennis today. We r not gonna make it. Sorry. -Aud*

Damn. I walked downstairs and snagged a bottle of wine and glass off the bar and headed to a private area of sandy beach to chill out and relax before driving home. I was in a contemplative mood and didn't feel like making small talk at the party with a bunch of people that I didn't know. I was sipping wine feeling sorry for myself when I was interrupted by a deep masculine voice.

"Alexandra Brown, right?" he questioned. "I'm a huge fan."

I looked around to find the source of the male voice and saw the stranger looking at me. He was seated on the sand not to far away from me, and was looking at me expectantly.

"Thanks," I replied. "And you are?"

He got up and walked to where I was sitting.

"I'm Will Jeffries. May I sit next to you?"

"Sure, you can help me drink this," I said gesturing toward the wine bottle. "Do I know you? You look familiar?"

Will Jeffries had a well-built physique, strong jaw line, bold blue eyes and was sexy as hell.

"You may have seen me in some print ads or commercials, but I promise I'm not just another pretty face."

"Oh, yeah. Prove it?"

"How would you like me to convince you?"

I winked. "I'm sure you could think of something?"

We drank numerous bottles of wine, shared a few "green" brownies, joked and flirted and I was having a good time. He didn't like to talk about his modeling career, but he did like to talk about directing which was his life long dream. I also found out he was an avid soccer and baseball player.

"I'm supposed to meet some friends at a club. Do you want to get out of here?" he asked his eyes roaming over me with undisguised longing.

Did I want to leave the party with this guy? I was torn. I kept thinking about what Tom and Lydia had said to me, but the thought of being alone was depressing and he was hot and fun. I decided that one more night of mindless fun was OK and that my straight-laced lifestyle could start on Monday.

"Yeah. Let's get out of here!" I replied giddy from all of the wine and brownies I had consumed and energized by the prospect of an exciting night ahead.

***

The shrill sound of the telephone ringing for the third time and the putrid smell of vomit penetrated my inebriated slumber. My head hurt and my throat was dry and sore. I opened my eyes and watched as the strange room came into focus. Where was I? Who kept calling me? I sat upright in bed trying to adjust my eyes and figure out the time. It was 6:10 am Sunday morning and someone was persistently trying to reach me. That's when I realized I was sitting in a pool of vomit...*gross...shit.*

I was disgusted and quickly scurried off the bed. My uncoordinated feet were wobbly and I held on to the wall in an effort to steady myself. I went into the bathroom to urinate and wash myself off. I couldn't believe my reflection. I had vomit in my hair and several hickeys on my neck. I went into the shower and started to pour the mini bottle of shampoo all over my scalp. I hoped there was enough shampoo to get the vomit out? I remembered leaving the party and going to a club with Will (or was it Bill?). We were with a group of people drinking champagne and fancy cocktails and then I remembered giggling in a cab and making out with him. From there we checked into a hotel. Which hotel? I couldn't remember. *Fuck.*

I realized with dread that I was probably recognized and photographed in the club and that it would most likely hit the news today...*damn it.* Tom, Lydia, Sandy, and my family – everyone was going to be so angry with me. This was certainly not the way to build my new clean, professional, and sober image. *Shit...why did I keep doing this?*

My phone rang again and I dashed into the room to get it.

"Hello?" I croaked, and I could hear the distinctive gravelly sound of my voice.

"Thank god you picked up!" Lydia cried. "Where are you?"

"I…I'm…uh, hold on," I stuttered grabbing a pad of paper from the desk in my hotel room and looked at the logo. "I'm in the JW Marriott in Santa Monica. What's wrong?"

"Why the hell are you there?" Lydia yelled. "Never mind, I'm just glad you're ok."

"Why wouldn't I be ok?" I asked.

"Audrey called me early this morning, because she couldn't reach you. Apparently, you were at Riley Scott's Malibu party last night?"

"Yeah, that's right Lydia. What's wrong?" I questioned trying to keep the alarm out of my voice.

"Riley died of a Heroin Overdose last night, the story broke a few hours ago and it's all over the news," Lydia answered. "Did you try any?"

"Of course not." I answered defensively.

"Good." Lydia said sounding relieved.

"Shit!"

"What's wrong?" Lydia asked.

"My car is still there and I just realized that I think I left my purse in it…" I trailed off angry with myself for being so stupid and irresponsible. "We need to get it Lydia."

"What about you? Do you need a ride home? What room are you in?" Lydia said taking charge of the situation.

"Hold on," I said as I got up and looked at the door number. Happily, no "papzz" seemed to be lurking around. Then I went over to the bed to try to wake up my snoring date, to see if he had a car nearby, but he was passed out and unmovable. Plus, I was fairly certain that we took a cab from the club to the hotel as both of us were totally wasted and couldn't drive last night. I resumed my phone conversation. "Room 610 Lydia."

"Ok. Hang tight," she said hanging up the phone.

The loud knock on the door an hour later startled me. *Wow*…Lydia had made it fast. I opened the door, and standing before me was a very *pissed off* looking Tom Hunter. He scowled at me and then quickly brushed me aside as he shut the door behind him.

"You look and smell like *shit* Alex," he fumed and then he grabbed me by the wrist dragging me into the bathroom.

"What the *hell* are you doing Tom?" I yelled.

He ignored me and forced me into the shower. I was fully dressed, but that didn't stop him from putting the cold water on and spraying me down.

"What the f*uck* Tom! Will you stop?" I screamed at the top of my lungs.

Tom shut the water off, and held me tightly. His angry face was only inches from me. "Will I stop?" Tom shouted, gnashing his teeth together. "I think you have it wrong Alex. When will you stop and grow up? Do you really want to *piss* it all away?"

I didn't answer his question. "Why are you here?" I said quietly, taking a step away from him and grabbing a towel in a wasted effort to dry off my dripping clothes.

"Lydia called me and told me what happened," he fumed. "She is getting your car in Malibu and will drop it off at your house. Come on, I'm going to drive you home now so if you want to say goodbye to your ah...*friend* and I use the term lightly, you better do it without delay."

I glared at Tom and stomped over to the bed. How could this guy have slept through Tom and I screaming at each other? He was really out of it. I put my hand on his shoulder and gently tried to shake him awake. "Will?" I said softly. *Nothing.* I shook him harder. "Will?" I said loudly. "Bill?" He made a grunting sound and rolled over, never opening his eyes.

"You don't even know his name?" Tom laughed harshly. "This is priceless."

"Let's go." I said walking swiftly to the door.

"Don't you want to leave *Prince Charming* your phone number?" His voice was mocking.

"Go to *Hell* Tom!" I said through clenched teeth opening the door and slamming it loudly behind me.

"Hey wait up!" Tom called as he caught up to me. "Wear these?" he ordered handing me a hat and sunglasses.

"Thanks." I acknowledged taking them from him and putting them on.

We stood at the elevator door not talking to each other. I was angry at the way he treated me, but at the same time, I was mortified and embarrassed by everything I had done. It was still very early for a Sunday morning and the sixth floor was quiet and deserted. We rode the elevator down to the underground parking garage and quickly made our way to Tom's car.

"Get in the car!" Tom barked.

"Would you mind lowering your voice? I have a headache." I hissed as I climbed into the soft leather seats.

"I bet you do!" he said dryly, his voice dripping with sarcasm.

There was no further conversation between us and we drove in silence back to my townhouse. When we got there, Lydia wasn't back yet with my car and purse.

"Do you have keys to get in?" Tom asked abruptly.

"We can get in through the garage. Hold on," I said climbing out of the car. I quickly entered the 4-digit PIN on the wireless keypad and the door opened.

When we entered the house, Tom quickly moved away from me and started looking for something in the kitchen.

"What are you doing?" I asked raising my voice.

Tom ignored me and started collecting the wine and alcohol from the kitchen and bar areas and poured the contents down the sink.

"You are unbelievable Tom!" I hissed. "I am not an *alcoholic* and you have crossed the line."

Tom ignored me until he poured the last bottle of alcohol down the drain. Then he started to search the other rooms for who knows what? What exactly did he think he would find?

"Have you had enough of your scavenger hunt yet?" I asked sarcastically.

"Just getting started!" he answered, his voice severe.

"Fine, knock yourself out Tom," I conceded. "I'm going to take another shower."

"Good, you stink!"

I glared at Tom, but he just ignored me. I silently cursed him and walked away.

When I got out of the shower, and dressed in clean clothes, Tom was waiting for me in the kitchen and I smelled the aroma of freshly brewed coffee. I noticed my bottle of prescription medicine on the table. He had some *nerve* evading my privacy like this.

I stomped over to the coffee pot and poured myself a hot steaming mug, and then I pulled the milk out of the refrigerator and slowly added it to the cup. I was angry, and had my back to Tom.

"Are you ignoring me Alex? That's very *mature*."

"Screw you Tom!" I stated flatly, the irritation clear in my voice. "I don't appreciate you going through my stuff and treating me like some drunk pill popping druggie out on the street."

"If you don't want to be treated like one, then stop acting like one." Tom said dryly, glaring at me from across the room.

I glared back. I opened my mouth to say something and then I stopped.

"Do you really need these?" Tom asked holding up the bottle of antidepressants.

"Not that's it's any of your business, but I will be off it shortly. I'm on my last dose."

"Good."

"I'm not an alcoholic Tom," I said quietly.

"Prove it?" he challenged.

"How would you like me to do that?" I asked mockingly.

"No alcohol for six months." His voice was stern. "If you can stick to that, then you'll gain my trust back."

"My trust too." Lydia said walking into the room and joining our conversation.

I watched Lydia put my purse and car keys down on the table. Then I saw her and Tom exchange glances. I felt like they were my parents - it frustrated me to be treated this way.

"You also need to cut down on the partying Alex," Tom said.

"And what's with the string of different men?" Lydia asked, the concern obvious in her voice.

I didn't say anything as I contemplated what they had said. I was full of conflicting emotions. I did *not* have a problem. On the other hand, I cringed at the thought of what happened last night and this morning. My life was empty and out of control. How much longer could I push the limits before causing real harm? No alcohol for *six* months. I thought about the upcoming press tour, premiere, and parties for *Tarzan & Jane 2*...it would be miserable to suffer through it without one drink. I cringed. Did I have a problem if I couldn't go without alcohol for six months? I jutted my chin out defiantly. I would show them...of course I could do it!

"Fine, no alcohol for six months. I'll prove to you both that I don't have a problem, but I better not hear complaints if I don't appear *friendly* enough with the press," I warned. "There's only so much acting I can do."

Lydia nodded. "One more thing," she plowed on. "I thought I would stay in your guest room for awhile if you don't mind?"

"I don't need a babysitter!" I nearly growled at them.

"We think you do," Tom said with authority, "at least for a little while until you prove us wrong."

"Fine Lydia, move on in." I said, feeling defeated and suddenly very tired from the conversation.

"Are we done now people?" I asked irritated.

Tom rose from his seat. "Yes, we're done for now. See you bright and early tomorrow at six sharp."

"Six?" I questioned raising my eyebrow. "Our meeting is at nine."

"I know," he smirked. "I'll meet you here first. Wear your running clothes."

I nodded as Tom grinned and then he sauntered away from me. I heard his chuckle right before the door closed.

## Chapter 25: The Road to Recovery

ALEX BROWN CLUBBING AGAIN! NEW HOTTIE KISSING ALEX BROWN AT CLUB! ALEX BROWN & WILL JEFFRIES SEEN LEAVING CLUB TOGETHER! ALEX BROWN TRIES TO HIDE AS SHE LEAVES CLUB WITH MODEL! ALEX BROWN LOOKING DRUNK & DISHEVELED AT CLUB!

I perused the headlines once more and was relieved that my car and attendance at Riley Scott's star-studded Malibu Beach party had not been discovered. I was also very lucky that my shenanigans with Will (I knew that was his name!) received very little attention as all eyes were focused on the shocking news of Riley Scott's Heroin and Alcohol Overdose. Riley was dead at twenty-four. A shiver ran down my spine as I realized that he was the same age as me. In a few months, I would celebrate my twenty-fifth birthday, but Riley never would, that thought sobered and frightened me.

The buzzer on my door broke through my reflections and I quickly got up to answer it. "You're five minutes late Tom," I said with a smirk.

"You won't be smiling for long once I'm done with you," he promised arrogantly.

"You won't even be able to keep up, old man!"

"Who was the athlete in school?" he protested. "And who is the one who has been partying and drinking like a fish for fifteen months?"

"Refresh my memory Tom, but how long has it been since you played sports in school?" I said raising my eyebrow in mock horror at him and walking out to stretch. "Hi Jeff!" I called to my bodyguard.

"Hey Alex! Hi Tom!" Jeff said. "I'll be right behind you."

"I hope we won't slow you down too much Jeff?" I said with a wink and then I took off.

"Hey, I haven't stretched yet!" complained Tom.

"Whose fault is that?" I yelled back.

It was a good, long run. Tom ran at a slower pace than me, but he was good at distance so we added a few extra loops around the UCLA campus before heading back up the steep hills on Sunset Blvd. My body felt great after the run and I was starting to feel more positive about myself, especially since I was the first one to make it back to the house.

Tom walked in as I was making coffee.

"Are you limping old man?"

"You think that little run would make me limp?"

"Well, you did stumble over that trashcan."

"Wipe the smirk off you face Alex or next time I'll make you sprint up the UCLA stadium stairs."

"Bring it on!" I challenged.

"I'll do that. Hey, do you mind if I take a shower here before I hit the road?"

"Go ahead, towels are in the closet next to the bathroom."

"Thanks, but before I hit the shower, let's try something other than coffee this morning," Tom said pulling two smoothies out of the refrigerator.

"When did you get those?" I asked.

"Lydia got them for us," he said. "To our health."

"To our health." I concurred and we clinked glasses.

***

I couldn't help but notice that Tom cleaned up well as I took a seat in his office, and waited for him to finish his phone conversation.

"Mandy, don't worry about it," Tom growled quietly on the phone. "I know I have the kids this weekend. I'm their father I think I can figure it out."

I looked up, surprised by the coldness I heard in his voice. Tom was not looking at me, so I took the opportunity to closely study his face as he continued to argue with his wife in hushed tones on the phone. He looked tired and his face was drawn. I also noted that he hadn't shaved, which was unlike him. I suddenly felt embarrassed that it had taken me so long to notice the subtle changes in him. It occurred to me that Tom looked sad and wasn't acting with his usual *joie de vivre*. I truly felt awful that I hadn't noticed before and that I had taken him away from his family this weekend to deal with my shit. I wondered what was wrong? I owed him an apology. I truly was a selfish friend.

He hung up the phone with a thud and got up from his desk and walked over to me. If I had not watched him so intently, I almost would have missed the faint expression of sorrow on his face.

"I'm sorry that you had to hear that," he said smoothly radiating his usual charm and exuding power and confidence. "Let's get down to business Alex."

Tom projected such competence that if I didn't know him better I would have been fooled. However, he couldn't hide the sadness in his eyes, at least not from me.

"Tom, before we get started," I said clearing my voice that was unexpectedly thick with emotion, "I want to thank you for everything you've done for me. I know I've been a tough client this year and I'm truly sorry. You've been more than just a great agent to me, and although I haven't shown it, I'm grateful for everything you've done for me."

He looked at me surprised and Tom Hunter was rarely surprised or caught off guard. His features softened for a moment. "You're welcome Alex," he said kindly. "I know it's been a rough year for you, but you're the not the first person in the world to go through this kind of thing. Heartbreak is universal. At least when you're young, the recovery period is usually faster and without so many complications."

"Have you experienced it?" I whispered softly.

"A few times," he admitted. "I think you should know that Mandy and I have separated."

"I'm sorry Tom," I said honestly. "Any chance of reconciliation?"

"We were in therapy for a while and that was horseshit!" he said with a grimace. "We are taking it slow, because of the children, and I'm fond of the phrase *Never Say Never*, as anything is possible, but the prospects don't look good. I think we're fucking done."

"How are the kids taking it?"

"It was very painful on everyone when I moved out," he said, the hurt clear in his voice. "I'm renting a place close by the house so that I can see my children as much as possible, but with my schedule it's been challenging and difficult on everyone."

"Is there anything I can do to help?"

Tom stared at me and unexpectedly took my hands. "Promise me that you will stop this destructive behavior and live to see your full potential?" he said intensely. "I know that your heart was broken, but don't let it break the very best things about you. You have a tremendous gift, and I know that you can be a great actress Alex, but it won't happen unless you stop this downward spiral. Don't give up?"

"I will *try* Tom," I said quietly.

"That's not good enough Alex, I want you to promise me that you *will* do it." Tom said fervently.

He continued to stare at me and I looked down at the floor as I pondered his request. I thought about the first talent agent who discovered me when I was ten years old and the countless auditions I went through before I landed my first real break. I realized that there was one thing I loved more than James and that was acting. For the last fifteen months, I had lost sight of that fact and I had almost lost myself in the process. I drew in a deep breath and squared my shoulders.

"I promise Tom," I said with determination. It was time to reclaim my destiny.

***

With a new strength of mind and a fresh attitude, I reinvented myself. The months flew by in a busy whirlwind of activity. It was like I had been a bear hibernating in a cave and I had finally woken up from a deep slumber. I got a trainer and worked out an hour a day, five days a week. Honestly, it was a crazy workout schedule, but I whipped myself into the best shape of my life and committed myself to a better lifestyle of good nutrition, healthy eating habits, and eight hours of sleep per night.

When I wasn't with my trainer, I did yoga, kickboxing, Pilates, and strength and flexibility conditioning. If that wasn't enough, I took numerous singing and dancing classes, and I even started to work with a voice and dialect coach who helped me to learn to adjust my breathing as well as project my 'actors' voice better.

My rebirth coincided with the promotional tour for *The Adventures of Tarzan & Jane 2*, so it was a good time to show the public and those in the industry the new and improved Alexandra Brown. I was prompt and polite for interviews and events to promote the film. I attended dinners with producers and executives targeting investors. I graciously followed the advice of my publicist and fashion consultants, and did my best to dazzle fans and foes alike.

Throughout the numerous dinners and events, I didn't drink; instead I sipped seltzer, after seltzer after seltzer. I did *not* miss the actual drinking, what I missed was the "high" and "temporary escape" that came from drinking. Drinking made me less inhibited. It loosened me up. I knew I was bolder and more fun when I had a few drinks. Without alcohol as a crutch, I had to "bear and grin" the unending mob of people, press, and events completely on my own.

On the other hand, it was a relief to be sober again as I couldn't believe the things that I had done during the last fifteen months of my life. It was nice to *own* my decisions again. It was like someone had pulled the blinders off and I was clearly conscious of my universe and the people in it again. Nothing escaped my observation.

I threw myself into this new lifestyle with relish. I did everything I could think of to make up for wasted time and clean up the mess that I had left behind. When I wasn't promoting the film, I made special appearances at children's hospitals, senior centers, animal shelters, and charitable events in an effort to clean up my image and generate some positive news stories.

My rebirth did not come without challenges. In those rare quiet moments, when I actually took the time to take stock of my life, it felt awfully empty. I knew that I had a loving group of family and friends, and I was fortunate enough to do work that I was passionate about and skilled at, but none of that negated the fact that I could never quite forget James and that I was lonely.

After the split, I obsessed about James compulsively and googled his name daily for even the smallest, most trivial, crumbs of information. I knew that most of the stories were probably phony and inaccurate, but that didn't stop me from fixating on a story about him and some woman and it would literally drive me mad. My imagination would come up with one unsettling image after another until finally one day I had to stop.

Still, I obsessed. Until one day I pretended that he was dead. It was easier to pretend that he was dead than to acknowledge the reality that I had pushed him away by doing the sequel to *Tarzan & Jane*. Then out of spite, I topped it off by having an affair with Jon. How could I have done something so selfish and hurtful to the only man I had ever loved? That question haunted me and I did not have a good answer for my actions. The affair was an act of stupidity and loneliness during a bad time in my life. What was harder to acknowledge was *why* I had chosen to do the film in the first place? I knew it had something to do with my occasional feelings of inadequacy. Part of me thought that I was *not* good enough for James and The Prescott's. On some level, I didn't think I was worthy of his love, so I pushed him away, rather than dealing with my insecurities and fear of abandonment. I blamed my actions on a mixture of immaturity and lack of confidence in myself.

Yet, in spite of my guilt, I did not take full responsibility for our break up. I was also very angry with James and I blamed him for leaving me alone and heartbroken. The truth was that I never understood how he could have walked away, and how I let him. I blamed it on our youth, the strain of the media attention, our lack of trust and forgiveness. Truly, I did not understand how a love so powerful and all consuming could have withered and died.

In my most insecure moments, I feared that he had been bored with me and used our problems as an excuse to escape so that he could "play the field". Those thoughts were so painful; that I found it easier to pretend that James did not exist rather than the alternatives I conjured up in my head. I mourned and grieved and did my best to move on and forget James. Without alcohol, wild nights, and unending parties to divert my attention, it made it almost impossible to entirely forget him or the nagging thoughts that ate away at me over our break up.

I threw myself deeper into work and packed my schedule so tight that it left little time for these late night introspections. On the few occasions that I slipped and thought of him, I told myself that it was water under the bridge, because it didn't change anything. James was dead to me.

***

Lydia woke me up the morning after the LA premiere for *The Adventures of Tarzan & Jane 2* with a big smile on her face.

"Read this!" she said happily throwing me a copy of the *LA Times*.

I sat up in bed and read the article: "…Alexandra Brown, 24, wowed in a figure hugging black dress. The gorgeous actress showed off her impressive physique in an ensemble that emphasized her incredible figure and toned legs as she signed autographs for adoring fans until it was time to watch the film."

"…The sequel hit the right mix of action, adventure and romance and is sure to be a box office hit with pleasing performances by its stars Jon Hanley and Alex Brown. In particular, Brown gave a strong performance elevating the character of Jane to a smart, highly capable female who gets in on the action, too."

Lydia interrupted. "All of the reviews are similarly positive to the one you're reading from the LA Times."

In a comforting gesture I crossed my fingers. "I hope the fans like it as much as the critics."

"Regardless, you should be proud of yourself for delivering a strong performance and for your hard work these past few months," Lydia praised like a mother with her child. "It's starting to pay off."

The ring of the telephone distracted us. "Do you want to get that?" Lydia asked.

"No, it's probably Jon again. He was not happy that I ducked out on him last night."

"Any regrets?" Lydia asked.

"I'm not sure. Jon got me through a difficult period of my life and for that I'll always be grateful. But it wasn't my brightest moment either."

"I guess you should call him back to have the quote-unquote *talk*?"

"Yeah. It's time." I replied feeling genuinely lighter for the first time in a very long while.

***

*The Adventures of Tarzan and Jane 2* was released worldwide on June 6th and won the box office it's opening weekend with \$68 million domestic, \$98.4 global. Reviews were generally positive from critics and fans alike, and it was considered commercially successful.

Sandy forwarded me a review with the headline: HANLEY & BROWN RETURN IN HIGH-ACTION ADVENTURE AS TARZAN & JANE! The article went on to review the movie, and there were a few sentences written about me. Sandy underlined one sentence in particular for emphasis. I found the words inspirational so I cut it out and read it whenever I needed encouragement: "…It's terrific fun to watch Brown on-screen again. She is a dynamic heroine who kick's butt in the role. After a downward spiral and a year off from acting, it looks like the young actress has turned her life around and is ready to work again. We certainly hope so as <u>she is potentially one of the best young actresses of her generation</u>."

With the success of *Tarzan and Jane* under foot, and my life falling back into order, Hollywood seemed willing to give me a second chance as long as I stayed out of trouble and out of tabloid fodder.

During this period, which I termed the 'clean up' stage of my life, my sole focus was to get my career back on track. Although milestones happened like me turning 25 years old, victoriously passing *six* months of sobriety (I was now "allowed" to have three drinks, but I kept it at two to be on the safe side), and Lydia, who I affectionately dubbed my "babysitter," moving out of my townhouse, I hardly took time to notice it at all.

In fact, these events went by in a blur, as did time in general, because I worked relentlessly round the clock reading scripts, doing interviews (which I hated), and making special appearances to prove to the world that I was ready to be a serious actress again.

## Chapter 26: The Comeback

It was on a beautiful September afternoon when I received the call from Tom about a script that I had to read. He felt it was the perfect comeback role for me and that it would illustrate my strengths as a serious actress.

I fell in love with the script and in a surprising twist of events the film director was George Wally, the creative and outspoken genius, that I had met two years earlier at The Avery's Anniversary party.

George Wally and the producers wanted me to co-star in the film, but it was not a done deal until I first met with George and the legendary actress, Madge St. Claire, who was regarded as one of the most talented actresses of all times. The role I was targeted for would play Madge St. Claire's character's daughter in the film. Our meeting was not an audition per se, but an informal *chemistry* audition to see how Madge and I would get along.

George had sent me some key scenes to review and I was invited to high tea with them at the glamorous Peninsula Hotel in Beverly Hills. Afternoon tea was served in the chic hotel's Living Room, which was a sophisticated salon, accompanied by a classical harpist.

When I arrived, I was greeted and taken to an intimate table where George and Madge were already seated.

Madge was a regal woman in her late fifties. She wore her blonde hair pulled back in a sleek chignon and had laugh lines around her eyes. She was wearing a stylish white dress and colorful scarf, and I immediately had the sense that this was a woman who was self-assured and comfortable in her own skin.

"Hello," I said warmly as I greeted them at the table.

"Ah … the lovely Alexandra. So nice to see you again," George said, taking my hand and giving it a friendly squeeze.

"Likewise, and thank you for thinking of me for the film. *Family Madness* is a fascinating story."

"That it is," George agreed. "May I introduce you to Madge St. Claire."

"Ms. St. Claire, it's an honor and a privilege to meet you," I said with genuine admiration. "I'm sure you hear this all of the time, but I'm a huge fan and great admirer of your work."

"Thank you, but please call me Madge," she said pleasantly as she delicately shook my hand.

Over tea and finger sandwiches, we chatted and got to know each other and after a few minutes together I started to relax. George was a genius, but a genius that could communicate. He came *alive* as he talked about the script and described technically and emotionally exactly what he was looking for in the relationship of the mother and daughter characters in the film. Madge was equally as impressive. She was a true artist who could play any role. I enjoyed talking with them both and I liked them immediately. They were clever, quick-witted, and well versed on so many subjects that there was never a lull in the conversation.

George got an important phone call from the studio and excused himself to take it in private. During his brief absence, Madge's sharp eyes appraised me. "Darling," she begins, "I'm not one to beat around the bush. I've read and heard some troubling things about you, and although I don't put a lot of stock into half of it, I'd like to be able to trust you. So tell me can I count on you to deliver if you play this character?"

"I know that you don't know me Madge, but you can be rest assured, that my wild party days are behind me." I said softly, but with conviction. "If I have the honor of working with you on this film, please know that I will work tirelessly on it."

"So *no* chance of a relapse?" Madge questioned.

"No. I promise you that I will *not* let you down." I said firmly.

"That's all I needed to know," Madge said kindly. Then she took a closer look at me. "Remember what doesn't kill us, makes us stronger."

"So I've been told," I responded with a smile.

"You know in my era, one could have a star-powered career and still maintain a private life. It's a lot harder today for you young actors. The only way to be successful and survive in this business is to grow a thick skin and keep your head down. Nothing goes on forever, so know that every situation, good or bad, is temporary.

I paused to let her words sink in, and then I smiled. "Thanks Madge."

George returned to the table. "What did I miss?" he asked.

"I think we've found my co-star," Madge said smiling back at me. It was the start of a beautiful friendship and an opportunity for me to take the ultimate leap and show my dramatic abilities. It was time to prove *exactly* what I could do.

\*\*\*

ST. CLAIRE & BROWN SHINE IN NEW FILM! ST. CLAIRE & BROWN, GREAT ACTORS! ST. CLAIRE & BROWN DAZZLE IN *FAMILY MADNESS*! CAN *FAMILY MADNESS* WIN ST. CLAIRE ANOTHER OCSCAR? CAN *FAMILY MADNESS* WIN ALEX BROWN AN OSCAR?

*Family Madness* was generally well regarded by critics and moviegoers and was a surprise box office success, prompting many rave reviews, and grossing over $305 million worldwide. The bittersweet story centered on the estranged relationship between a mother and daughter who is forced together to deal with the declining health and mental illness of their beloved husband and father, as he grows more unhinged.

It was the first project that I had worked on that had Oscar winning potential and where I was strongly praised. Critics described my performance with words like "captivating," "charming," and "a young woman who demonstrates maturity beyond her years" and the film was described as "beautifully acted," "delivering true emotion," and "a funny, touching, and poignant story that's relatable with its naked truth and utterly human characters, in a few words *extraordinary*." The Academy apparently agreed and *Family Madness* was nominated for 12 Academy Award nominations and both Madge and I were among the nominees for Best Actress.

When I first found out the news that I had been nominated for an Academy Award, I should have been overjoyed, but instead my *reaction* was unexpected and I momentarily slipped into a state of melancholy.

"Let's celebrate!" Lydia yelled ecstatically when she entered my house. But then she saw my tear stained face, which stopped her dead in her tracks. "What's wrong?"

I could have lied and told her that I was being overly dramatic, but I chose the truth. "When I heard the news, my initial reaction was to call James. I know it's pathetic. Who get's nominated for an academy award and of all the people in the world wants to call their ex-boyfriend? It's been almost three years ... when am I going to forget him Lydia?"

"Shhh…" Lydia said giving me a hug. "It's a natural reaction."

"No…it's pathetic. Since the split, he hasn't tried to contact me even once. Nothing. It was so easy for him to walk away…and…and it's three year's later and I'm still pining for the guy." I admitted unable to look Lydia in the eye.

"That's not entirely true," Lydia said softly.

"What?" I asked not understanding.

"While it's true that James has never contacted you directly, Ken calls and checks in with me every few months to say hello and hear how you're doing."

"Why haven't you ever told me that until now?" I asked.

"Because you get hostile and upset every time I try to bring up the topic."

"Well, that's nice that Ken checks in with you, but Ken is not James."

"Oh come on now, surely you can read between the lines."

Then, after considerable silence, she added, "Obviously James has asked Ken to do this."

"Big deal. If James really cared, he would call me directly."

"Or you would call him," Lydia stated dryly looking me squarely in the eye. "Why don't you just call him and get it over with already?"

"I have nothing to say to him." I stubbornly refused.

"You have unfinished business with James and until you reach some kind of closure, it's always going to haunt you."

"So be it. That's my problem." I said defiantly.

There was a loud knock on my door.

"That could be Tom or your family as they were planning to come over for an impromptu celebration!" Lydia declared. "I'll get it and give you a few minutes to get yourself together."

"Wait Lydia," my throat was tight as I got the words out, "please forget today's conversation and don't tell anyone."

"It's forgotten," she said, closing the door behind her.

***

Madge St. Claire and I had bonded during the filming of *Family Madness*, developing a close friendship, so it could have been awkward that we were both nominated for the same Academy Award, but it wasn't. She took me under her wing and offered me career tips. I really admired all that she had accomplished in her life and I looked up to her both professionally and personally. She had a calming affect on me and was very kind and nurturing. Madge inspired everything that I wanted to be. She was a brilliant actress, had a successful marriage, three children, and was known as a "perfectionist," who strived for authenticity while still walking to the beat of her own drummer. Madge stood for everything that I loved about acting, and she made me want to strive for *greatness*.

I ended up losing the award to Madge, but I was gracious about it and just happy to be part of such an amazing project. Madge surprised me by including me in her acceptance speech: "...I want to thank the Academy for recognizing my work in *Family Madness*, but I need to share this award with my co-star Alexandra Brown who deserves the award as much as I do. Alex worked passionately on this project and I could not have given this performance without her incredibly beautiful performance spurring me on. Thank you Alex."

*Family Madness* went on to win five Academy Awards that evening. George won the Academy Awards for Best Picture, Best Director, Best Adapted Screenplay, while Madge won her third Academy Award for Best Actress, and Daniel Weston, who played the role of my father, won for Best Supporting Actor. It had been an unbelievable experience and I was eternally grateful for it. To date, it was probably the best work experience of my adult life.

Professionally, life was about as good as it gets. I was flooded with scripts, and quickly accepted three new projects that I was excited about. I had just wrapped up work on one film, and was doing pre-production on another, when Tom sent me a script with a note: "READ THIS NOW!" I read it and fell in love with it. I loved everything about it and I wanted the role desperately. The story, *Shattered: An Ivy League Brain*, chronicled the life of "Natalie," a brilliant college woman attending Harvard who got into a car accident that left her with brain damage. Natalie was told that the damage she sustained in the accident was permanent and that she no longer had the intellectual ability necessary to finish her degree. With extensive rehabilitation and against all odds, she goes on to complete her Harvard degree, and eventually a medical degree from Stanford University becoming a successful Neuroscientist and expert in cognitive brain disorders.

It was an inspiring story with a strong female character. I knew that amazing scripts like this didn't come around often, so I lobbied hard for the role, but Tom said that they didn't think I was right for it. I wanted to prove them wrong and asked them if I could audition for it anyway. I flew to New York on a red eye during a short break in production from my current film. I dressed in Brooks Brothers, braided and colored my hair strawberry blonde, and wore glasses like the character of Natalie. I poured my sole into that audition, and after three grueling hours, I walked out knowing that I nailed it. The next day they called Tom and offered me the role.

Since my first acting role as a child, I'd always picked things up fairly quickly, and didn't need a lot of directing, but even with my fast-learning abilities and natural emotional instincts, I never could have anticipated the range and flexibility I was capable of achieving. It was with great satisfaction that I knew that I was growing and honing my skills as one of the most versatile young actresses in Hollywood.

With my Oscar nomination from *Family Madness*, I'd become a hot property again and I found myself in the position of being a very bankable Hollywood star. Professionally, I was reaching new heights, but I still yearned for *more* and I missed having a man in my life. I started to date again, but there was no one really special in my life. When I needed a date for an event, I usually asked Tom to accompany me and he didn't seem to mind. He was in the final stages of his divorce and he needed a friend as much as I did.

With Tom it was always easy and he was fun to be around. He was charming, witty, handsome, rugged, athletic, loyal, and had a mind like a steel trap. Of course, he was also ferociously competitive, tenacious, outspoken, and an egomaniac. Those traits might have made me nervous if I was meeting him for the first time in another context, such as a romantic one, but Tom was my friend and agent, so I never thought about him beyond those roles. It wasn't that I was oblivious to his charms, because of course I had noticed that he was very attractive, and from time to time I caught myself thinking about what it would be like to kiss him, or feel his arms around me, but I chalked it up to my feelings of loneliness. I missed the intimacy of a relationship, but Tom was fourteen years older than me, and he was my agent, and therefore, I considered him *off limits*.

It was during this time that I decided it was time to put some roots down and buy a house. I had always wanted to live on the beach, and originally set my sights on Malibu, but I still hadn't found the right place, so I cast my search far and wide and decided to keep looking until I discovered my dream house. It was my mom who found it.

"I know you said you wanted a beach house Alex, but remember the architect Wallace Neff's Mediterranean-influenced 'California-Style' home in the movie *The Holiday*? You know the one that you adored and drooled over?"

"No way mom! Is it for sale?" I asked unable to hide my excitement as I conjured up images of the beautiful contemporary house. "Let's go see it."

"Hold on a minute," my mom said. "If it was for sale you'd be living inside Sony Pictures Studios."

"I don't understand Mom?"

"The interiors of that house were elaborate sets built on a soundstage and the exterior of the real house is in Pasadena," she replied.

"Well, that's disappointing," I said. "Why did you bother to bring it up *then*?"

"Do you remember Betty Friedlan, my friend the real estate agent?

"No, should I?" I asked distracted, quickly losing interest in the conversation.

"Hey, stop looking at your phone and reading your messages," she scolded. "Can I have five minutes of your undivided attention?"

"Sorry mom, go ahead." I said trying to be patient until she finished talking. My mom had a tendency to go off into tangents, and a story that should be only two minutes long could easily turn into a full-length novel.

"Betty is representing a young couple, the husband is a talented 'up and coming' architect and his wife is an interior designer, and they are selling their house in Brentwood that they built three years ago. According to Betty, it is divine and was inspired by the house in that film," my mother stated proudly.

"If it's so great, why are they selling it?"

"He is becoming a partner in a top architecture firm in San Francisco, so they are moving to the Bay area. Betty said the house is going on the market next week, but that if you wanted a showing ahead of time, she could get us in."

"Ok Mom, you've peeked my interest. Let's go see it."

The gated property was everything that I had hoped for and more. When I walked in, I couldn't help, but smile. The clean design was simple with a neutral color palette and warm rich undertones that took my breath away and I immediately fell in love with it.

My mom saw my reaction, "I told you it was worth a look," she gloated.

I nodded my agreement as we walked around. The wood floors were dark-almost black, and there was a large modern sweeping staircase with a sea grass runner that led to a second floor, creating a sophisticated and contemporary elegance that was stunning, yet casual and relaxed at the same time. The home had great light, high ceilings, and a large, open floor plan with the living room, dining room, and kitchen flowing into each other. There were floor to ceiling windows and French doors throughout the space that let in plenty of natural light, and opened to a large patio overlooking the most lovely gardens, grounds, and pool that I had ever seen.

On the second floor was an exquisite master suite and sitting room with Carrara marble bathroom and walk-in closet. Off the master were an additional four bedrooms, which was more space than I needed as a single woman, but instinctively I knew it was the right place, and that I would grow into it in the future. My mom and I stood on the balcony off the master bedroom overlooking the pool and breathtaking view of the mountains. I could feel the cool breeze on my face and I had the impulse to crack open a bottle of wine and stay all day.

"Thank you Mom, the house is perfect!"

"I know dear," my mom smirked.

I made an offer that day, which was accepted, and I moved into the house two months later.

Over the next several months, I went furniture shopping with my mom, Lydia and Audrey and we had a ball decorating the place. During that time, my dad and brothers pointed out that the four-car garage was looking *pitifully* empty and that they would be *happy* to help me go shopping for new cars. We started to test-drive every make and model we could think of and my brothers convinced me to upgrade my old Audi convertible to a new special edition one. It was sleek with a black exterior, and body elements highlighted in red including red-rimmed wheels, and boy could that car go FAST! As a thank you for helping me shop, I surprised my dad and brothers with shiny new sports cars for all of them and a Mercedes sedan for my mom.

Next I turned my attention to dressing more fashionably while still reflecting my personality. I'd always been comfortable dressing down in jeans and a t-shirt, or in yoga pants and a tank top, and while I still preferred simple, I was learning that simple could look amazing! I let my fashion choices showcase my more mature and eclectic personality and I took the fashion world by storm with stylishly confident, edgy, and chic looks.

I was living the high life and overall I was happy, as happy as one can be when they are single and unattached. After years of grieving over James, and countless rebounds, I was ready for a man. The question was who and when?

## Chapter 27: Clear Green Eyes

"You have to come!" Audrey declared over lunch. "It's not a proper reunion if you're not there."

Audrey had been coaxing and cajoling me for the better half of an hour about me attending a casual get together with some of the cast and crew of *Galaxy Drifters* at Cecconi's in West Hollywood, a classic Italian restaurant that we all used to dine in. The get together was scheduled on a Thursday night, the following month, in the semi-private Butterfly Room adjacent to the restaurant's main dining area. The informal reunion was just a few days before I flew out to Boston to film *Shattered: An Ivy League Brain.*

"I repeat for the tenth and final time...will James be there?" I asked with growing fatigue.

"And for the tenth and final time...I don't know!" Lydia replied haughtily.

"I'm sorry Audrey, but if he's there, I cannot come." I regrettably replied.

"It's been like almost four years, can't you guys be in the same room together and act civil to one another?" she questioned.

"I don't know," I retorted. "But do you honestly think I want my first run in with him to be so public?"

"I'm surprised that you've avoided it for so long especially because you guys ..."

"What?" I questioned sharply.

"Um...never mind." She shrugged. "Well, don't you think it's time to grow up and act like mature adults *already*?"

"You think it's immature of me to want to avoid a public *debacle*?"

"Of course not," Audrey quickly said. "I know how private you and James are. It's just really awkward for everyone involved. We want you both to be there, but we do understand that's it would be incredibly uncomfortable for you guy's to be in the same room together and have to brave a front for everyone. I just wish things were different..."

"I know," I said quietly. "But it's not."

"I'll ask Mark to call James to see if he is going to attend," Audrey replied. "If James doesn't go, will you promise me that you'll come?"

"Yes," I promised. "If James isn't going to attend, there is no reason that we should both miss out on seeing our friends and co-stars."

***

I arrived at Cecconi's through a private entrance and was eager to see my friends. Audrey told me that Ben and Sue Avery, Mark, Sean, Ellie, Owen Stevenson, Sally Clark, Andrew Mitchell, Kelly Wayland, and Jonathan Banks and his wife were all planning to attend. Rounding out the party was Audrey and I. James was on location out of town, and would not be able to attend.

We were all planning to have cocktails first in the plant-lined patio, and then we would follow with dinner in the private area. I spotted The Avery's and The Banks' getting a drink at the bar and I joined them. Although we were in the public dining area, all the diners respected our privacy, no one came over or interfered, so I started to relax and enjoy myself.

Soon after, Audrey, Mark, and Ellie joined us, and we made our way out to the patio. I was happily chatting with my friends when Jeff, my bodyguard, came in and quickly whispered something in my ear.

"I'm sorry…what did you say Jeff?" I asked.

"The paparazzi are outside and a crowd is starting to gather."

Before Jeff could finish speaking, I heard a loud commotion from the front entrance of the restaurant and in my gut I knew that it was James. I turned to Audrey and Mark in anger. "Jesus Christ! You told me that James wasn't coming?"

"He said he wasn't!" Mark replied defensively.

"I'm sorry folks, but the paps are outside, so I'm gonna go before there's a scene." I said turning on my heel to leave before anyone could protest. What I didn't say was: *I'm a chicken shit afraid of running into my ex-boyfriend!* Because believe me…seeing James was much more threatening then a run in with the "papzz" and "looky-loos." Jeff escorted me toward the private entrance and I saw the flash of a camera, which surprised me, because taking photos of celebrities inside the restaurant was not allowed. Then I heard the hum of excited, high-pitched female voices from behind me. "It's him, that actor from *Galaxy Drifters*." "Wow!" "He's gorgeous." "I wonder who he's meeting?" "Do you think he's single?" I avoided looking back toward the animated chatter and quickly followed Jeff to the exit, but in the excitement, a waiter accidently knocked a drink down next to me and I moved to the right trying to get around it. It was in that brief instant that I saw his absurdly handsome face again. He was staring intently at me from across the room. Our eyes locked. I froze and stared back at him, absorbing every detail no matter how small or trivial. I was riveted to my spot watching him, dazed and confused, and utterly unsure of what to do next.

Jeff grabbed my hand interrupting the moment and got me out the door in record time, ushering me quickly into the waiting SUV. The cameras lurking outside were a spectacle to behold and the parking area and sidewalk were jammed with photographers and fans as we quickly sped away from the scene.

***

Seeing James at Cecconi's, although fleetingly, brought on a tidal wave of unresolved emotions – I could no longer pretend that he was dead. I wanted to forget the expression on his face when our eyes locked, but the more I tried to forget, the more it haunted me.

I waited with bated breath every time my iPhone buzzed. I was convinced it would be James, but he did not reach out to me. In the days that followed, I thought about calling him, but I never knew what I would actually say so I remained silent. Seeing James again had shook me up badly. I couldn't seem to get the moment, or the man, out of my head.

## Chapter 28: A New Romance

Alcohol and prescription drugs were once my crutches, but now I realized that I had a new crutch and his name was Tom Hunter. I couldn't pin point exactly when I realized that I had feelings for Tom, but I knew our romance had started with a soccer game.

"Dad, I got a goal! Did you see how fast I was?" Tyler yelled with excitement.

"Way to go!" Tom said to his son, giving him a *high five*.

It was Sunday afternoon, and I was with Tom and his daughter Samantha, watching his son, Tyler's soccer game. It was three days after the incident at Cecconi's (or what I referred to in my head as the "James Sighting") and I was still disturbed by it. I kept replaying the moment when I saw James again, and although the moment was brief, I blew it up into such epic proportions, that the vision appeared in slow motion and significantly longer and more dramatic in my head.

It was an ironic twist of fate, I laughed to myself, that just when I had decided that I was ready for a new man in my life, reminders of James reared their ugly head in my consciousness again. Although time had helped soften my heartache, seeing James at Cecconi's, had triggered a fresh wave of nostalgic reminders of our past together and how much I had loved and adored him.

If seeing James was the *icing on the cake*, then surely tomorrow was the *cherry on top* as I was travelling to Boston and Cambridge, both cities that I closely identified with James, to shoot my new film, *Shattered: An Ivy League Brain.* Those cities held so many memories of James and I, and his family, that every time I thought about it, my stomach would drop, the way it used to when I would go to the amusement park with my brothers and they would dare me to ride the biggest and scariest roller coaster in the park. I would hate to miss out or be called a "sissy" so I would ride it even though I had this terrible fear of roller coasters and I was sick to my stomach the entire time.

"Defense Tyler!" Tom yelled to his son pulling me away from my wandering thoughts about roller coasters, the Prescott family, fear of running into Mrs. Prescott during my shoot at Harvard University, a sea of North Face jackets, mahogany sailboats, and clear green eyes. Then Tom looked at me quizzically. "Are you ok Alex?"

"I'm fine Tom, sorry if I've been distracted today," I said as I refocused my attention back to the present soccer game. "Just thinking about last minute preparations, before I fly out tomorrow."

"Yeah, right Alex," Tom said dryly. He looked like he wanted to say something else, but then thought better of it. "By the way, have you noticed that no one seems to be in awe of your presence at the games anymore?"

I looked around and smiled. This was about the seventh or eighth game I had attended, the first few had caused quite a "stir" and I had signed lots of autographs and taken a few photos with fans, but now I sort of just blended in with all of the other spectators and "soccer moms and dads" in attendance which included a few local celebrities, doctors, lawyers, one wealthy producer, a sleazy director, a local television weatherman who was graying at the temples and a morning talk show host who recently had an eyebrow lift.

"I'm *old* news," I replied with a grin.

"No you're not Alex," Tom's daughter, Samantha said with such earnest conviction, that Tom and I just smiled at each other. "You're going to come back to the house for dinner, right?"

"I'm not sure Sam, it's getting late, and I have a lot to do," I replied honestly.

"You have to come to dinner, because I have a new dress that I want to show you and I'm not sure the next time I'll see you?"

"Are you sure it's no trouble?" I said more to Tom, then to Samantha.

"No trouble," Tom and Sam said in unison.

"Ok, it's a date!" I replied with a wink.

Since the first day I had met Tom, he was always running around like crazy, but since the divorce, he had made it a priority to be with his children, so on the weekend's he did his best to be there for them.

When I wasn't traveling to a film location or to promote my next movie, I fell into a pattern of spending time with Tom and his kids on Sundays. Occasionally, Tom or I would be dating someone new, but it never seemed to last long for either one of us, and over time it had become a sort of unspoken ritual to hang out together.

After seeing Samantha's dress, and playing five games of "Go Fish" with Tyler, the kids were finally watching a movie. Tom and I were talking outside sharing a glass of wine on his patio when it started to rain. At first it was just a few raindrops, but then a massive storm moved in pelting us with rain and wind and I could see lightning in the distance. We ran quickly through the glass door into the shelter of the kitchen, and started to laugh as we stood their drenched dripping all over his kitchen floor. Tom said that he would get me a towel and some dry clothes, but then he hesitated. That's when he suddenly took a step forward and started to kiss me. His kiss was unexpected, but when I didn't pull away, he intensified the kiss, and pushed me against the glass door until I started to kiss him back. We kissed each other for a long time until I started to shiver. I wasn't sure if I shivered, because I was cold and wet or from his expert lips?

When it was time to say goodbye, we shared one last lingering kiss, and it was a kiss filled with longing, desire, and anticipation of things to come. "Hurry back," Tom whispered in my ear.

*** 

It was a cool crisp autumn day when Lydia, Jeff, and I arrived in Boston. We checked into the Ritz-Carlton, Boston Common where the cast was staying during the movie shoot. Pre-production and cast rehearsals had started in LA a month ago, so I was already at ease with the director, Christopher Howard, and my fellow actors, and we were ready to jump right into principal photography and shooting the next morning.

*Shattered: An Ivy League Brain* was a beautiful story with a lot of compelling emotional material, an exceptionally talented group of actors and a passionate and driven director.

Because movies are often shot out of sequence, we had to shoot one incredibly emotional scene during our first week of filming. In order to make it as genuine as possible, we ended up shooting the scene for about three days until Christopher was satisfied that it was flawless. It was such a draining scene for all of us to pull off, that we had to wait about ten minutes between each individual take so that we could recover from it. Over and over again, Christopher looked at my fellow actors and I, and said "one more," although we were exhausted, we became extremely eager to squeeze out "one more" performance until it was "just right."

The last take was perfect.

I overheard Christopher say that he was "pleased with the exposed vulnerability that I brought to the role of Natalie and the rawness of the last shot" and I was absolutely positive that it would be the shot used in the final cut.

*Family Madness* had been an unbelievable experience and sometimes I questioned whether I would ever find another project comparable. I knew that it was very rare to find a really amazing script with a remarkable director and cast, and I was grateful, because I knew that *Shattered: An Ivy League Brain* was another gem. I worked day and night to deliver incredibly honest, dramatically moving, and physical scenes. I thought it was my best performance to date.

The shoot was so emotionally and physically exhausting that I underestimated just how much the whole week would take from me, and the second week was a carbon copy of the first. Although I felt completely exhausted, it was a wonderful sort of exhaustion as I felt like we had really achieved something brilliant with each progressive shot.

The emotional material in the film sparked something deep within me and I found myself in a contemplative frame of mind. Before I could consider starting a romance with Tom, I first needed to close the door once and for all on my long-dormant emotions about James. I could think of no better place to do that, then a day revisiting my past. It was in this mood and spirit that I prepared for my journey to Portland, Maine the next weekend.

"Lydia, could you do me a favor and rent an extra car in your name for me next weekend?"

"What's wrong with the car we have?" Lydia questioned.

"Nothing, but you and Jeff will need one car, and when I have a break from shooting, there is someplace that I need to go by myself which will require the second car," I said. "I don't want to be rude, but I don't want company when I do it."

Lydia examined me closely, concern clear on her face. "If you go to a public venue Alex, I don't think it's wise for you to go off on your own without a bodyguard."

"I'll be fine Lydia," I said, the sound of my voice defensive. "I'll be gone for a few hours, please don't be concerned," I said, working to soften my tone.

Lydia nodded, frowning. "Are you sure you don't want company?"

I smiled, but nodded *no*. "Thank you, but this is something that I need to do solo."

***

The drive from Boston to Portland took under two hours. With each passing mile, I started to feel foolish and considered turning around. I was nervous that someone would recognize me, so I did my best to dress inconspicuous in loose clothes that hid my figure. My hair was strawberry blonde for the role of Natalie, and I wore it pulled back into a ponytail with a baseball cap and big sunglasses.

My journey began at the Portland Yacht Club, but I never got out of my car. I was tempted a few times to walk over to the marina to see if I could find the Prescott's motorboat. Instead, I stayed seated in my parked car and contented myself with a short trip down memory lane as I thought about the first time I came here with James when I was eighteen years old and the power of our young love. It was liberating to think about it again. Almost like discovering your old photo albums and yearbook covered in dust in the back of your closet, and deciding to take a peek inside.

I continued my journey at Casco Bay Lines Ferry terminal where I boarded a no frills mail boat that carried passengers, mail and freight daily to the islands of Casco Bay. It was mid-October, and chilly on the water, thus I zipped up my jacket, and wrapped my scarf tightly around my neck. I took my seat and I quickly became lost in the past again, but this time I thought about my last trip to Maine ... *the stunning Prescott residence, the glamorous anniversary party, the feel of James arm's around me as we danced, and the words of his father and grandmother.*

I thought about everything and I started to cry. I remembered nights staying up until the wee hours of the morning talking and giggling with James. Other times, there were no words, as we basked in each other's quiet embrace not needing to fill up the stillness with speech. In particular, I remembered quiet moments spent on his boat. The sound of crashing waves and the smell of the sea mixed with the faint odor of diesel from the engine, citrus scented boat cleaner, and sex.

I thought about our amazing physical attraction and the mind-blowing sex that we had together. Most of all, I thought about our friendship and how I could talk to James about anything and everything, and how truly unique it was to find a friend and lover like that.

Then, I reflected about the bad stuff... *Julie, Jon... infidelity... lack of trust... jealousy... paranoia... anger... negative news stories... hate mail... stalkers... obsessive fans... zealous papzz.* I considered our meteoric rise to fame, and the good and bad that came along with the lifestyle and how we handled it.

Portland shimmered in the distance and I knew that it was almost time to say goodbye to James and our past. The tears fell silently down my face as I let myself mourn for what could have been, but was no longer.

As land approached, I took a sip of the cold stale coffee that I had been holding for hours. I thought about Tom, and the future, and what it would be like to have a romantic relationship with him. I was attracted to Tom and he was my friend, the question was could I love him? I mean really love him? Tom was like a mad bull in a china shop with an abundant supply of never-ending energy – would that drive me insane some day? He could be abrasive and argumentative at times, and he had lots of baggage. On the other hand, Tom was charming and sharp-witted and there was no question that life would never get dull with him as a companion. I was reminded of a favorite quote: "The journey of a lifetime begins with a single step." I didn't know where my steps would lead, but I was ready to find out.

When I returned home from Boston, my steps took me directly to Tom, and we started where we left off. It was a fun and passionate relationship. Tom was a maddening man, who drove me crazy, but to my surprise, he had a soft and loving side, and I found myself laughing out loud and smiling every irritating minute with him. Being with Tom was nice and I finally felt complete, safe, whole, and happy again.

## Chapter 29: An Unexpected Offer

"To us," Tom said as we clinked champagne glasses. "Happy Anniversary!"

It was the one-year anniversary of our first kiss, and while I wasn't convinced that this particular day signified the start of our relationship, Tom disagreed with me. We were having dinner at one of our favorite places, RivaBella, on the Sunset Strip's western edge celebrating in lavish style. While I loved the expansive wine cave, my favorite part of RivaBella's was the atmosphere. The sprawling indoor-outdoor space had wood trellises, cushioned booths and lush greenery, reminding me of a sleek, yet rustic farmhouse. In typical Tom fashion he secured us one of the best tables, which provided us with just enough privacy, so that we could relax without distractions, but would also allow him to view the other fashionable diners so that he could socialize or conduct business at his whim.

I was pushing a piece of crusty bread around my plate to soak up the last drop of pistachio pesto when Tom handed me a jewelry box, "This is for you Alex."

I dropped the bread and looked directly at him. "Tom, you promised me no gifts," I gently scolded, pressing my napkin to my mouth.

"I know...I lied." Tom chuckled. "Open it Alex."

I opened the box and inside was a stainless steel Cartier tank watch. "Tom this is too extravagant. I can't accept it."

"Of course, you can accept it Alex and everyone need's a good watch. Maybe now you won't be late to your meetings with me."

"Thank you Tom," I said, my voice thick with emotion. "I love it."

"Shall I put it on for you?" Tom questioned. "It's a size small, but your wrist is so tiny, that you may need to have some links removed."

I nodded my head yes and put my arm across the table. Tom took the watch out of the box, but instead of putting it on my wrist, he took my hand and raised it to his lips. He kissed my hand and stroked my wrist with his finger in a slow sensual circular motion moving gradually down the length of my arm. My reaction was immediate and I could tell that my cheeks had reddened as desire coursed through my body. I saw Tom's blue eyes darken as he witnessed my reaction and continued his *assault* with butterfly kisses.

I cleared my throat and gave him my most alluring smile. "I think we should go home now."

***

Life with Tom was exciting. He knew everyone in Hollywood, and he knew everything about them, the good and the ugly.

In many ways we were opposites. Tom had a big personality and was often drawn to the spotlight. I preferred low-key, and more privacy, but somehow are pairing worked well together, and we thrived.

The gleam in my eye and skip in my step that I hadn't had since my days with James, had returned, and I was happy.

One night, Tom and I, were at a family dinner with my parents, Peter and Zach, and their respective girlfriends, Jenny and Sue, who I had both grown fond of.

Peter had met Jenny at UCLA where she was a fellow surgical resident with him and they seemed very serious about each other. I couldn't tell if Zach, who was my more light-hearted and irresponsible brother, was serious about Sue (who he affectionately called "Suzy"). Sue typified the blonde-hair, blue-eyed California girl. She was a full-time yoga instructor who also loved to surf, and they were always laughing and having fun together, thus time would tell if she was "the one."

Anyway, we were all having dinner together when Tom, Peter, and Jenny started talking about "America's Healthcare Crisis" and I braced myself for an argument. My family was very liberal and I feared that Tom would take the typical "business owners" argument, and offend someone at the table, but he surprised me that evening by taking an entirely different viewpoint then what I expected. Every time I assumed something about Tom, he usually did the opposite. He wasn't someone you could easily pigeonhole, and I liked that about him.

After dinner, I was in the kitchen with my mom as she brewed a fresh pot of coffee.

"I haven't seen you this content in a really long time Alexandra."

"He's good for me, mom." I acknowledged with a smile.

"I can see that you're happy," she said. "But your father and I still have some concerns."

"Such as?" I inquired with a slight frown.

"Well, for one, there is the age difference," she said with a scowl. "He is divorced and has two kids, and he is known in the industry for his bullying and profane outbursts."

"*Wow*...don't hold back mom," I teased with growing irritation. "Now tell me how you really feel?"

"Alexandra, you're being a *smart aleck* and I don't appreciate it. I'm telling you these things, because I love you."

"Seriously, mom. I love you too, but you have to trust me. I know about Tom's reputation. You also left out the good things, like he is super-creative, unbelievably loyal and not afraid of failure."

I knew she was worrying, and I locked eyes with her, and quietly added. "Most important above all, Tom has remained at my side, during the good and bad. He has been there for me in my darkest moments."

She stared at me, uncertainty plain on her face. I knew that she was still concerned.

"What can I say mom to make you stop worrying?"

"I'll always worry Alex, that's my job as your mom," she joked. "I had to be honest and tell you our concerns, but I see how happy you are with him and he is *growing* on us. If you *really* fall in love with this man and decide that he is the one, we will learn to like him too."

She hugged me and we spent the rest of the night giggling. I felt like all the important people in my life were collectively coming together, and like a jigsaw puzzle, the pieces were at long last fitting.

***

The moment I received the wonderful news that I had been nominated for an Academy Award for Best Actress for my role as Natalie in *Shattered: An Ivy League Brain,* I was overjoyed and

filled with happiness. The state of melancholy that I had experienced
when I received my first nomination for my role in *Family Madness*
did not rear its ugly head again. This time around, I was ready to
rejoice!

Tom and I were driving in his car on our way to a celebratory
party to meet with my family, Lydia, her boyfriend, Andy, and
Christopher and my co-stars from the film. The movie had swept the
Academy with 14 nominations, and spirits were high that evening. I
was in a bubbly mood as I chatted happily in the car to Tom, but I
realized that the conversation was one-sided and that he wasn't
paying attention to anything that I'd said.

"Is everything ok, Tom?" I questioned, the concern obvious in my
voice.

"Nothing that I want to trouble you with tonight," he said
sounding anxious.

"So there is something?" I quizzed.

"It's just business," he said sweeping it under the rug. "It can hold
until tomorrow." Then he looked at me and smiled enthusiastically.
"TONIGHT WE CELEBRATE!"

***

The next morning we were in bed, and I wrapped my arms around
him. "Ok, Mr. Gloomy, fess up? What's wrong?"

"Nothing is wrong. It's actually a very lucrative opportunity for
you."

"Then why do you look like someone *died*?"

"I do not, Alex. It's just the offer has some *strings attached*. Let's
discuss it over breakfast," he said. "But first things first," he said
grabbing me and kissing me … breakfast could wait.

After a leisurely morning of sex, Tom and I had finally showered
and dressed and we were eating breakfast in my kitchen.

"Ok Tom, spill…what's up?" I asked, curious to see what had
him so unhinged.

"Have you heard of the novel, *Opposite Sides of the Aisle*?" Tom
asked.

"Isn't that like asking me if I've heard of *The Bourne Identity*?" I teased. "Of course, I've heard about it. I actually read it and I couldn't put it down. It was riveting and very suspenseful. Why?"

"You forgot *erotic*," Tom said wryly.

"Well, it's not *Fifty Shades*, but yeah, it was *steamy*," I agreed. "You still haven't answered my question…what's up?"

"It's being made into a film with the potential for sequels and I've received a call from the producer and they are interested in you for the female lead… "

"That's great Tom," I interrupted. "Diane is a dynamic character, strong, intelligent, challenging. I would be very interested in reading the script."

Tom brushed a piece of hair off his forehead, and was quiet. He seemed preoccupied like he was deliberating something.

"Tom?" I questioned.

"Alex, like I said earlier there are strings attached to the offer…"

"Like what, Tom?" I prompted. I started to feel like I was pulling teeth to get Tom to talk to me.

"The offer is contingent upon you and your co-star working together as a team," he said, sounding almost surly.

I looked up at him then; surprised by the hardness I heard in his voice and realized that his strong jaw was set in anger.

"I'm sorry, have I missed the punch line?" I asked baffled by his behavior.

"Your co-star would be James. They want you both. If one of you refuses, the offer is rescinded."

I frowned. "Is this a sick joke?"

"No," he said flatly, his eyes guarded.

"Tell them to go to *hell*," I muttered, and then added more clearly, "Actually, tell them that I am *insulted* by the offer and that they can *fuck off.*"

I was fuming and really irritated as I thought about the *cunning* offer and the nerve of the studio execs and producers who came up with it. It wasn't that I didn't see the logic or cleverness in the idea. Getting James and I for the central characters was original and actually quite ingenious. I thought about the strong attraction and instant chemistry of the protagonist's in the book, and I certainly recognized how James and I could give strong, believable performances that might make us ideal for the leading roles. Even so, to put us in such an awkward position, albeit tempting, was unethical, bordering on cruel.

Was it *tempting*?

If I was honest with myself, one part of me was tempted. The novel was good, and if the script measured up; it could be a phenomenal film. But could I work with James again? What was I *thinking*? There was NO WAY that I could consider such a *crazy* proposal.

Tom cleared his throat. "James is interested."

I felt like someone had *literally* knocked the wind right out of my sails. I glared at Tom and wondered why, exactly, this sick joke was happening *now* when I finally had put my past behind me and was happy in my life?

"I didn't realize that you had *already* spoken to James," I said, working to sound indifferent.

The tone of my voice caught Tom's attention and he looked troubled, bordering on uneasy.

"I didn't speak to James," Tom clarified. "My partner, Curt did."

"Since when does James work with Curt Wescott?" I asked surprised, forgetting my earlier annoyance.

"Since we started dating Alex," Tom admitted. "I still represent James for the most part, but our relationship has become strained, so I usually deal with Ken, his manager, directly. However, if Ken is not available or when James need's to be involved, we've found it easier if he work's with Curt instead. Then, Ken or Curt will pull me in as needed."

"I see," I said stunned, processing the news. "I don't understand why your relationship with James has become strained … is it because of me?"

"Neither one of us have ever come out and admitted it, but yeah you are certainly the cause." Tom said with a wry grin on his face.

"I don't understand. My relationship with James is ancient history; surely he cannot hold a grudge against you, simply because we are dating?"

Tom looked up at me and stared at me, his expression mocking.

"*Seriously*, Alex?" Tom scolded me like I was a child. "Whose *ex* would want to work closely with their former lover's boyfriend? Especially considering how you both left things?"

"What is that supposed to mean?" I asked with exasperation.

"It mean's you didn't have a clean break and you never experienced closure. You were a basket case for years."

"That's *untrue* Tom," I replied unable to look him in the eye.

"I'm sorry Alex, but the truth hurts."

"Relationships are messy," I quickly pointed out. "Not everything can end on a clean note, but it's water under the bridge. C'est la vie!"

"Well, aren't you full of quaint *colloquialisms* today," Tom said dryly.

"Why are you giving me such a hard time about this Tom?" I asked raising my voice in frustration.

"James wants to meet with you alone to have a private conversation and discuss the offer."

The moment the words were out of Tom's mouth, I could feel the tightness in my throat and the stirrings of anxiety in the pit of my stomach. *James wanted to meet with me?* This couldn't actually be happening, could it? I felt like the room was spinning around and I quickly took a seat before Tom could see my reaction. Why did James want to meet with me, certainly he must hate me for filming *The Adventures of Tarzan & Jane 2* and for my affair with Jon. Perhaps, enough time had gone by that he didn't hate me anymore? I started to feel hopeful that maybe he had forgiven me for my past transgressions. Even so, what good could possibly come from us meeting now? The thought sent shivers down my spine and my heart began to race at the prospect of actually meeting with him face-to-face.

"Why? He couldn't seriously be considering it, is he?" I asked with uncertainty.

"You'll have to ask him that yourself." Tom said with a hint of disdain in his voice.

"Does that mean you think I should meet with him?" I questioned.

"I think you and James have *unfinished business* and it would be good for the both of you to wipe the slate clean and have a conversation like two grown ups…"

I went over to Tom, and looked at his face with probing eyes. "Tell them that my answer is no."

"Why?" he asked.

"I made a mistake doing the sequel for *Tarzan & Jane* and it cost me dearly. I've learned my lesson and I will not do that to you."

"While I appreciate the sentiment Alex," Tom said roughly, "if you can't even meet with the guy after this much time has gone by, then you are *lying* to yourself and to me that you are over him. I don't think it will ever be *ancient history* to you."

"Why are you doing this Tom?" I asked, slightly irritated. "Are you trying to cause a fight and push me away?"

"Of course not, I'm just sick of you lying to yourself and to me," he said, sounding tired. "I think you need to deal with it head on and meet with him. If after the meeting, your decision is no, then we can finally move on."

"Why do you think I'm being dishonest about my feelings?" I asked, holding his gaze.

"Because you have never once looked at me Alex, the way you did at him."

"Tom, you're being foolish," I protested. "For crying out loud, I was seventeen when I met him. Don't be so insecure."

"There's nothing insecure about me Alex and you know that," he said. "I just don't want you to waste my time if I'm your consolation prize. Have the courage to finally confront him and figure out what you really want. If I'm the man you truly desire, then I'll be here waiting."

"And if we decide to do the movie together, could you live with that decision?" I asked lightly, hesitantly trying to test the waters.

Tom looked me squarely in the eye. "I will stand by whatever decision you make, Alex, but I think we should take a few weeks apart until you meet with James and figure things out."

His expression was calm, but I could tell that he was tense and that he was putting on an act to cover up his anxiety. I wanted to tell him that I had figured things out and that I didn't need to meet with James, but I couldn't do it. Instead, I put my hands on each side of his face and tenderly kissed him. "Thank you Tom."

## Chapter 30: The Reunion

The big day was here. Today I would finally meet with James. A month had passed since my emotional conversation with Tom and we hadn't seen each other since. It wasn't that it came as a shock. I understood why Tom was keeping me at arms length. I had never really gotten over James and deep down Tom knew it and so did I. Tom didn't want to get burned and quite frankly, I was grateful that he was avoiding me. Pure and simple, I was a bundle of nerves.

With trepidation, I entered the Beverly Hills Hotel bungalow and the first thing I noticed was the floor-to-ceiling design which provided a lovely tranquil perspective of the pool and outside patio. At first I thought I was alone, and I enjoyed the moment of privacy, something I seldom got to experience.

Then he spoke, "Can I get you something to drink?"

I knew his voice in an instant and for one second I closed my eyes. It was the voice of a familiar, beloved stranger.

I was still too unsettled to look at him, so I answered instead. "A sparkling water would be great."

As James prepared the drinks, I stole my first glance and studied his face intently. I tried not to notice his looks, but it was hard to overlook. He was sexy as hell. Time had not changed him. If anything, he was more handsome and irresistible than I had remembered. Still, I wondered what lay underneath? Was he still the man I had fallen in love with? Then he looked up and our eyes met. Neither one of us said anything; we just continued to look at each other from across the room.

James walked over first and handed me a drink. "Alex," he finally said, studying my face. "It's good to see you. Um…how have you been?"

The heat from his hand burned into my hand, but I ignored it. I raised my chin defiantly. *How had I been?* Is this really how he was going to play it? I moved away from him then and took a large sip of my drink trying to quench my now suddenly dry throat.

I let out the breath I'd been holding. "It's good to see you too."

He looked at me intently. "Um, congratulations on the nomination. I hope you win."

"Thanks, but the competition is tough. It's a long shot." I said, my voice wavering. *Damn...I was nervous.* I felt my heart pounding in my chest and I willed myself to calm down. Straightening my shoulders, I took another step away from him.

"I think you have a good chance." He smiled graciously. "Anyway, you've been recognized by your peers so you're already a winner. Regardless of what happens, I think it was your best performance to date and that you deserve it. You were amazing."

He *saw* the movie? I couldn't *believe* it? I cleared my throat to speak. "Thanks. Um, I wanted to wish you congratulations as well."

"For what?"

"Your Grammy awards."

"Oh." he said with a faint, quick smile.

"Yeah, Mr. Overachiever. It's like...a big deal." I teased. "Seriously, James, your music is beautiful. I listen to some of your indie pop ballads when I'm running. I think it's some of your best work."

"Really?" he volunteered, sounding in disbelief. "I'm surprised that you've listened."

"Why?" I gestured toward my phone. "Do you want to check my running playlist?" I offered, trying to keep the lighthearted banter going.

"No...I believe you," he said quietly, his face suddenly grave and contemplative.

I waited for him to continue to speak, but he didn't and an awkward silence followed. I opened up my mouth to say something, but then closed it again. It seemed like we were finished making small talk, so what next? I was tense and I could feel my stomach churning. James leaned against the wall, staring intently at me. I wanted to say something to break the uncomfortable atmosphere, but I stubbornly refused, because *honestly* I didn't know what to say?

Suddenly with two long strides he was next to me. We stood so close that when he exhaled, I could feel his breath on me. To a casual observer, our close proximity may have looked intimate. In reality, we faced each other as if we were in a duel, our expressions were grim, our postures defensive.

I braced myself for him to speak.

"I'm sorry," he finally said, his voice thick with emotion.

"Are you?" I questioned unable to keep the bitterness out of my voice. "You just caste me aside like some selfish prick. Not one phone call, email – nothing."

"It wasn't like that…I missed you every day," he said dropping his gaze and running his hands through his hair in a gesture that he always did when he was nervous or uncomfortable. "I mean, I guess I was wrapped up in my own shit for awhile. I was pissed about Hanley and trying to cope with all of the bullshit. I'm sorry for hurting you."

I took a step back as I tried to process his words and come up with a proper response. "I'm fine, you needn't feel guilty James," I lied, managing to keep my voice even and calm. "It was a long time ago."

He looked at me carefully, closing the gap between us again. "I don't believe you Alex and I'm calling your bluff," he stated coolly.

"What do you want from me, James?" I asked losing my composure, and raising my voice. "Do you really want to re-hash the past?"

He ignored my question and stated plainly. "A day hasn't gone by that I have not regretted my actions. I miss you," he murmured.

"You left me – remember?" I said through clenched teeth. "Why didn't you call?"

"Just because I didn't call, doesn't mean that I didn't think about you." James stated defiantly, his jaw clenched. "That night at Cecconi's, I was in London, filming six days a week, but I changed my plans so that I could fly in that night to see you. I thought if I could see you in a neutral setting, that maybe it could be a first step in trying to *fix* things and open up channels of communication with you. When I saw you walk out of the restaurant, I felt like it was a slap across the face, and that you didn't want anything to do with me."

"Don't you think showing up at a public place for our reunion was a flawed notion?" I asked. "Did you really want our first conversation after like three, almost four years to be in front of everybody? Think about it James…it would have been broadcasted everywhere."

He stared at me, understanding dawning on his face. "I guess I didn't give it enough thought."

"I wish you had just called," I said wistfully.

"I'm sorry," he murmured.

"Me too," I whispered in a small tired voice.

His head shot up. "What?"

I squirmed uncomfortably. "I should not have done the movie. I'm sorry, James. It was a shitty thing to do." I put my head down, ashamed to look at him or see his reaction. "I'm so very sorry – especially about Jon - I was wrong."

He moved unexpectedly closer and put one hand on my shoulder. "We both made mistakes."

The minutes ticked by, as we were both lost in a sea of emotion. I turned away to stare out the window. *How had something so good turned so bad?* I started to pace the floor as I tried to explain to him all of the bottled up emotions of the last five years.

"I never meant to hurt you James…I was young and immature. Our relationship was so serious so fast - I handled things poorly. When you left, and we said goodbye, I felt like a part of me was dead, the very best part. After that, I built a wall around me. For a few years, I went nuts. I was seriously wild and self-destructive. Partying every night, excessive alcohol, and banging myself up in all sorts of careless ways. Then one morning I woke up in a sea of my own vomit in some strange hotel and it dawned on me that my life had gotten out of control and that I was miserable. After that, I cleaned up my lifestyle and things got better."

"And now?" he asked, his voice anxious, probing. "Are you okay?"

I knew he was worrying, and I wanted to give him a truthful answer.

"Yeah, I'm good James, and before this meeting, I would have ventured to say that my life seemed almost perfect. But now I'm not sure."

"Why?" he asked tentatively, staring at me.

"If it was perfect," I said mustering up my courage, "I wouldn't be sitting here calmly contemplating this *foolish* offer." I sighed silently and met his gaze. "How could we possibly consider working together *again*?"

He smiled sheepishly at me. "About that – I don't want to do it."

"What? You don't?"

"No fucking way! Listen - in all seriousness – six cars followed me this morning when I left my house. They sit outside my house every day. If we were to do this movie, it will probably be ten or twelve or twenty cars. It will be pandemonium all over again." He shuddered.

"I don't understand? Then why…" I trailed off. "Why are you here James?"

"I wanted to see you," he murmured. "I've missed you and I've been worried about you. I wanted to make sure that you were ok."

There was so much I wanted to say, but somehow I was dumbfounded so I looked out the window without saying a word.

"Say something." He cleared his throat. "Listen - if you really want to do the film, then I guess I could be convinced to sign up for that insanity again?" he said shrugging his shoulder, emotion thick in his voice. "I try my best to deal with it, and to a certain extent that requires work. We could work on it together; we try our best, nobody's perfect, but there's no one I'd rather try with."

"But you don't want to do the film?" I probed.

"No."

"Well then, what have you been up to for the last five years?" I asked offhandedly, my tone casual, but it was the question that had been burning in the back of my mind for years.

"Mostly work Alex."

"And?" I asked unable to hide my interest any longer.

"Well, after the *Elvis* movie wrapped up, I did another three movies quickly in succession. I think that was probably around the time that you were on your wild rampage and I was pissed off and angry with you. After that, I went sailing for a few months on my own."

"Alone? Isn't that dangerous James?"

"I was cautious Alex, and sailing provided me a good opportunity to spend some alone time and reflect."

"Reflect on what?" I questioned.

"I wanted to leave the stress of the world behind for awhile so that I could think without all of the noise, confusion and distraction from my daily life."

"What did you do after that James?"

"I bought a place in New York and started focusing primarily on my music career. I still act if I'm passionate about a role, but for the most part, I've been composing and singing and it brings me a lot of joy."

"Um, what about women ... Is there someone special in your life?" I asked, biting my tongue nervously.

"There's no one in my life at the moment." James stated smoothly, and then he casually glanced at me for my reaction.

I gave a nonchalant shrug, trying to project indifference. "I find that hard to believe?" I questioned cocking an eyebrow.

"It's true."

"Come on...your answer is lame."

He stood looking at me for a minute and there was a rather awkward pause as he deliberated over my question. "I've been in a couple of relationships, but only one was serious."

"What happened with the serious one? Is she still in your life?" I asked, surprised by the sudden feeling of overwhelming panic in my chest as I waited for his answer.

"She was Rachel's college friend and roommate. Her name is Sadie Kelly and she is a violinist on the East Coast. I met her about two months after the incident at Cecconi's. We recently broke up."

"That's too bad." I said with a smug smile.

"Not really," he said.

"Well, your family must have been devastated as she sounds like the *perfect* girl for you." I said with a slight trace of sarcasm as I recalled how his parents had treated me.

"It doesn't matter if my family liked her. Sadie wasn't the *one*, Alex." He stated boldly, staring at me intently until I dropped my gaze from him.

"Oh."

"Now it's time you answer some questions for me. Why are you *actually* here today?" he asked with deliberate slowness.

"I wanted to see you."

"Why?"

"To say sorry and to find out if you hated me?"

"I was mad as hell at you for a long time Alex…But I never hated you…how could I? I loved you…I'll always love you."

"U-um," I struggled to find the right words. *I had no idea what to say?* I played nervously with a loose thread that was hanging from my dress. "So what now?"

"I think we should try the friendship thing...what do you say?" James whispered, cocking his head to one side, and flashing me his well practiced, knowingly sexy, boyish grin. His seductive smile and charm were momentarily disarming, but I pushed my wayward thoughts aside.

"James, you're not playing fair."

"I know Alex," he acknowledged. "Let's try it," he urged, his voice passionate, compelling. "Will you be my friend?"

He looked so sincere as he gazed at me, waiting for me to respond. My heart pounded frantically as I considered his request. Could I go down this path with him *again*?

"Come on Alex…give us a second chance?"

I automatically tallied the pros and cons in my head. Could I be his friend again, and what would it cost me? I counted all the ways that I could get hurt again. Was it worth it?

"What do you want to do Alex? Do you want to try?"

"I don't know James," I said gravely, closing my eyes.

"Is this about you and Tom?" he asked with a little hostility. "How is our favorite power-broker doing these days?"

"He's fine." I huffed.

"I need to know Alex…do you love him?" James asked, his voice tense. "If you do, I will respect that and I'll walk away. Otherwise, give us a second chance?"

"My feelings for Tom are complicated," I blurted out.

"It's a yes or no question Alex?"

"Yeah, I love Tom, but…but not the way I loved you." I said in a whisper, putting my head down, to ashamed to look at him. Unexpectedly, James crossed the room and cupped my chin so that I was forced to look at his face, but I pushed away from him taking a step back. "What's love got to do it with it anyway, James?" I said emotionally raising my voice. "When we tore each other to shreds, being in love didn't help keep us together."

"Don't run away Alex, the way you did that night from Cecconi's," James warned. "I know you're scared *shitless* and so am I. We have both made mistakes. I know that I've learned from those mistakes and I think you have too. Let's not make a mistake a second time. There are no guarantees in life, but you need to have the courage to go after what you really want."

"A second chance at *precisely* what?" I clarified. "What do you want from me James?"

James ran his hand through his hair, and examined me warily.

"I don't know Alex, but I want you to trust me again. I can't erase the past, or the hurt that we've inflicted on one another, but I never stopped loving you and I want you back in my life."

For years I had dreamed of hearing James utter those words, but that was before my relationship with Tom. I knew the sensible response would be to shut the door permanently with James. If I did that *right* now, Tom would be waiting and I could continue my life happy and uninterrupted. The problem was that the pull towards James could not be denied, and I could *no* longer lie to myself *nor* drown my inner voice. I was not here today for closure. I was here to find the courage to follow my heart and intuition.

James moved slowly toward me, "Please?" he whispered, his eyes probing mine.

I looked at him – I mean I really looked at him and I saw that young man I had fallen in love with so long ago, the one I could never quite forget. "Okay," I murmured quietly.

He closed his eyes and nodded, a smile of relief clear on his face. "Thank you," he breathed, and leaned down to press his lips to my forehead.

I smiled and nodded as a feeling of contentment washed over me as I realized that James Alexander Prescott was back in my life.

## Epilogue: One Year Later

All I saw was blue. But not any shade of blue. The stone flashed a blue-fire brilliance that made me blink. We had been engaged for three weeks and I could not hold back the cheesy grin from forming on my face every time I looked down at the ring and thought about him. Well really, every time I thought about us...about marriage, kids, the future, and everything I still wanted with him.

I guess, I'm more romantic, than cynic, but still the road to get here, was not easy. After that first meeting with James at the Beverly Hills Hotel, almost a year ago, we eased our way into our newfound friendship with baby steps. The key was moderation. I took it one day at a time. What else could I have done?

I didn't want to make any hasty decisions about James or Tom, deciding that being on my own for a while, was healthier. But something happened. It was just a little thing, but it turned my stomach. It was my first meeting with Tom, after seeing James, and it was a tense one. I guess Tom found it hard to look at me, because he acted different and kept his distance during the entire time we met. I thought Tom would be relieved when I told him the news that James and I had decided to decline the film and not work together, but instead he threw up his hands and sounded annoyed. "Jesus Christ, Alex! You're killing me...there's nothing to fuckin' think about. You guys are insane if you give this up."

His words were unsettling and I begin to feel nauseous. "I thought you would be happy Tom." I murmured.

"Well, clearly I'm not."

I tried finding a reason to hang on to Tom - But his tone during that one meeting told me everything I needed to know. Soon after, we officially broke things off. It did occur to me that Tom could have lied, but if he did, I refused to consider it. Whether it was an act of kindness to let me go easily or the greedy actions of a fast talking hustler – I didn't want to know the truth. In any event, I stayed away from Tom for a while – it was just too painful to be around him. And although he wouldn't admit it, I suspected that it was painful for him too.

Time went by.

As Tom and I fizzled out, James and I heated up. No matter where each of us was on the globe, James would call me every night and we would talk until our voices sounded sleepy and our eyes grew heavy. Gradually, the Skype sessions, phone calls, emails and texts turned into real life dates and little by little I fell in love with James all over again.

I waited to go to bed with James until I was sure that it wasn't just nostalgia dictating our actions. Then one morning, he surprised me by showing up at my house unannounced. He had Lydia clear my schedule and asked me to pack my bags. He took me to a beach house located atop a bluff at the end of a winding, secluded road, somewhere along the Northern California coastline.

"I want to show you something," he said taking my hand. "Wear comfortable shoes."

He took me down a broad dirt path that suddenly narrowed and twisted down steeply towards a woodland area just above stone steps. The steps led down to a private beach with a dock, float and boat mooring. I shielded my eyes against the glare of the sun, and blinked. That's when I saw it. At first, I thought it was the wooden sailboat the *Crescendo*, but then I realized it was a replica. The new sailboat was the *Alexandra James*. I wandered over and squeezed my eyes shut so that he wouldn't see my tears. "When did you get her?" I asked, my voice thick with emotion.

"A couple of years ago," he said vaguely.

"A couple of years?" I questioned. "I thought you were pissed at me."

"I was," James laughed. "She remained nameless until about a year ago. Do you like her?"

"You know I do."

Since that weekend, James and I have been inseparable. Funnily enough, the sex was even hotter the second time around.

Tom is still my agent and I heard from Lydia that he is fine. Actually, I think her exact words were "fucking excellent". He landed some huge 'deal of the century', and for Tom, making deals will always be his oxygen. It's what makes him tick. I don't know about the status of his love life nor do I really care, but I imagine that my shoes have probably been filled by now.

James and I now live in California and we just bought a place in Maine. We plan to live in Maine each summer and it will also be the location for our September wedding.

I don't really believe in soul mates and all of that crap, but I do believe in James and I. Like the mighty Oakes, that produces the hardest and strongest of wood, this time around we're learning to create the kind of environment that can help our love grow and withstand the test of time...*and we lived happily ever after*.

THE END

A NOVEL BY EDIE BLACK

From the coastal region of Boston's North Shore to the high finances of Wall Street: The tale of one girl, two brothers and a love triangle of sorts.

*The Cortship* is the story of Samantha "Sam" Nottingham, a pretty girl from a suburban middle class family and her whirlwind 'cortship' with the wealthy and privileged Cort Family. At the age of six Sam meets outspoken and rich girl, Heather Cort, and they quickly become best friends. Soon after, Sam is introduced to Heather's brothers, Brian and Matt. She is captivated by the popular and handsome brothers, especially Matt, whom she develops a crush on. Both brothers are also drawn to her. The attraction, however, stirs up tension and jealously between the brothers, particularly for Brian who feels that he always loses to Matt.

During the summer before Sam's senior year of high school, Matt returns home from Stanford and asks Sam to join his crew for the Beringer Bowl; an overnight sailboat race from Marblehead to Provincetown, Cape Cod. While in Cape Cod, Sam and Matt have sex and a passionate romance between the two unfolds. But their newfound relationship is shattered when Sam discovers that Matt has been lying to her. Heartbroken, Sam cannot forgive Matt and the two separate. After graduation, Sam moves, and loses touch with the Cort family.

Eight years later, Sam meets the Cort brothers by chance at a business conference in London. With their reappearance, Sam slowly becomes intertwined with them again and is forced to confront her love-hate-love feelings for the larger-than-life family and the man that she could never quite forget.

35929756R00174

Made in the USA
Middletown, DE
19 October 2016